AND NOW A WORD FROM OUR SPONSOR . . .

The apparition appeared on the TV right after the start of the *NBC Nightly News*. One moment there was anchorman Gary Elliot doing the lead-in to a story, and the next he'd been replaced by the face of some weird cartoon-like skull. Gibson blinked in amazement. Then it spoke to him, addressing him by name in a high-pitched, Mighty Mouse voice.

"Don't worry, Joe, be happy. It's always darkest before the dawn, Joe. And you got a visitor coming. You should do yourself a favor and talk to him. Way to go, Joe. Have a nice day."

And then the cartoon skull vanished and NBC was back. Joe's hands shook as he picked up his drink. One thing he knew for sure: there was no way he was going to open the door for anyone . . .

By Mick Farren
Published by Ballantine Books:

THE ARMAGEDDON CRAZY
THE FEELIES
THE LAST STAND OF THE DNA COWBOYS
THE LONG ORBIT
MARS—THE RED PLANET
NECROM
THEIR MASTER'S WAR

NECROM

Mick Farren

A Del Rey Book
BALLANTINE BOOKS • NEW YORK

This one's for Susan

"This is funny . . ."

—The last words of
Doc Holliday

The White Room

JOE GIBSON WAS alone in the narrow white bed in the narrow white room in the small but very expensive clinic. Bursts of hysterical applause blasted from some idiot game show on TV. In the very expensive clinic, the TV was mounted high on the wall, out of reach, and even if he had stood on a chair to get to it, it wouldn't have done him any good. The TV was some special hospital number with no buttons or switches. No channel selector. Nothing. He couldn't even turn it off.

Gibson saw the TV as the key to his situation. In the very expensive clinic his programs were selected for him. The doctors and the nurses who operated the clinic—the ones he thought of as the people in white—seemed not to believe that patients were capable of free choice. Gibson had a different view of it: when a man lost control of his television, he lost his foothold in the world. He wondered if all the patients in the place got the same TV programs or if each one had a prepared schedule tailored to his or her emotional profile. Gibson suspected that it was the latter. It was the kind of detail that the customers paid for in a place like this. He had noticed that he was fed a hell of a lot of game shows, and he wondered what that said about him.

Not that he thought much about the TV. Most of the time they kept him too doped up to think about anything. Only in these periods, the half hour or so before the nurse was due to give him his shot, did he start to get riled by the whole setup. It was only in this half hour that his own memories were at their most intact. After the shot, the confusion started again, and what he believed he knew for real became hopelessly jumbled with

1

what the nurses and doctors, the people in white, wanted him to believe.

As with so many episodes in his life, it had started with a hangover and a loss of memory of a very different kind . . .

Chapter
One

JOE GIBSON GROANED out loud.

"Not again. Oh, God, not again."

It would have been a lie to say that the pain was indescribable. He was able to describe it all too well. He knew it like the backs of his hands, or maybe like the insides of his eyelids. Over the last few months, since Desiree had walked out on him, citing cruel and unusual behavior, the pain had been with him more mornings than not. The morning's suffering followed the evening's excess as surely as day followed night. His tongue was glued to the roof of his mouth. The knife stabs were working on the nerves at the back of his eyes, and blood was trying to force its way into a brain that felt like an old dried-out sponge. This post-alcohol purgatory had become so familiar that it was now routine.

Equally familiar was the sudden elevator drop into the black, empty shaft of no memory, no recall of getting home or much of what had gone before.

With the drop came the fear. Joe Gibson's head fell back onto the pillow, and he groaned aloud. "Oh, God, what did I do this time?"

He closed his eyes, hoping in vain for the darkness to return so the awful moment of actually getting up could be delayed for an hour or so. The darkness refused to oblige. He was on his own with the day. Not that there was all that much of the day left. The green numerals on the VCR at the foot of the ridiculously huge bed told him that it was 4:19 in the afternoon. The daylight was all but shot, and his vampire status safely intact.

Anxiety was the natural aftermath of a drunken blackout. He firmly repeated this litany to himself. Most of the time the fear was unfounded. Most nights it turned out that he hadn't really

3

done anything so terrible. Maybe he'd stumbled, maybe he'd upset a waitress or a maître d' or else pissed off a cabdriver. It was possible that he'd heaped unreasonable abuse on some unfortunate whose only mistake had been to fall for his rapidly fading legend and have the good grace to ignore the tarnish on his charisma and to be blind to his public fall from favor. Of course, there had been the other occasions, like the time that he had stormed into the Plaza, roaring like a psychotic moose, waving a bottle of Jack Daniels and bent on telling Morgan Luthor, a guest in there at the time, what he thought about him and his stupid twelve-piece band and his brand-new, big-ass double-platinum, megahit album. He had finished up in jail after that escapade. His only consolation had been that his notoriety had gained him a cell to himself and he had managed to come out of the experience with both his boots and anal virginity intact. The media had made a meal of it, though, and the pictures of him coming out of court, disheveled and once again hung over, had confirmed to an already convinced music industry that he was washed-up, burned-out, and uncontrollable. It had been right after the incident at the Plaza that Desiree had left.

In his more private moments, he tended to forgive himself the Plaza fiasco. It had, after all, been at the end of a four-day, no-sleep, bourbon-and-Coke jag, and Luthor had made some snide crack about him on *Entertainment Tonight*. Worse than that, Gibson had never had anything but contempt for the man's dumb songs. The fact that they sold zillions of units didn't make them anything other than trite commercial garbage. And what did the media expect? Where did they get off writing all that stuff about him? *Stone Free* particularly could go screw itself. The damn magazine was nothing more than a criminal waste of trees. When he'd been up there, they'd been down on their knees lapping up every last fleck of his self-destructive bullshit. Damn it, they had fawned over him as though we were Lucifer incarnate, coming for to carry them home. Did they really expect him to change his trim just because his career had slipped a little? They probably resented the fact that he hadn't died five years earlier like some of the others.

There was a pack of Camel Lights and a book of matches in among the debris on the night table. He shook one out, stuck it between numb lips, and lit it. The matchbook was a garish pink and advertised a set of phone-sex numbers. "FOR THE PASSION OF PAIN—1-900-976-LASH. ALL MAJOR CREDIT CARDS ACCEPTED." And they called *him* degenerate. He inhaled the first smoke, started coughing, and knew he had to sit up immediately. He swung his legs over the side of the bed but was forced to drop his head between his knees as the coughing escalated to the dry heaves.

"Sweet Jesus Christ!"

When the coughing fit subsided, he examined the floor at his feet. The fur rug had once been pristine white, but now it was a dirty gray. He had trouble keeping staff. Housekeepers couldn't handle him, and au pairs ran out screaming and sent for their things later. At the moment, he was reduced to Arthur, the out-of-work dancer who came in one afternoon a week and disposed of the worst of the wreckage. Arthur didn't ever get as far as shampooing the rugs. Gibson's clothes were strewn across the floor, lying where they had fallen. He could see only one of his red snakeskin boots, but otherwise he seemed to have made it home fairly intact. So far so good. Then he spotted the other clothes mixed in with his: a laddered black stocking, a leather miniskirt. The sound he made was not so much a groan as a whimper.

"Oh, shit, there's someone here."

He stood up. His head revolted at being elevated so quickly, and a wave of giddiness gripped him. He gritted his teeth and went into the connecting bathroom, and the reek of stale Scotch. A pair of gold, high-heeled, slingback sandals sat side by side on the floor, and a broken glass lay in the basin.

"Goddamn it, how the hell did that happen?"

He had no recollection of bringing anyone back with him. The best he could dredge up was a vague blurred image of leaning on a dark bar staring into a shot of tequila while some woman with a lot of lipstick and eyeshadow endlessly babbled at him. Was she the owner of the miniskirt and laddered stockings? All he knew for sure was that there was a strange woman somewhere in his apartment.

Mercifully, she wasn't in the bathroom. He removed the worst of the broken glass and ran the cold tap. The running water made him want to piss. He took care of that and then swallowed three Advil. As he splashed the cold water on his face, he realized that he was only assuming that the leather skirt and gold heels belonged to a woman. It wasn't beyond the realm of possibility that the stranger in the apartment was some demented transvestite. It wouldn't be the first time. Woman or man, it was a reasonable bet that whoever it was would be three parts crazy. That was the only kind who seemed to go for him these days.

He picked up one of the shoes and examined it. It was a size seven. If it did belong to a man, he had tiny feet. Did transvestites go in for foot binding? There was still no recall.

He became aware of the smell of coffee. Oh, Christ, she was being domestic. That could bode ill. If she started cooking anything, he would probably throw up. Something had to be done. He slipped into his black silk Christian Dior robe. There were dubious stains all down the front, but he was too sick to think about grooming. He went back into the bedroom and blearily took stock of the room. Where were his Ray-Bans? A man needed a measure of protection. Outside, on Central Park West, the sun was still up. Finally he spotted the sunglasses and his missing boot on the floor beside the art-deco dressing table, the one that Desiree had bought in that place down in SoHo. He picked up the Ray-Bans and clamped them firmly on the front of his face. Feeling a little more protected, he started down the corridor that led to the kitchen. The sunglasses made it a little hard to see, but he didn't care. He knew what the apartment looked like, all twelve, white elephant rooms full of his accumulated junk. He was cultivating a serious dislike of the apartment that was primarily self-protection. If the IRS had their way, soon he would be living in a refrigerator carton on Avenue C. He might as well prepare himself for the worst.

She was sitting at the kitchen table with her back to him. She was eating cornflakes and wearing one of his shirts. Romantic, darling, he thought sourly. Just like in the TV commercials. The bitch hadn't stopped to think that it might be his last clean shirt. Her hair was an untidy mess of blond curls with the roots coming in dark, cut in a style favored by heavy-metal babes and porno stars. As he walked in, she looked around. Her small, rather vapid face wasn't improved by the panda smudges of the previous night's smeared eye makeup. She definitely wasn't the one who had been babbling at him while he had meditated on the tequila. Her mouth was set in a small, tight, disagreeable line. She clearly wasn't in misty-eyed, slack-jawed love with him. There must have been a problem.

"Fuck you, Joe Gibson."

Joe Gibson sighed. There had been a problem. "So what did I do?"

"Not much except swill cognac and abuse me until well after dawn."

Joe Gibson knew that he didn't have the strength to accept a load of guilt before breakfast, particularly from a woman he couldn't even remember. Desiree had handed him a lifetime's supply of that kind of shit. He resorted to blunt rudeness.

"So why don't you leave?"

The woman wasn't going to let go of it. "Do you realize that I used to idolize you?"

That was all he needed. A bloody fan who thought he owed her something for a lifetime of adoration. She had fastened only two of the buttons on his shirt, and as she twisted round in the chair to face him, he had a clear and gratuitous view of her left breast. It was a good breast, small and young-girl firm. He was tempted by that perverse, swamp-thing lust that was the paradox of hangovers. Maybe he should take her back to bed and lose himself in her warm feminine moisture. Slurpings at the portal, smelling the smoke and perfume in that hair—although maybe he should brush his teeth first. Then part of him revolted. Good grief, no! That would only complicate matters. He didn't want to encourage her. It was a nice fantasy, but it had to remain a fantasy. Next thing he knew, she would be moving in.

"Is that coffee?"

"Do you realize that when I was a kid I thought you and the Holy Ghosts were the next best thing to God?"

Gibson peered at the Krups coffeemaker that was dripping happily. "We weren't. We weren't nothing but a rock 'n' roll band. Be assured of that." Despite himself, he grinned. "We did have our moments, though."

"How did it all go so wrong?"

That was a good question.

"Maybe too many people thought we were the next best thing to God."

"Be serious."

He poured himself a cup of coffee. "I don't have the energy. Blame it on eight years of Reagan. Just say no. One way or the other, we fucked up. What did everyone expect? We were the grand fuck-ups. Nobody played it harder than us and then suddenly it was Perrier and the Jane Fonda workout, ego enhancement and the Nissan Imperator. It's not easy to be an unreconstructed leftover from the sixties."

On the other side of the kitchen there was a huge, almost life-size photo portrait of him that had been taken back in the glory days when he and the band had thought they owned the world. His image stared coldly down at the two of them. Elegant and wasted. Flowing black hair like Charles II, black leather, the curl of the lip that he had learned from Elvis, shadows under his cheekbones, and arrogant hooded eyes. Jesus, he had been magnificent. Maybe that was what the girl was seeing. Yesterday's rock princeling, not today's has-been in a stained silk robe. She looked as though she was working up to tears.

"I would have done anything for you."

Maybe he should take her back to bed and damn the consequences. The coffee was too hot and burned his lip. He cursed and put down the cup. The woman didn't appear to notice.

"When I saw you in the bar last night I could hardly believe it. It was like a teenage dream come true."

What bar? There had been a great many bars, running one into the next like some dark melting Rembrandt. It was always the same on the nightwatch. How was he supposed to know what bar? He couldn't even remember her face.

"So you came home with me and it turned into a grown-up nightmare."

"Why are you so bitter?"

"Honey, I'm not bitter. It's just that my ability to laugh at it all is getting a little threadbare."

"But you've had everything. How can you act the way you do?"

There was a catch in her voice. The tears were very close. To start his day with an emotional disaster right in his own kitchen was more than he could face. Why me, Lord? He was about to ask her name but he bit off the question. Maybe he really ought to take her back to bed. It might stop her becoming hysterical.

"Listen, why don't we go back to bed and try to be nice to each other?"

She didn't exactly jump at the offer. "It's the evening already. Maybe I ought to just go."

"You've got something to do?"

She shook her head. "No."

"So?"

She was still shaking her head. "This is too weird."

"What is?"

"Ten years ago, I would have killed to be here like this."

Gibson said nothing. The girl looked up at him in the hope that he would somehow bail her out. Finally she stood up and came toward him. The shirt had fallen open and he could now see both of her breasts. He put his arms around her. Her body was stiff and reluctant. He steered her back down the corridor, past the gold records and the photographs, the award plaques and the posters and all the rest of the trash that was the tangible backwash of his career. He had to suppress a shudder. The place was a museum, a home for some rock 'n' roll Addams Family. In the study there was a life-size cardboard cutout of him posing with his shirt off. There had been a week when copies of that cutout had been in record stores across three continents. Maybe the best solution would be to let the IRS take the whole wretched mess.

An hour later, they lay naked, side by side in the gloom of the bed, but there was no real contact. She was propped up on one elbow, staring at his face. Her look was definitely not one of adoration. If anything, she looked depressed. Perhaps she was holding a solitary wake for the illusions of her youth.

"I think I should go."

Gibson nodded. There was really nothing else to say. She threw back the covers and slid out of bed. He watched her in silence as she dressed. With her clothes—first the garter belt and the ruined stockings, then the leather mini, the lace blouse, the chain belt—she assumed a tough sexuality that she wasn't able to maintain while she was naked. When she started putting on her shoes, he, too, rose and slipped once more into his robe.

"I'll see you to the door."

She didn't answer. At that moment the phone rang, and Gibson picked it up.

"Could I please speak to Joseph Gibson?"

The voice sounded very old and was strangely accented, possibly South American.

"Could I please speak to Joseph Gibson?"

Gibson was immediately suspicious. "Who is this?"

"My name is Don Carlos Gustavo Casillas."

"This is Joe Gibson, but I'm afraid I don't have a clue who you are."

"That's understandable, Señor Gibson. We have never met."

"What do you want, Mr. Casillas?"

"I want to talk to you."

"About what?"

The girl signaled that she would see herself out.

Gibson put a hand over the mouthpiece of the phone. "Wait a minute . . ."

Either she didn't hear him or she wanted to pass on the farewells. She was gone down the corridor. A moment later the front door slammed.

"Are you still there, Señor Gibson?"

"Yeah, I'm still here. Someone was just leaving." Gibson didn't know for the life of him why he was explaining anything to the stranger on the other end of the phone.

"I wish to come and see you."

Gibson was unconsciously shaking his head. "I don't think so. I don't see many people these days."

Casillas was persistent. "This is a matter of some importance."

"I should warn you that I don't have any money anymore."

"Believe me, Señor Gibson, I am not in the least interested in your money. This is something far more important."

"If you're one of those people who have a scheme to put the band back together for some reunion show, forget it. It'll never happen. Pretend we're all dead."

"I'm not interested in your band, either."

"So what is your interest?"

"It would be impossible to explain over the phone. I would have to see you in person."

Gibson was shaking his head again.

"No. I really can't go along with that."

"You might also be in some degree of danger, Señor Gibson."

Joe Gibson was suddenly angry. Who did the old fool think he was? "Are you threatening me?"

"I'm not threatening you, Señor. Quite the reverse. All I want is to meet and talk with you. Might I suggest I call on you at eight this evening."

"I won't be home at eight."

"I think by eight you may want to see me. I'll call anyway."

And with that, Don Carlos Gustavo Casillas hung up.

Gibson was left standing, listening to the dial tone. He was not at all happy. First the hangover and now this. What was he supposed to make of it all? Although he'd initially been angered by the suggestion that he might be in danger, in retrospect it gave him something to think about. He glanced at the VCR. It was after six. He had less than two hours to decide what to do about Señor Casillas.

He went into the living room. Here the clutter was much more high-tech—guitars, a computer, a DX7 keyboard. A monolithic bank of recording equipment shared a wall with the big David Hockney nude drawing of him. He went to the window, parted the curtains a couple of inches, and peered out. A black helicopter was hovering over the park. For no conscious reason, the helicopter disturbed him. He closed the curtains again.

It was only a matter of minutes before Gibson made up his mind what he was going to do. He would pour himself a stiff drink, put the security chain on the door, turn on the TV, and if the doorbell rang at eight o'clock, he'd ignore it.

The apparition appeared on the TV right after the start of the *NBC Nightly News*. One moment there was anchorman Gary Elliot doing the lead-in to a story on corruption in the Justice Department, and the next he'd been replaced by the face of some weird, cartoon-skull demon, an animated mosaic, like the wall of an Aztec temple brought to life by Hanna-Barbera. Gibson blinked in amazement.

"Now what the fuck is this?"

His first thought was that it was some arty commercial that he hadn't seen before, cued in at the wrong place. That was a better idea than wondering if he was losing his mind. The trouble was that even arty commercials usually had music and a voice-over. The only audio behind the skull was the sound of labored breathing, as though the thing was suffering from bronchial asthma. Then it spoke to him, addressing him by name in a high-pitched, wheezing, Mighty Mouse voice.

"Hey, Joe, whattaya know?"

Gibson slowly put down his drink. Now he had to seriously consider the possibility that he was losing it. DTs? He'd had only a couple of shots. He was aware that he was topping up his blood alcohol from the night before, but he shouldn't have been that far gone so fast.

"What is this?"

"You're a bit of a mess, Joe."

Gibson couldn't believe it. Could DTs come from the TV? Had someone cut into his cable to try to drive him crazy? He was suddenly frightened.

"I'm going to quit drinking."

The skull thing's face stretched into an insane grin. The jaw actually detached itself from the upper part of the skull.

"Come on, Joe, you say that every morning."

"What the fuck is going on here?"

"Don't worry, Joe, be happy. The tide always turns. It's always darkest before the dawn. That's the reason for the season. It's just the ebb before the flow, Joe. And you've got a visitor coming. You should do yourself a favor and talk to him. Way to go, Joe. Have a nice day."

And then the cartoon skull had vanished and NBC was back as if it had never been gone. Gibson stared uncomprehendingly at the end of the piece on Justice Department corruption. He was terrified. What was happening to him? On the screen, Gary Elliot had started into a health piece about botulism in pancake mix. He grabbed for the remote and killed the power. His hands were shaking as he picked up his drink. Was it him or was the whole world taking get-weird pills? One thing he knew for sure: There was no way that he was going to open the door to Casillas. He wasn't going to answer the door to anyone.

Gibson should have remembered that it was always a mistake to make hard-and-fast predictions. If he had learned anything from the way his life had gone, it should have been exactly that. As the clock on the VCR moved from 7:59 to 8:00, the intercom beeped. Despite his resolve, Gibson pushed the button.

"Mr. Gibson, this is Ramone the doorman."

"What is it, Ramone?"

"You have a visitor, Mr. Gibson."

"Who is it?"

"He says his name is Casillas."

Ramone sounded as though he didn't quite approve of the visitor. Then again Ramone didn't approve of most of Gibson's visitors.

"Send him up."

Gibson couldn't believe that the words had come out of his mouth. The very last thing he wanted was some weirdass in his apartment, and yet he seemed to have lost all will to resist. He looked round like a condemned man seeking a way out of the inevitable. What was happening to him?

Two and a half minutes after Ramone's call, the doorbell rang. The set of chimes that played the first two bars of Howling Wolf's "Smokestack Lightning" was one of his more absurd rock-star purchases, and normally he took a childish pleasure in it, but this time the final note was a funeral bell tolling gloomily in the air. Like a zombie, he stood up and walked to the door. His legs didn't feel as though they even belonged to him. He took off the chain, snapped back the two deadbolts, and opened the door. The man standing there looked at least a hundred years old. His face was like an ancient walnut, deeply etched with a thousand lines and creases. The eyes, however, that looked out from beneath bushy white eyebrows were bright with a penetrating intelligence. He was not only old but very small, a tiny birdlike figure in a set of clothes that were totally incongruous not only for a man of his age but for practically anyone else. It should have belonged to a pachuco zoot-suiter from the early forties. His shoes were two-tone; his pants wide-cut, draped and pleated; the black coat reached almost to his knees; and his watch chain hung in a long, three-foot loop. His tie was skinny, and the brim of his hat was wide. When he removed it, a full head of snow-white hair was revealed, neatly brushed back into an immaculate DA.

"Mr. Gibson?"

Gibson nodded and held the door wide open. "Please come in, Mr. Casillas."

The old man stepped across the threshold, moving with an energy that also wasn't in keeping with his apparent years.

"I believe your TV had a word with you earlier."

They had walked through into the kitchen. The odd little man seemed no more real to Gibson than the thing that had interrupted the NBC news.

"You did that?"

"I felt that I needed to get your attention."

Gibson took a unopened bottle of Scotch from the Welsh dresser. He cracked the seal with a brisk, businesslike twist and poured himself a large shot. Before he drank it down, he held the glass up to the light. He had to believe that something was real.

"Are you telling me that you interrupted a network TV broadcast just to get my attention?"

Casillas shook his head. "Believe me, I didn't interrupt anything. I only borrowed the facility. Besides, the skull was instructed to appear only on your set."

Gibson poured himself a second shot. "Do you want a drink?"

Casillas shook his head a second time. "Alas, I am unable to indulge in alcohol anymore, but please feel free to do so yourself, as much as you want. I can still enjoy watching a young man drink."

Gibson drank half the shot. "I'm not that young anymore."

"You're but a child from where I stand."

In an attempt to restore some minor normality to the situation, Gibson sat down at the kitchen table and indicated that Casillas should do the same. There had to be a way to find a point of perspective on all this, a position from which he could handle what was going on. It wasn't easy, not when faced with Casillas's preposterous clothes and even more preposterous suggestion that he could alter someone's television programming at will. And yet the skull had appeared on his TV. Gibson was starting to feel that it was going to be a long night.

"What exactly is this all about?"

"It is complicated."

Gibson sighed. "You know something? I rather thought that it might be."

"We also have very little time."

"We do?"

"Very little time."

When Casillas had first entered the kitchen, his eyes had moved around the room, darting from side to side, watchful, cautious; the jerky gaze, plus the small, fast motions of his head, and his delicate, fragile-looking bones gave him such a resemblance to an inquisitive bird, but once seated he fixed Gibson with an unwavering stare.

"Very little time indeed," he repeated.

Gibson leaned back in his chair. He didn't like that stare at all. The old man's eyes seemed to radiate power, as though they could bore into his head and read his very thoughts.

"Maybe you could start by telling me how you put that thing on my TV?"

Casillas looked sad. "I don't want you to think me rude or feel insulted, but if I did try to explain it, I very much doubt that you would understand. Shall we just say that my associates and I have considerable resources at our disposal?"

Gibson raised an eyebrow. "Associates?"

"I'm not acting alone here, Mr. Gibson. I am the representative of a much larger organization."

"Do you want to tell me what this organization is?"

"No yet. For the moment it will have to remain anonymous."

Gibson lit a cigarette. His patience was wearing a little thin. "This is all a bit too mysterious, Señor Casillas. If you don't want to tell me anything, why did you come here?"

Casillas sat up a little straighter in his chair and neatly folded his hands in front of him. "I have a problem."

Gibson regarded him expressionlessly. "We all have problems, señor."

"I seriously fear that you may have difficulty believing much of what I have to tell to you."

Despite himself, Gibson couldn't help grinning. "I've seen more than my fair share of the weird."

Casillas nodded. "I know that. That's why I'm here."

"So try me."

"My first reason for coming here was to see you, to look at you face-to-face and decide if you really were the person we were looking for."

"Are you telling me that this is an audition?"

Casillas smiled. "If you want to think of it like that."

"It's been a long time since I auditioned for anything."

"You could also think of it as the first phase of a recruiting process."

"And do I get the part?"

Casillas's smile faded. "Unfortunately, I think that you do. If you're agreeable, that is."

"Unfortunately?"

"I still have a number of reservations regarding your erratic and self-destructive life-style. You live in a serious state of denial, Mr. Gibson."

"I'm sorry I'm such a disappointment."

Casillas's fingers flexed. "Would you be willing to come with me and meet my associates?"

Gibson was on guard again. This was something new. "Right now?"

"There's no time like the present."

Gibson started to shake his head. "I'm not sure that I can do that."

Up to that point, Gibson had been prepared to let Casillas ramble on, figuring that he would get to whatever was on his mind in his own good time. To have the crazy old geezer sitting in his kitchen was one thing. To go out into the night with him was quite another.

Casillas had placed both hands flat on the table. "I can't urge you strongly enough. I realize that I'm expecting you to take a great deal on trust, which must be hard for a paranoid individual such as yourself, but this really is a matter of the utmost urgency."

Something was happening to the old man's eyes as he spoke: they seemed to be growing in his head, making it impossible for Gibson to look away. With a major effort of will he pulled loose from the bright-eyed stare and focused his attention instead on the portrait of himself on the wall.

Anger overtook Gibson. "This is a fucking charade."

The old man wasn't amusing anymore. It was an invasion, first of Gibson's home and then of his free will.

Casillas tilted his head slightly. "A charade, Mr. Gibson?"

"Yeah, right. A charade. I have the distinct impression that you can make me do pretty much what you want. First you cause some Aztec human-sacrifice demon to take over my TV and then . . ."

"Actually it was a rather benign mortality demon, low-level and virtually harmless beyond the odd prank."

Gibson pressed on regardless, feeding on his own fury. "And then you show up at my door, and I'm damn sure that if there hadn't been someone or something working on me I never would have let you in here. When it started, it was intriguing, but the idea of someone having the gall to sit right here in my kitchen and try to hypnotize me makes me good and mad. I don't give a fuck what the problem is or how little time you and your associates have got, but I'm not going anywhere with you or anyone until I know what all this is about. You can go on trying to work your mojo on me, but it's hard to put something over on an angry man."

Casillas was actually smiling. "You seem very adept at detecting what you call a mojo."

With a boldness that verged on recklessness, Gibson looked straight back into the bead-bright black eyes. "I've been around."

"That's exactly why I'm here."

"So start talking."

Casillas, seemingly aware that he had gone too far, took a deep breath. "You must understand that my associates and I are under a great deal of pressure and it tends to make us a little high-handed in our dealings with others."

Gibson nodded. "I know how that goes."

Casillas's expression was suddenly very hard and very cold. "You do?"

"Like I said, I've been around."

The old man seemed about to respond with an anger to match Gibson's, but then he controlled himself with a visible effort.

"The world is a nervous place, my friend. Already it dances from one real or imagined fear to the next. Although it doesn't know it yet, it now has very good reason for fear. A catastrophe is building of a magnitude that will surpass anything humanity has ever witnessed. Indeed, if it comes, it will be more destructive than anything ever witnessed by any life on this planet. It will be the worst thing to happen since the asteroid Telal exploded and wiped out the dinosaurs."

Casillas looked to Gibson for a reaction. Gibson was in the

process of surrendering. If this was madness, it was madness on a refreshingly lavish scale. Getting no response, Casillas went on.

"We live in a multidimensional universe, and by far the greater part of it is not, and possibly never will be, understood by human beings. We do, however, live in it, and when forces are unleashed across those dimensions, they can threaten and even destroy us whether we understand them or not."

Casillas once again looked for a response, but Gibson was biding his time, just letting the idea of a multidimensional universe flow over him. He hadn't even started to consider what truth there might be in any part of the bizarre tale.

"Few of us, with the possible exception of Albert Einstein, have the math to even approach a grasp of the dimensions immediately aligned with our own. We have yet to do better than the Chaldeans, who, simply and succinctly, described the universe as consisting of the Earth, the zones above the Earth, and the zones below the Earth. They, at least, could accept the idea that there are other realities and existences about which we have little or no awareness. How about you, Mr. Gibson? Are you able to accept that?"

Gibson nodded. "Round about now, I could accept almost anything."

"Please don't be flippant."

"I'm not being flippant, it's just the sound of one mind boggling."

The old man half smiled. "Just try and stay with me."

"I'll do my best."

"In normal times, these various dimensions move forward in unison along the time stream with little or no interface one to another. From time to time there have been leakages, minor print-throughs. The UFOs with which we have become so familiar are a product of exactly one such recent occurrence. There are, however, moments of major confluence, and these have the potential for the kind of disaster that we seem to be approaching. At such times it is briefly possible for entities with the necessary knowledge to pass from one reality to another. History is littered with the stories and legends of these beings—Zeus, Azag-Thoth, Jesus of Nazareth, Abdul Alhazred the so-called Mad Arab, Vlad Tepes the Impaler . . ."

Gibson blinked. "Are you telling me that Dracula was from another dimension?"

Casillas made a dismissive gesture. "Did you ever think otherwise?"

Gibson sighed. "I guess I'm a little slow."

"We are approaching an era where the slow may lose everything."

"I'm guessing that all this is the lead-in to your telling me that this disaster that's on its way is going to come screaming out of another dimension."

Casillas nodded. "Exactly that. A prime confluence is very close. Even under normal circumstances this would be a time of confusion and possible global danger. These, though, are far from being normal circumstances. There is an entity."

Gibson raised an eyebrow. "An entity?"

"He was known to the ancients as Akhkhara and later he was called Necrom."

"Necrom?"

"Necrom." Casillas let the name sink in. "Necrom is one of the most massive and malevolent intelligences in the as yet realized universe. He normally occupies a dimension that is so far removed that it scarcely even impinges upon ours and the others near us."

"So why do we have to worry about him?"

"For millennia, Necrom has slept but, very soon, he will wake. And his waking will coincide exactly with the major confluence. If, once he is risen, this being, this awesomely powerful and unbelievably evil thing, is able to roam loose, to move, as he is quite well able to, from dimension to dimension at will, the potential for destruction on all levels of the universe would be beyond description."

Gibson had become numb. Necrom? The multidimensional universe? If he had let it, his head would have been reeling, but his hangover, which was still very much with him, made it simpler to go numb. What he needed was some handhold by which he could pull himself back into the infinitely more comfortable world where he drank too much and took too many drugs, where his career was a shambles and the record companies put him on hold, where he owed a cool half million in back taxes. Necrom or the IRS? It was a questionable choice, and he unashamedly scrabbled for disbelief. The best he could do was to hold up a hand to cut Casillas's flow.

"Okay, okay. Even if, for the sake of argument, I go along with all this, what does it have to do with me? Why have I been picked out for a private, personal warning? You like my old records or something? It seems to me that there isn't too much I could do about Necrom if he ever decided to come after me."

Casillas smiled sadly and shook his head. "This isn't a warning, Joseph Gibson. This is a request for help."

Now Gibson's head was reeling.

"You want my help?"

"That's right."

Gibson couldn't stop himself. He burst out laughing.

"Let me get this straight. You want a drunken, broken-down ex-rock star to go out and fight Necrom? Give me a break, will you?"

Casillas was expressionless. "Nobody would expect you to go anywhere near a leviathan like Necrom. Those of his own kind will do their best to deal with him."

"So what do you want of me?"

"He is not the only entity that will be on the move during the confluence. Hundreds of others, from simple tricksters to the brilliantly malign, will be stirred up by the rising of Necrom. Like the tiny scavenger fish that swim in the wake of a great whale, they will stream through the wormholes created by the confluence to wreak whatever mischief they can on a whole spectrum of realities. These will be our adversaries and, believe me, they will be more than enough to test the limits of our strength. Accordingly, we are recruiting anyone we think might have the potential to aid us in the coming conflict."

Gibson covered his shock by slowly lighting another cigarette, doing his best to stop his hands from shaking.

"What the hell makes you think that I'll be of any use to you? I mean, look at me. I can hardly manage my own life, let alone save the multidimensional universe."

"We have studied enough of your background to know that you are no stranger to the paranormal. Even though it was the fleeting interest of the dilettante, you have attempted to gain a measure of enlightenment and seem to have managed to avoid the path of universal evil. That in itself is a rarity in these blighted times. You attended a *yage* ceremony in that apartment in Mexico City and a coven in the Scottish Hebrides. You have eaten peyote with the Hopi and—"

"But that was just dabbling," Gibson protested, "what we used to call kicks, an extra twist on sex, drugs, and rock 'n' roll."

"Even dabbling can produce a certain insight, but I think you protest too much. That ceremony in the graveyard in Port-au-Prince went a good deal further than mere dabbling.''

Gibson swallowed hard. He had always assumed that no one had known about that grisly and thoroughly terrifying Haitian escapade beyond those who had been present at the time.

Casillas grinned as though he actually was reading Gibson's thoughts. ''The most important fact about you is that you have the energy and you have the aura. The aura may currently be tarnished and the energy low, but you can be built up again. The latency is still there. Without it, you could never have been what you were, and an aura is something that you cannot lose.''

Gibson mashed out the cigarette. Nobody had ever wanted him for his aura before, at least not in so many words.

''You keep talking about 'we' and 'us' and your associates. Who is this 'us'? Do you and your associates have a collective title?''

''We are the Nine.''

Gibson frowned. ''I've heard of the Nine.''

''You've heard the legends.''

''And now you're going to tell me the truth?''

Casillas nodded. ''In ancient times, the Nine were the overseers of humanity's occult destiny, the custodians of this dimension and this reality. When we discovered, this time around, that there had been nine of us contacted, we took the title. It seemed only reasonable. We are fulfilling the same function. We are the new guardians.''

''When you say 'contacted,' what exactly do you mean?''

''We have been in contact with beings from elsewhere.''

For Gibson, that was the final straw. Clearly the old geezer was barking nuts.

Casillas saw his reaction and quickly went on. ''I know it's hard to believe but I beg you to retain an open mind. We are nine human beings, nine mortals who, by differing routes, have become partially aware of the true nature of the multidimensional universe. When the threat presented by the coming confluence became known, we were brought together by representatives of the dimensions nearest to us with a view to forming a defensive alliance.''

''You're telling me that you've been to another dimension?''

Casillas wearily shook his head. ''Alas, no. All contacts have so far been in this world.''

The old man was starting to look very tired. For the first time, his energy seemed to match his apparent age. He raised both hands.

"I really can't talk any more. If you want to learn more, please come with me. That's all I can say. Come with me now."

The White Room

NURSE LOPEZ WAS late. He could tell she was late because the *NBC Nightly News* had already started. Lateness was something that almost never happened in the very expensive clinic. Nurse Lopez usually arrived before the news to administer the shot, the one that messed up his memory. She usually arrived before the news because the people in white, the doctors and the nurses, were aware that, with the previous shot wearing off, the news tended to upset him. The doctors had discovered this when he'd first been brought to the hospital. What disturbed him was the fact that the regular anchorman, Gary Elliot, had been replaced by someone called Tom Brokaw. The weird, altered details were the first phase of his coming unhinged and the hideous slide into screaming panic. A car that he knew as the Nissan Imperator was being advertised as the Infiniti. Solly the Sailor was suddenly known as Popeye, although mercifully he was still created by Max Fleisher. Everyone he asked claimed never to have heard of Gary Elliot or the Imperator or Solly the Sailor. It was as though they were products of some elaborate fantasy that was exclusively his. At first they'd simply shut off the TV, but he'd dug his heels in and demanded that it be turned on again. After that they had simply made sure that he was doped to the eyeballs when Popeye or this Brokaw came on. The dope also helped him hide from the more important differences, the ones that would have him baying at the moon if he wasn't sedated.

He heard Nurse Lopez outside the door. The shot had arrived. It was time to go down into the happy, unfeeling depths again. Joe Gibson sighed. He was starting to wonder if they were right. Maybe he was insane. Christ, if only he'd never given in to the whim and taken that first ride with Casillas.

Chapter
Two

THE TWO OF them rode down in the elevator without speaking. Casillas leaned impassively on his cane, and Gibson wondered what the hell he was thinking about going anywhere with the weird old man. This time he couldn't blame it on the old man using any ancient Mexican whammy. Don Carlos Gustavo Casillas had been very insistent that Gibson came of his own free will. His own reckless curiosity had to take sole responsibility for the fact that he was leaving the building on his way to an unknown destination to meet a group of people who claimed to be in touch with other dimensions. After all those years, he really should have known better. His curiosity had certainly landed him in enough trouble to teach him some sort of a lesson. Most of his current problems had started with that small but devilish voice that always began its arguments with a grin and a shrug and the exclamation, "Ah, what the hell." In this case it was, "Ah, what the hell, suppose everything that Casillas said is true. Wouldn't that be a kick in the head?" Of course, that would also mean that Necrom was real, and he didn't like the sound of Necrom one little bit. But one thing at a time. First he'd see what the Nine were all about and then take it from there. The odds were that it'd be a total letdown and they'd turn out to be the kind of loonies who also sent messages to Venus by banana-powered radio. He just couldn't resist the temptation to see for himself.

As they walked through the lobby, Ramone stared curiously at them but made no comment. Gibson nodded and Ramone nodded back with that look of supercilious disapproval that was unique to the doormen of expensive Manhattan apartment buildings. Fuck you, Ramone. You ought to be used to it by now.

Weird visitors going to and coming from his apartment were hardly a novelty anymore.

Outside, on Central Park West, Gibson finally broke the silence. "Do we get a cab?"

After all that Casillas had been saying, Gibson was mildly surprised that he wasn't levitating the pair of them to wherever they were going.

The old man shook his head. "My car will be here in a moment."

He didn't explain how whoever was driving the car would know that he was waiting for it.

An immaculate, midnight-blue Rolls Royce Silver Ghost with whitewalls and tinted windows was majestically commanding the inside lane. The other traffic seemed actually to defer to it, and Gibson knew instinctively that it belonged to Casillas. Sure enough, it slowed to a stop right in front of them. A tall, black chauffeur in pearl-gray livery and with Stevie Wonder braids under his formal peaked cap climbed out and walked round to open the near-side rear door.

Casillas glanced at Gibson. "This is Amadeus."

Gibson nodded to the chauffeur, who returned his gaze as though he wasn't particularly impressed.

Casillas concluded the introduction. "This is Joseph Gibson."

It was Amadeus's turn to nod. He was curt in the extreme. "I know. I used to see him on TV."

Gibson didn't see why he should stand for this hostility. He smiled right back at the chauffeur. "I hope you enjoyed it."

"I never enjoy seeing a white boy ripping off Chuck Berry and James Brown."

Gibson nodded. At least he knew where the two of them stood. Casillas terminated the exchange by ducking quickly into the car. After a moment's hesitation, Gibson followed, and as soon as Amadeus was behind the wheel, the Rolls quickly pulled out into the stream of traffic.

They seemed to be heading downtown, rounding Columbus Circle and then along Central Park South to turn down Fifth Avenue. The early-evening traffic was light and moving rapidly and, in short order, they were passing the blank-eyed bronze eagles that flanked the steps to the Public Library. Casillas didn't seem to want to talk, so Gibson stared through the smoked-glass windows as they continued south. No one seemed willing to tell Gibson anything about where they were going. It wasn't until they passed Twenty-third Street, with the landmark of the Chelsea Hotel on the corner, that Amadeus broke the silence, and then it turned out to be an emergency.

The chauffeur glanced sharply back at Casillas. "I think we're being followed. There's this guy who's been sticking to our tail since just below Forty-second Street."

Casillas cursed softly in Spanish. "What kind of car is it?"

"A black Jeep Cherokee with crash screens and the whole bit."

Gibson swiveled in his seat and peered through the Rolls's narrow rear window. Sure enough, there it was, just as Amadeus had described it, equipped with every kind of exterior gizmo short of machine-gun mounts and finished in a dull black that gleamed dimly as it passed under the streetlights and cheap neon around Fourteenth Street; it might have just been a trick of the light, but the car seemed to carry with it an aura of profound menace.

Gibson suppressed a shudder. "Are they really following us?"

Amadeus nodded. "And making no secret of it, either."

Gibson looked at Casillas. "Do you know who they are?"

The old man's face was tight. "Whoever they are, I don't think they mean us any good."

"Maybe you ought to let me off here."

Casillas didn't even consider the idea. "It's too late for that."

Amadeus glanced into the rearview mirror. "You want me to take evasive action?"

Casillas frowned. "They may be hard to lose."

"I'll do my best."

Amadeus, who up to that point had been maintaining a fairly dignified speed, quite in keeping with the stately demeanor of the Rolls, suddenly put the hammer down. There was no more dignity in the car's engine. The snarl of raw power drowned out the ticking of the clock. Someone had done a superb job on whatever was under the hood. Unfortunately the Jeep also had the horses, and it stuck with them. Now they were down in the Village and the traffic was heavier, complicated by cabs dropping off and picking up in front of bars and clubs and restaurants. Amadeus, however, maneuvered his way through it, swerving and weaving like Steve McQueen in *Bullitt*, ignoring the horns and the cursing that he left in his wake.

Gibson was now thoroughly alarmed. "Listen, I'm not kidding. I want to get out. Right now."

Casillas glanced behind. The black Jeep was just two car lengths behind. "It wouldn't do you any good. On the sidewalk, you'd be a sitting duck. You're much safer with Amadeus."

Gibson didn't care if his voice sounded desperate. "I don't have any beef with these people, whoever they are."

Casillas's expression was politely regretful. "I'm afraid, as far as these people are concerned, you became one of us the moment you got into the car. Guilt by association."

"What do they want?"

"They want us, Mr. Gibson. They want us. Although I wouldn't care to speculate what they intend to do with us if they get us."

Gibson felt sick. "Jesus Christ."

Amadeus turned in his seat and flashed Gibson a broad grin. Three of his front teeth were gold. "Life's a bitch, ain't it, Joe?"

They were through the Village and headed for Canal Street. The three towers of the World Trade Center loomed luminously in front of them. Amadeus ran the lights by the ball court at Houston, but the Jeep came through right behind them in a drawn-out, discordant fanfare of angry New York horns.

Amadeus was shaking his head. "These guys just don't give up. With your permission, *padrone*, I'm going to swing into the Holland Tunnel and try and shake them on the Jersey side. Jersey got a mojo all of its own."

Casillas nodded. "Whatever you think."

Amadeus left the turn until the very last second and then screamed the Rolls across three lanes in the hope of faking out the Jeep's driver and leaving him racing fruitlessly toward the Battery. Again, the drivers around him leaned on their horns in protest. It was a good theory but it didn't work. As the Rolls plunged into the smell and dirty tiles of the tunnel, the Jeep followed as though it were glued to them. Amadeus swore bitterly, using what sounded like African curses.

"It's like the motherfucker knows what I'm going to do before I do it."

Casillas nodded gravely. "They may have help."

"So when does our side come through with some?"

"We'll just have to wait and see."

"Shee-it. You better hold on in the back there. These guys are coming for us."

Casillas and Gibson grabbed for handholds as Amadeus swung the Rolls from side to side across the width of the tunnel. The

Jeep was aggressively jockeying to move up beside them. Something black and cylindrical protruded from a slit in the mesh screen that covered the right-hand passenger window. Gibson's stomach lurched and knotted as he recognized it as the snout of an assault rifle.

"They've got a gun, goddamn it!"

Amadeus grunted. "We're lucky they ain't got a fucking rocket launcher."

A voice shrieked in Gibson's head. Get out of here! Get out of here! It was only the last shreds of a self-destructive pride that stopped him from sliding to the floor of the car and huddling there whimpering.

Amadeus only managed to keep the black Jeep at bay by making it impossible to get past the Rolls in the narrow confines of the tunnel. The tunnel, however, wouldn't go on forever. The two vehicles came out on the Jersey side like twin shots from a cannon. The Rolls howled past the tollbooths and startled faces gaped from the cars waiting for the lights. The Jeep swung wide, running abreast of the Rolls, and muzzle flashes chattered from the weapon aiming out of the side window.

Amadeus was yelling, "Get down and keep hanging on!"

A stammer of bullets raked the Rolls. Gibson now had no reservations about hitting the floor. The old man was crouched beside him. The left rear window starred but didn't shatter.

"Armored glass?"

He found that his voice had gone up an octave.

Amadeus grunted as he wrenched the wheel around and spun the car into a side street. "Inch thick."

He made four more fast turns and then eased off slightly. There was no sign of the Jeep Cherokee.

"I think we may have thrown them off for the moment."

"Don't speak too soon."

Amadeus kept looking back. "I don't see them."

Casillas eased himself back into the seat. "Just keep going, drive around for a while, and then we'll try to slip back into Manhattan."

Gibson was also up off the floor. He looked out of the window. He didn't have a clue where he was except the vaguest idea that they were somewhere in back of the Jersey City waterfront. They were passing factories and warehouses and two-story houses punctuated here and there by the lights of a liquor store, corner grocery, or fast-food joint. After almost twenty minutes of zigzagging through this kind of terrain, Casillas decided that it might be safe to make for the Lincoln Tunnel and back to New York. In just five blocks, he was proved wrong. Once again it was as though whoever was in control of the black Jeep Cherokee could read their minds. They made a turn and there it was, coming straight at them, the wrong way down a one-way street.

Amadeus yelled a warning. "Motherfucker's going to ram us!"

Amadeus's feet tap-danced, heel and toe, across the brake, clutch, and gas pedals as he spun the steering wheel. The moonshiner's turnaround. Gibson had heard of it but never actually seen it done outside of a movie. He was thrown sideways as the car spun on its axis with a scream of tires and tortured suspension. The front wheels were up on the sidewalk. The Jeep swerved to intercept. For a stretched moment of confusion Amadeus fought with the wheel. A lamppost was coming up. Amadeus stomped down on the brakes. Casillas lost his hold and was thrown forward. He cracked his head on the partition separating the driver from the passengers.

As the Rolls lurched to a stop, Amadeus gestured urgently to Gibson. "Out of the car! Run! Save yourself!"

Gibson looked down at Casillas. He seemed to be out cold, maybe even dead. "What about him?"

"I'll take care of the old one. Go quickly. The armor on this thing is good but it won't stand up to a concerted close-range attack."

Joe Gibson didn't need a second urging. He hit the ground running. The Jeep had come to a stop maybe twenty to thirty yards up the street and was backing up, but he didn't pause to look. In the old days, he'd done a lot of running to and from cars. Back then, the threat had been from hysterical fans who had wanted to tear his clothes off for souvenirs. God knew what the shadowy denizens of the sinister Jeep wanted to do to him.

Gunfire echoed around the buildings behind him, but he didn't look back. He could all too easily imagine bullets tearing into his back. His overwhelming instinct was to dive for a doorway and huddle there, but common sense kept him pounding down the sidewalk. Police sirens wailed intermittently in the distance. For Christ's sake let them get here. He couldn't think of anything better right there and then than being arrested. By the end of three blocks, he was winded. His lungs were laboring and his legs were threatening to cave on him. Too much booze and too many cigarettes—dear God, he was out of condition. There was no sound of footsteps behind him and so far he hadn't been shot, but after another block he couldn't force himself to go any farther. He stopped for a moment and leaned on a fire hydrant, gasping for breath. For the first time, he looked back and immediately wished that he hadn't. The Jeep had reversed up alongside the Rolls, blocking it from moving. Worse than that, though, two men were loping down the street on silent running shoes, obviously coming for him. He took one look and started off again. They had to be from the Jeep. Sweatsuits and porkpie hats, black wraparound sunglasses at night. Both were carrying weapons—which looked uncomfortably like machine pistols— at high port. Over and above the hardware, there was something else that kept Gibson running down that back street in Jersey City. The two figures bore a terrible resemblance to the *tontons* that he'd seen cruising the street that time in Port-au-Prince. They'd also had a thing about Jeep Cherokees. Just the sight of one of them, with crash bars and black windows, was quite enough to strike mortal terror into the average Haitian, and it was doing much the same for Gibson right then. There was nothing he could think of that scared him more than the idea of falling into the hands of a couple of *tonton macoute* with a grudge. The very thought of them set his mind racing in nineteen different directions like a gang of roaches suddenly hit by the light. The things that these voodoo gestapo were rumored to do to their prisoners were the subject of fearful looks and glances over the shoulder. Between the electric shocks and the rubber hoses and the juju chants and zombie powder, they were supposed to not only be able to break man's mind and body, they also came for his soul. Gibson was so scared that it didn't even occur to him to wonder what the hell they might be doing running all over New York and New Jersey and, in particular, why they were coming after him.

He pushed himself off the hydrant and fled on down the street. It was quite enough that the world had stopped making sense with a viciousness that defied even his imagination. The blood was pounding in his head, and his heart threatened to burst. He chanced a glance behind. They were still coming. In fact, they'd gained on him. Not shooting, but just padding effortlessly, a Zulu lope, like hunters running down a wounded buck, seemingly content to let him run himself out. He came to the end of a block and quickly turned the corner. Lose them, he told himself, lose them. He knew in his heart that these guys would be hard to shake, but he had to tell himself something. His sanity was at stake. Why him? What had he done? The new street was nothing more than a black industrial wall thick with graffiti to the height that a kid with a spray can could reach. No yards or back alleys, no place to hide. The *tontons* came round the corner and that moment was close at hand. He searched the night for a bodega or a liquor store that was open. Maybe they wouldn't try anything if there were other people around. There was nothing—no kids hanging out, not even the red light of a Budweiser sign. Gibson could only see the red that was pulsing behind his own eyes. His legs could scarcely lift themselves. It was the point in the nightmare when you woke up, except this was no dream. Gibson knew that he was through; not even mortal fear and certainly not effort of will was going to stop him dropping in his tracks. He was about to faint.

And then the third car was on the scene. The white Cadillac Eldorado came out of the night like the Lone Ranger. As it swept toward him, Gibson dropped to his knees and then to all fours, completely exhausted. He was past caring what this new twist was going to mean, although his pursuers apparently didn't like the look of it. They halted and readied their weapons. The Cadillac slowed to a halt a matter of feet from where Gibson was on his hands and his knees, silhouetting him against the double headlights. He slowly raised his head and stared blindly into their glare. He could almost have sworn that he was being inspected. Nothing happened for a full five seconds. Then the car's doors flew open. Dark figures were moving with the speed and precision of highly trained professionals. What the fuck was this? Mossad? The SAS? He had no more assumptions. Anything could happen.

As Gibson's mind boggled his knees also buckled, and he fell over on his side in the road. It was only a burst of wild gunfire from one of the *tontons* that galvanized him back to life. He curled his body into a tight fetal ball and hugged his head with his arms. His eyes were tightly closed. When the firing suddenly stopped, he hesitatingly opened just one of them. The vision that presented itself had the crystal clarity that only comes when the mind is about to save itself by going into shock. A physically perfect young man was standing beside him. He was wearing neat, dark-blue coveralls with small gold sun symbols at the throat. Lank blond hair hung over a pale face, his knees were bent, and both arms were at full stretch, aiming a hand weapon that was like something out of *Star Wars*, a collection of parallel tubes mounted on an elaborate pistol grip and frame. One of the *tontons* loosed another burst of fire. Gibson curled tighter, but the young man took his time. When he did fire, there was a pair of twin white pulses of light at what was the weapon's approximation of a muzzle and the nearest *tonton* simply vanished. He was gone. No muss, no fuss, not even a puff of smoke or a beam-me-up-Scotty shimmer. Just gone. In the next second the other *tonton* disappeared in exactly the same way as more twin pulses came from the other side of the car.

The young man looked down at Gibson. He could have been a high-tech avenging angel or have come from a flying saucer.

"Streamheat. Just stay put."

"What?"

"We're the good guys, stay right where you are."

And then he was gone. The Cadillac was swerving around Gibson and speeding off down the street, presumably to help Amadeus. It was only at that point that Gibson realized that the Cadillac hadn't made a sound. He eased himself into a sitting position. Gibson could only suppose whoever else had been in the Jeep had gone the same way as their two brothers. Although what way that might have been was something that he didn't want to think about.

It was almost five minutes before they came back to see how he was. He was still sitting in the road. This time the Cadillac halted beside him and two young men in overalls stepped out.

"You'd better get in the car."

Gibson was through. He didn't care if he sat there until the end of time. "Fuck off."

The two perfect young men looked down at him. "You want to sit there all night?"

Gibson petulantly folded his arms. He was aware that he was making an asshole of himself in front of rescuers but he didn't care. "It's my goddamned inalienable right, if I want to. And what the fuck is streamheat anyway."

"Why don't you get in the car and stop causing grief?"

The young man's voice had the paper-thin patience that law-enforcement officers the world over use on the drunk and the difficult. Gibson had heard it plenty of times before, and he couldn't help going for that little extra mileage.

"I told you to fuck off. I'm not getting in any more strange cars."

"Please don't be difficult."

Gibson abruptly changed the subject. "What's happened to Casillas?"

"He's okay. Amadeus is taking care of him. It's taken a lot out of him. Contacting us nearly fried his brain."

Gibson scowled. "He's not the only one with a fried brain."

"So we see."

"Do you wonder at it?"

"Get in the car."

"I told you, fuck off."

Without a word, the two perfect young men reached down, gripped him under the armpits, and started to lift. Gibson had enough common sense left not to resist. He didn't want to go to wherever the *tontons* had gone. They lifted him with no apparent effort, and all he could do was to mollify the old rebel in him by shaking himself free of them when they had him on his feet.

"Okay, okay, I can walk."

He ducked in to the backseat of the Cadillac without any help. The interior had that brand-new leather, fresh-from-the-factory smell, which was a little strange since, as far as Gibson could see, it was an old Caddy, maybe 1964 or 1965. A woman was already sitting in there on the far side of the car, the exact female counterpart of the young men. She was wearing the same coveralls with the same gold sun insignia. In fact, the three of them were so alike that they could have been siblings.

She smiled coldly at Gibson as he sat down beside her. "You really shouldn't be difficult."

"I think I've earned the right."

The woman shrugged. At least he was in the car. The two men got into the front. As the car pulled away, Gibson looked round belligerently. "So who are you? What's all this stream-heat stuff?"

The woman was even better at professional patience than the men were. "We're agents of the Time Stream Directorate."

Gibson looked at her bleakly. "Silly me. I should have known."

"We're part of a multidimensional task force formed in response to the Necrom crisis. I'm Smith—" She indicated the man driving. "—he's Klein—" She pointed to the remaining young man in the front passenger seat. "—and he's French."

Gibson nodded. "Smith, Klein, and French. Am I to understand that you are another three of the Nine?"

Smith laughed. "Us? Hell, no. We're just a set of out-of-town triggers."

"And which town are you out of?"

"You wouldn't know it."

"Try me. I'm widely traveled."

"We're not from this dimension."

Gibson sighed. "Something else I should have known?"

Smith regarded him as though he was a particularly tiresome, low-grade moron. "It's hard to grasp at first."

Gibson allowed himself a long time to digest this. Damn straight it was hard to grasp. He could feel himself slipping again. The interior of the Cadillac had provided a brief illusion of normality. He'd been in a lot of Cadillacs in his time. Now even that was melting away. Once again his cake was in the rain.

"So where are you taking me? To Ganymede? Alpha Centauri?"

The woman may have had more patience but it was quickly ebbing. "You're going to a secure loft in SoHo. You wouldn't like Ganymede."

"And what happens to me when I get there?"

"That will be up to Casillas and his associates. We were only called in as backup."

"Suppose I don't want to go? Suppose I want to go back to my own home and forget all about this lunacy?"

Smith shook her head. "You wouldn't want to do that."

Gibson's eyes narrowed. "Why? Because you'll make me vanish with one of those weird fucking weapons of yours?"

Smith shook her head. "You wouldn't vanish, you'd just fry."

"What are those things anyway?"

Smith touched the weapon at her hip. "The DL20? If I explained, you wouldn't understand."

"Why don't you try me? There seems to be a real shortage of straight answers around here."

French turned in his seat. "Maybe that's the result of a real shortage of straight questions."

The chill silence that followed this shutout was only broken when Gibson finally pulled out his battered pack of cigarettes. "Is anyone going to object if I smoke?"

Smith shook her head. "We don't get cancer."

"Well, good for you." Gibson stuck a Camel Light in his mouth and lit it.

"Maybe you could tell me one thing. If us humans are so dumb and weak and cancer-prone and all-around inferior, how come you superior beings bother?"

French's lip curled. "Just following orders."

Gibson noticed that his hands were shaking. He was in delayed shock. A certain detached part of him wondered how he was managing to adapt so fast to this multidimensional craziness. The weird part was that he wasn't only accepting all that was being thrown at him, but that he was now thinking very clearly. He was even becoming suspicious, and that had to be a good sign.

Gibson eyes swiveled sideways. "Or maybe you aren't really bothering with us. Maybe we're just the inconvenient natives on a prime piece of strategic real estate. Is that it?"

All three streamheat looked sharply at him. Even Klein took his eyes off the road. Gibson seemed to have struck a nerve. He knew it was going to take a lot for him to trust these individuals, even though they had rescued him from the *tonton macoute*. They were just too slick and certain. He loathed people who came on superior, even if they were. He wondered if Chilean peasants looked at the local CIA man in the same way. Smith seemed to sense the way his thoughts were riding and climbed down a couple of notches.

"Listen, Gibson, we know the last few hours must seem like a fever dream to you, but try and go with the program. We've got orders to look after you and that's exactly what we're going to do, whether you cooperate or not. If you have any questions about us, please ask them and I'll do my best to answer in terms that you can understand."

Her tone was still condescending, but at least she seemed to be trying for minimal common ground. The shreds of Gibson's rationality advised him to go along.

"Why me?"

"Why you, what?"

"Why is it me being rescued? Why is it me being chased by *tontons* in the first place?"

Smith's face blanked over. "I don't have any information about that. We just had orders to come and get you. You, Casillas, and the chauffeur. Maybe they'll tell you more when you get to SoHo."

"I thought you were going to answer my questions?"

"I can't tell you what I don't know."

"So what do you know?"

"Try me."

Gibson took a long drag on his cigarette. "What happened to

those guys back there? People don't vanish like that. It's against the laws of physics."

French's expression was pure John Wayne. Gibson almost expected the man to call him pilgrim. "We brought our own laws with us."

Smith shot French a hard warning look and then attempted to answer Gibson's question. "In simple terms, our weapons returned them instantly to their dimensions of origin."

Gibson slowly rubbed his jaw.

"Are you telling me they were also from another dimension?"

"That's correct."

"Suppose they'd really been human?"

"We're all human, more or less."

"But suppose they'd been from this dimension."

"Like I said before, they would have fried. When the weapon's used on an individual who's in his or her dimension of origin, there's nowhere for the energy to vent to. A circle burn starts in the molecular structure. *Fizzipp.* High-speed sizzle."

Gibson was a little sickened by the idea. He eyed the weapon on Smith's hip.

"Nothing left?"

French laughed nastily.

"Maybe a grease spot."

Gibson was still having trouble with it all. The more he learned the greater the confusion. One thing he knew for sure, though—he really didn't like the streamheat.

"I don't get it. Why the hell should a bunch of cats from another dimension want to disguise themselves as a Haitian death squad?"

"Habit. And maybe because they enjoy it. Haiti has been a major entry portal to this dimension for more than a century."

"The voodoo lets them through?"

"Among other things."

Gibson sagged in the seat. "This is getting out of hand."

Klein spoke for the first time. "Makes your head spin at first, doesn't it?"

Gibson nodded. "You can say that again." He thought for a moment. "Let me get this straight. These guys slip through and your job is to zap them back again?"

"That's putting it a little crudely."

"But those weapons do zap them back?"

Smith nodded. "Right back to their own dimension."

Gibson snapped his fingers.

"Just like that?"

Smith smiled. It was the first time Gibson had seen any crack in the cold efficiency. "Just like that. Sometimes they arrive intact and sometimes they don't. Sometimes they come out at ground level but other times they materialize in the middle of a mountain or a thousand feet up in empty air."

"You sound like you don't particularly care."

"We don't lose any sleep over it."

Something occurred to Gibson. It was one of those thoughts that one immediately regrets thinking. "You say that everyone's human, more or less?"

"More or less, except those who aren't."

"Are you?"

Klein laughed. He must have seen Gibson's expression in the mirror. "Don't worry, we can't turn into the Dunwich Horror right before your eyes."

Gibson turned to Smith for help.

"This is more than making my head spin."

"That's because you have no real grasp of the multidimensional universe."

"Perhaps you'd like to explain it to me?"

Smith frowned. "Not really. I don't have the time, and you don't have the math."

Gibson was starting to come out of his shock, and the repeated double-talk was starting to make him angry. "You call this answering my questions?"

Smith did her best to placate him. "I'm not trying to be difficult. It's just that you keep asking questions that only show you don't even understand the fundamental principles. I mean, you probably think that when I'm talking about another dimension, I'm referring to things that are—" She gestured airily to beyond the car window. "—over there somewhere."

"Well, aren't they?"

Smith shook her head. "Quite the reverse; thousands of dimensions exist at once in the same relative space."

"So how come we aren't knocking into each other all the time?"

"Because different dimensions exist at different levels of reality, at different wavelengths if you like. Like the different channels on a TV set if it helps to think of it that way."

Gibson nodded. "I understand wavelengths. One zigs and the

other zags so the twain never meet. There seems to be quite a lot of meeting of the twain, though. I mean, you guys are here."

French half smiled. "He's really quite smart for a primitive."

Gibson scowled. "That's what Custer said about Sitting Bull."

Smith ignored the exchange. "In normal times, the worst that happens is a degree of leakage."

"But these aren't normal times."

Klein snorted. "There's leakage all over the place. Things are getting real messy."

Gibson was thoughtful. "So, when you travel from one dimension to another, it's really a matter of tuning, of changing wavelengths?"

"You could look at it that way."

"How do you do it?"

"How do you do what?"

"Travel from one dimension to another?"

Smith shook her head as if talking to a child who amazed her with its relentless questions. "There are dozens of ways, maybe hundreds. They range from primitive, animalistic energy rites to the most sophisticated subpartical—"

French quickly cut in. "You think you should be telling him that?"

Smith looked surprised. "I'm hardly giving him a course in how to do it."

"I think all that Gibson really wants is a reassurance that we aren't monsters disguised as humans."

French was right, but Gibson greatly objected to the way that he said it.

Smith spread her hands. "Back in our own dimension, we're as human as you are. There are certain minor changes that take place when we go through transition. Local adaptation is part of the process; it's integral to the dimension crossover. It quite literally comes with the territory. Much depends on subjective perception but, all in all, we are all very similar, certainly not monsters."

Gibson didn't sound quite convinced. "Just our brothers on another wavelength?"

"Right."

"That's a relief."

"I thought it might be."

Gibson looked at Smith. She really was a good-looking woman.

"So what I see is what I get?"

"Quite."

"And how do you see me?"

"The adaptation process is really a two-way street. It allows us to interface in all the normal ways."

Despite his confusion, Gibson managed to raise a flippant grin. "And does normal interface include sex?"

Smith's eyes became steely. "It's possible, but try anything with me and I'll break it off."

They were back in the Holland Tunnel. In a couple of minutes, they'd be in SoHo, and Gibson decided it was time to concentrate on psyching himself up as far as he could in preparation for whatever might be coming next. He didn't doubt that their destination would deliver a whole new set of shocks and surprises. They were passing the Four Roses Bar on Canal Street, and he was forcibly reminded how badly he needed a drink. Damn but he could use a shot before they got to where they were going. He had half a notion to ask Klein to pull over, but then he pictured the three streamheat—even if they could be persuaded to stop at the bar, which he didn't imagine they could—marching into the Four Roses, with their neat uniforms and whitebread-clone good looks, while the disco lights flashed and James Brown pumped out from the jukebox. They'd clear the place. The clientele of the Four Roses, as Gibson remembered it, would assume that the trio were some new kind of narco task force and instantly vanish for parts unknown.

They turned up Lafayette and then doubled back on Broome Street. Finally they turned into Greene. The Cadillac slowed to a stop in front of a loft building with no lights showing.

Klein turned off the engine. "This is it."

Smith looked at Gibson.

"Stay put until we're sure there's no problem."

Although apparently deserted, the place was covered by what, even to Gibson's untrained eye, had to be a considerable screen of discreet security. Two heavyset thug types in dark suits flanked the totally unremarkable entrance, like the doormen of some clandestine nightclub. Two others, junior mob in leather jackets and those stone-washed jeans that were so big with Italians, were stationed under the streetlamp on the other side of the street. Every so often, one of them would mutter something into his cupped hand as though he was holding a small transceiver. A black van with darkened windows and Virginia plates was parked at the curb.

Smith, Klein, and French looked round carefully. It was only when they seemed thoroughly convinced that everything was in order that they started to make a move. Smith fixed Gibson with an I'll-only-say-this-once stare.

"We're going to get out of the car and walk directly to the door of that building. Don't worry about the two men standing there. They have orders to let us through. Whatever you do or whatever happens, don't stop. Don't stop for anything. Do you understand?"

Gibson nodded. "I keep going, no matter what, until I'm inside the building."

"Okay, let's go."

They were out of the car and walking smartly across the sidewalk. From what Smith had said, Gibson wouldn't have been too surprised if the air had suddenly been filled with *tontons macoute* paratroopers in Ray Charles sunglasses. As it was, nothing happened at all. One of the men in the entrance pushed open the street door and they were inside. Two more security goons waited in the small lobby, inner-circle Nation of Islam with faces hard enough to cut glass. The Nine seemed to draw their muscle from the most diverse sources. While Gibson and the three streamheat waited for the elevator, they were inspected at length by the cold black lens of an automatic surveillance camera. A second camera inside the elevator gave them an equally thorough going-over. The walls of the car were lined with armor plate, and no less than three very complex electronic locking devices were mounted on its sliding doors. Gibson didn't find the level of security exactly comforting. It was nice to be protected, but it also indicated that those who occupied the building appeared to consider themselves to be in some considerable danger.

Gibson wasn't exactly sure what he'd expected to see when he stepped out of the elevator, but what confronted him when the doors slid back certainly wasn't it. The major surprise was the absolute normality. The black-glass reception area could have belonged to any trendy SoHo office space: an overly hip real-estate broker; a young, happening rock 'n' roll lawyer; a model agency. The wall behind the designer Swedish reception desk bore the legend Group Nine in a foot-high, slickly corporate typeface. Only two things didn't fit the contrived image of Lower Manhattan yuppiedom. One was the large framed William Blake print. The fiber-optic sculpture was okay but the Blake was a tad too mystic. The other was the thick steel door that led to whatever else the loft might contain. This was simply incongruous. It belonged in a bank or on the bulkhead of a nuclear submarine. No amount of interior decorating could disguise the fact that it could probably withstand a concerted attack with thermite and explosives.

A sleek young woman with straight, Nordic blond hair was sitting behind the reception desk. She stood up when Gibson and his escort came out of the elevator.

"Mr. Gibson?"

"That's me."

"We've been expecting you."

The black rollneck sweater and leather skirt showed off a slender thoroughbred figure that could have been featured in *Vogue*.

"If you'd like to follow me, the members are waiting for you."

"The members?"

"Please follow me."

She walked over to the massive steel door and tapped an eleven-figure code into a keypad on the wall beside it. The big door slid back absolutely silently, no mean feat of precision engineering considering that the door proved to be almost a foot thick. What the hell were these people using for money? He'd only seen the tip of the iceberg so far, but already the tab was up in the millions. More important, what were they scared of? The area beyond the door was closer to Gibson's imagining than reception had been. He'd expected the extremely strange and now he was unquestionably getting it. He found that he'd stepped into some weird-science hybrid of NORAD and the Temple of Thoth. It had to be the next best thing to visiting another planet. Even the air was far from normal. There was an almost vibrant metallic bite to it, as though it had been filtered through some run-amok comfort system.

The receptionist smiled back at him as though she'd read his thoughts. "You're in a controlled and sterile biospace, Mr. Gibson. It's heavily over-oxygenated and, of course, the equipment gives off a lot of ozone."

Of course.

"It takes a little getting used to at first but, after a while, you don't really notice it, and the extra oxygen gives you so much more energy. Of course, you can't smoke."

Of course.

"The only places that you can smoke are in the designated areas. I can't stress this strongly enough, Mr. Gibson. Smoking outside the designated areas is extremely dangerous."

Message received and understood.

"I was out of cigarettes anyway."

The receptionist was leading Gibson and his streamheat minders down the central aisle of a very large loft. So large, in fact, that it must have run all the way through to the other side of the block. On one side of the central aisle, there was an area that looked for all the world like a compact version of NASA mission control or possibly the launch center of an MX-missile complex. Lines of computer workstations were arranged in semicircular rows facing the big board, a multiple split-projection display the size of a small cinema screen. The main display was a simplified map of the world according to Mercator. This was surrounded by a bank of smaller displays, some twenty in all; the majority of these small screens showed the layouts of familiar cities— New York, London, Paris, Los Angeles, Beirut, Jerusalem, Tokyo, Rio—but others were showing places that Gibson didn't recognize, either by name or configuration.

The large map was dotted with a hundred or more bloodred points of light. In the main they corresponded with the major centers of population, but here and there there were dots in some of the most inaccessible spots on the face of the Earth. There were two in Antarctica, two more in remote parts of the Andes, three up the Amazon, and no less than six in the Australian outback. Here and there, two or more dots had merged to produce irregular shaded areas that resembled the blemishes of an unpleasant disease. The planet on the big board looked sick and infected, and Gibson knew in his heart that this wasn't just an error in design. The big board was plotting some very bad news. He searched out Haiti. It was one solid red island. The area of Tibet was similarly shaded.

Gibson transferred his attention from the display screens to the people who sat hunched over the rows of computer terminals. Most were the kind of shirt-sleeved, crew-cut young men one might expect to find at a military installation; there was also a sprinkling of beards and rock-band T-shirts that might be more in keeping with MIT or Caltech. Right in the middle, however, there was a shaved head and a saffron robe. What the hell was a Buddhist priest doing running a state-of-the-art computer?

Something else caught Gibson's eye. He paused in midstride and leaned over the shoulder of one of the operators in the back row and looked at his terminal. The characters that were traveling from the bottom to the top of his screen, green and orange out of black, were completely alien, like nothing that Gibson, who prided himself on being pretty well traveled, had ever seen before.

The receptionist immediately snapped him to heel. "Please don't linger, Mr. Gibson. The members are waiting."

The other side of the aisle was even more fantastic. Gibson didn't even recognize the components. A circular area of floor, about twenty feet across, had been surfaced in what looked like either black marble or some sort of plastic substitute. Lines of a red substance were inlaid into the marble like giant symbols or possibly even a huge printed circuit. A pair of sturdy translucent pillars, some two feet in diameter, stood in the center of the marble circle and extended almost to the roof. They were sunk into gold floor settings, and they terminated in two large gold spheres. Inside the pillars, a dimly glowing, green-tinged liquid energy writhed and undulated, making the pillars look like two giant lava lamps arranged side by side. The space between the pillars appeared to pulse with an indistinct shimmer like the heat haze on a blacktop in the afternoon sun. Although there were no people in this part of the loft, the whole area seemed to be alive with abnormal and unearthly energy.

At the end of the aisle there was a pair of double doors. Gibson was a little relieved to see that they were simple mahogany with plain brass fittings. It pleased Gibson that they hadn't been constructed to withstand a small nuclear attack. They were, however, flanked by two more young women in leather skirts and black rollnecks. Unlike the receptionist, though, these women had sidearms strapped around their hips in military-police style, white webbing holsters. The overall effect was not unlike an old sixties Matt Helm movie, and it added a definite touch of the absurd to what had previously just been outlandish and impossible.

Gibson's party halted in front of the doors. Smith raised a hand. "This is where we part company."

Gibson was too overawed by the place to think much about the streamheat. If anything, he was glad to be rid of their certain superiority and condescension.

"Yeah, okay. Thanks for pulling me out of the shit back there in Jersey."

French nodded. "It was nothing personal."

With that, the three of them turned on their heels and walked back the way that they had come.

The receptionist exchanged curt salutes with the two guards.

One of them turned and opened the right-hand door, and the receptionist indicated that Gibson should go in.

After the bizarre combinations of technology in the outer area, the inner room was more like something out of the Middle Ages. The space was dominated by a long conference table of solid dark wood. Its top, polished to a mirror finish, was empty apart from a foot-high gold pyramid and a long, very old double-handed broadsword. Gibson wasn't pleased to note that the blade was pointed directly at him. The lights were dim, going on gloomy, and the walls of the chamber were hung with deep-purple drapes. The only concession to the modern world was a smaller version of the big board outside, mounted on the wall at the head of the table where he might have expected a heraldic coat of arms to be given pride of place. The screen showed the same map of the world with the same scattering of ugly red dots.

"Welcome, Joseph Gibson, enter freely and remain only from your own choice."

Casillas and three other men were seated at the far end of the table. It had been one of the others who had spoken in greeting and who now held out a hand indicating the single chair that had been placed at his end of the table.

"Please be seated."

The lone, isolated chair was too much like the kind of seat that might be offered to a prisoner who'd been hauled before the Inquisition. Gibson sat down in silence, inwardly reminding himself that this wasn't fifteenth-century Spain but New York in the 1990s. Just beyond the purple-draped walls there were the crowds on West Broadway; the bars, nightclubs, and bustle of downtown in full swing. Men and women were out there going about the everyday business of looking for lovers, copping drugs, getting drunk, hustling for status. There were people in nearby buildings watching TV, making themselves snacks, or fucking. There was probably at least one individual getting mugged within a matter of blocks. Life was going on as usual, in blissful ignorance of interdimensional conflict and impending disaster. It was a reminder that didn't provide much comfort. For Gibson, reality had become this purple room, and he didn't like that one little bit.

The man who had greeted him was seated on Casillas's right. He was black, thickset, and completely bald. From the lines etched in his face, Gibson could only guess that he was at least in his early seventies, but everything else about him gave the impression that he was as strong as an ox. Indeed, that was the overall feel of the man: the old bull, the unquestioned monarch of his herd. Visually, he was easily less plausible than the ancient Hispanic. He was dressed in a silver, three-button mohair suit with narrow lapels, a black shirt, and a white tie. The outfit was completed by blue mirrored aviator glasses. He looked like either the venerable star of a Motown singing group or a retired Detroit pimp. When he spoke, there was the faintest trace of a French accent. For almost a minute he looked at Gibson; then he loudly cleared his throat.

"We realize that you have been through a great deal during the last few hours and that you are very close to being in a state of shock. We who have been dealing with this situation for so long now are apt to forget the trauma that can be produced when an ordinary individual is precipitated without warning into our world. In an ideal situation, we would have preferred to allow you a more gradual and humane introduction to all this. Unfortunately this is not an ideal situation. To put it bluntly, we are at war. It matters not that the great majority of the human race has yet to become aware of the conflict. Their lack of awareness doesn't render the circumstances any less dangerous. We are fighting for the very existence of civilization, the survival of this planet, and, in war, it is not always possible to regard the niceties of humane behavior."

Casillas glanced at the big man and smiled. "I think we may find Señor Gibson a good deal more resilient than it would first appear."

Gibson, in fact, had something other than his potential resilience on his mind right at that moment. He was wondering if the man in the mohair suit was yet another Haitian. There seemed to be far too many Haitian connections in all this. First the pseudo *tontons* and now this French accent. Haiti still scared the hell out of him. The time that he and the band had taken that ridiculous trip to Port-au-Prince, although he hadn't admitted it to Casillas, had been an episode of terrifying stupidity. They had gone completely out of their depths, and he'd come close to things that he still preferred to keep locked down in the deepest recesses of his memory.

He looked guardedly at the four men. "You know who I am. Perhaps you ought to start by telling me who you are."

Go for it, Joe. Take the high ground. Let these bastards start coming up with some specific answers. Enough of this "you're too dumb to understand" bullshit.

"We are four of the Nine."

This first answer did a lot to take the wind out of his sails. There was no easy way to deal with people who called themselves the Nine. The answer had come from the individual on Casillas's left. This new speaker was nothing as flamboyant or exotic as Casillas or the man in the silver mohair, but he quietly radiated an intense personal magnetism. His prominently curved nose and broad, flat cheekbones clearly identified him as Native American, probably from somewhere in the southwest. His long hair was pulled back into a ponytail, and he was wearing a conservative, Western suit of the kind that might be favored by an Arizona banker. His only flourishes were a silver-and-turquoise bolo tie in the shape of the traditional thunderbird and a matching ring on the third finger of his left hand.

Gibson resisted giving in to intimidation. "So where are the other five?"

The Indian had the hardest pale-blue eyes, an extreme rarity among Native Americans.

"They are in a number of different cities across the globe. This is only one of our worldwide crisis centers. The pressure has already become so strong that we've been forced to abandon the single original monitoring base in Lhasa and divide our strength. This New York center is of sufficient importance to warrant the presence here of four of us."

Gibson jerked a thumb at the doors behind him. "There are more setups like this?"

The Indian nodded. "This is one of the more sophisticated ones."

"How many other bases are there?"

"That's one of our best-kept secrets."

Casillas, who seemed to be playing the role of mediator at this initial meeting, cut in quickly. "Perhaps, before we go any further, I should introduce everyone." He gestured toward the Indian.

"This gentlemen on my left is William Storm Eagle. He came to us from the Ghost Society of the Lakota Nation."

William Storm Eagle nodded impassively.

Casillas went on. "To my right, in the sunglasses, is the Very Reverend Houn'gan Jean Paul Le Blanc Agassou."

Gibson let out a slow breath. "Sure is turning out to be a day for voodoo. First *tontons* and now a houn'gan."

The mirrored shades flashed as the houn'gan minutely inclined his head. "Remember I am a houn'gan, Mr. Gibson, a minister of the white light and the true path. Don't confuse me with the *macoute* and the *bocor* witchmen who control them. I don't practice the Petro, I don't draw the *veve*, and I don't take council with evil."

It was one weird statement to hear in a place that came equipped with NASA-style computers. Gibson bowed his head, thoroughly put in his place. Casillas tactfully went on with the introductions. His hand extended to the last of the quartet. "At the end here, beyond the Reverend Agassou, is Mr. Sebastian Rampton."

Gibson couldn't help himself. Despite all his efforts to remain a paragon of cool, his eyebrows shot up. Sebastian Rampton might not actually have been a household name, but he was certainly notorious on both sides of the Atlantic. His followers looked on him as the natural successor to Aleister Crowley. After a number of lurid scandals and a sensational court case centering around orgies, animal sacrifices, and underage girls, he had been saved from serving time only by a seven-figure lawyer and a couple of very reluctant witnesses. As a result, the popular press had started treating him like the embodiment of pure evil. A couple of TV preachers had loudly expressed the opinion that he was the Antichrist and busily solicited funds to fight him. Back in the old days, Gibson had been approached on a number of occasions by Rampton's people looking to hook him into their trip and probably relieve him of a great deal of his money along the way. Around that time a number of rock 'n' roll bands had fallen under his influence. Gibson, showing what he congratulated himself on as unusual common sense and foresight, had decided in front that they were too seriously creepy and refused to see them.

Rampton, who was sitting well back in the shadows, smiled wanly. "I see you recognize the name."

Gibson nodded. "Your reputation does tend to precede you."

"Why don't you just come out and say it, Gibson? Rampton the Satanist. Isn't that what they called me? The tabloid media seem to have this habit of confusing me with Charles Manson."

Rampton looked exactly like his photographs. A black-and-white combination of corpse and mortician, with a touch of the renegade Jesuit or defrocked priest. His black suit was Victorian in its severity, and his small, round, and very thick eyeglasses gave him a myopic, fish-eyed stare. The glasses bore an unfortunate resemblance to the kind that had been worn by Heinrich Himmler. What was a maniac like this doing working along with those who at least professed to be the good guys? The whole business of multidimensional conflict was hard enough to swallow under the most favorable of circumstances. To find that an individual who was rumored to have a thing about virgins and dead goats was one of those who were running things tended to stretch the suspension of disbelief to its limits. Gibson looked to Casillas for some sort of explanation, but it was Rampton who answered the question that he hadn't even asked.

For the first time, he leaned forward into the light. His hands were folded in front of him like a pair of dormant albino spiders. "Understand one thing, Gibson, this is not a cozy conflict of good and evil. We are dealing here with power and counter-power. If the power that threatens us cannot be deflected by any means available to us, we will all be destroyed. Such a situation can produce some very odd alliances."

"So it would seem."

An Indian mystic, a voodoo priest, whatever the hell Casillas was supposed to be, and the leader of a highly publicized occult sex cult? This bunch was going to save the world? Gibson inwardly shrugged. He was in now, and nobody seemed to be offering a way out.

Agassou interrupted to put an end to the exchange between Rampton and Gibson. "In the near future, you may find that alliances will become considerably stranger. Up to this point in time, we have relied heavily on help from other dimensions to protect our world and our reality. Unfortunately, the enemy is pressing hard on all fronts and we find ourselves having to organize a very rapid process of humanization."

"Humanization?"

"We are expected to play an expanded role in our own defense."

"You make us sound like South Vietnam."

"The analogy is not inapt."

"Am I part of this humanization?"

"You were to be."

Gibson didn't like the sound of that.

"Were?"

"The original plan was to recruit you to our side and, after a period of basic training, to place you in control of one of the points of penetration." He indicated the display map with its red dots. "After the night's events, however, we have been forced to change our plans. For some reason known only to them, the enemy appears to have assumed that you are much more important than we ever thought you were. Either they are mistaken or they know something that we don't.''

This was something else the sound of which Gibson didn't like.

"If that's the case, it's something that I don't know about, either. I haven't been important to anyone for years.''

Rampton's lip curled. "The enemy moves in mysterious ways, but I must confess that I see no reason why the fellow travelers of Necrom should be interested in a broken-down ex-rock star.''

Agassou treated Rampton to a cold look. "As you say, the enemy moves in mysterious ways.'' He turned his attention back to Gibson. "The way things stand, we are now forced to move you to some safe location until the situation either resolves itself or the reason for the enemy's interest in you becomes apparent.''

Gibson thought about this. He wasn't too taken with the idea of being moved to some safe location. It was too much like a euphemism for protective custody. "Wouldn't it be a whole lot simpler if I just slipped away and minded my own business? I mean, if the enemy does have its eye on me, it's going to be quickly apparent that I'm not a threat to anyone.''

Rampton smiled. "It's far more likely that, once you've left our protection, the enemy will merely eliminate you, just to be on the safe side. I know that's what I'd do.''

Even after their short acquaintance, Gibson didn't doubt that was what he'd do. He raised his hands in a gesture of surrender. "Okay, I give up. What do you want to do with me?''

This time it was Casillas who answered. "For tonight, you will remain here. I very much doubt that the enemy has anything like the strength in New York City to mount an all-out attack on this installation. In the morning, we will attempt to transfer you, without the enemy's knowledge, to a less high-profile location. To be truthful, we have yet to formulate a plan to remove you from the city. This has all taken us rather by surprise. I would suggest that we all retire and reconvene in the morning.''

"I'm staying here?''

"For the moment.''

"There are a lot of things that I need to know. I—''

Casillas cut him off. "Please. We will attempt to answer your questions in the morning. We have all had a very arduous evening. It is time to rest.''

"There are also a couple of people I ought to call. Let them know where I am."

Storm Eagle shook his head. "That isn't possible. Outside calls would be far too dangerous."

Rampton's sneer was back. "You've been thoroughly researched, Gibson. There's no one out there who gives a damn where you are, except maybe some IRS agents."

"So why go to all this trouble to get me here?"

"It wasn't my idea, believe me. I was of the opinion that you were simply a worthless burnout and nothing that I've seen this evening has done anything to convince me otherwise."

Something inside of Gibson finally snapped. He'd been listening to this shit for a couple of years now and he was sick of it. He wasn't going to take it. He slowly stood up and faced Rampton.

"I don't know what's going on here and I don't know how a man with your track record got here, either. In fact, I don't know anything. All I know is fuck you, man. I didn't ask to come here so don't be busting my fucking balls. You hear me?"

Gibson suddenly felt good. For the first time in months, he stopped feeling sorry for himself and was genuinely angry. Out of the corner of his eye he was surprised to see that the other three—Casillas, Agassou, and Storm Eagle—looked almost approving. He turned and started for the door. The receptionist was standing there waiting for him.

"If you come with me, Mr. Gibson, I'll show you to your room."

"Gibson."

Rampton's voice stopped him in his tracks.

"I may have a checkered history, Gibson, but the reason I'm here is that I've been all the way in. Can you say that?"

Gibson smiled and shook his head. "No, but I've been a lot farther than most and that must count for something."

He followed the receptionist out of the meeting room.

The White Room

JOE GIBSON FLOATED. The narrow white bed
was a warm, easy cloud. The narrow white room was a protective heaven. Nothing could get to him and nothing could hurt
him. The shot that Nurse Lopez had given him had fully kicked
in and ended the pain, the confusion, and the puzzlement. *The
Dating Game* was showing on the TV, but Joe Gibson didn't
give a damn.

"Bachelorette Number Three, if you were an animal, what
kind of animal would you be?"

Best of all, the shot cut him loose from the dreams. Almost
from the moment that the thing had started, sleep had quite
literally become a nightmare.

"I think I'd be a white fuzzy rabbit so you just couldn't resist
picking me up and cuddling me."

It had started that first night on Greene Street with the dream
that all but totaled his mind . . .

Chapter
Three

HE WAS IN a tunnel made from hard, bright, reflective material, and he was terrified. A dazzling white light was all but blinding him. He didn't have a clue where he was except for an uncertain feeling that the way out was somewhere up ahead. The most important thing was that he had to keep going. This he knew for sure. Keeping going was of a life-preserving importance. There was something behind him, something coming after him down the tunnel, and if it caught him he was dead meat.

The diameter of the tunnel was getting smaller. He was having to walk in a semicrouch with his knees bent and his head hunched into his shoulders like an ape. If the tunnel got any narrower, he'd be forced to crawl. He heard noises behind him but he didn't look back. He couldn't look back. All he could do was to keep hurrying on, doubled over in the knuckle-trailing, simian shamble. It wouldn't do any good to look back. The pursuit sounded as if it was gaining on him, and the bright tunnel continued to shrink. As well as shrinking, it was taking on a definite downward incline. He was running back down the slippery slope of evolution. It was like that chart on the wall in school: the Ascent of Man. Except he was going in the opposite direction. Any moment, he'd be developing a tail. The sounds behind him were even louder—coarse laughter and the crash of heavy boots. He couldn't take any more. Despite his fear, he turned and looked for the first time.

Rats.

Not real rats scuttling on all fours but anthropomorphic rats the size of five-year-old children. Maybe twenty of them. Rats in engineer boots. Rats in sunglasses. Rats in Nazi helmets. Rats wearing bandoliers and carrying tommy guns. Rats that walked on two legs with oversize heads and humanoid bodies. Rats that flashed disgusting yellow rat teeth as they laughed and called out to him in B-movie Mexican-bandito accents.

"Hey, gringo, we gonna get you. We don't need no stinking badges."

Their leader wore a black patch over his left eye. He was the one setting the pace, making sure that his men took their time, stringing it out, relishing this game of rat and mouse.

"Hey, Gibson, we gonna get you."

They weren't cartoon rats. He hadn't washed up on the dark side of some surreal Looney Tune. They weren't even Roger Rabbit technology. These bastards were for real, far too real. Filthy fur formed into greasy spikes; the cuts and sores on their bodies were gross and suppurating. They smelled bad. They stank of sewers and foulness. A detached part of Gibson's mind marveled at this. Joe Gibson had very little sense of smell, having progressively destroyed it during the years when cocaine had been the public display of having too much money. It hardly ever played a part in his dreams.

Dreams! It was a dream. He was dreaming, damn it. All he had to do was wake up.

Wake up!

He couldn't wake up. No matter how he tried, he couldn't wake up. Stop this dream! Let me out of here!

He turned and fled. The tunnel was even narrower and it sloped more steeply. He slipped. His feet went out from under him and he fell heavily on his ass. There were shouts of laughter from the rats. They enjoyed a good pratfall. The tunnel was now so steep that he started to slide. He couldn't stop himself. He was picking up speed. The tunnel had become a spiral. Round and round he went, down and down he went. He curled himself into a fetal ball. What was this? The DNA helix? True devolution?

He shot out of the chute. For a moment he was in midair, weightless. Then he hit the water and went under. It was foul and stank worse than the rats. His feet found bottom and he struggled to stand. Snaky things slithered around his ankles, but he didn't even want to think of them.

"Wake up!" A voice rolled across the foul water, but he couldn't wake up. With most nightmares, once the realization came that he was was only dreaming, it was always possible to make the effort and come out of it. This one, however, had him locked in. It wouldn't let go. Any minute, he'd be running into Freddy Krueger.

He was standing up to his waist in black, filthy water in what had to be the heart of all the sewers of the world. A huge man-made cavern with walls of slimy stone, a dank and dripping cathedral with cascades and waterfalls where pipes and conduits spilled their contents into the central confluence.

And there was something wading toward him. It wasn't Freddy. In fact, there were nine of them. More Nazi helmets, except that these were on the heads of real live Nazis. Almost-live Nazis. Corpse-white, hollow-skull faces and ragged, filthy uniforms, pushing through the water with weary, dead-eyed determination, holding their rifles above the water, survivors of Stalingrad on the long, long retreat through hell.

"Ve haf come for you, Gibson, you piece of *scheiss*."

This time it was B-movie German. "We have ways of making you talk." He had to get out of this dream.

"Wake up!" The disembodied voice spoke again.

"Wake up!"

"Come on, Joe, wake up. It's just a dream."

Now there were two voices, Gibson didn't understand. The voices were urgent, concerned. For a moment, faces looked down, shouting and shaking. Then the faces blurred and, instead, a skeletal hand with an SS ring on its third finger was reaching into his face.

"Quick, give him the shot, he's slipping back."

A needle was going into his arm.

Gibson started to struggle. "What?"

"Psych attack."

He was struggling out of the dream. "What?"

"They tried to get you on the dream level."

Gibson was shaking his head. He was stretched out on the bed in the guest room. A woman, either the receptionist or her double, was bending over him. A second Nordic blond, enough like the receptionist to be her sister, had just pulled the needle of a disposable syringe out of his arm and was wiping the skin with a swab. He felt the quick chill of surgical spirit. Casillas was standing in the background looking concerned.

The receptionist or her double put an arm under his shoulders. "Can you sit up?"

Gibson eased into a sitting position with her half-lifting him. She was exceedingly strong. Gibson sighed. He'd always had a thing about girls who could beat him at arm wrestling.

He shook his head, trying to clear the craziness. "What was that all about?"

This time Casillas answered. "You have been under what we call psych attack. While you were sleeping, the enemy attempted to infiltrate your dreams."

"Infiltrate my dreams?"

"It's a very basic technique. Fortunately we were able to wake you in time."

"And what would have happened if you hadn't?"

Casillas stepped forward so Gibson could see him better. "I imagine there was something in the dream that was trying to get you, to do you harm?"

Gibson nodded. "Rats and Nazis. What would have happened if they'd got me?"

"You would have retreated into catatonia."

Gibson took a deep breath. "Thanks for the early call."

The last thing that he remembered was being taken to a small functional guest room, little more than a cell, and stretching out on the narrow single bed to think about the day's revelations. He must have fallen asleep almost immediately, and that was strange in itself.

He looked at the receptionist's sister, who was disposing of the syringe. "What did you shoot me up with?"

"A combination of tranquilizer and Methedrine."

Gibson half smiled. "No shit."

Casillas had an excellent bedside manner. "It's important that you don't sleep for the next few hours."

"I don't think I'm going to be able to."

"You may not be able to resist."

"So I'm on speed for the duration?"

"Until we get you to a safer location."

"I thought that I was supposed to be safe here?"

"Apparently not. The enemy seem to be incredibly interested in you."

"So where do I go to now?"

"London."

"You're putting me on! London, England?"

"It's clearly not safe for you in New York."

"But why London? Why not Cleveland?"

"We have an associate in London who I believe may be equipped to hide you. Why? Would you rather go to Cleveland?"

Gibson quickly shook his head.

"Hell, no. I was just curious."

The door opened quietly and William Storm Eagle entered. "Is he okay?"

Casillas nodded. "He made it."

Storm Eagle came to Gibson's bedside. "How do you feel?"

Gibson grinned like an idiot. The chemical cocktail was kicking in. "I feel fine. It was just some old dream."

Storm Eagle didn't smile. "It was more than a bad dream."

Gibson was feeling better and better, and the temptation was to minimize what had just happened. "I think it's time that we had a talk."

Casillas shook his head. "You should rest."

"The hell I should rest. I've just been shot full of crank and I haven't felt so talkative in years. Besides, I think you people owe me a couple of explanations."

Storm Eagle glanced at Casillas. "He has a point."

Casillas seated himself in a chair beside the bed. "What do you want to know?"

"Know? I want to know anything you can tell me. I heard a bunch of stuff about dimensions and wavelengths, but nobody has given me anything like a satisfactory explanation of why I'm a part of all this. How did you people, you Nine, hook into me? All I've had so far is double-talk."

William Storm Eagle sat down on the edge of the bed. The unusual blue eyes scanned Gibson. "You have the mark of the coyote on you."

Gibson shook his head vigorously. "That's not what I want to hear. I've had enough bullshit mysticism. You know what I'm saying, Chief?"

Casillas sighed. "The problem that we have here is one of language. William says you have the mark of the coyote, another of our number might say you had a manifest destiny, a third would describe it as a dark aura. The detector provided by the streamheat gave you a reading of two-hundred-percent normal."

Gibson's head snapped round. "Are you telling me that the streamheat have given you some gizmo that you use to select recruits to your cause?"

"Without their help, we'd be virtually blind."

"Isn't it putting a lot of trust in those guys?"

"We have no other choice."

Gibson had a vision of Casillas and the rest of the Nine sneaking around in the New York night with something that looked like a Geiger counter, looking for a few good men to battle Necrom.

"Jesus Christ."

Casillas's voice sounded weary. "You are not here as a result of the device alone. The mark, the aura, manifest destiny, they are all ways of saying that you are an exceptional individual and that it seems you have a definite role in the coming conflict."

"So what is that role? Are you telling me that I'm the fucking Ringbearer or the Defender of the Universe?"

Storm Eagle sternly shook his head. "Probably nothing as grand. It may be that you are only a pivot, a catalyst of some kind. To be frank, it was a major surprise when the enemy took an immediate interest in you."

"That's the other big-ticket question. Who exactly is the enemy? Who sent the *tontons* or whatever they were? Who caused the dream attack?" The speed was giving Gibson's voice a desperate edge. "Who's out to get me?"

It was the first time that Gibson had seen Casillas look helpless. "That's something for which we don't have a precise answer."

"No kidding."

"There really is no single enemy as such. You have to think in terms of various marauding groups coming into this dimension. Some of these marauders we've known about for a very long time. They are the demons of old, set in motion by the approach of the confluence. Others are entirely new entities who have seen a chance to expand their power to other dimensions and are making the most of it. The confluence and the waking of Necrom are moments when massive power will be free for the taking. There are a great many ruthless and power-hungry entities in this universe, both human and nonhuman."

"But why do so many of them seem hell-bent on heading for our dimension and causing trouble?"

William Storm Eagle stood up. "Because we are vulnerable, Joseph Gibson. Over the last few centuries, this has become a particularly material world, obsessed with technology. Much of what we once knew about the multidimensional universe has either been lost or has been relegated to the level of mythology and folktale or else clouded by superstition. This is also why we have to rely so heavily on the streamheat. There is so much that we have to relearn."

Gibson lay back on the bed. "I really need to think about all this."

Casillas got to his feet and stood beside Storm Eagle. "I'm afraid you are going to have to do your thinking on the run. There is no time to linger. You'll be starting out for London very shortly."

As the two men left the room, William Storm Eagle turned and looked hard at Gibson.

"One thing, Joseph Gibson."

"What's that?"

"Don't ever address me as 'chief' again."

If all those years on the road had taught Gibson anything, it was that travel gets easier the less that you have to do with the mechanics of it. The car takes you to the airport, the airline takes your luggage, the cabin attendants bring you drinks. They are paid to do these things; as far as you're concerned it's their reason for being. They maybe even enjoy it. Fuck-ups were inevitable but there was no way to beat the process. The only answer was to become as passive as possible. Insure as much comfort as you could, but, after that, behave as closely as possible to a piece of luggage and let them do it for you.

The trip to London was arranged in what had to be record time, and Gibson's role in it was nothing if not passive. He didn't even have anything to pack. It had been decided that under no circumstances should he return to his own apartment. Within the hour, a chartered executive jet was waiting at JFK, a phone call to the home of a highly placed State Department official had covered his lack of a passport. Smith, Klein, and French had once again been assigned as his bodyguards, although they hadn't seemed exactly overjoyed to be saddled with the task.

"We thought we were through with you, Gibson."

"The feeling was mutual."

Klein had slowly shaken his head. "London, huh?"

Gibson had nodded. "You were hoping for somewhere a bit more exotic?"

"I'm always hoping. I guess it won't be for long, though. We've only got to stash you and then we're done."

"That's what they said the last time, wasn't it?"

Klein had looked at Gibson curiously, as though wondering for the first time if he might have had the rudiments of intelligence after all.

"You may have a point there."

The first phase of the operation was to move Gibson out of

the building and into the car. The entire Greene Street security force was assembled in the lobby. Before Gibson was even allowed to enter the elevator, patrols with hand radios were sent out to nearby intersections and up to the roof. It was only when they reported back that everything seemed safe that the party for the airport and its considerable protective shield started to move out. Gibson found that he didn't even make it into the first elevator. This was entirely filled with security whose job was to cover the short distance between the building entrance and the car that would take him to JFK. Gibson had been the focus of hired protection before, but even on the Self-Destruction Tour, when that bunch of psychotics who called themselves the Order of the Cleansing Flame had been threatening to cleanse him, there had been nothing on a scale that could approach this.

"I guess this is how Nixon felt."

One of the guards, who was standing right beside him in the tightly packed elevator, grunted. "Or maybe Jack Kennedy."

Gibson turned his head and regarded the man bleakly. "Thanks a bunch."

"Any time."

When he hit the street, he was almost too hemmed in to see anything. The white Cadillac was waiting. As he was hurried to the car, he craned around to see as much as he could of what was actually going on. To his surprise, he found that the block had been sealed at both ends by the regular NYPD. There were the familiar crowd-control sawhorses and parked blue-and-whites with red flashing lights that reflected off the officers' nylon jackets. The street was completely clear of both vehicle and pedestrian traffic, and the building's security force was able to fan out with weapons at the ready, looking every which way for possible threats. How the hell had the Nine managed to persuade the cops to cooperate at such short notice? They might be strange but they seemed to have a wealth of connections on every level.

"How's all this being explained to the general population?" Klein grinned.

"We're making a film. It seems that in this town, a movie crew can do about anything it wants."

They were in the car. Just Gibson, Smith, Klein, and French. A police cruiser in front of them immediately whooped into life and, as its lights started slowly rotating, they followed as it eased forward. They were on the move, up the block at little more than walking pace. The police barriers were drawn aside, and they nosed through a small crowd of curious onlookers. The moment they were clear, the two cars rocketed away. Gibson was pushed back into his seat by the sudden acceleration. By the time he'd struggled to lean forward again, they were running red lights at seventy miles an hour, the police car in the lead with its sirens howling a warning while the Cadillac followed behind flashing its own signal—one of those magnetic flashers that stuck to the roof of the car. They touched ninety on Delancey Street but had to drop to just fifty crossing the Edward R. Koch Bridge (named for the very popular mayor after his 1988 assassination) to avoid running into a truck. After that they were on the BQE and weaving in and out of traffic, following the signs to JFK at speeds that weren't actually suicidal but frequently came very close. Nobody was going to take them on the highway.

To reach their chartered jet, they had to use an extremely exclusive side entrance to the Pan Am terminal that led directly to the airline's most isolated and protected ultra-VIP sanctuary. This was the place that was used only for the likes of Margaret Thatcher, Fidel Castro, or Michael Jackson. A quartet of Pan Am officials was waiting for them. There was an undercurrent of excitement in the superplush suite of rooms, as though the Pan Am people thought they were participating in some real-life James Bond epic. Gibson wondered what story they'd been told regarding the reasons for this sudden no-expense-spared flight.

Smith went straight to work. "Is the aircraft prepared for takeoff?"

"It's fueled and stocked but it'll be about twenty minutes before it can be integrated into the traffic pattern and given clearance. Would anyone care for a drink while you're waiting?"

Smith began to shake her head, but Gibson quickly interrupted. The Methedrine was riding roughshod over the tranks that they had given him, and if he didn't have something to mellow him out a little, he'd be chewing on the inside of his lips. "Yes, I would. I'd like a very large Scotch, please, the oldest single malt you have behind your bar."

One of the Pan Am officials beckoned to a hovering waiter. "Ralph here will take your order."

Gibson repeated the order to Ralph. To his surprise, as Ralph walked away, Klein beckoned to him. "I'll have one, too."

"Certainly, sir. What would you like?"

"I'll have the same as him."

Gibson raised an amused eyebrow. "I didn't know that you people drank."

Klein winked. "You'd be surprised what we do. I have a feeling that this is going to turn into a long and grueling trip, and I thought I might settle in just a little."

The drinks arrived before he could elaborate. Two very large Scotches on a silver tray with separate glasses of ice and water and a bowl of mixed nuts. Klein put two ice cubes into his and topped it off with a little water. Gibson took his straight. As the first sip hit his tongue, he let out a delighted gasp.

"Like a dancing angel."

It was possibly the finest whiskey that he had ever tasted.

All too quickly, as far as Gibson was concerned, the flight was ready to board and he found himself being ushered toward the escalator that led out onto the dark tarmac. The twin-engine executive jet was standing by itself under cold floodlights in the parking area reserved for large private aircraft. There was no other traffic that late at night, and they had the area to themselves. The plane was white with gold trim, and as they hurried toward it, one of the Pan Am officials attempted to fill in a little of its background.

"I think you'll enjoy traveling in this aircraft, Mr. Hoover . . ."

Hoover? Who the hell did they think he was? Didn't the guy recognize him? It wasn't that long since he'd been a regular in *People* magazine.

". . . it was originally built for an Arab oil prince and it really is on the cutting edge of luxury."

Gibson glanced curiously at the official. "What happened to the prince?"

"He was assassinated by his brother-in-law. That's how the aircraft became available for private charter."

If pink leather couches, concealed lighting, gilt cherubs, and a fifty-inch projection TV were the cutting edge of luxury, then the Pan Am official was right on the money.

As he stepped into the cabin, Gibson looked around in wonder. "Christ, it looks like a flying whorehouse."

The captain was waiting to greet them. He smiled and nodded. "I believe that was what its first owner used it for most of the time. I'm Captain Donovan, and my crew and I hope that you enjoy your flight. Flying time to London will be just under seven hours."

Gibson wondered if all airline captains were turned out from the same mold: calm, tall, mature, good-looking and slow-spoken, laugh lines at the corners of their eyes, and gray at the temples—the very image of capable reliability.

Once again, Smith had no time for pleasantries. "Will we be leaving right away?"

"We're going through the final clearances right now. As soon as you're settled in, we'll start to taxi out to the runway."

"Which airport will we be landing at?"

"We'll be coming into Luton. It was thought to be less conspicuous than Heathrow."

"We'll need a suitable car waiting when we arrive."

The captain nodded. "As soon as we've reached our cruising altitude, I'll call ahead and make the arrangements."

Smith thought about that. "I'd rather this was left to the last moment, say when we're an hour or so out from London. That way there'd be less chance of word of our arrival leaking out."

The captain was nothing if not anxious to please. "Whatever you suggest." He indicated the cabin attendant, who up to that point had been standing in the background. "I have to go forward now. This is Janine, she'll be happy to answer any other questions that you may have and generally make your flight as comfortable as possible."

Janine stepped forward with a professional smile. "Hi, if you'd all like to take your seats and strap in, we'll be getting under way."

If anyone had ever needed a model for the perfect stewardess, Janine would have admirably filled the role. She had lavish red hair that might have belonged to Ann-Margret in her Vegas prime. Her figure was long-legged showgirl perfect and shown off to total advantage by the short tailored uniform that matched the pink and gold of the decor. As he dropped into his seat and fastened the seat belt, Gibson wondered idly how well acquainted he and Janine might become during the seven-hour Atlantic crossing. There had been a time when stewardesses had fallen all over him, but since his very public descent from grace, their ardor had cooled to nothing more than routine courtesy.

As soon as they were in level flight, and the seat-belt sign was off, Gibson stood up and started to explore the possibilities of the aircraft. The speed made it virtually impossible for him to sit still. The first thing that he discovered was a smaller rear cabin that was taken up by an enormous circular water bed and a second projection TV. When he saw it, Gibson laughed out loud.

"Jesus, it really is a flying whorehouse."

Janine stepped through the connecting door behind him. "The ex-prince had very distinctive taste."

Gibson looked along a shelf of videocassettes beside the bed. They were mainly S&M porno punctuated by Clint Eastwood and Sylvester Stallone movies. "I don't think that even Elvis would have gone for decor like this."

He prodded the yielding surface of the water bed. "Did you work for the prince?"

Janine laughed and shook her head. "Definitely not. From what I heard, he expected things from his cabin crews that were far beyond my job description. I work for the charter brokers. The day after tomorrow I'll be dressed like a butler, serving cognac to a Japanese electronics mogul in a walnut-paneled Learjet that looks like an English stately home on the inside."

Gibson sat down on the bed. "That seems like a waste."

Janine reverted to formality. "Would you care for a drink, Mr. . . . Hoover?"

Gibson looked at her with a who-are-we-trying-to-kid expression. "Hoover?"

"I was given strict instructions to not know who you were. The passenger list reads 'J. E. Hoover and party.' "

"I was starting to think that I'd been totally forgotten."

"Actually, I used to have nearly all of your records."

"Used to?"

"I still have them . . ."

"You just don't admit it in polite company anymore?"

"You did rather screw up, didn't you? I mean, telling the whole of Madison Square Garden to eat shit and die and then stalking off the stage was hardly a great career move. I was there, you know."

"I did worse than that."

"Yes, I read about it."

Gibson wasn't sure if her expression was sympathetic or just professional. "Maybe I'll have that drink now."

"Scotch?"

"How did you know?"

"I told you. I used to be a fan. You gave up drinking Rebel Yell bourbon and switched to good Scotch because the hangovers weren't so bad. I read that in the big *Stone Free* interview."

"The one with me on the cover."

"I'll get your drink."

With that, she was gone.

Gibson lay back on the water bed, producing a medium swell. He'd never really liked water beds. They made him feel seasick when he was drunk, and after his first couple of experiences with them he'd dismissed the whole concept as an overpromoted Californian aberration. Janine returned with his Scotch. "If you want anything else, just ring."

Gibson nodded. "Indeed I will."

After she'd gone, he muttered under his breath, "You know how to ring, don't you? You just stick out your finger and push."

Outside the window a night-flight ghost world of moonlit cloudscape drifted past. For the first time, he realized that it was either a full moon or a close approximation. In New York, you tended not to be aware of the night sky. He picked out the movie *High Plains Drifter* from the shelf of cassettes, fed it into the VCR that was attached to the projection TV, lit a cigarette, and settled down to let Clint keep him amused for the next hundred minutes or so.

Just as the movie was coming to an end with Clint destroying the whole town without ever once telling anyone his name, Smith looked into the rear cabin. "I think you'd better come out here."

Gibson sat up. "What's going on?"

Smith looked at the screen with an expression of distaste. "The captain has just told us something."

"What?"

"You'd better hear it for yourself."

Gibson followed her into the main cabin. The captain was standing there looking a good deal less than happy. "I've just been telling your companions that I believe a strange aircraft is shadowing this flight."

Gibson pushed his hair back out of his eyes. He was about at the point where he'd believe anything. "What kind of aircraft?"

"That's a part of the problem. It has a radar configuration like nothing I've ever seen before. Its progress is also extremely erratic."

Gibson looked round for Janine. She seemed to have secreted herself in the galley. "What exactly are you trying to say?"

"I've never encountered a UFO, but this thing does tend to conform to a lot of the reports that I've read."

Gibson closed his eyes and took a deep breath. "Are you trying to say that there's a flying saucer following us?"

Captain Donovan looked very uncomfortable. "Those aren't the words that I'd choose."

"But they're close enough for rock 'n' roll."

"Right."

Gibson turned to Smith. "You know anything about this?"

Smith shook her head, at the same time giving a hard look that indicated that he should keep his mouth shut. "Absolutely nothing."

Gibson peered out of one of the cabin windows. Donovan indicated that he was wasting his time. "You won't see anything. Whatever it is has been staying between twenty and thirty miles behind us. It maintains approximately the same altitude, but there are wild fluctuations in its airspeed, and it keeps executing these crazy zigzag patterns that would be quite impossible for a normal aircraft."

Gibson turned angrily from the window. "Does anyone want to tell me what the fuck is going on?"

Smith moved toward him. "We don't know what's going on."

"The hell you don't."

Smith glanced at the captain. "Could you give us a few minutes to talk in private?"

"Of course, but, if you do know something about this thing, I'd be grateful if you'd let me in on it."

For the first time, Gibson saw Smith showing signs of stress. "Please, Captain, just give us a few minutes."

Without a further word, the captain turned and went back to the flight deck. His calm and patience seemed to be fading fast. Gibson's was totally in shreds. The Methedrine was gnawing at his nerves, and nothing would have pleased him more than to hurl something at the wall and start screaming. He could see no reason why anyone should retain their cool when they were thirty thousand feet over the North Atlantic being chased by a UFO.

As soon as the door had closed behind Donovan, Gibson rounded on the three streamheat. "Somebody had better start coming up with some answers pretty damn fast."

French raised a warning hand. "Can the crew listen in to our conversation?"

Smith shook her head. "No, they can't. I had the plane checked out for privacy before it was chartered. Its previous owner was particularly obsessive about privacy."

Gibson's anger continued to build to a flareup. "I don't give a damn what the crew can hear or can't hear. All I want is some answers, and I want them now."

Smith fixed him with a cold stare. "Don't throw a tantrum, Joe. We don't know everything. This is as baffling to us as it is to you."

"I wonder why it is that I don't believe you?"

"Maybe because you're a paranoid on amphetamines."

Gibson could feel himself becoming terminally ratty. "Or maybe because you're lying through your teeth."

Smith faced him. "You have my word. We know nothing about these things. Except that they turn up in just about every inhabited dimension with which we've ever had contact."

"You have them in your dimension?"

Smith nodded. "We not only have them but they also seem to be stepping up the frequency of their appearances. In recent years, it's gone as far as hands-on experimentation."

Gibson's eyes narrowed. "Kidnapping? Genuine abductions?"

Klein nodded. "Kidnapping."

"I thought that was just tabloid bullshit."

"Way up all over in the last five years."

Gibson clutched at a straw. "But they don't generally attack expensive private jets?"

Klein jerked the comfort of the straw from his grasp. "They've downed a few military interceptors."

"Yeah, but isn't it usually two guys called Vern and Bubba out fishing in the swamp who get themselves carried off by a gang of little green men? They have large heads and they stick tubes up Vern and Bubba's nostrils."

Klein didn't crack a smile. "Green skin, large heads, and slanted almond eyes. The reports are very common."

The Methedrine made it all too easy to take the situation at face value. After everything else that had happened in the last twelve or so hours, why shouldn't he be chased by a UFO? Gibson couldn't help an involuntary glance out of the window, to the rear of the plane, as if, at any minute, the UFO would come into view. "So are we in any danger?"

"It would seem unlikely. There are virtually no reports of these things being overtly violent without provocation. There are, of course, literally millions of people, aircraft, boats, even cars and trucks, that have simply vanished into thin air. They could be UFO victims. The shame of it is that we have so little data."

"You're a cheerful bastard."

Klein made a gesture with his hands. "You wanted to know the facts."

Smith looked at Klein. She was plainly not amused by his talking to Gibson. "While you're giving out all of this information, have you considered what story we're going to feed the captain?"

Before Klein could answer, the captain himself came through the door to the flight deck. "I'm sorry to interrupt you, but, if you go to the starboard windows, whatever this thing is should become visible very soon. It's been steadily closing on us for some minutes and should be alongside any time now."

For Gibson, everything else ceased to matter. What Smith, Klein, and French intended to say to the captain became irrelevant. What weird ideas Donovan might be entertaining were equally unimportant. He went to the window, pressing close to the glass to see as far as he could. In a minute or so he'd know whether he was going the same way as Vern and Bubba. There was a strange sense of detachment. Events were now so far beyond his experience and control that he couldn't even feel fear. All he could do was watch and wait. The others had also moved to the windows. Janine was in the cabin, standing beside him. Donovan had returned to the flight deck.

At first, it was almost nothing, a smudge of red light a long way off in the darkness. It was, however, changing fast, growing and expanding. The single red light split into a dozen or more tiny pinpoints that formed themselves into a circle, a spinning ellipse like a ruby necklace thrown through the night sky. The sky itself had also started to change, distorted by a shimmer like heat haze, except how could there be heat shimmer thirty thousand feet over the ocean in the dead of night? Then came the cathode flicker of distant, silent sheet lightning that seemed to judder clear to the horizon. Against the flare of the lightning, it was possible to see that there was a dark shape contained within the ring of red lights, an ovoid that was black as a hole in the heavens. And then it was no longer black. The dark of the shape turned deepest purple. But this was only another phase. Both the sky and the purple shape grew lighter. The sky was an eerie blue. Not the blue of the dawn but a cold, unholy, alien color, as though the atmosphere had become suffused with chill metallic energy. The ovoid continued to take on color. Now it was a violet glow, streaked with veins of liquid gold like the circulatory system of a god. The spinning red lights were also going through a metamorphosis. They grew from simple glowing points to large misshapen globules of throbbing power. For some seconds, they whirled at high speed and then extended laterally and merged into each other to form a continuous band girding the ovoid.

Klein was slowly shaking his head. His voice was an awed whisper. "It's amazing. It's like it's powering up for something, progressively raising all its energy levels."

As far as Gibson could tell the UFO was twice, maybe three times the size of the jet, and it rode in the air some hundred feet off their right wingtip, matching their speed and maintaining a constant distance.

He glanced at Klein. "What do you think it's doing? Taking a look at us?"

He found that he also was whispering. Klein was transfixed. "Who the hell knows?"

For more than a minute, the UFO seemed quite content to maintain its distance. Then it started to swing closer. At the same time, it glowed brighter, a relentless surge of energy that hurt the eyes. Damaging raw power, now brilliant white and bright enough to blind, was filling up the sky. The interior of the cabin was brighter than day. The terrible light took over everything, hard radiation that seemed actually to be streaming through the very fuselage of the aircraft.

"God help us!"

It was Janine who had spoken, but a similar thought had to be on everyone's mind. Gibson felt himself blacking out and then, with no perceivable transition, he found he was picking himself up from the floor. The others were doing the same.

Donovan came into the cabin. He looked shaken. "Are you all okay?"

Smith answered for them. "It would seem so. What happened?"

Donovan frowned. "I don't know, but the UFO has vanished without trace and we seem to have lost ten minutes."

"Who was flying the plane during this lost ten minutes?"

"No one. We were all out cold. We really ought to be in the sea by now, but as you can see, we're not."

Smith faced Klein and French. "This isn't good. Anything could've happened in ten minutes."

She turned back to the captain. "Are we where we're supposed to be?"

"If there's nothing wrong with the instruments, we're on course and on schedule."

Smith avoided Donovan's eyes. "I don't quite know how to put this, Captain Donovan, but are we also when we're supposed to be? Is there anything at all on the radio or radar that might not exactly be consistent with the late twentieth century?"

Gibson raised an eyebrow. Did Smith know more about UFOs than she'd admitted?

The captain gave her a hard look. "If you mean did we pass through the Twilight Zone and come out in ten million years B.C., no, we didn't. Everything seems normal."

"Did you check the commercial broadcast bands?"

"I got an FM rock station out of Thunder Bay. Bruce Springsteen as usual. No Glenn Miller or speeches by FDR. There are, however, three military jets out of an RAF base in eastern Scotland on an intercept heading for this position."

"What does that mean?"

"I imagine their radar must have picked up that thing and they're scrambling to investigate. People get nervous when a UFO shows up and closes on a commercial flight that immediately goes off the air."

French stepped into the picture. "Do you have a story ready, Captain Donovan?"

Donovan looked coldly at him. "What do you mean by that?"

"I mean that, when we land, you're going to be asked a great many questions if, as it seems, this UFO has caused enough of a flap to get fighters up in the air."

"If you're thinking of asking me to forget the whole thing, that's out of the question. The radar sightings and the instrument readings during the time we were out are all on the flight recorder, and I can't pretend that entire episode didn't happen, much as I'd like to. Right at this moment, my first officer is on the radio trying to explain how we went off the air."

"What about the visual sighting? Are you going to tell them about that?"

Gibson had to admire the sheer gall of the streamheat. Minutes earlier, they'd been knocked out by a UFO and they were all but trying to blackmail the captain into keeping quiet about it. Donovan was silent for a very long time. When he spoke, it was with a cold distaste. "No, I don't think so. I'll leave it as a purely electronic phenomenon. All of the crew will almost certainly be up for drink and drug tests and psych examination as it is. I see no reason to make our lives even more difficult."

He paused and looked hard at Smith, Klein, and French. "Why do you people fill me with a deep and instinctive distrust?"

Smith put one hand on her hip and faced the captain. "That's a good question, Captain Donovan. Why do we?"

French backed her up.

"Maybe that's something else that might be a good idea to keep to yourself if you don't want the airline and FAA shrinks climbing all over you."

Donovan thought about that and answered with the expression of an honest man who finds himself compromised. "I take your point."

He turned to go back to the flight deck. In the doorway, he glanced back. "I'll be very happy when all of you are off my aircraft."

The White Room

THE TV FINALLY went off in the white room in the very exclusive clinic. The lights followed five minutes later. Joe Gibson lay in the darkness too drugged to move. He didn't miss the TV. How many back-to-back game shows and reruns of *M*A*S*H* could he watch? He didn't even miss the light. In the darkness, he could let his imagination wander and create pictures. In the light, he was clamped into a sterile reality with the TV as the only escape. Not that his imagination worked too well after Nurse Lopez had administered the shot. It was sluggish and had difficulty grasping on to entire concepts; fragmented images and disjointed words and phrases were mostly all it could manage. Right at that moment, two words, a name, kept going round and round in his head. The words were Gideon Windemere. He couldn't put a face or a personality to the name. It stood alone, unconnected to events or memories. Gideon Windemere.

Deep in his mind, though, in the area that the drug tried so hard to suppress, and even to obliterate, a single tenuous link remained. The name came from somewhere in the lost memories, the ones that the doctors wanted to take away from him, the memories they claimed had never happened and were making him sick. He groped around, fighting the drug and going as deep inside his mind as he was able. Gideon Windemere. There had to be something else, something tangible to which he could anchor the name and force it to start making sense. Gideon Windemere?

Chapter Four

WINDEMERE PASSED THE ornate silver-and-ivory pipe to Gibson. "The problem with contemporary culture is that it suffers from the metallic KO, so to speak."

Windemere had a definite tendency to pontificate, but Gibson didn't mind. In the hour that the two of them had been together, it had become very obvious to Gibson that Gideon Windemere had a decidedly superior mind, and if he tended to become a little arrogant in the way that he delivered his ideas, the quality of the ideas certainly entitled him to a degree of self-congratulation.

Gibson sank into the deep leather armchair. He was exhausted, but the Methedrine that Smith had shot into him just before the plane landed wasn't going to let him sleep for a while, if at all. Apparently they thought that he still ran the risk of succumbing to psych attack if he closed his eyes. Sprawling was the next best thing. He applied the flame of a Bic lighter to the bowl of the pipe and sucked hard. The smoke went deep into his lungs and filled him with a sense of heavy-limbed well-being. It was a mixture of premier Lebanese hashish and opium, and it did a great deal to take the edge off the speed. He and Windemere were alone in the man's crowded study. He passed back the pipe. Windemere took it and relit it without missing a phrase.

"The industrialized society thinks in terms of metal. Cans and containers, generators and dynamos, magnetism and electricity, even chemistry is aggressively mundane. We take a trip to the moon in a steel-and-plastic container while the gossamer wing is relegated to the realm of song and fantasy. Everyone can drive an automobile but few can astral travel and almost no one can levitate. Not even the medical arts can be raised above the knife, the isotope, and the pill. The metal mind is so bloody unyielding. It doesn't flex. It entertains no alternative to its hammer and anvil. Even simple bioenergies are all but ignored, and advanced bioenergies are still looked on as witchcraft.''

Smith, Klein, and French were in some other part of the house inspecting the security with Windemere's two live-in minders, Cadiz and O'Neal. The house was Number Thirteen Ladbroke Grove, a three-story detached town house that from the outside looked perfectly normal, apart from the way the small front garden was heavily overgrown, but on the inside was anything but. Windemere's home was also museum, a chaotic jumble of art and objects. Warhols and Mondrians rubbed shoulders with models from the various productions of *Star Trek*. In the hallway, an Edward Hopper was mounted next to a framed original poster for the show that Hank Williams had been due to play the night after he died, ''if the Good Lord's willing and the creek don't rise.'' Gibson could only stand in awe. Windemere's home was even more crammed with junk than his own apartment on Central Park West. It was quite understandable, though. Now in his mid-fifties, Windemere was not only fabulously rich and extensively traveled but he was also one of the great unsung outlaws of the sixties and seventies. He was unsung because he had always avoided being caught. Gideon Windemere was the one, above all, who had been too smart for them. He'd made his first fortune by being one of the great Owsley Stanley III's major subdistributors during the acid summer of 1967. The very few photographs that remained of him from those days were paparazzi shots of the Beatles, Jimi Hendrix, or Morgan Luthor, in which he could be seen blurrily lurking in the background. During the seventies, he surfaced again as the inventor of the designer hypnotic Mandrake but almost immediately had to vanish, one step ahead of the DEA and the Hell's Angels. Rumor had it that he'd hidden out on the private tropical island of a legendary movie actor. Somewhere along the line, he'd also acquired an intimate knowledge of the back hills of Afghanistan that greatly exceeded that of the CIA, a fact that later insured his liberty during a brush with the Roy Cohn Justice Department in the mid-eighties. His studies of the occult and allied subjects, the reason that Casillas had entrusted Gibson into his care in the first place, went back to even before his acid days, and he had, according to Casillas, delved in quite as deep as Sebastian Rampton. He had certainly been on nodding terms with the Manson Family, but fortunately nothing had rubbed off. Unlike

Rampton, he had never courted publicity, although it virtually went without saying that there had been times when he'd behaved with equal weirdness. As a consequence, nobody went around calling him the Great Beast or the Antichrist. Gideon Windemere simply lived in strange semiretirement in his large house at the smart end of one of London's traditional rock 'n' roll neighborhoods, just up the street from the local police station.

Gibson and the streamheat had driven in from Luton in another white Cadillac that was almost identical to the one that they had left at Kennedy Airport. After the UFO, Gibson had ceased to sweat the details or worry about how the streamheat could find identical cars in strange cities at a moment's notice. He was doing his best to learn relaxation, to float on the stream of events. The banana boat had left, and he was irreversibly on board with no chances of swimming back to shore.

It had been some years since he'd been in Ladbroke Grove, and at first he had scarcely recognized the neighborhood. There were still reminders of glory days when it had been the stronghold of hippies and punks, rudies and dreads, and a large assorted population of the down-at-heel and plain crazy, but all over there were the same signs of creeping gentrification common in so many once-bohemian enclaves in the big cities of the west. It was no longer the place were Gibson had once lounged around smoking ganja with a bunch of Rastafarians and a couple of guys from The Clash. Sometimes it seemed that the whole world was going to yuppie hell.

Windemere began carefully refilling the pipe. Gibson wasn't sure if it was the excellent dope, but he felt perfectly relaxed around the man. The retired swashbuckler was the kind who, having done most everything, had nothing left to prove. He was open, assured, seemingly very generous, and Gibson was left with the feeling that, if he was safe anywhere, it was here at Thirteen Ladbroke Grove.

Windemere leaned forward and again handed the pipe to Gibson. "Why don't you light this while I find us something to drink? You do drink, don't you?"

Gibson nodded. "Oh, yes."

Windemere stood up and left the room, and Gibson had a chance to look around the man's study. It was the dense epicenter of the clutter, the heart of the anarchic museum, and Gibson marveled at how trusting the man was to leave someone he'd just met alone with his treasures. The study was literally bursting at the seams. The only empty space in the room was the smoke-stained ceiling, and even that had its complement of elaborate cherub moldings. All four walls were lined with dark mahogany shelving. Three were filled with books and dozens of small pictures and knickknacks—a lava lamp from the fifties, a set of impossibly large crystals, a human skull from God knew where—while the shelves on the fourth wall contained records, CDs, tapes, and electronic equipment. Gibson stood up and ambled over to look at the record collection. He noted with satisfaction that Windemere had a copy of everything that he'd ever released, both with the band and the later solo albums. At least that put the two of them at about level pegging, egowise.

Windemere returned with a dusty bottle that had no label and a pair of brandy snifters. "How do you feel about cognac?"

Gibson smiled. "I feel pretty good until the hangover sets in."

Windemere held up the bottle. "This is almost a hundred years old."

"No shit."

Both men sat down again, each in an old leather armchair, on opposite sides of Windemere's antique desk. A mellow golden light came from a Tiffany desk lamp, endowing the study with a rich, shadow-filled comfort. Windemere carefully poured one cognac and passed it to Gibson. Then he poured himself one and raised his glass.

"Your good health."

Gibson returned the toast. "Thank you. I'll do my best to keep it."

He slowly inhaled the fumes in the top of the balloon snifter and then took a first experimental sip of the cognac. "This is very fine."

Windemere nodded with the agreement of a proud host. It was no empty compliment; the brandy was truly remarkable. After allowing a decent interval for contemplation of the liquor, Gibson went back to the original conversation.

"You know, all this stuff you've been saying about bio-energy. It sounds an awful lot like Wilhelm Reich's orgone theories."

Windemere nodded enthusiastically. "Of course, it is. It's exactly that. Old Reich was coming very close to grasping the handle. Why else do you think the man was impaled so quickly and efficiently by the FBI, the guardians of capitalism and the transactional universe? If indeed it actually was the FBI."

"Who else would have busted his ass?"

"A lot of people over the years have tried to hang it on the Men in Black."

"The Men in Black who show up after close UFO encounters and tell Vern and Bubba to shut the fuck up or else."

"The very same."

"Does anyone really know who or what they are?"

Windemere shrugged but his eyes twinkled. Beneath his English gentleman's veneer, he was all piratical rogue. "The only time that I crossed paths with them, I got the distinct impression that they were something other than us."

The twinkle had started Gibson wondering just how real Windemere really was and how much of his act was master-class put-on.

Windemere's thoughts took a sudden, sideways, grasshopper leap. Either the hashish or the brandy was getting to him. "Talking of impaling, did you know that the idea of incapacitating a vampire with a wooden stake was actually an invention of Bram Stoker?"

"I always thought that it was just poetic justice for Vlad the Impaler."

"The real tradition was iron stake. What does that suggest to you?"

"That they were grounding the vampire?"

"Exactly, dear boy. Running its energies to an earth. Isn't that a nice phrase? Grounding the vampire."

"What do you mean by the transactional universe?"

Windemere was sucking on the pipe. "It's just another phrase."

Gibson had enough Meth in him not to settle for any Zen double-talk. "Yes, but what does it mean?"

"Simply that our metallic world's other great error is to look on everything according to a capitalist model. Everything is a transaction. The sun shines and the crops grow. Everything's a deal. You do a deal to cop some fossil fuel and your car carries you to Birmingham. You smoke too many cigarettes and you get cancer. We look at energy as a transaction, as a commodity. Almost no one except Albert Einstein ever thought of it as an interface with the universe, as a dialogue, so to speak. We release energy constantly without a clue to its possible effects—sexual energy, philosophical energy, the massive jolt that comes with the moment of death."

"Death?" Gibson didn't like the word.

"Yes, death. This century in particular can be viewed as little more than a sequence of death cults."

"You mean the Manson Family and stuff like that?"

Windemere laughed. "Charlie? Oh, dear me, no. Old Charlie was nothing more than a very lowly servant of Abraxas. All he did was snuff that Polish movie director and his starlet wife, and a bunch of other decadent rich folk. He just got too much media coverage. No, I'm talking about the generals who ran World War I or Adolf Hitler or Pol Pot or Edward Teller, the father of the H-bomb, and all the others who babble about limited nuclear war."

"Surely they aren't cults, though, are they? Monsters but not cults?"

Windemere's face became grim.

"What do you think World War I was but a conspiracy by old men to maintain power and potency by the mass sacrifice of the young? In one afternoon on the Somme, the British general, Haig, lost almost twice the American casualty list for the whole of Vietnam. Think about the trouble that the Aztecs caused with just one sacrificial victim and a pyramid amplifier and then think of the power that Auschwitz must have put out in a single day."

Gibson wanted to ask what trouble the Aztecs had caused, but Windemere was still running.

"That is exactly the kind of stuff that wakes Necrom."

"You know about Necrom?"

Windemere nodded. "Oh, yes, I doubt that Carlos Casillas would have sent you here if I didn't."

"Do you have any idea why I'm getting so much attention? Do you know that we were followed by a UFO on the way over here?"

Windemere's eyes narrowed.

"No, nobody told me that. All I heard was that a bunch of *tontons* tried to ice you and Don Carlos."

"I think they were actually trying to take us alive."

"Every dark cloud has a silver lining."

"With *tontons*, dying may be the decided lesser evil."

Windemere topped up Gibson's drink. "You have a point there, old son." He paused to fill his own glass and then changed the subject. "You say that you saw a UFO over the Atlantic?

"We didn't just see it. It played tag with our plane and put us out for something like ten minutes."

"Out?"

"Gone, unconscious, dead to the world, everyone on the plane."

"You really do seem to be attracting attention."

Gibson twisted uncomfortably in his chair. "But why me, goddamn it?"

"Maybe someone thinks that you're a threat."

"I doubt I could be a threat if I tried."

Windemere laughed. "That's something you really can never know."

"I'm glad you find it amusing."

"If you can't see the cosmic joke, you're liable to go crazy in the process."

"I can't help feeling that I'm still waiting for the cosmic punch line and I may be the one falling over on the cosmic banana peel."

"That's the chance that you take."

"Thanks."

"Lighten up, Joe. You're in safe hands right now."

Gibson sighed and sipped his cognac. "I'm sorry. It's been a hard day."

"Tell me about the saucer. What did it look like?"

Gibson wondered if Windemere was really interested or whether he was merely decoying him away from his latest attempt at self-pity.

"In fact, it wasn't a saucer, it was more like an egg."

Windemere grinned wryly. "Shades of *Mork and Mindy*."

Despite himself Gibson also had to grin. "I hadn't thought of it that way."

"So what did this egg do?"

Gibson shrugged. "Up until it put us out, nothing very much. The captain said it was zigzagging a lot when he first picked it up on the radar. Then it came alongside and mostly just kept on changing color."

"And what happened when it put you out?"

"There was a blinding light, like a massive burst of radiation, and that was all she wrote. Next thing, we're waking up ten minutes later. You have any inside track on UFOs?"

Windemere shook his head. "Not much, aside from what I've read, and, as far as I can see, about ninety percent of that is pure bullshit."

"That's pretty much what the streamheat said."

Windemere looked at Gibson questioningly. "The streamheat claimed that they didn't know anything about UFOs?"

Gibson nodded. "That's what they said."

"I thought they knew everything."

"Apparently not."

Windemere leaned forward and lowered his voice. "Maybe I shouldn't say this while they're in the house, but I don't altogether trust your newfound chaperones."

It was Gibson's turn to look questioning. "Why not?"

Windemere frowned. "I don't know, it's just a feeling. They're a little too . . . metallic, if you know what I mean."

Gibson nodded. "I know what you mean."

Windemere held his brandy glass, warming it between his cupped hands and staring thoughtfully into the amber liquid. "It could be that someone out there believes that you're some sort of catalyst or pivot, that somehow some minor action of yours is going to trigger major events."

"William Storm Eagle said something of the sort."

"He's a wise old bird, Storm Eagle."

Gibson winced at the terrible pun. Windemere spread his hands. "It just came out."

"What makes you think I'm a catalyst?"

Windemere inhaled the fumes from his glass. "It's one explanation of all the shit that seems to have come down on your head since you hooked up with Casillas. You certainly don't seem to have done anything to merit it, unless there's something that no one's telling me. I very much doubt that UFOs are chasing you because some alien doesn't like your old records."

"Are you telling me that all this is happening to me because of something I might do in the future?"

"You have to remember that telling the future is a big deal in what, for want of a better term, gets called the paranormal. Projection's a growth industry, and there are a lot of people, not only in this dimension, that are very hung up on plotting the future. You should talk to your streamheat friends. From what I've heard, their dimension has made a high-tech science out of trying to figure out what's going to happen. They've got data banks from here to Thursday chock-full of nonlinear projection models and societal convection rolls and ways of suppressing the sensitivity to initial conditions. It's all very grand, but I have a sneaking feeling that it's all just fortune-telling when you get down to it, and I've never really trusted fortune-tellers. Even Nostradamus tends to fuck up. It's hard enough to predict a crap game, let alone the whole of everything interacting. If Lorenz's butterfly proves anything, it's that there's only so much you can do to constrain chaos.''

Gibson put his brandy glass down on the desk. He had lost Windemere about three sentences back, but he didn't really care.

''How does all this affect you and me?''

''You mean in terms of your remaining here when it seems like half the multidimensional universe is down on your ass?''

''I'd hate to find myself out on the street.''

Windemere gestured dismissively, as though his continued hospitality went without saying. ''There's no chance of that. I gave my word to Don Carlos that I'd take care of you, and I don't intend to go back on it. On the other hand, though, if it gets hairy we may have to come up with some sort of backup plan.''

''Do you have one?''

''Not yet, but I'm thinking about it.''

''Do you mind if I ask you something?''

Windemere laughed. ''It doesn't seem to have stopped you so far.''

''Why aren't you one of the Nine?''

Windemere hesitated before answering. ''I guess basically because I didn't want to be. I didn't want to be involved in something that also involved Sebastian Rampton.''

''That's been puzzling me ever since I was at that place on Greene Street. How did a sleaze like that get to be one of the great guardians of the Earth?''

''Rampton may be a very unpleasant individual, but there are areas about which he knows more than any living human. When the Nine were selected, nobody was talking morality or even likability. They were dealing in terms of knowledge and power and, God knows, he's got both.''

''But can he be trusted?''

Windemere's expression was matter-of-fact. ''I doubt it. It's always been my opinion that he was a power-crazed geek who fancied himself as *ubermensch*. I never thought that it was just coincidence that he wore exactly the same glasses as Heinrich Himmler.''

''Isn't his being one of the Nine downright dangerous?''

Windemere nodded. ''We'll just have to hope that his interests go on corresponding with those of the rest of them.'' Windemere swirled his brandy in the glass. ''It's not just Rampton. I doubt that I would have joined the Nine even if he hadn't been one of the other invited candidates. I don't exactly share all of their principles. I guess when it comes down to it, I'm too much of a nihilist. The Nine are altogether too strong on preserving civilization as we know it. Me, on the other hand, I'm not even sure that I like civilization as we know it.''

"I thought that if Necrom woke up, it'd be the end of everything, that he'd eat us alive.''

Windemere shrugged. "That's more fortune-telling.''

"So what will happen?''

"Damned if I know. It could be that Necrom will usher in a whole new golden age, although, having lived through the sixties, I'm not sure we'd recognize a golden age if it jumped up and bit us. The only real hope I can see is that we survived the last one and maybe we'll survive again this time round.''

"Survived the last what?''

"The last influx of superbeings.''

Gibson blinked. "When did that happen? Did I miss something?''

"This planet was occupied for about ten thousand years by Necrom and his kind.''

Every time Gibson thought that he was starting to get a handle on the events that had been thrust at him from the moment that Casillas had come knocking on his door, someone or something came along and kicked all previous logic out from under him.

He took a deep, cleansing breath and then spoke slowly and carefully. "There were superbeings actually living on Earth?''

"Right.''

"Right here on Earth.''

"Right.''

"For ten thousand years.''

"That's correct.''

"When was this?''

"From about 25,000 to 15,000 B.C.''

"How come we never heard about any of this?''

"It's just another of those little things that metallic science doesn't like to think about and therefore refuses to believe ever happened. The evidence is there if we care to look.''

"Where?''

Windemere picked up a small rope of worry beads from his desk and twisted them between his fingers.

"It's actually the lack of evidence that's the most overwhelming factor. For the whole of this period, there are no conventional human archeological remains. That's a hell of a period just to misplace. And we know that man was around during that time. It wasn't that he hadn't appeared on the scene yet. Jesus, the Leakeys have found bones in Africa that go back five million years. It's just that we appear to vanish for about ten millennia."

"Are you going to tell me about it?"

Windemere applied a lighter to the pipe. "Don't have much else to do."

"So what happened?"

"Really I don't know that much. Just bits and pieces that I've gleaned along the way. Otherzoners can become amazingly tight-lipped when it comes to telling us stuff that we don't already know."

Gibson nodded. "I've noticed that."

"Anyway, for what it's worth, it seems that round about twenty-seven thousand years ago a bunch of superbeings showed up and colonized this planet in this particular temporal reality."

"Huh?"

"This dimension, if you like. A bunch of parallel dimensions, too, for that matter. Superbeings don't do that kind of stuff by half."

"What did they want here?"

"Who the hell knows? Why does anyone go out and colonize anywhere? Why did Columbus risk sailing off the edge of the world? To prove a point? Maybe all sentient beings are possessed of insatiable curiosity."

"And what did they do?"

"Usual colonial power stuff. Dragged us monkeys out of our caves and forced their idea of civilization on us. Used the place as a playground and probably as a staging point for their inexplicable adventures elsewhere."

"How is it that no trace remains of them?"

Windemere grinned. He was warming to his subject.

"That's the point, there are traces. It's just that we either don't recognize them or we make excuses for them. The whole planet is covered with improbable objects, roads, pyramids, giant structures that may have been constructed according to some big superaesthetic: the Great Pyramid, the Black Stone at Mecca, Easter Island. We're up to our ass in superbeing stuff."

"Superbeing art?"

"Why not?"

"No reason, I guess."

"Artifacts aside, by far the greatest traces of this occupation remain in our own minds."

"They do?"

"Sure. Our gods, ancient and modern, are certainly nothing more than a handed-down memory of Necrom and his kind, although saying so, up until comparatively recently, could get you burned at the stake."

"You don't believe in any kind of religion?"

Windemere looked almost angry.

"I don't believe in gods, full stop. We have quite enough troubles of our own without inventing more. I used to agree with Einstein that the need to create gods was an aberration of our species, maybe a by-product of being at the top of the food chain—how did he put it, 'fear or ridiculous egotism'? Now I suspect that it's all the result of trauma. The arrival of the superbeings left us with a dent in our ego that we still haven't worked out. Our collective consciousness took a terrible hammering. First these superior entities show up and we have to admit that we're no longer number one with a bullet, and then, to add insult to injury, after ten thousand years, just as we're getting used to the idea of being the pets of giants, they dump us and fuck off. We've never recovered. We still keep watching the skies, straining to get up there, promising ourselves that we'll go there when we die. The later pyramids, the spires of cathedrals, Stonehenge, the lines at Nazca, are all appeals to the gods to return. Daddy come home. The truth is, we're a bunch of bloody cargo cultists."

"But how come there are no human remains left for that period? There were plenty of us running around, right?"

"I'm not sure that we were running around. I have a feeling that we were rather more doing what the superbeings wanted. We may have been in reservations or zoos or we may really have been pets inside the residences of the gods. They may not have approved of wild humans, violent and inquisitive, and generally an all-round fucking nuisance. I'm also pretty sure that they left the place as they'd hope to find it, underpopulated and primitive, and they did one hell of a job clearing up, too. They must have practically leveled everything. The catalogue of disaster in legends would seem to confirm it. All the floods, the earthquakes, the nuking of Sodom, they're all likely memories of the superbeings wiping the place clean. The few survivors crawled off to lick their wounds. A few may have struggled for a while, trying to hang on to a little of what they learned, but the majority were too dispirited by the whole business to do anything but head back to their caves and start over."

"You're saying they almost wiped out humanity."

Windemere raised an eyebrow. "Plus all surface trace of their having been here. Does it surprise you?"

Gibson shook his head.

"Not really. It must have been something of a task, though."

"Not for Necrom's bunch, believe me."

"Just how super are they?"

"It's inconceivable. It's like a poodle contemplating Bertrand Russell. Don't let it get you down, though. The point is that we did survive. A pack of angry poodles can bring down a single philosopher if they have a mind to. Don't forget that. Of course, why they should have a mind to and the ethical questions contained therein are a whole other can of worms. That's maybe another reason I didn't join the Nine."

There was a quiet knock on the door. Windemere looked up.

"Yeah, come on in."

The woman who came in was in her mid-twenties and moved with a grace that immediately appealed to Gibson, who automatically rose from his chair. Windemere made the introductions.

"Joe, this is Christobelle Lacey. Christobelle, this is Joe Gibson."

Gibson turned on the charm. "Christobelle is a lovely name."

Christobelle smiled. "Thank you. You know, I saw you play once."

"I hope you enjoyed it."

"Oh, I did, but you rather fucked up later, didn't you?"

Gibson put on his rueful face. "So they tell me. I think I was a little mad at the time."

"We all get twisted at one time or another."

Gibson maintained the rueful smile. "Not all of us do it so publicly, though."

Christobelle nodded. "You did rather make a production out of your paranoia."

He was already wondering about the relationship between Windemere and Christobelle Lacey. What was she? Wife, mistress, employee, friend? Gibson found her exceedingly attractive. The bone structure of her face was solid and patrician, but this was offset by a full, sensual, and very generous mouth. Her white-blond hair was cut punk short and combed straight back. A short leather skirt revealed a pair of very good legs, and even the man's white dress shirt couldn't hide the hard points of her breasts. Christobelle had that same provocative British androgyny that Annie Lennox of the Tourists had exploited into a career. He wondered if the androgyny was limited to style or if androgynous was as androgynous did. You never could tell about the English.

Windemere smiled and half answered the question without being asked. "Christobelle is my secretary. This house would fall into total disorganization without her."

Gibson realized that he'd been staring with this fatuous expression on his face. "I'm sorry, I think the speed is starting to wear off."

Windemere was suddenly very businesslike. "Well, we won't have to worry about giving you any more for the moment."

"I don't think its a good idea for me to fall asleep. The last time I tried it, it was very nearly permanent."

"You're quite safe here."

Gibson looked a little uncomfortable. "I don't want to insult your hospitality or anything, but that's what they told me back on Greene Street. When it came down to it, the psych attack ran all over them."

Windemere slowly nodded.

"I think you'll find that you'll be a good deal safer here from dream invasion. They do rather tend to live in the material world, what with their Mafia rent-a-goons and Muslims straight out of Attica. We tend to be a little more organic over here. Why do you think I've been feeding you hundred-year-old cognac and good opium for the last couple of hours?"

"I thought you were showing me a good time."

Windemere grinned. "Well, that, too, but I was also hardening up your dreams. An opium dream is practically inviolate on its own, but surrounded by a layer of good booze, it's rock steady. They can psych away all they want, but you'll be in blissful oblivion. I don't really approve of amphetamine as a way of life. Without sleep, you just grow less and less sane. Just to be on the safe side, I have some heavy-duty blockers built into this humble abode that are, although a little more funky than the stuff they have in the Nine's little Disneyland on the Hudson, a great deal more effective."

Gibson was still a little doubtful. He wanted to think that Windemere was okay, but it was taking a hell of a risk. The rats and the Nazis were still horribly vivid in his memory.

"I have to take your word for all this?"

Windemere nodded. It was almost casual. "That's right. You do."

"I need to talk to Smith, Klein, and French about this."

This time Windemere shook his head. "I'm afraid that here in my own small magic kingdom I call the shots, and the first one is that you have to make your own decision. As far as my protecting you, it'll be done my way or not at all. Don Carlos knows this and the streamheat know it. It's really a case of take it or leave it, Joe."

Gibson thought hard about this. He really was exhausted and would like nothing better than to stretch out and go to sleep. "If there is an attack, will you have people on hand, ready to pull me out?"

"Of course."

Gibson took a deep breath. "Okay, then. I'll try and get some sleep."

Windemere looked at Christobelle. "Would you mind showing Joe to his room? I have some thinking to do. I fear the multidimensional universe is going to a war footing sooner than I expected."

Christobelle stood up and smiled at Gibson. "Would you like to come with me?"

At the door, Gibson turned back and grinned at Windemere. "Thanks for the hospitality."

Gideon Windemere waved a hand in airy dismissal. "You're more than welcome."

As Christobelle closed the door, she winked solemnly at Gibson. "You should take Gideon's bullshit with a pinch of salt."

Gibson was surprised. It seemed like a decided lack of loyalty. "You mean all that he was telling, he was just making it up?"

Christobelle quickly shook her head. "Oh, no. I don't know what he was telling you, but Gideon always tells the truth as he sees it. The bullshit's in the presentation. Do you want a Valium?"

Gibson thought about both the statement and the question. "No, I don't think so. The opium will more than do it for me."

Windemere's study was in the ground floor of the house, and they were out in the main hallway that led in one direction to the front door and in the other to an imposing staircase. Christobelle started toward the staircase. As she began to climb, she glanced back at Gibson.

"Did you really kill your roadie?"

Gibson wearily halted. How many times did he have to go over that old, old story? "You know, that whole thing has been blown out of all proportion. We were all drunk and the gun went off. Damn, he was out of the hospital and back on his feet inside of a week.''

''But you did shoot him?''

Gibson sighed. ''That's right. I did shoot him. I pointed the gun and shot the son of a bitch.''

Christobelle seemed to realize that she'd gone too far. ''I'm sorry. I wasn't making any kind of judgment.''

''You just wanted to hear from the horse's mouth if the stories were true.''

''Something like that. I suppose a lot of people ask you the same thing.''

Gibson nodded. ''One or two.''

''I really am sorry.''

''That's okay. Don't worry about it.''

The sound of footsteps was coming down from the second floor, and he and Christobelle were confronted by Smith, Klein, and French and Windemere's two minions on the first-floor landing. Windemere's minions were a choice pair. Gibson had no difficulty figuring out which was Cadiz and which was O'Neal without any formal introductions. Cadiz looked fresh out of a Cuban maximum-security prison. He was a small swarthy man with a flat nose and broad cheekbones. His black hair was slicked straight back, and three tattooed tears ran down his cheek from the outer corner of his right eye. The mythology was that each tear represented a homicide. If Cadiz was from the joint, O'Neal looked as though he'd learned his business in some extreme faction of the Irish Republican Army. His hair was shoulder-length and his features were hard and florid, and both men faced down the world with expressions that were totally devoid of the normal signs of either humor or pity. Gibson wondered how a seemingly cultured individual like Windemere stood living with this duo of cold killers hanging around.

Smith stopped on the landing and looked questioningly at Gibson. ''Are you okay?''

Gibson nodded. ''Yes, I'm fine.''

''What are you doing?''

Gibson scowled. Smith continued to behave as though she were his goddamn governess or something.

''Windemere suggested that I should get some sleep.''

''Is that a good idea after what happened in New York?''

''I'm prepared to take the chance.''

''We're responsible for your safety.''

"I thought Windemere had taken over that role?"

Smith glanced back at Cadiz and O'Neal.

"I don't think this is the time or place for this discussion."

Gibson stood his ground.

"And I don't think that it's a good idea to be shooting me up with any more speed. I'm going to wind up crazier than I am already. So, despite your misgivings, I'm going to avail myself of Mr. Windemere's hospitality and go to bed." He stepped past Smith and looked at Christobelle. "Would you like to show me to the guest room?"

Christobelle eyed Smith, Klein, and French coldly.

"Of course, whatever you want."

The two of them started up the next flight of stairs. Nothing more was said, but Gibson had the distinct feeling that somewhere along the line Smith would make him pay for his demonstration of independence.

The guest room was on the top floor. In the days when the house had originally been built as the home for a well-to-do Victorian family, the room had probably been part of the servants' quarters. On one side, the ceiling angled down, following the line of the roof. Most of the floor space was taken up by a king-size brass bed and a small bedside table. On the table there were two twelve-ounce Cokes cooled in a bucket of ice, and a copy of Stephen Hawking's *A Brief History of Time* appeared to be set out as suggested bedside reading. How the hell did Windemere know that Coca-Cola was Gibson's favorite hangover cure? There was a framed print of Andy Warhol's *Electric Chair* hanging above the mantel. The room wasn't exactly cheerful, but the bed looked comfortable, and right at that moment it was all Gibson cared about. As they entered the room, a very large black Persian cat with the amber eyes of a demon jumped up from where it had been sleeping and streaked past them and out of the door. Gibson started but quickly recovered himself.

"What was that? Windemere's familiar?"

"That's Errol. He shares his home with us and we feed him. He's a bit neurotic and doesn't altogether trust strangers."

Christobelle closed the door behind the animal. "You think you'll be okay here?"

Gibson was a little surprised when she closed the door; he couldn't really believe that she intended to remain through the night with him on so brief an acquaintance. He picked up the book and leafed through it, doing his best to look casual. "I'm sure I will. I could sleep on a cement floor if I had to."

Christobelle dimmed the bedside light and turned back the covers; then she started unbuttoning her shirt. Gibson glanced up and raised a questioning eyebrow. "You look as though you're planning to stay?"

She grinned at him. "Unless you have an objection."

Gibson sat down on the bed. "No objection at all. I just didn't expect it."

Christobelle wasn't wearing a bra.

"Didn't you think that well-brought-up English girls did this sort of thing?"

Gibson chuckled.

"Hell, no, I've met a few well-brought-up English women in my time. They didn't act any different to anyone else."

"So why the look of amazement? You must have had girls throwing themselves at you all the time."

"Windemere isn't going to be put out by us being here like this?"

"Why should he?"

"I was wondering how he might feel about a total stranger debauching with his secretary."

"Listen, Gibson, Gideon Windemere's secretary debauches with whom the hell she wants. Don't you forget that."

She was sliding the leather miniskirt over her hips. Her panties were plain black cotton. She sat down beside him and put her lips close to his ear. "If you want to, you can look at it as just a little more dreamstate reinforcement. Or put it down to the fact that, when I was little, I always wanted to be a groupie."

Gibson could feel the warmth of her breath, and he needed no further urging.

After all that he'd been through, making love to Christobelle Lacey was close to a hallucinatory experience. He was beyond exhaustion and far from certain that he'd be able to respond at all. Fortunately, Christobelle seemed to have no reservations about taking control, and Gibson was more than happy to relax and leave himself in her capable hands, lips, arms, mouth, and all the other parts of her body that continuously drifted in and out of his soft-focus opium half-dream. She moved against him sinuously. She stretched and writhed. There was muscular, feline joy in each slow variation of her movement. She was a jaguar crouching over him, purring and sighing, hot breath on his face. Momentarily, her teeth clamped into the flesh of his shoulder, and he later tasted blood on her lips. As if from a great distance, he could hear his own gasps of pleasure, and despite all that he'd been through, he found himself rising with her, coming up for annihilation, drawing a strange new strength from somewhere in the depths of complete unreality. The only disturbing part was that each time he opened his eyes he found that he was looking at the Warhol *Electric Chair* on the wall that faced the end of the bed. Who was it who said that there was only a fine line between orgasm and death? You said a mouthful there, Jack.

When they were both finished, Gibson lay on his back, panting, watching red explosions beneath his eyelids. Christobelle rested her arms on his chest and looked down at him in the gloom with a wicked but contented grin on her face.

"Did you like that, Joe Gibson?" He noticed that she had very sharp little incisors. He opened his eyes and smiled.

"That would be an understatement. I feel like a violin that's been played by a master."

"Or maybe a mistress?"

Gibson laughed. "Top-of-the-line, five-thousand-dollar hooker couldn't have done better."

Her teeth were very white in the darkness.

"You really know how to sweet-talk a girl."

"Were you ever a top-of-the-line, five-thousand-dollar hooker? Maybe in another life?"

Although Gibson knew that it was probably the gentlemanly thing to stay awake and talk, he couldn't fight his sinking mind and wilting intelligence. Within minutes, he was fast asleep. His dreams were a procession of ragged fragmented images, weird but not terrifying and certainly not imposed from outside. At one point, he floated on his back in a warm, buoyant sea while an entire armada of stately UFOs, rainbow-colored and in an infinity of configurations, slowly crossed the jet-black sky in multiple formations. Christobelle or someone very like her swam beside him, occasionally reaching out a soft hand to touch his body. There was nothing in this part of his dreamstate to warrant any complaint.

Waking was a whole different matter. Christobelle was gone, replaced by O'Neal and a headache of Godzilla proportions. O'Neal was standing at the end of the bed. He was wearing a zipped-up nylon windbreaker that made him look like a narc.

"You'd best be getting up."

His voice had the harsh rasp of Catholic Belfast. Gibson sat up. For a few moments, he had no idea where he was. Then it all came back to him. It was hardly a pleasant sensation. Even less pleasant was the taste in his mouth. He reached for one of the Cokes on the bedside table. The ice had melted, but it was still cold.

"What's going on?"

"Windemere will fill you in. You'd best get some clothes on. Everyone else is waiting for you in the drawing room."

The White Room

IT WAS THE shrink hour at the small but very exclusive clinic. That is to say, it was shrink hour for Joe Gibson. It was plainly a very self-centered attitude to think that the clinic revolved around him, but there was nothing to give him any greater perspective. They had him completely isolated, and he had absolutely no idea what went on in the rest of the place. Monday through Friday, he spent one hour a day with Dr. Kooning. Indeed, the only way that he could recognize a weekend was by the lack of Dr. Kooning's hour and the change in the TV schedules. Monday through Friday, they came for him in his white cubicle with the ceaseless TV set, put him in a wheelchair, and wheeled him through the bright, sterile corridors of the clinic to the equally white interview room with the garish, orange-and-yellow floral curtains. Gibson couldn't figure the logic of transporting physically healthy mental patients from one part of the clinic to another by wheelchair. Why in hell couldn't he be allowed to walk and maintain some shreds of his dignity? Did the patients being in wheelchairs make them easier to subdue? Gibson had learned more than he really cared to know about subduing procedures at the clinic when he'd made that first futile attempt at a breakout.

Dr. Kooning was a small woman with scraped-back, graying hair, rather prominent teeth, and very thick, circular glasses that she wore balanced on the bridge of her nose. Her face was locked into a permanent expression of distaste. Gibson wasn't sure exactly what she found so distasteful: humanity at large, the nature of her job, or maybe just him. He didn't believe that it was him alone. She'd appeared to have been wearing the expression so long that almost all the lines of her face conformed to it. Dr. Kooning had been viewing the world with distaste long

before he'd shown up. That was, however, no reason for her
not to make him the focus of it during their sessions. They had
clashed immediately. One of Gibson's first ploys was to refuse
to lie down on the couch. Another token maintenance of dignity.
He would sit on the couch, he'd lean on the couch, he'd sit on
the couch hunched in a corner with his legs curled up under him,
or in a full lotus position. The one thing that he wouldn't do was
lie flat on his back on the couch.

"What frightens you about the couch, Joe?"

"I'd get too anxious and I wouldn't be able to concentrate.
I'd be too worried that someone would suddenly jump on my
stomach with both feet."

The thing that annoyed him the most about Dr. Kooning was
that she always tried to insinuate herself into the picture.

"Do you fear that I'd jump on you?"

"No, but one can't be too careful."

After about a week of sparring, Dr. Kooning had accepted
Gibson's attitude regarding the couch. She still brought the matter up at roughly weekly intervals, but the initial fight seemed
to have gone out of her. Instead, she had recently taken to challenging his fundamental belief in himself.

"So it was only when you returned to this particular dimension that you began to believe that you didn't exist?"

"I didn't say that I didn't exist. I said that all evidence of my
existence had been erased."

"Isn't that the same thing?"

"Only if you take a very Orwellian view of the world."

"Are you angry that you've been erased?"

"I'm not very pleased."

"Do you feel that you're being punished?"

"No. I think something tipped over on its side."

"Or maybe that the world isn't grateful. It took away your
fantasy of being a once successful entertainer."

"It wasn't a fantasy."

She'd stay with the same question like a dog worrying at a
bone. "Maybe the world isn't grateful enough?"

"Why should the world be grateful to me?"

"For saving the universe."

"I didn't save the universe. My world has gone."

"Perhaps that's why you're being punished."

When this kind of concentric looping of the subject didn't get
anywhere, she had him go over his story in the minutest of
details.

"Now, Joe, if I remember correctly, when we finished yesterday, you were about to tell me how you woke up in that house in London."

"The house that doesn't exist anymore."

"Forget about that for the moment and just tell me how you felt when you woke up that first time. You'd briefly felt safe and you'd made love with a woman who'd given you more satisfaction than you'd experienced in a while. Very quickly, though, you began to feel as though it was all slipping away . . ."

Chapter
Five

"GO TO THE window and look out."

Gideon Windemere's drawing room was on the first floor of the house. The big bay windows with their small wrought-iron balcony commanded a perfect view of the street out front. Gibson walked over to the window, pulled aside the heavy blue velvet drapes, and looked out. Windemere was standing behind him.

"Tell me what you see."

A light drizzle was falling on the town. The road surface was slick, and cars hissed by with windshield wipers flicking. Water dripped from the plane trees that lined both sides of Ladbroke Grove. Even in the house, there was a smell of dampness.

Gibson considered the scene in the street below him.

"There's a large black car across the street. An old Hudson, '51 or '52, the one with the small narrow windows that looks like a big turtle."

"Anything else?"

"There's a man leaning against the car. I'd say at a guess that he's watching the house. The funny thing is that he doesn't appear to be getting wet."

"Describe him."

"He's wearing a long raincoat of some kind of dirty off-white material—it's a bit like a duster—and a black cowboy hat with studs around the band."

"Can you see his face?"

Gibson shook his head. "No, it's hidden by the brim of his hat. Who is this guy? Is the Jesse James look big in London this year?"

"When he's in this dimension he calls himself Yancey Slide, and he's nothing to do with London."

Gibson turned and looked at Windemere. "What is he?"

"He's an extremely dangerous entity."

Gibson looked out of the window again.

"This cat in the cowboy hat is a superbeing?"

"No, but he's hardly human."

As O'Neal had told Gibson, everyone had been waiting for him in the drawing room. Christobelle was sitting in a deep leather armchair. She was comfortable in torn and faded Levis and a bulky fisherman's sweater. As Gibson walked into the room, she gave no indication that the previous night had ever happened. There was no quick smile or fast intimate eye contact. Cadiz and O'Neal flanked the door. Smith, Klein, and French sat side by side on the leather couch that was part of the same set as Christobelle's armchair. Windemere presided over the room, leaning on the mantel of the marble fireplace, in which a small log fire was burning.

"Yancey Slide is what was known in Sumerian as *idimmu*, a minor demon."

Gibson was still staring out of the window with his back to the others. "You're telling me that a minor demon is standing in the rain on a street in London in broad daylight, leaning on a 1951 Hudson? I don't see no horns or tail and certainly don't see no smoke rising or smell any brimstone."

Christobelle rearranged herself in the armchair. "He isn't getting wet, is he?"

"That is a little weird," Gibson conceded. He slowly turned. "At risk of sounding overparanoid and being accused of believing that I'm the center of the universe, does the fact that this guy is lounging around across the street not getting wet have anything to do with the fact that I'm here?"

Windemere half smiled. "It would be pushing coincidence not to recognize that there could well be a relationship between you turning up and then Yancey Slide arriving just twenty-four hours later."

"So what about this character? What do you know about him?"

Windemere scratched his ear and looked a little unhappy. He glanced at Smith.

"You want to field this one?"

Smith shook her head with a quick but very smug smile.

"It's all yours, Gideon. I don't do demons. They're not my field."

Gibson looked slowly from Windemere to Smith and back

again. She was calling him Gideon? Had there been something going on between these two last night? What went on between an otherzone cop and a weird-ass, postmodern philosopher?

"So which of you is going to tell me about Yancey Slide? This waltzing around is making me nervous."

Smith looked to Windemere for a response. Windemere stared long and hard at the rattlesnake skeleton that was coiled in a glass dome on the mantelpiece. Finally he straightened up and went and stood beside Gideon. The gray afternoon light in the London drawing room was suddenly detached and alien, and there was a chill in the air despite the fire.

"It's funny that you should mention Jesse James. In many respects, Yancey Slide is the very same kind of morbid, psychotic, ethnopath white trash. Except, of course, that he may be as much as twenty thousand years old. He seems one and the same as Yanex, the servant of Maskim Xul during the first occupation, although it's very hard to know with *idimmu*. There's one theory that they're immortal, much in the manner of the vampire, while another suggests that they might be a series of entities that consecutively take up residence in the same personality."

"Kind of like renting an apartment?"

Windemere seemed pleased that Gibson was taking it so well.

"Exactly. There's definite evidence that Slide has always had an affinity with the southern part of the United States. He appears to have started a vampire plague in New Orleans around the beginning of the nineteenth century and later roamed the settlements along the Mississippi as a professional witch-finder. He's recorded as hanging seventy-three women and sixteen men in one summer of operations. It's also likely that he may have been present at the burning of Lawrence, Kansas, so the Jesse James connection is more than just sartorial."

"You're going to tell me next that he rode with Attila the Hun."

"Attila the Hun didn't keep records."

Gibson peered at the man in the street, but this time he did it from half behind the curtain. Slide hadn't moved.

"Can he be stopped?"

Windemere spread his hands.

"Stopped? I doubt it. Deflected might be possible."

Gibson turned to Smith, Klein, and French. "Can't you zap him with one of your weapons and send him back to where he came from?"

Smith shook her head. "It's not possible. Slide's much too complicated for that."

"Silver bullets? Stake through the heart? Holy water? Exorcism?"

Windemere was shaking his head. "None of the above."

"So?"

"So I suggest we go and see what he wants."

Smith looked up in amazement. "Have you taken leave of your senses?"

Windemere shrugged. "You have a better idea? We can't zap him, and I certainly don't intend to cower in the house until he gets bored and goes away. If we talk to him, at least we know what he wants and if there's any chance of negotiating."

Gibson didn't like the sound of the word "negotiating." He could all too easily see himself as the subject of the negotiations.

"Hold up there a minute."

Windemere quickly turned. "Don't worry. We won't be giving you away to him unless we absolutely have to."

Smith still looked less than overjoyed by the idea. "Are you sure you can handle this?"

Windemere nodded. "I think so. It's my turf, after all."

Gibson stood up very straight. "I'm going with you."

Windemere and Smith responded in unison. "Don't be ridiculous."

"I'm going."

Windemere was busily shaking his head. "Your being there is just the kind of distraction that Slide could use to pull something."

"I don't want to argue about it."

Smith fixed him with a look that should have left freezer burn. "We're not arguing. You're not going out there."

It may have been the look that snapped it or it may have been the tone of her voice. Gibson wasn't sure which. All he knew was that he was suddenly as mad as hell. He jabbed a finger at Smith.

"Listen, lady, we had the start of this discussion last night. I'm getting mighty tired of being told what to do and being expected to obey without question. I don't do that sort of thing. I spent a lifetime not doing that sort of thing and I'm not about to start now. I'm extremely grateful for you pulling me out of the shit in Jersey, but nobody appointed you either my babysitter or the custodian of my life. If they did, they were acting well outside their authority. I'm a grown man and I make my own decisions, and here's the one for today. I intend to have myself a very large Scotch—'' He glanced at Windemere and made a slight bow. ''—if I may—'' He returned his attention to Smith. ''—and then I'm going to walk out of the front door and find out what this Yancey Slide wants with me.''

Windemere laughed. He went to the sideboard and started pouring from a decanter of amber fluid.

Christobelle's voice came from the depths of the leather armchair. ''You'll need a raincoat. It's raining out and you don't have Yancey Slide's power to mysteriously remain dry.''

Windemere handed Gibson what had to be a triple Scotch.

''She's right, you know. You came in with what you have on, dressed for autumn in New York. This is London and it's damp and chilly. Besides, you'd attract attention walking round soaking wet in a lightweight suit.'' He turned to Christobelle. ''Joe and I are roughly the same size, why don't you have a look in my wardrobe for something suitable?''

Christobelle stood up. ''Whatever you say, boss.''

She left the room. Smith, meanwhile, seemed to be in the grip of high, controlled fury. ''I still think this is a very bad idea.''

Gibson was halfway through his Scotch. ''Your protest is noted. If things fuck up, you'll have the satisfaction of having told me so.''

''Maybe we should leave you altogether.''

Gibson could have sworn that, in her own icy way, Smith was pouting. ''That's for you to decide.''

Smith shook her head angrily. ''Unfortunately, I can't just dump you. I made an agreement.''

''Then there's nothing to discuss. All you have to realize is that protecting me is not the same thing as holding me prisoner.''

Christobelle returned with a black Italian trenchcoat over her arm. She held it out to Gibson. ''Try this. It ought to be appropriate for the occasion.''

''Aren't you worried that I'm going outside to get myself killed or worse?''

''I'm sure you'll do whatever you have a mind to.''

There was still not the slightest intimacy or warmth. Gibson downed the rest of his Scotch and slipped into the coat. Christobelle looked him over and nodded.

''Yeah, that'll do. Turn your collar up in the back like a hood.''

Windemere took Gibson's empty glass. "Take care of that coat, I'm quite fond of it."

Gibson pulled a wry face. "I'll try not to get blood on it."

Smith looked from one to the other of them. "How many of us are going?"

Windemere glanced quickly at Gibson and then faced Smith.

"I thought just Joe and I. We don't know how much Slide knows. It hardly seems like a good idea to give him the gift-wrapped chance to look you three over. We are hoping this isn't going to be a confrontation."

Smith nodded curtly. "We'll be watching from the window."

O'Neal stepped forward. "You want me to come with you?"

Windemere nodded. "Now, that might be a good idea, a bit of terrestrial bulk." He looked from O'Neal to Gibson. "Okay, so it's the three of us. Shall we go, gentlemen?"

As Windemere was putting on his own raincoat, he suddenly grinned at Gibson. "You seem to be getting the measure of our streamheat friends."

"I just don't like to be treated like that. I never cottoned to be nursemaided."

"Just don't underestimate them." He placed a dark-brown fedora with a wide black band on his head and tilted it at an angle. "By the by, I don't think this is a very good idea, either."

Gibson started for the front door. "Then you'll be able to say You told me so, too."

Windemere followed him and O'Neal brought up the rear. Outside on the pavement, they waited for a break in the traffic. Even in a neighborhood that had its fair share of odd sights, the three of them must have presented a fairly bizarre spectacle. O'Neal looked like a terrorist; Windemere, in his fedora and Burberry, had turned into Sam Spade; and, for himself, Gibson had the distinct impression that the black coat made him look like an Italian pimp circa 1972. And they were all off to see the eighteen-thousand-year-old demon dressed like a refugee from the Civil War. Good-bye cruel sanity.

When Ladbroke Grove was clear, they walked straight across the road, straight toward the figure leaning against the big black Hudson. Yancey Slide didn't move. They were only halfway across the street when Windemere called out to him.

"Mr. Slide. My name is Gideon Windemere, and I own that house behind us. I was wondering why you were showing such an interest in it?"

Yancey Slide didn't move. It was only when they were right

up to him that he finally pushed back his wide-brimmed hat and
Gibson saw his face for the first time. Wherever and however
Yancey Slide had acquired his human form, he'd gone for dramatic impact. It had clearly been modeled on Clint Eastwood,
except it was a Clint who had engaged in such a wealth of
prolonged and elaborate depravity, both ancient and modern,
that it hardly bore thinking about. There had been no attempt to
disguise the eyes. They just weren't human. The narrow, ice-
blue slits were like looking into the heart of some deep frozen
hell.

"Gideon Windemere. I've heard of you. And Joe Gibson.
You know, I saw you perform once? And the third gentleman I
think I might know by sight. Didn't we once go kneecapping up
the Falls Road? Or was that someone else, Paddy? I'm damned
if I know. All you boyos look alike to me."

Slide's voice was little more than a ruined whisper, a dangerous reptilian rasp that sounded as though he might really be
eighteen thousand years old. Gibson turned and looked at
O'Neal. He seemed seriously taken aback. This surprised Gibson. He wouldn't have thought that the implacable Irishman had
it in his repertoire of responses.

Windemere quickly tried to cover the disarray of the moment.
"Perhaps we should all step onto the pavement."

It was a practical suggestion. They were standing on the off
side of the Hudson with black London taxicabs hurtling past just
inches from their backs.

And, with that, they were on the pavement.

With no movement or even a sense of discontinuity and in
less than the blink of an eye, they were standing in another place
some ten or twelve feet away. Slide was still leaning on the car
in exactly the same thumbs-in-his-belt gunslinger posture, except he was now leaning on the other side of the car. His smile
was a fraction less faint.

"Excuse the parlor trick, *mis amigos*. Sometimes I just can't
resist."

Gibson was speechless. If the man—he was still thinking of
Slide as a man, "demon" a hard word to use with conviction
even after everything he had seen—could instantly move them
through space, what the hell else could he do? Windemere, on
the other hand, seemed completely undaunted.

"I'm suitably impressed. Now perhaps you'd like to tell me
why you're taking such an interest in my house."

Slide fumbled in the pocket of his duster and pulled out a thin black cheroot. "You know who I am?"

Windemere nodded. "I know who you are."

"Then you're showing a hell of a lot of balls for a human, coming out here like this."

He held up his right index finger. A blue flame appeared at its tip. He lit the cigar from it and then extinguished the flame with a shake of his hand.

Windemere watched him without expression. "If you're trying to frighten us, you're not succeeding. We've seen magic acts before."

Slide slowly nodded. He tapped softly on the black glass of the front passenger window of the Hudson. The rear door swung open and a man and a woman climbed out. They were equally impressive. If Slide's human form had been modeled on Clint Eastwood's, the woman was a hybrid of Cher and Elizabeth Taylor with a liberal dash of heavy metal—a stunningly beautiful Amazon road warrior, over six feet tall with high, jet-black hair and, as Little Richard put it, "a figure made to squeeze," although anyone squeezing her right at that moment might find himself hampered by the chrome studs, the chains, the metal plates, and the reinforced, tuck-and-roll leather. The only truly feminine parts of her costume were the torn fishnet stockings and spike-heeled ankle boots. The man was a totally bald sumo wrestler in a suit that looked as though it had been constructed by a tentmaker. It was a yellow-and-black plaid, cut in a style that Gibson hadn't seen since the passing of Nikita Khrushchev.

"These are my traveling companions, Nephredana and Yop Boy."

Gibson wondered if these two had the same nonhuman eyes as Slide. It was impossible to tell since they were both wearing impenetrable Ray-Bans. Then Yop Boy let his coat swing open, and Gibson stopped wondering about the eyes. He, Windemere, and O'Neal were treated to a brief glimpse of an elaborate, ultralight assault weapon strapped to the huge man's massive thigh. It was a design that Gibson had never seen before. It looked something like a deluxe version of an Uzi that had been fitted with a weird set of gas ports under the ejector, finished in gold leaf, and then fitted with mother-of-pearl grips and a top-mounted laser sight. Gibson suspected that he was looking at a weapon that had been brought through from another dimension. He was also puzzled. Why should a demon, seemingly with all manner of supernatural powers, resort to such a temporal show of force?

Windemere seemed to be thinking the same thing. He faced Slide with an amused smile. "You want to watch that. This is London and people here are a little down on firearms."

Slide's smile had disappeared altogether. "I don't think we'll have any trouble."

Gibson wasn't so sure. He was surprised that they hadn't had trouble already. In daylight, on a street with heavy traffic and with the local police station just a block away down the hill, the Hudson alone should have been enough to cause comment. Combined with the appearance of the six of them, the sight should have been enough to stop traffic, and yet no one was giving them a second glance.

Windemere was still facing Slide. "I sincerely hope we won't."

Slide looked Windemere up and down. "There are places where walking up to a man and demanding to know his business is construed as a hostile act."

Again, Windemere wouldn't allow himself to be intimidated. "I believe there are other places where to watch a man's home is a way of making the man in question exceedingly paranoid."

Slide took the cheroot out of his mouth and spat on the pavement. "And this paranoia is the reason for all the firepower?"

Windemere's face was a picture of injured innocence. "Firepower? The only firepower I've seen is strapped to Yop Boy here."

Slide's eyes narrowed dangerously. "Don't bullshit me, Windemere. I know about the three streamheat inside your house, and your other bodyguard, standing in the doorway over there, undoubtedly has some sort of weapon under his coat."

Both Windemere and Gibson looked across the road at the house. Cadiz was standing at the front door and there almost certainly was a weapon concealed under his loose combat coat. Gibson couldn't see anything inside the bay window on the first floor, but he knew that it was safe to assume that Smith, Klein, and French were inside watching.

Windemere shrugged. "These are troubled times. You can't be too careful."

Slide looked up and down the street and around at the nearby buildings. He flipped his cheroot away, and for some reason the butt vanished just before it hit the ground.

"I suspect that we could probably make a tolerable mess of

this particular corner of merry old England if we were to fall to fighting. Is that what you want, Gideon Windemere?"

Windemere shook his head. "No, of course not."

"So, having established the basic standoff, shall we start talking? You want to know what I'm doing here—what I want with you people—is that correct?"

"You can't blame me for being curious."

"Then you'll understand when I say that I'm here because I was curious myself. I wanted to see why the focus of so much attention should show up at your home."

Gibson stiffened. "You mean me?"

Slide pushed himself away from the car. "Yes, you. Anyone who has what you people call a UFO chasing him across the Atlantic needs watching. I hate fucking UFOs."

Gibson wasn't buying the impartial-observer routine. "You're just here to watch? You don't want to kidnap me or kill me or anything like that?"

Slide made a sighing sound that was his approximation of a laugh. "Why should I want to kill you, Joe? I already told you. I saw you play. I enjoyed it. I like rock 'n' roll, Joe. I was a personal friend of Jim Morrison." A slow hand indicated Nephredana. "She was there."

Nephredana's face was impassive behind the Ray-Bans and the red lipstick. Her voice was husky, down in the Marlene Dietrich range, and almost as burned-out as Slide's. Was she eighteen thousand years old, too? "He was a personal friend of Jim Morrison's. He also went on a three-day drunk with John Lennon in Hamburg when the Beatles were starting out."

She produced a stick of gum, unwrapped it, and folded it into her mouth. Although the wrapper was the same color scheme as a standard pack of Bubblicious, the lettering was in a strange alien script. She dropped the wrapper and it, too, vanished just before it touched the sidewalk. The little display didn't help Gibson in any way to accept the premise that having been a drinking buddy of both Jim Morrison and John Lennon confirmed Yancey Slide as nothing more than a curious bystander.

"There have been a lot of strange people trying to get me in the last couple of days and it's made me a little distrustful of strangers."

"You know why all these strangers should be out to get you?"

Gibson shook his head. "That's the worst part. I don't have

a clue. All I know is that this old Mexican guy shows up and
says this group called the Nine wants me to join up with them.''

Windemere looked at him sharply but Gibson was damned if
he was going to shut up on order. ''Since then, all hell seems to
have been breaking loose.''

Slide's lip curled. ''So you've become a lackey of the Nine?''

Gibson eyed him coldly. ''I'm no one's lackey, friend. I'm
just—''

He broke off abruptly. Two constables in blue uniforms and
those improbable Victorian helmets had come down the steps of
the police station, apparently at the start of a foot patrol. They
were walking up the hill toward the group by the Hudson.

''What do they call them here? The Old Bill?''

Slide glanced at the two London cops. ''I wouldn't worry
about them.''

To Gibson's amazement, the officers proceeded to walk
slowly past them.

''They didn't even see us.''

Slide nodded. ''I took the precaution of making us invisible.''

''Invisible? You can make people invisible?''

''I'm a demon, kid, I do shit like that. If you notice, you're
also not getting wet.''

For the first time, Gibson noticed that the drizzle wasn't getting to him. There was no slick of moisture on his raincoat. It
was as though there was a kind of force field a millimeter or so
out from his body.

''I appreciate you keeping me dry.''

Slide laughed. ''I'm not doing it for your comfort, boy. I'd
look kinda dumb if there was an empty shape in the air that the
rain was going around.''

It was while Slide was talking that a figure at the top of the
hill caught Gibson's attention. There was a black man with
dreadlocks perched on a ten-speed bicycle, on the opposite side
of the street from the church, looking in their direction. He not
only seemed able to see them but apparently didn't like what he
was seeing. He took off on his bike with a look of considerable
alarm and disappeared over the brow of the hill. No one else
appeared to have noticed, so Gibson kept his mouth shut.

Slide leaned closer to him. ''I think the only real answer to
your fears, Joe, is that, if I'd wanted you, I would have had you
by now.''

This was easier to accept. Gibson was in no doubt that Slide
hadn't showed them even the introduction to his bag of tricks.

Slide seemed to sense that he'd at least marginally won Gibson over, and he turned his attention to Windemere.

"It's really kind of pointless standing around in the street. Why don't we go into your house and talk in a bit more comfort?"

This was clearly the last thing Windemere wanted. "I'm not inviting you into my house."

Slide's eyes became angry slits. "Never invite an *idimmu* across the threshold? That's vampires, my friend."

Windemere refused to give ground. "Is there that much difference?"

"Find a vampire and I'll show you."

"I'm not letting you into my house."

"You may regret this, Windemere."

"That's always possible."

Slide gestured to the others to get back in the car. He took a final look a Windemere.

"Don't start feeling too pleased with yourself. I'll still be around. If you make a move, I'll know about it."

"Could your being here have something to do with the rumors that your master is about to wake?"

Slide was in the process of getting into the driver's seat of the Hudson. He stopped and slowly turned. To Gibson's surprise, he suddenly looked weary, as if eighteen thousand years had just dropped hard on him. "Master? My master? You don't know what you're talking about, Windemere. You really don't."

"I heard that Necrom will soon be on the move."

"If you knew anything, you wouldn't even mention the name."

The car door closed. Then the window rolled down and Slide fixed Gibson with those alien eyes.

"You should be very careful, Joe. You're running with some people who may not be all that they appear."

The window rolled up and the Hudson squealed away from the curb, laying smoke and rubber. When it reached the top of the hill, something happened to its shape. It seemed to distort and shimmer, and Gibson wasn't sure whether it had disappeared over the hill or just disappeared. He suddenly felt as though a cold, clammy hand had closed over him. The drizzle was noticeably wet.

"I guess we're back in the visible world."

Windemere indicated that the three of them should return to the house. "I think a drink is in order."

Gibson fell into step beside him. "That could have been a lot worse."

Windemere was thoughtful. "I don't think we've seen the last of Yancey Slide."

Cadiz met them at the door. The outline of what looked like a sawed-off shotgun was easy to make out through his combat coat. Once, years before, Gibson had been instructed in the lore of the sawed-off shotgun. Backstage at one of the band's concerts at the Wembley soccer stadium, a bodyguard called Big Cyril, who'd been hired on for the tour, had waxed lyrical, claiming that, in his youth, he'd broken legs for the notorious Kray Twins. "What makes the sawn-off shotgun so favorite is that it appeals to the imagination, like. All you got to do is point one at a geezer and he immediately imagines himself splattered all over the wall like a Sam Peckinpah film. Me, I don't hold with killing. I use a gun to avoid killing. I want a gun that so terrifies people they do exactly what you say and no bother. You know what I mean?" Gibson had hastily assured him that he knew what he meant. Big Cyril had later been fired for his violently overzealous handling of teenage fans.

Cadiz looked a little anxious. Within the limitations of his considerable macho, he all but clucked over Windemere. "Are you okay, boss? I didn't like the look of those guys. They had this aura about them. A bad aura, like the yellow light before a storm."

Gibson was amazed that Cadiz—who on the surface seemed little more than a Central American thug who should have been carrying an Uzi for the Medellín Cartel—talked so matter-of-factly about auras. Then he remembered that, five hundred years ago, his ancestors were probably performing human sacrifices on the tops of pyramids.

Windemere was quick to reassure Cadiz that all was well. "I'm okay. There's no problem."

Gibson wondered about the loyalty that Windemere received from his strange household. There was a great deal more to Gideon Windemere than appeared on the surface. Which was exactly what Yancey Slide had said. Windemere questioned him about this as they took off their coats.

"How do you feel about Slide's parting shot?"

Gibson looked at him guardedly. "You mean about things not being what they might seem."

Windemere nodded. "That one."

Gibson looked unconcerned. "It seemed like a crude attempt to induce a few doubts."

"And did it?"

"I've been around paranoia so long that it now takes more than a minor demon to get me going. UFOs and other dimensions are quite enough. Besides, I'm living proof that things aren't what they appear."

Although he made light of it, Slide had in fact started Gibson thinking. He had no guarantee that these people that he was with were the Good Guys. All he had was their word on it. He'd been quite impressed with Yancey Slide's style and the show that he'd put on, and Nephredana had been something else again. Slide's trio seemed as though they'd be a good deal more entertaining than Smith, Klein, and French.

"What exactly is an *idimmu*?"

Windemere shook his head. "It'd take too long to explain right now. One thing to remember, though, is never to underestimate them." He started up the stairs to the drawing room. Halfway up, he looked back. "Don't be charmed by them, either."

The sun went down behind the Shepherds Bush high-rise projects, the streetlights came on, and the drizzle continued. After a fairly perfunctory couple of Scotches with Windemere, Gibson found himself left alone. He was aware that things were going on in the rest of the house in which he wasn't being included. Everyone seemed to have private stuff to do and people to talk to after the events of the day, and all he could do was make the most of an evening of comparative peace and quiet.

The high point of being left to himself turned out to be making the acquaintance of another member of Windemere's staff. Rita was a large Jamaican lady who cooked for Windemere and the rest of his household and who served Gibson the best meal that he'd had in a very long time: lamb chops with mint sauce and new potatoes, a bottle of Guinness, and apple crumble with egg custard to follow. Even before the adventure had started, Gibson had eaten like a drunk, either greasy or not at all, and at the moment that he finished the last mouthful of dessert, he would have cheerfully fought with anyone who said anything bad about English cuisine. After Rita had served him coffee and cognac, this time only a mere eighteen years old, he was left alone with the television.

This suited him down to the ground. He had a great deal of

thinking to do and he had always found that he thought most creatively while staring blankly at a TV screen. British TV took a little getting used to, with its impenetrably mannered comedies, ultraviolent cop shows, and documentaries that seemed determined to educate the masses whether the masses liked it or not, but it was TV and it was in English and it would suffice. He wished that he had a little more of Windemere's opium but he felt that it would be churlish to come right out and ask. Contenting himself with the cognac, he stretched out on the drawing room couch and attempted a review of his situation.

He didn't imagine that he'd make any real sense of what was happening to him, but he was getting heartily sick of the way that his ignorance was being used to constantly force him into a role of total passivity. Okay, so he was a drunk and a wastrel, and a bunch of stuff that he had never dreamed of in his philosophy was dropping on him like the proverbial shitstorm, but he had to start making his own moves. One of the few constants in the whole sorry business was that everyone he encountered went to some pains to warn him not to trust anyone else. The streamheat didn't trust Windemere, Windemere warned him against the Nine, everyone warned him against Yancey Slide, and Slide played right along with the game by telling him not to trust any of them. Let the circle be unbroken. Unfortunately the circle was wrapped around the outside of his skull and being slowly tightened. His first task was to break out and stop allowing himself to be run from hither to yon like a lab rat in a behavioral study. Independence of action had to be the next item on the agenda.

He wasn't going to achieve independence, though, until he found out why everyone was so interested in him and why the explanations of that interest were so uniformly vague. If he was playing a role in this movie, it was high time he got himself a copy of the script. Enough of all the Shirley MacLaine bullshit about fulcrums, auras, and destiny—if no one was going to tell it to him straight, he was going to have to figure it out for himself. There had to be one among this bunch who knew the score. The streamheat definitely knew a great deal more than they were telling, but he didn't think any one of them was going to get stinking drunk and spill the beans or otherwise let anything slip. He wished that he'd been able to talk to Slide for a while longer. The demon seemed inclined to boast, and after eighteen thousand years, he ought to know a thing or two. In spite of Windemere's warning about not letting himself be charmed,

Gibson couldn't shake the feeling that Slide and his bunch were probably fun to be around.

The ITN *News at Ten* carried a small joke item about the crew of an Air India 797 claiming to have spotted a UFO over the Atlantic the previous night, and this somehow added to his general sense that nothing was quite real. After the news, he found himself faced with *The Poseidon Adventure*. He drifted with the ponderous stupidity of the inverted ocean liner without coming up with any fresh revelations. Sure, he knew what he had to do; how to go about doing it was the hard part. It was about the point Shelley Winters was making her heroic underwater swim that his peace and quiet started to noticeably decay.

Through most of the evening muffled sounds had drifted up from somewhere below; for a while it had been a high-pitched electronic hum, and then that had been replaced by shouts in a strange language, bursts of drumming and clusters of sub-bass harmonics. He had assumed that Windemere was doing something in the basement and left it at that. It was only when a strange smell seemed to be creeping through the house—a jungle-sweet, heavy scent like damp vegetation burning—that it became impossible to ignore. The smell clung and infiltrated and seemed to insinuate its way into his pores. His legs and arms grew heavy, and a dull weight settled on his brain. At first, he resisted, but very soon just let it drift around and over him while he listened to the increasing volume of sound that came from the basement. The random bursts of harmonics had been replaced by an almost hypnotic pulsing, and Gibson caught himself nodding in time and all but drifting into a shallow trance.

Gas! The smell was a colorless gas. He didn't want to think about gas. It was just a smell. He had to focus his eyes and concentrate. Thinking required effort, as did willing himself back to functioning reality, and, once back, he was both suspicious and a little alarmed. Was someone trying to fuck with him again, or was the effect a by-product of the party down below? Either way, he decided that he had the right to take a look. Just a glance down the basement stairs to see what he could see was hardly an invasion of his host's privacy, particularly when whatever his host was doing in private was noticeably leaking through into the rest of the house. He stood up, turned off the TV, and suddenly felt dizzy. Was the smell causing it, or just a delayed reaction to the events of the last few days? The world seemed to have taken on a greenish tinge. Indeed, the greening of the room seemed to have extended to his own face. He groaned as he caught a glimpse of it in the mirror above the fireplace.

"You poor-ass bastard, you look like the walking dead."

He leaned into the mirror and pulled down the lower lid of his left eye. The white of the eye was more than bloodshot. It looked like a color photograph of the planet Mars.

"No wonder, this shit's killing you."

He took a deep breath but it didn't help; the smell was still there, like a warm night on the Amazon. He started for the door. He was definitely going to have a look in the basement.

The pulse was louder and the smell thicker and more pungent as he stepped out onto the first-floor landing. He looked down the stairs into the ground-floor hallway. The door that led to the basement was open, and weirdly oscillating lights were reflected in the polished wood—red, yellow, and orange, like strobing electronic hellfire.

He reached the front hallway but hesitated at the top of the basement stairs, standing just outside the door, just listening to the complex weave of the outlandish rhythm pattern. It wasn't merely a pulsing hum. Rising and falling tones were punctuated by shimmering flutters and mutters that could almost have been human voices except that, without warning, they would lift through eight-octave runs like the music of an Inca sundance and then roll away with the finality of a breaking wave.

He pushed the door open a little wider and put his foot on the first step. He knew that he was completely out of line, and he was suddenly a little scared. Windemere could be doing practically anything down there. Suppose it was something serious and bad? He took another step; now he was committed.

Going down the basement stairs, he could see only a small area of floor. The red and orange lights flashed through curls of heavy vapor that slowly undulated across it like phantom snakes.

As he reached the bottom of the stairs, he realized that he had intruded on something decidedly private. He was turning to go when Cadiz bore down on him and seized him by the arm with an angry, almost desperate whisper.

"Not here, Señor Gibson. Not here."

As Cadiz propelled him back up the stairs, Gibson wondered at what he had seen. Windemere had been sitting naked inside a pyramid in the center of the floor that appeared to be constructed out of some kind of sheet crystal. Windemere wasn't alone in there. A woman was with him. She was also naked, muscular and very black, and her body was in violent motion. Her mass of braids swung like whips each time she moved her head, and she was moving her head a great deal. Windemere and his companion were seated facing each other with their naked torsos pressed together and their legs and arms wrapped around each other's bodies, but within these confines they writhed against each other like twining snakes. Light reflected from bodies that were slick with either oil or mingled sweat, and Windemere's back was daubed with a large single ideogram that seemed to have been painted in what looked uncomfortably like blood.

The pyramid itself was maybe eight feet high and wide enough at the base to contain the two seated people. It glowed as though it was alive with energy and the sheet crystal was somehow conductive. It stood on a solid, square platform that appeared to be constructed of alternate sandwiched layers of bright metal, polished steel or maybe silver, and strata of dark, compacted organic fiber. Some kind of supercharged orgone box? The most elaborate sex aid that Gibson had ever seen? The rest of the room looked like nothing more than a very expensive recording studio. The ceiling was filled with pulsing track lights, and the sound came from eight large speaker bins. The four walls were lined with ranked racks of electronics, each unit powered up and highlighted by its own set of rippling and flashing LEDs. If Windemere was practicing witchcraft, it was a form that could only have been developed in some dark subbasement of NASA or MIT.

When they reached the inside hallway, Gibson turned and faced Cadiz. "What the hell are they doing down there?"

Cadiz shook his head. "No questions, señor. No questions."

"What's that pyramid thing?"

Cadiz's eyes flashed with implacable warning.

"I said no questions, señor. Just go on upstairs and forget everything you have seen."

The threat didn't have to be stated. The tattooed teardrops said it all. Cadiz stood in the hallway, watching Gibson as he climbed the stairs. He hesitated outside the drawing room door. Perhaps he should have a nightcap and think about all this.

Cadiz called up to him. "It would be better if you went to your own room, señor."

Gibson wanted to snap back that he wasn't about to be ordered to his room like a naughty child, but he restrained himself. At the top of the next flight a second voice called out to him.

"Joe Gibson."

This time, it was Christobelle. What now? If she wanted to frolic again, he wasn't sure if he was in quite the right mood. One door on the second landing stood slightly ajar, and her voice was coming from inside.

Gibson stopped at the top of the stairs. He was more than a little wary.

"Yeah, right. That's me."

"Please come in here."

Gibson shrugged to himself. What did he really have to lose? The spectacle in the basement had put an end to any ideas of sleeping in the immediate future. If Christobelle had decided to be nice to him again, who was he to refuse? It sure beat brooding. He went to the door and stepped inside, feeling a little like a character in a French farce. The bedroom was large and dark, and the spacious bed was quite capable of accommodating four or five people with no effort. Christobelle sat alone in the middle of it, cross-legged with her toes curling into the black fur cover. It was a very different Christobelle. The androgynous daytime severity had been replaced by a houri straight out of some sultan's fantasy. Chiffon scarves in soft pastel colors were draped around her neck and did nothing to hide her breasts. The scarves and the collections of gold chains and bells and bracelets on her wrists and ankles were all that she was wearing apart from a gold Balinese headdress that would have delighted Mata Hari. She was backlit by a collection of a half-dozen candles in a floor-standing candelabra on the far side of the bed.

Gibson stopped in the doorway and took in the display. "What was the word the Victorians used? Odalisque?"

Christobelle nodded. "Odalisque, a female harem slave."

"Is all this for my benefit?"

"I called you, didn't I?"

"I thought you weren't friends with me anymore."

"What made you think that?"

"I haven't had a kind word from you all the livelong day."

"I like to maintain a professional distance during working hours."

"But now you're off duty?"

Christobelle slowly spread her arms. "Don't I look off duty?"

Gibson grinned. "That depends what your duties include."

"Why don't you stop talking and come to me."

He didn't immediately go to her. Instead, he peered around the room. It didn't look at all like Christobelle's bedroom. It was too masculine. Framed prints were hung along one wall in a geometric arrangement: Guido Crepax's illustration for the works of the Marquis de Sade, the ones from the notorious Private Portfolio, and a set of Robert Mapplethorpe nudes. The starkness of the prints was offset by Afghan hangings that looked ancient and extremely valuable, Moroccan wooden screens, and a large Louis Quinze dresser, but it still didn't add up to Christobelle.

"Who's room is this?"

"It's Gideon's."

"Might he not take exception to us romping about on his bed? Some people are kind of territorial about their bedrooms."

Christobelle's eyes sparkled in the candlelight. "Gideon is otherwise engaged. He won't surface until morning."

"I know. I caught a little of the act."

The sex languor instantly drained from her face. Christobelle looked worried. "You saw him?"

"I went to the basement. I was curious about the noise and that weird smell."

"That wasn't a very smart thing to do."

"Cadiz gave me that impression."

"You also ran into Cadiz?"

"He hustled me out of there *mucho pronto* and sent me off to bed."

"You're lucky he didn't break your arms and legs as well, just to impress upon you the desirability of minding your own business."

"It seemed that he wanted to but someone had given instructions not to."

"Like I said, you're lucky."

"People keep telling me I'm lucky. I don't think they see it quite from my perspective."

Christobelle's voice softened. "Why don't you take your clothes off."

Gibson sat down on the edge of the bed. "What exactly was Windemere doing down there?"

"You went down there, you saw."

Gibson pulled off one of his boots. "He takes his loving very seriously. That setup must have been burning thousands of kilowatts."

Christobelle smiled.

"The electricity bills can be a little steep."

Christobelle was obviously trying to divert Gibson's queries, but he hung on like a terrier. "There was more to that than a little expensive fun."

Christobelle abruptly lost patience. "Of course there's more to it than fun. You really can be very naive at times. Gideon's generating psionic energy. He's energizing the house and everything in it. We may need all the power we can get. First you show up and then Yancey Slide. Who the hell knows what's going to come next? I wish he didn't feel that he had to do it with that black bitch but that's his decision."

It was a definite flash of jealousy. Gibson wouldn't have thought that Christobelle had it in her. It occurred to him that Windemere might actually maintain a real harem here. You never could tell with the very rich and very powerful. He started to unbutton his shirt. Christobelle was visibly working on regaining her composure. Her breasts rose and fell with each measured, regulated breath. He didn't say a word, just went on undressing. When he was naked, he stood up and faced her. She leaned over and lit a thick, yellowish green stick of incense. The smell of the smoke was the same smell that had been coming from the basement. She turned back to him and held out her arms, apparently not noticing his look of suspicion.

"Come here."

Realizing that it was far too late to back out, he crawled across the bed toward her. The fur felt good. He was about to make a playful grab for her when she fended him off.

"Just sit facing me."

Gibson did as he was told. Whatever she had in mind was almost certainly worth going along with. He crossed his legs and sat upright with a straight back. Their faces were about eight inches apart.

Christobelle smiled. "As with many things, the secret of the tantric arts is that less is more."

Gibson had done his share of the Kama-sutra but he kept quiet and let her go on. "In the *jab-yum*, the key is to do as little as possible as slowly as possible. All I want you to do is to sit very still."

"Windemere wasn't sitting still."

Christobelle sighed. "He'd already been at it for over two hours. Now shut up and do what I tell you."

Her right leg snaked around him in a yogic move that brought her heel to rest against the small of his lower back. Using pressure from her foot, she eased him closer to her.

"Now put your leg over mine in the same way."

Gibson smiled and shook his head. "I don't think that I can. I've been living a life of indolence and sin, and I'm not as limber as I used to be."

Her hand was on his knee, gently guiding him. It was far easier than he'd imagined. A couple of muscles initially protested, but he found that he had his leg around her waist and the seemingly impossible had been achieved with only minor effort. The room was thick with the pungent jungle-rot smell, and Gibson was once again in the cloying grip of euphoric drift.

"Use your own leg to draw me closer."

Gibson gently flexed his calf. Their bodies were now very close; she twisted her torso in a slow, languorous undulation and her breasts brushed against his chest.

"Now the other leg. I'll put my hands on your shoulders and we'll do it together."

Once again the impossible was achieved with comparative ease. They were now in a strange double-lotus position; their upright bodies were pressed closely together, and he could feel her contours along the length of his chest. The nearness of her was quickly arousing him, and as his erection grew it eased inside her as though by osmosis, with no conscious effort on his part. She whispered hypnotically in his ear.

"Slowly . . . slowly . . . you are very, very, slow . . . slow as the movement of mountains."

They were like one multilimbed being, a Hindu god, a child of Shiva. Christobelle's fingers performed the lightest of dances up and down his back. They felt like moths fluttering against his spine. Tiny shudders of pleasure ran up his body.

"Slowly . . . slowly. You need do nothing . . . you need to feel nothing. You are the world and you have all of time. Take nothing for yourself and all will be yours."

He was just starting to drift in the direction of oneness with the sensual universe when, completely uninvited and in some far-off part of his mind where logic and self-preservation still wearily held the line, a realization dawned.

"We're doing the same thing that they were doing in the basement."

Christobelle's whisper was no longer hypnotic. "Of course we are."

Alarm eased out euphoria. "So what's all this, then? A little backup ritual?"

"Something like that. Is it a problem?"

"I've got to think about this."

She leaned away from him slightly. "What's the matter? Did you think that I went to all this trouble because you were so damned irresistible?"

"It's a little cold-blooded for my taste."

"You have something against fucking for a higher purpose than simple personal gratification?"

"I thought you were enjoying this, and now I find that you're just going through the prescribed moves."

Christobelle's voice took on an angry edge. "For your information, Joe Gibson, I enjoy it very much. I was enjoying this very much until you felt the need to inject your note of crude morality. I can only believe that if I can generate energy over and above my own pleasure, it can only be for the greater good. Fun and a bonus, too. It's like gift stamps. It's also the philosophy of the Earth Goddess and that's why I've made it my calling."

"Fucking for victory?"

"It makes a great deal more sense than killing for it."

"I've really got to think about this."

He tried to disentangle himself from her, but they were too complicatedly entwined. Her legs tightened around him as if she was trying to calm his fears with her physical presence. Her voice again took on the hypnotic quality.

She crooned in his ear. "Don't think, Joe Gibson, just be. You are safe here for tonight. Don't think, just be. You are safe in my arms."

The scent was closing in on him and he did feel safe in her arms. He was also growing inside her again. Again she crooned to him.

"Let it go, Joe. Slowly let it go. You're safe. Nothing can hurt you. Slowly let it go."

Joe was letting it go. His mind was floating away, and his body was at long last taking over. The little spasms of pleasure started again.

"Go with it, Joe. Just let it happen."

Her breath was hot against his ear. His legs were so firm around her that he seemed to be melting into her.

"Slowly, Joe. So slowly. Soooo slowly."

The whisper was deep in her throat.

"So good, Joe. Sooo gooood!"

Her pelvis had started to gradually rotate.

"Slowly, Joe. Sooo slowly."

Now he could feel it. He could feel himself growing and expanding. He could feel the power flowing around him.

"That feels so good."

"Slowly."

"That feels so right."

"So slowly."

They seemed to be rising together.

"Oh, God, that feels good."

"Sooo slowly."

Neither of them was moving a muscle, and yet there was sweat running between their bodies.

"Oh, God, that feels good."

"Soooo slowly!"

The smell of them was combining with the jungle reek.

"Oh, God, that feels so good."

"Sooo . . ."

"Oh, God!"

Their sighs and whispers blended together, breath mingling.

"Slowly!"

"Feels good."

"So good!"

"Too good!"

"Slow!"

Somehow, he could feel the two other bodies in the pyramid downstairs. He could feel them also joining.

"Oh, God!"

"Oh!"

"God!"

"Oh!"

"God!"

"OH!"

"Slow!"

"Ooooh!"

"OOOOOOOOH!"

And, at that moment, deep inside the house and deep in the real world from which they were trying so hard to detach themselves, there was a fearful pounding on the front door.

The White Room

"IT'S ALL A matter of playing their game."

Joe Gibson regarded the man blearily. "Game? What game?"

The drugs made it so goddamn hard to focus on anything. He knew that the man's name was John West.

"You have to let them believe that they're curing you, that's the only way you'll ever get out of here."

A new innovation had occurred in the very expensive private clinic. It had come after Gibson had been there for, as far as he could calculate, about three weeks, although the drugs that they were feeding him made it almost impossible to keep track of time. He'd tried for a while to keep a record by marking each day on a secret slip of paper, but they'd found that and taken it away. The innovation was known as "patient interaction." Boiled down, this meant that every day, right after *Love Connection*, he was taken from his room and his private TV and wheeled by an orderly down to a large, white, sterile common room with too much light where he and a dozen or so other doped-up individuals sat in chrome wheelchairs, in varying states of vegetation, and lethargically watched a communal television. This so-called interaction was timed so that he always seemed to end up watching *Gilligan's Island*. Which was weird in its own way since, back in what he was increasingly thinking of as his old world, there had been an almost identical show except it had been known as *Finnegan's Island*. On the screen, the castaways were trying to use a misdirected NASA Mars probe to get themselves rescued. Beside him, John West seemed to have a theory to expound. "Of course, it depends on who put you here in the first place and who's picking up the tab. There are some of us in here who aren't ever going to get out. Too much of an embarrassment to either families or the people that they

118

used to work for. I've heard that there are agency people who've wound up in here just because they knew too much.''

Gibson slowly nodded. The shot that they always gave him just before the patient interaction period made everything seem as if it were taking place underwater.

"It sounds like the old-time Soviets."

"Things don't ever change. If you don't fit, you're crazy."

"I think they put me here because I didn't fit."

He had been going to the interaction periods for over a week—once again, the calculations were a little uncertain—before John West had spoken to him. When West had wheeled himself over, pointed to the TV and muttered, "This is a fucking silly show for grown men to spend their time watching," it was the very first contact that Gibson had experienced with anyone in the clinic who wasn't staff. After that first observation, West had extended a shaking hand. "The name's West. John West."

Gibson had shaken the hand, glad of any contact that didn't come with a white coat and a professional smile. It was hard to tell what any given patient might have been on the outside. You had to read beyond the slack jaws, the vacant eyes, the hollow cheeks, and the uncoordinated movements. All these were a product of the relentless medication. When reading the faces, Gibson knew that he also had to remember that he was in as bad shape as anyone else. A certain residual strength was detectable in West's face, and, although his muscle tone was long gone, traces of what could have been an athletic physique still remained. Gibson suspected that West might well himself have been one of the ones who'd been incarcerated in the clinic because they either knew too much or thought that they knew too much. In all their conversations, West refused to say anything about his own background, although, from his claimed knowledge of the world, his travels seemed to have been extensive and exotic. They certainly would have fitted the profile for a heavy-hitting executive or a spook who later fell from grace.

He may have been reticent about his own past, but that didn't stop him closely questioning Gibson about his.

"So how do you figure you don't fit? What did you do?"

"It's like I told Kooning: I got involved with Necrom and this whole multidimensional thing, and I kept crossing from one dimension to another until, when I finally managed to get back home again, home wasn't home anymore. A lot of little things had changed. TV shows had different names, there were songs that I'd never heard of that were supposed to be classics, people

were still alive who'd died in my world, the world I'd left. The
worst part was that I didn't exist at all. All trace of me had
vanished. How d'you like that for not fitting in. Kind of absolute, huh?''

Gibson found that the medication allowed him to tell the story
with complete detachment. West, who'd been holding a Diet
Sprite unnoticed in his left hand for almost all of the period,
raised it thoughtfully to his lips and sucked on the straw.

After the first sip, he stopped and regarded the can with the
look of one betrayed. ''Damn thing's warm.''

''You've been holding it for all of the period.''

West carefully placed the can on the floor. His face showed
a sad amusement, as though at how far he'd managed to fall.
Then he straightened up and turned his attention back to Gibson.
''And before that, in your world, you were a washed-up rock
star?''

''That would be the blunt way of putting it.''

''And there's no trace of you.''

''Nothing. Me, the band, all erased, no magazine articles, no
recordings, zip. That's the worst part. It's not only me that's
gone, it's my work, too.''

''And what does the good Dr. Kooning say about this?''

''She says that an inability to accept thwarted ambition had
caused me to take a powder on reality.''

West nodded. ''That's a good start.''

There were times when Gibson wondered if maybe West
wasn't an inmate at all, just a spy for the doctors posing as an
inmate. He again stared at him blearily and discovered that he
didn't really care. ''What do you mean, 'that's a good start'?''

West leaned forward like a man making his point. ''It's like
I've been trying to tell you. If you want to even have a chance
at getting out of here, you have to convince them that they're
curing you.''

''How do I do that?''

West's face broke into a slack lopsided grin. There was no
way that he could be an undercover shrink and look like that.
''The trick is to start off acting real crazy, as crazy as you can,
and then you gradually ease off. They think that they're doing
it and they ease up on you. Easy. You dig?''

Gibson stared at him blankly. ''I don't know.''

West didn't seem to notice. ''Like I said, you're off to a good
start. What you have to do now is to start pretending to remember who you really are.''

Gibson looked dourly at West. "How the hell am I supposed to do that? I've never been anyone else. I'm me. That's all there is. There isn't any other me to remember."

West wheeled himself backward as though he'd decided that he was wasting his time. "Then you got a problem, pal. A problem that's going to keep you here for a long time."

On the TV, Gilligan/Finnegan had screwed up yet again and prevented the castaways from being rescued.

Chapter Six

WINDEMERE LIT A cigarette. It was the first time that Gibson had seen him smoke tobacco. "This is my home, damn it. You know what they say about Englishmen and their castles."

Abigail Voud regarded him calmly from behind her small square-cut glasses. Although she hadn't actually pounded on the door of Thirteen Ladbroke Grove with her own tiny fists, there wasn't a shadow of doubt that she was the absolute instigator of the nighttime disturbance. Madame Voud was quite as old as Casillas and equally as frail. "Don't get so angry, Gideon. This is not an invasion. We have to assume that we are all working for the common good." Her head turned slightly so the three streamheat were included in her penetrating gaze. "At least, we have to assume that for the moment, until we have information to the contrary." Also in common with Casillas, the eyes behind the wire-rimmed glasses appeared far younger than her apparent age.

Windemere's anger seemed to be the only thing that was keeping him on his feet. Wrapped in a hastily donned bathrobe, he looked haggard and exhausted, as though the rite in the basement had totally drained all his reserves of energy.

"When someone comes beating on my door in the middle of the night, backed up by an assault team of the local dreads, I tend to treat it as an invasion, even when that someone is one of the Nine."

The pair of tall, burly Rastafarians who stood on either side of the chair in which Abigail Voud was seated maintained implacable stone faces that silently cautioned Windemere he could rant and rave all he wanted but if he went any further, he was dead meat. That this seemingly fragile old lady could recruit herself a personal bodyguard from the pubs and shebeens of the Portobello Road said a great deal about her personal power. It was rare that these hardman Rastas, heavyweights who ran with the London end of some of the baddest posses out of Trenchtown, would demean themselves to take orders from a woman, particularly a woman who stood little more than four feet tall and was old enough to be their great-great-grandmother. It went against every grain of their intractable Jamaican machismo.

Once again, the entire household had assembled in the drawing room of Number Thirteen Ladbroke Grove, roused from their beds by the beating on the door and the sudden intrusion of Abigail Voud and her hastily assembled entourage.

"I flew from Paris when I heard that Yancey Slide was out of the woodwork. I'm sorry that I couldn't give you warning or arrive at a more genteel hour, but I felt that you had a situation building up here."

"I'm handling the situation."

"The way that you've been powering up this place has set the whole neighborhood in an uproar." Somewhere outside a dog was barking, hysterical and out of control. Abigail Voud slowly shook her head. Gibson marveled at the way that she seemed to be talking to Windemere as if he were some headstrong schoolboy. "Did you really think you could load on that much psionic energy in an area as densely populated as this without anyone noticing?"

The Rasta standing on Abigail Voud's right—a thickset, bearded six-footer in a combat coat and camouflage pants, with his locks tucked into a red, green, and black wool cap, whose name was Montgomery, and who was reputed to control a sizable chunk of the West London wholesale ganja market—nodded in agreement.

"You can't be doing shit like that round here, Windemere. We got enough rasclat troubles without all this nonsense, see?"

The tension in the room was downright dangerous. Cadiz and O'Neal were still holding the weapons that they'd grabbed when the disturbance had first started. Gibson, barefoot and bleary-eyed, in the shirt and pants that he had thrown on when people had begun streaming into the house, felt himself at a distinct disadvantage. Christobelle had removed the Balinese headdress and wrapped herself in a floral-print robe, but the bangles and beads of her odalisque outfit still clanked and jingled on her wrists and ankles. Even Rita stood angrily at the back of the room in a pink housecoat and with her hair in rollers, muttering about no-account rude boys and ready to join in any fray that might develop. Only the streamheat remained pin-neat and apparently unconcerned.

Windemere was adamantly shaking his head. "You're pushing me too far, Abigail. I mean, look at it from where I'm standing, I didn't ask to take charge of Joe Gibson. The Nine dumped him on me and now the Nine, through you, are complaining about the way I'm handling things. Either you let me do things in my own way, or you get Gibson out of here and stash him someplace else."

Abigail Voud raised a thin, blue-veined hand. "Calm down, Gideon, please. I'm not here to criticize you. None of us were aware that matters would escalate so quickly. We, the Nine, made the original mistake in assuming that the attacks on Gibson were a purely localized, New York threat. Nobody expected either Yancey Slide or a UFO."

Windemere's mouth twisted into a half smile. "Nobody ever expects Yancey Slide or a UFO." He had, however, calmed down quite considerably.

The authority that seemed to be contained in the old lady's tiny body amazed Gibson. Wrapped in a heavily embroidered purple sari that made her look like a cross between Indira Gandhi and the Witch of Gagool, she seemed easily to assume control of the whole room. Nobody had taken time out from this latest crisis to fill Gibson in about what it was in her background that qualified her for a place in the Nine, but from the look of her Gibson could only assume that she was extensively traveled in whatever secret labyrinth linked the occult undergrounds of Europe, Africa, and the Indian subcontinent. Gibson knew that during colonial days, strange crossovers had taken place and links had undoubtedly been forged that had lasted to the present, and he wondered what she must have been like when she was young. Perhaps she had been one of those mysteriously seductive dragon-women who, according to legend, film, and fable, moved, fingernails clicking and eyes flashing, through the dark intrigues of the twenties and thirties, spreading chaos and disorder as they played off British military intelligence against the Abwehr and Manchu warlords against the Imperial Japanese Secret Service in that long-gone twilight zone of steamship voyages, romance behind bamboo shutters, and secret assignations in Cairo or Shanghai.

Madame Voud's spectacles flashed as she quickly agreed with

Windemere. "Exactly. It's simply that none of us foresaw how the situation would build."

Montgomery glanced over his shoulder. "Seems you got a situation building on the street right now, mon."

"Oh, Jesus." Windemere quickly crossed to the window and inched back the curtain. "Damn it to hell."

Gibson moved to look for himself. "What is it?"

"You see those two white vans parked across the way there?"

"Cops?"

"SPG. That's all we needed."

"What's the SPG?"

Montgomery supplied the answer. "Special Patrol Group, the heavy mob. They keep them bastards in cages and feed 'em on raw meat, vodka, and copies of *Mein Kampf*. Only let 'em out when heads gotta be broke."

Smith stood up. "I can deal with the local law enforcement. May I use the phone?"

Gibson continued to peer out of the window. Ever since Voud and her Rastas had come beating on the door, a small silent crowd had been standing on the sidewalk staring at the house as though waiting for a sign. The majority of them were wearing dreadlocks or sculpted hip-hop hairdos, but there was also a sprinkling of leftover hippies and other local weirdos. Three teddy boys even stood with hands thrust into the pockets of their long drape jackets. This was a little odd, given the average ted's extreme and overt racism. The uniformed figures inside the white Ford Transit vans, with the screens over the windows and the riot-control cowcatchers on the front, were now watching the crowd on the sidewalk, and a good many of the crowd were looking right back at them with challenging hostility. For decades, the Ladbroke Grove area had been famous for its riots, and all the ingredients for another one were rapidly gathering right outside the house.

Montgomery seemed to sense this, and he squinted at Smith. "I hope you can pull this off, lady. It's like Windemere say, we don't need the aggravation."

Smith appeared to be on hold. Abigail Voud glanced up at Montgomery. "Can't you get your people to go home?"

The big Rastafarian shook his head. "No chance. Too much blood between jah man and pig rasclat SPG. Pride, see? You know what I'm talking about?"

Smith was now talking fast into the phone. Christobelle glanced at French. "Can she really get the SPG pulled out?"

French nodded. "We maintain close ties with the locals in all the major cities in which we operate."

Gibson caught the remark. The more he learned of the stream-heat, the more they started to resemble an interdimensional CIA, and he was feeling more and more that he trusted them about as much as he would trust the domestic version.

Smith put down the phone. "It's done. The SPG are being removed."

Montgomery looked at her disbelievingly. "How you do that?"

Smith shrugged as though it was the easiest thing in the world. "All under the blanket of national security."

Sure enough, within a matter of minutes, the headlights of the first of the two white Transits came on and it pulled away from the curb, quickly followed by the second. A ragged cheer came from the crowd outside as though they thought the official retreat had been a result of their own hostile stares and intractable attitudes.

Gibson turned away from the window. "They've gone."

Abigail Voud brought the meeting back to order. "Now we have to decide what's to be done with Joseph Gibson."

Every eye in the room turned in his direction, and Gibson felt profoundly uncomfortable. "I'm getting a little tired of listening to people discuss what's to be done with me."

Everyone ignored the remark except Montgomery, who glared at him. "You gotta go, mon, before you cause any more bother."

Gibson stood his ground.

"And doubtless someone's going to tell me where I'm going to be shipped off to next and what drug I'm going to be filled with to keep me quiet on the trip."

Smith's face was cold, as if, as far as she was concerned, he was little more than a recalcitrant package. "It's my opinion that we should take you out of this dimension entirely."

Gibson's jaw dropped. "Say what?"

"I think the only answer is to transport you out of this dimension entirely. While I'm not totally convinced that all the phenomena that are showing up are solely attracted by you, I think the situation has become far too unpredictable for you to remain."

Abigail Voud was nodding in agreement. "This is also the opinion of the Nine. Although I don't share some of my colleagues' absolute faith in our extradimensional friends, I believe that, in this instance, they are right."

Gibson couldn't have controlled his anger even if he'd wanted to. "Hold everything just a goddamned minute! Being flown to London is one thing, but being shipped out to another fucking dimension is something else entirely."

French raised an eyebrow. "You have a problem with transfer to another dimension?"

Gibson was close to snarling. "Damn right I have a problem. I've got a serious problem."

"I doubt you have a workable alternative, however."

"I've got one, a real good one. I'm not going, so think of another plan."

The chill of Smith's expression dropped another twenty degrees. "You're being ridiculous."

Gibson finally lost it. "Oh, yeah? I've been chased, scared shitless, followed by UFOs, and visited by demons, and you're telling me I'm being ridiculous because I don't want to go rushing off to someplace that I can't hardly conceive except as some abstract science-fiction concept. Oh, sure, excuse me, I'm being ridiculous." He turned in appeal to Windemere. "Do you have anything to say about this?"

Windemere shook his head. "It's out of my hands."

Gibson's mouth twisted into a sneer. "Fucking great. Even in the occult, passing the buck seems to be a fine art."

Christobelle straight away sprang to her boss's defense. She glared at Gibson. It seemed that the ties formed by lovemaking were peripheral compared with home-team loyalty. "You can't blame Gideon for this. He's done the best he can for you. It's not only a matter of protecting you from whatever may be coming after us next. Already we've got a mob outside the house. If things go on as they've been going, it's highly likely that one of the locals will become sufficiently pissed off with the weirdness going on here to toss a Molotov cocktail through the front window. What are you going to do then, Joe?"

Gibson felt himself being backed into yet another corner. He rounded on Abigail Voud. "Do you and your eight chums have anything to say about this? Is your best idea just to hand me over to the goddamned streamheat and let them do what they want with me? I didn't ask to be brought into this. Casillas dragged me in on behalf of the Nine and, the way I figure it, the Nine are responsible. You started this shit and you've got to come up with something a bit more satisfactory than handing me over to these three cold bastards and pretending that I never happened."

Abigail Voud was very calm. "We're not pretending that you never happened or ducking our responsibilities. I've already told you that I don't put as much faith in the streamheat as Carlos Casillas and some of the others, but, in this instance, I can't see another viable alternative."

"Viable alternative? Shit! You're the Nine. You're supposed to be defending the planet, and you can't even protect one man without outside help. You claim to have secure installations all over, so why don't you take me to one of those? Hide me out in Tibet or somewhere like that."

Smith was staring at him with open contempt. "We were in Lhasa just a week ago. Believe me, it's a lot less safe there than it is here."

Christobelle joined in. She seemed quiet adept at herding Gibson in directions that he didn't want to go. "Why don't you get real, Joe? You'd hate Tibet. There's nothing there but monks, yaks, and the army of the People's Republic of China. They don't even have decent booze. I would have thought you'd treat going to another dimension as an adventure."

Gibson scowled. "So you go. This boy's had his share of adventures. I'm sick of fucking adventures. That's why I became a drunk."

Klein made an attempt to cool him down. "Perhaps if you heard a little about the dimension we had in mind you might . . ."

"I don't want to hear shit. Read my lips, Jack. I ain't going. Hell I don't even know why I have to go. I still want to know what's so bloody special about me. Why's everyone after my ass?" He stabbed a finger at Abigail Voud. "You want to tell me? You got an answer to that? And I don't want to hear no aura talk, either."

Abigail Voud laughed, and her eyes flashed with an electrical sparkle that had to come from somewhere out of her past. The sparkle quite convinced Gibson that, once upon a time, she could have been a killer Dragon Lady.

"My dear boy, I don't know why you're in the trouble you're in, but you really ought to stop pouting about it. Pouting only hampers practical action. I don't doubt you'd rather not hear about auras, but ignorance is no protection at all, believe me, particularly as you're walking around with a black cloud hanging over you that would terrify the hardest old soothsaying crone on the Street of Mirrors. Are you sure you don't want to see it? Just as a part of your education?"

Gibson continued to pout. "I don't want to see anything. I'm sick of all this."

"You're scared?"

"Sure I'm scared."

"Maybe if you saw what you're carrying around with you, you might be more able to accept the things that are happening to you."

Gibson sighed. "Okay, okay, show me the fucking aura."

Smith made an impatient gesture. "Do we have to have more party tricks? Weren't Slide's this afternoon enough?"

Abigail Voud looked at her sharply. "I think it might help Gibson."

"I'm starting to think that Gibson's beyond help."

Madame Voud paid no attention to Smith's last remark and faced Gibson. She held up her right hand with the palm inward. "What I'm going to do first is show you a comparatively normal aura. Christobelle, do you mind if I use you for an example?"

Christobelle didn't look exactly pleased, but she nodded her assent. "Okay."

There was a ruby ring on the third finger of the old woman's left hand with a stone the size of a pigeon's egg. Abigail Voud closed her eyes and concentrated. The stone started to glow.

"This isn't going to hurt, so don't be frightened."

Christobelle's eyes widened as tiny points of blue light sparkled in the air around her. They increased in both number and density for about a minute, and then Madame Voud lowered her hand. The lights around Christobelle and the glow of the ruby both faded.

Abigail Voud opened her eyes. "Now that was a normal aura. Are you ready to see yours, Joe?"

"What do I have to do?"

"Just stand still and don't panic at anything that happens."

Gibson stood still. Abigail Voud held up her hand again. The ring began to glow. At first nothing happened, and then, just as Gibson was about to open his mouth to protest, he was suddenly enclosed in a pillar of cold black flame.

"Jesus Christ!"

Through the weird flames, he could see everyone in Windemere's drawing room staring at him open-mouthed. It was like he was looking at them through dirty water. Montgomery's eyes were wide with shock. Even though there was neither heat nor pain, Gibson's first instinct was to try and beat out the flames, to shake them from his body—but then he remembered Voud's warning not to panic. When he spoke, though, his voice was far from stress-free.

"Okay, I think you made your point. Could you stop this please?"

Madame Voud lowered her hand, the ruby ceased to glow, and the flames around him vanished.

"That's my aura."

"That's your aura, Joe."

"I think I'm in a lot of trouble."

"That's what we've been trying to tell you."

Gibson sat down. "I need to sort my head out."

Smith stood up. "Don't take too long. The sooner we're out of here the better."

Gibson looked up. "Did I say I was coming with you?"

Smith's shoulders sagged slightly, as though she was weary of Gibson's objections. "What other real choice do you have? The Nine obviously can't do anything for you, and Windemere doesn't want you."

"Aren't you forgetting one thing?"

"What's that?"

"I'm still my own man. I didn't ask to get into this mess and I can walk away from it any time I want to."

"After what you've seen."

"After what I've seen, I don't trust anyone. I may be in a lot of trouble but I've been in trouble before and got myself out of it."

French sneered. "From what I've heard, you've mainly drunk your way out of it."

"So? At least everyone can be assured that a drunk isn't a cosmic danger."

Smith sighed. "And where exactly would you walk to?"

Gibson smiled for the first time since he'd been dragged out of bed by the hammering on the door. "I'd walk out of here and that'd be that. You wouldn't have to worry about me anymore. I wouldn't be your problem. The one thing that you're all forgetting is that I'm Joe Gibson. I know people in London. People you wouldn't even imagine. I'll make it."

"You think so?"

"Like I said, you don't have to worry about it."

"You wouldn't last through tomorrow morning."

It was Gibson's turn to sneer. "You think I'm completely helpless?"

Smith turned and faced him. "I think after the police get a call from me, they'll pick you up pretty quickly."

Gibson's eyebrows shot up. "For what?"

"For being an illegal immigrant."

"What are you talking about?"

"There's no record of you entering the country."

"It was all arranged with the State Department. Casillas told me that."

"I think you'll find that those arrangements have been quite forgotten. You entered the country as J. Edgar Hoover. Try convincing the London bobbies that you're the late director of the FBI."

Light dawned on Gibson. "Now you're blackmailing me."

"It's an ugly word."

"You really think I couldn't go to ground in London?"

"Without money and without papers? You might manage it, but would you like it?"

Gibson shrugged. "So what's the worst that could happen to me? I could be deported back to the U.S., right?"

"I imagine that there might be a couple of agents from the IRS Criminal Investigation Division waiting to arrest you when you got to JFK."

"Another phone call?"

Smith nodded. "Another phone call."

Gibson looked helplessly round the room. "None of this makes any sense. Remember me? Worthless Joe Gibson, the no-account, burned-out drunk. How come you streamheat are suddenly so keen to whisk me off to another dimension?"

Christobelle, who had been sitting quietly since Madame Voud had used her as a guinea pig, leaned forward in her chair. "Joe's got a point. You streamheat have done nothing but call him a drunk and treat him as an unwanted burden. Now you're all but putting a gun to his head to force him to go with you. Would you care to explain?"

Now everyone in the room was looking at the three streamheat. For the slightest fraction of an instant, Klein glanced at Smith to see what she was going to say, and, in that same fraction of an instant, Gibson knew beyond any shadow of a doubt that for some mysterious reason of their own, the streamheat wanted him; they had wanted him all along, and they'd been lying to him ever since they had all left New York on the private jet. It was like a weight being lifted. He still didn't know what they intended to do with him, but at least they'd shown a part of their hand and given him some slight idea of how to play his own sorry collection of cards. Smith's response to Christobelle only confirmed what Gibson was thinking.

"We haven't put a gun to his head yet."

Gibson almost smiled. "But you would if you had to?"

Smith realized she'd blundered by being too glib and hastily spun into damage control. "You have to face it, Gibson, what with the aura that Madame Voud showed you and all the things that have been happening, your best chance is with us."

Now Gibson did smile. "That's bullshit and you know it. For some reasons of your own that I can't even get near, you want to take me out of this dimension."

Silence filled the room like physical pressure, and the sightless eye sockets of the rattlesnake skull in the glass dome on the mantel seemed to stare into space as everyone waited to see what the streamheat were going to say or do next. Smith had the look of a woman backed up into a corner, and after being cornered so often himself Gibson couldn't help but relish the spectacle.

Finally she let out a careful breath. "Yes, you're right. It's our mission to remove you to another dimension. We received our orders while we were at Greene Street."

Gibson stood up and faced Smith. He allowed a few seconds to pass before he spoke. "So let me ask you one more time, what is it about me? Why am I so important?"

"I can't tell you that."

Gibson sighed. "Here we go again."

"I can't tell you that because I don't know."

Gibson's face was hard. "I don't believe you."

Smith was on the defensive. "All I know is that you are a key figure in one of our future projections. Because of that, we were ordered to get you to safety even if it meant transporting you to another dimension."

"You're just following orders?"

"Exactly."

Windemere coughed. "That phrase has unfortunate connotations in this dimension."

Gibson abruptly sat down again. "Does anyone have a cigarette?"

Montgomery pulled out a pack of Silk Cut and offered him one. "I think you getting screwed, mon."

Gibson looked up at the big Rasta and grinned. "So do you want to take me in and look after me?"

Montgomery shook his head. "Fuck, no. You too much trouble for jah man."

Gibson scanned the room. He'd miss it when he was gone. Despite the problems, the mysteries, and the dangers, he'd begun to really enjoy the company of Windemere and Christobelle. "So it looks as though I'm going to another dimension."

"I have a question." Madame Voud had apparently been deep in thought, but now she was looking at Smith. "Was it you that caused the psych attack on Gibson in New York?"

Once again there was a split moment of hesitation on the part of Smith. "Of course not. Why should we do a thing like that?"

"Perhaps you thought you had to convince Casillas and the others at Greene Street that Gibson needed your special protection."

"And we staged it? That's an outrageous suggestion, particularly coming from someone who's supposed to be an ally."

"Allies sometimes play games with each other. It's hardly unknown."

Smith took refuge in anger. "I suppose we also arranged for the UFO to follow our plane?"

Abigail Voud smiled from behind her glasses. "It was just a thought." Without pausing, she looked up at Montgomery. "I think we can leave now. Gibson will be going with the streamheat, so what we came here for has been accomplished."

To Gibson, this sounded too much like a dismissal. "So the Nine are washing their hands of me?"

As Montgomery helped the old woman to her feet, she looked sadly at Gibson. "These are troubled times, Joe Gibson. None of us is exempt."

Madame Voud and her Rasta escort had left the room with Windemere and his two bodyguards going along to show her out. Gibson and Christobelle went to the window to watch them go. When the old woman emerged from the house with her Rastafarians on either side, the crowd outside immediately surrounded them and, en masse, they headed up Ladbroke Grove on foot.

Christobelle put a hand on Gibson's arm. "Are you scared?"

Gibson glanced back at the three streamheat. They seemed to be locked in a muttered conversation in a language that wasn't

English. "I'm not crazy about going anywhere with that bunch, let alone to another dimension."

"You'll make it through."

Gibson raised an eyebrow. "You know something I don't?"

"Just a feeling that you're not the total fuck-up that you pretend to be."

Windemere came back into the room alone, brisk and businesslike, cutting short both conversations.

"So you're out of here, Joe."

Gibson nodded. "So it would seem."

"I'm sorry I couldn't do more to look out for you."

"That's okay, you did your best."

"I wouldn't worry too much. Another dimension shouldn't be so bad. A lot of them are very like our own."

"Have you ever been to another dimension?"

Windemere shook his head. "No, but . . ."

"So let me worry."

As soon as he'd said it, Gibson felt bad. Windemere had done his best for him and he didn't need to be on the receiving end of Gibson's panic and anger. After the near snub, Windemere turned to the streamheat to hide his resentment. "Where are you taking him?"

Smith looked at Windemere as though it was hardly any of his business. "A nearby semiparallel."

Gibson detached himself from Christobelle. "What's a semiparallel?"

"A dimension very like this just twelve or so points across the divides."

Gibson's face hardened. "I know it's company policy to not tell poor dumbfuck Joe Gibson anything if you can possibly help it, but since we're going to have to be traveling together, I'd suggest you start talking to me in terms that I can understand. We'll get on a whole lot better if you do."

Smith had the expression of a woman who'd been pushed far enough. "Okay, Gibson, this is the start of the first lesson. Semiparallel dimensions are those in very close tuning, ones that follow paths in the time stream that are only slightly divergent."

"How divergent?"

"Some parallels are very close, varying in only minor details. Others have undergone radical changes at some point in the past and, although they follow similar courses and share a broadly common pattern of events, the differences are major."

"And this one?"

"There are some significant differences."

"Like what?"

Klein answered this question with a grin. "Like this one never had a World War II the way that you did here."

Gibson thought about this. "It must have slowed them down some."

Smith looked puzzled. "Slowed them down?"

"Yeah, think about it. Here in this dimension, we went from the first powered flight to a landing on the moon in a little over sixty years, just one human lifetime, and a hell of a lot of the momentum for that dizzy surge of progress was World War II."

Smith nodded as though surprised that Gibson should have the brains to come up with an idea like this. "In fact you're right. The UKR in many ways resembles North America in the fifties."

"The UKR?"

"United Kamerian Republics. Our destination will be the capital city of Luxor. We have a primary installation there."

Gibson was thinking about something else. He turned to Klein. "The fifties?"

"Similar."

"Did they invent rock 'n' roll yet?"

Klein shook his head. "I really don't know."

Smith looked sourly at Gibson, clearly disapproving of this flippancy about rock 'n' roll. "There is a footnote to the lesson."

Gibson didn't like the sound of this. "Yeah? What's that?"

"You are now in my charge. The transition to Luxor can be either easy or hard. I suggest you remember that."

Gibson's gaze didn't waver. "So I've been warned, have I?"

"Indeed you have."

Gibson and Smith continued to stare each other down until Windemere stepped into the conversation. "How do you intend to make this transition?"

Smith finally turned away from Gibson. "We have to go to the south of Germany."

Windemere frowned. "Why Germany?"

"We have access to a hidden transition substation in the Bavarian Alps. It was built by the Nazis in 1944 with some extra-dimensional help. I believe it was designed to be an escape route for Adolf Hitler at the end of the war. Later it was carrier plugged and modernized."

"Did Hitler actually use it?"

Smith shook her head. "I've no idea."

French was eyeing Smith and frowning. "Should you have told him all that?"

"Any harm that could be done has been done already."

Gibson was thinking again. "How are we getting to Germany?"

"I imagine we'll have to take a scheduled Lufthansa flight to Munich and drive from there. There isn't time to do anything fancy."

"Isn't that kind of exposing ourselves?"

"Perhaps, but it can't be helped."

Windemere laughed. "You don't have to do that. There's a transition point just a couple of hours out of London."

Smith's eyes narrowed. "What are you talking about?"

"It's a very ancient one, near a village called Glastonbury. It's under a pyramid earthworks."

"Are you sure about this?"

"It's been there for fifteen thousand years."

Smith was not quite buying the idea. "You've used it?"

Windemere shook his head. "Not me, I've had quite enough fun to keep me busy here, but I do know a couple of individuals who have."

Gibson stuck his face into the conversation. "They came back intact?"

"They looked okay."

Smith glanced at French and Klein. "You think we should take a chance on this?"

Klein shrugged, but French looked doubtfully at Windemere. "I don't think we should trust either it or him."

Now it was Gibson's turn to start running out of patience. "You don't trust Windemere but you're prepared to trail all across Europe with me being a sitting duck for whatever may turn up next to have a shot at me? That's real smart, French."

Klein nodded. "I hate to say it, but I think Gibson's right."

Christobelle joined in. "I don't know if I'm supposed to have an opinion, but I also think Gibson's right. You say your orders are to get him to this Luxor place alive, and it would seem obvious that the less he's exposed to danger the better."

Smith actually looked worried. "I'd use the transition point in a moment, if I thought that it would actually take us to where we wanted to go."

Windemere poured himself a drink and then did the same for Gibson. "I imagine that it would be a damn sight more reliable than a bunch of botched-together Nazi mad-scientist gear. This is superbeing hardware. I don't know how much you people have studied this dimension, but that stuff was supposedly built to last to infinity." He glanced slyly at Smith. "Of course, if you don't know how to operate the ancient stuff, maybe you'd better stick with this Kraut setup of yours."

Smith wasn't going to let Windemere's slur on her competence go unchallenged. "I think what we'll do is go to this Glastonbury place and see what's there. If it doesn't seem right, we can always fall back on the Bavarian transition point."

French still wasn't happy. "Suppose Windemere's sending us into a trap of some kind?"

"That's a chance we'll take."

With a decision made, Smith got down to the details. "How long will it take us to drive to this place?"

Windemere put down his drink. "Two, maybe two and a half hours, but you could be there a lot faster if you used the lays."

"The lays?"

"The laylines, imposed tracks of magnetic force also laid down by the superbeings. This whole island is riddled with them. The Glastonbury Tor, that's the name of the earthworks, is a major convergence. Any line in southern England will take you right inside. I assume you have a Cody Groove?"

Klein nodded. "Sure, its hard-wired into the subframe of the Caddy."

"So all you have to do is hook into the wavelength and that's it. If you don't have a computer that can figure it, I'm sure one of mine can. Why don't you come down to my study and I'll show you some charts."

Windemere and the streamheat left the room. Gibson and Christobelle were alone.

Gibson put his hands on her shoulders. He suddenly felt a great deal of warmth for the woman. "You think we'll see each other again?"

"I'm optimistic."

Gibson raised an eyebrow. "You mean that?"

Christobelle looked him straight in the eye. "Yes."

Gibson stroked her hair. "I sure as hell hope so."

"Why don't you kiss me?"

He kissed her. She let her robe fall open and pressed herself against him. Her body felt good. "I wish there was more time."

"You're not the only one."

"Are you scared?"

Gibson buried his face in her hair. "I'm fucking terrified."

For a long time, they just held each other; then Christobelle pushed him away and held him at arm's length. She looked at him sadly. "I'm not going to stand at the door and watch you go."

Gibson sighed. "I'll just vanish into the night."

The first phase of the journey to another dimension was anticlimactically normal. They drove to the bottom of Ladbroke Grove and turned right onto Holland Park Avenue. There was very little traffic, just the odd taxi and a couple of newspaper trucks. The tree-lined street was still wet from the day's rain. At the start of Shepherds Bush Green, they passed a small gang of skinheads, no more than eight or nine of them in bother boots and ankle-swinger jeans, gathered round a banner, a Union Jack with a swastika in a white circle superimposed on it. They glared sullenly at the car as it went by.

Gibson watched through the rear window as they dwindled in the distance. "You think they know something?"

French shook his head. "What could they know?"

"A lot of people seem to know a lot of things."

Smith made a dismissive gesture. "They probably just resent big American cars."

Gibson, keyed up for the start of what promised to be the weirdest experience of his life, was surprised at how things continued to remain normal. Klein drove the Cadillac through the western suburbs of London like any other traveler getting a jump on the morning traffic. They might have simply been heading for Heathrow Airport rather than another dimension. Before the airport, however, they took the route to the M4 motorway. Gibson finally had to say something.

"What happened to the mystic laylines we were going to use?"

Klein glanced back at him. "According to Windemere, it isn't possible to enter the grid while we're still in the city. Most of the ancient access points have been built over and there are too many man-made magnetic fields. There's the underground rail network, the electrical power system; even home stereos and TV sets do their bit to distort the original pattern and make it unusable."

"So what's the plan?"

"Windemere claimed that our best option is to take the M4

until we see an exit for a place called Kings Ridley. We take that exit and follow this country road until we pass through the village, then we go on for another two miles. At that point we'll be almost over what they call a barrow, a prehistoric burial mound. It's also a grid access point. We simply engage the Cody Groove and that's it. Inside of a matter of seconds, we should be inside this Glastonbury pyramid. Unless, of course, your friend Windemere has been lying to us.''

There was a certain amount of traffic on the six-lane motorway, but not enough to conceal the fact that they were being followed. It was Klein who first spotted the tail. ''Slide's behind us.''

''Are you sure?''

''There can't be too many '51 Hudsons in this country.''

Smith didn't even bother to look round. ''Go. Use the overdrive.''

Klein stamped hard on the gas pedal. The Cadillac suddenly rocketed forward, pressing Gibson back into his seat. Klein shouted over the tortured howl of the engine. ''I have a feeling that we aren't going to be able to lose him.''

Smith leaned forward, holding on to the seat in front of her. ''I don't think so either, but this sudden burst of acceleration may take him by surprise and gain us a few minutes. I'd like us to have all the slack that we can get.''

Gibson looked out of the window. The Cadillac seemed to be traveling at an impossible speed. The speedometer was hard over, and the car appeared to be moving at something well in excess of the 120 mph that was showing on the clock. The trees at the edge of the highway were flashing past as though the Caddy were about to sprout wings and fly. He knew that there had to be some advanced gizmo from another dimension juicing the mill.

It seemed that Klein must also have had something juicing his reactions. The signs were coming too fast for Gibson to read, but Klein was quite able to spot the one for the Kings Ridley exit and send the car hurtling into the off ramp in a scream of tires.

On the country two-lane, they had to slow down considerably, but Klein was still able to throw the car through its twists and turns at an average of ninety. Kings Ridley was a picturesque piece of rural England with cottages set around a village green, a Saxon church with a squat, square tower, a pub called The Ox, and even a duck pond, but Gibson saw almost nothing of it as they roared through like a motorized banshee. Two miles outside the village, they halted, just as Windemere had suggested. Klein turned off the headlights, and Gibson looked through the rear window, but he could see no signs of Yancey Slide's Hudson. Smith peered out at the fields that surrounded them. The sky was overcast and vision was further hampered by the lack of a moon.

"Does anyone see this burial mound thing?"

Klein was also staring into the darkness. "There's something over there but it's hard to tell what it is."

Smith thought for a moment. "We can't go back with Slide somewhere behind us. I fear our only course is to engage the groove and see what happens."

French scowled. "If there's nothing there for the groove to lock on to, it could create a random displacement and that'd be the effective end of us."

"We're going to have to take that chance."

French was not only scowling but also shaking his head. "You're placing one hell of a bet on the accuracy of Windemere's information."

Smith nodded. "Believe me, I'm very aware of that. If there was an alternative course of action, I'd take it."

Gibson watched with a frightened fascination as Klein dropped the flap of the glove compartment. A complex keypad was built into its inside surface with three decks of keys, one marked with normal roman characters, the second with Japanese, and the third with an alien script. Klein tapped in a twelve-character code, six roman, four Japanese, and two alien.

All through the drive, Gibson had been bracing himself for the unexpected, but none of his fears or imaginings had prepared him for what happened next. For the briefest instant, the surrounding countryside was lit up as bright as day. It was as though the bomb had gone off, but then, as quickly as it came, the flash faded into retinal aftershocks and the very nature of the light itself began to change. Both land and sky took on brilliant emerald radiance as though a vast green fire had suddenly blazed at the core of the Earth. The horizon started to curve upward. It was like giant hands were attempting to roll the actual fabric of the landscape into a giant tube. Perspective was shot to hell by the curvature of this distortion, and Gibson reflexively grabbed for a handhold as the visual distortion tilted him sideways. Then the Cadillac started to vibrate. At first it was a smooth tremor, but it rapidly became more violent and erratic, and as Gibson was bounced up and down in his seat he became quite convinced that something was wretchedly wrong and the car was going to shake itself to bits. Then the buffeting stopped, and all that remained was a high-pitched whistle.

Klein's voice floated to him from a long way away. "We have groove lock."

With no apparent acceleration, the Cadillac started to move forward. It seemed to be floating down a huge emerald tunnel of merging earth and heaven. For the first fifteen seconds, the tunnel remained absolutely straight, and, still with no feeling of motion, the Cadillac began picking up speed. Suddenly the tunnel abruptly curved.

French voiced the general alarm as the Cadillac began to slide into the curve like a surfer entering the pipeline. "This isn't right."

"It's got to be a power plant or something throwing a stress pattern."

"It'd take more than a power station to produce a stretch-out like this."

Klein, who was no longer steering the car, just letting it take its own course, pointed through the windshield. "There's the culprit."

A glowing disk of bright white light surrounded by a blue aura had appeared in the area of sky that was contained by the unnaturally curved horizon.

Gibson's jaw sagged. "I don't believe it. Every time I step outside the house, I'm set on by UFOs."

Despite the tension, Klein grinned. "Maybe you should stay indoors."

A second white UFO with a blue aura appeared beside the first. Gibson turned anxiously to Smith. "What can we do about this?"

Smith looked at him blankly. "Your guess is as good as mine. It's like I told you on the plane, UFOs are way outside our field of expertise."

The first disk held its position, but the second one dropped into the path of the Cadillac. It was coming rapidly toward them.

French stared at it, transfixed. "This looks unpleasantly like the start of a strafing run."

A strange detachment had taken hold inside the car. Gibson knew that he should have been convulsed with terror, but he wasn't. He was frightened, but there was a distance to the fear. The environment had become so unreal that it was hard to relate to the idea that they were under attack by hostile UFOs. It was something that just didn't happen. The worst part was the unreal quiet. Events silently drifted. With no outside sound except the high-pitched whine, the UFO seemed to be floating at them through a vacuum. It rose and fell slightly but kept getting bigger and bigger, and with no idea of its size and no intelligible perspective, it was impossible to judge how far away it was and how soon it would be upon them.

Gibson shifted uncomfortably in his seat. "Can't we take some kind of evasive action?"

Klein shook his head. "Once you lock the groove, you give up all control. You're on a cosmic railroad."

Gibson groaned. "Mystery train and out of control."

A bright point of ruby-red light detached itself from the disk's leading edge. It zigzagged toward them. Gibson shut his eyes. He was certain that it was an alien missile. He opened them again just in time to see it explode short of the car. He wasn't even sure that it was an explosion. For a brief instant the world as he could see it turned scarlet, and then it returned to the way it had been. All that remained was a column of glittering vapor. The Cadillac plunged into it, and where the car came in contact with the mist a blue-gray deposit was left behind on the bodywork.

Gibson looked at the others. "I think we're okay."

Smith was peering suspiciously at the blue-gray deposit on the outside of the windows. "Don't speak too soon, we've no idea what this stuff may be doing to us."

The UFO lifted slightly and passed over them. As it did, their hair stood on end and Gibson was aware of an acute electric tingle running through him. He twisted around in the backseat and peered out of the rear window. The UFO seemed to be turning in preparation for another pass. Gibson was surprised to see the amount of room the UFO had to maneuver in the weird, enclosed sky. The emerald world beyond the car's windows was starting to slowly corkscrew along its length, like an Escher drawing in which the normal rules of spatial relationships had been canceled and comparative distance made no sense at all.

"I think it's coming back!"

The UFO had completed its turn and started to drop again. Two more ruby points of light detached themselves from the white disk, but, once again, they exploded short in two more brief, silent flashes of red. Again, they were apparently unharmed, but now the original UFO had started dropping from its previous vantage point and was coming at them, seemingly joining the attack, if indeed it was an attack.

Klein glanced out of the side window and grunted a warning. "Uh-oh. Here's an added complication."

Three more UFOs had appeared on the scene, coming in from the right-hand side of the car, following the up curve of the landscape, and moving in a tight triangular formation. They were completely different from the white disks. These had the traditional flying-saucer configuration that resembled the detached top of a Victorian streetlamp, the central turret with its circle of portholes, the conical skirt, and the three hemispheres on the underside.

Gibson shook his head in amazement. "Adamski saucers."

Smith looked at him sharply. "What's an Adamski?"

"Not what, who. Adamski was a guy back in the early fifties who wrote a bunch of books claiming that he'd been abducted by aliens. He had photographs of flying saucers exactly like these."

"What happened to him?"

"Nobody believed him. They said his photos were fakes and everyone assumed that he was running a con. I guess in the end he just kinda went away."

The saucers headed straight for the two white disks, and revolving golden stars flashed from their turrets. The disks immediately took what seemed to be frantic evasive action.

"What are these new guys? The cavalry?"

The white disks ran an evasion pattern of short dashes and abrupt changes of direction, doing anything to get away from the golden stars. Finally they seemed to concede defeat. They broke from the engagement and began climbing away. The saucers went up after them. Inside of a second, all five of the strange craft had vanished. Inside the car, there was a general sigh of relief. Gibson wiped his face. Somewhere along the line, he'd broken out in a cold sweat.

"So what the hell have we been watching? The war of the worlds?"

There was no time for discussion, however, or even answers. The curve in the emerald tunnel was straightening out, and the Cadillac accelerated to a dizzying speed. After a moment of blur and shimmer the lights went out and Gibson was in a darkness more complete than anything that he had ever experienced before. His first assumption was that he'd died. He'd become discorporate. He was in limbo between dimensions. He put a hand up to his face and was somewhat amazed to find that his face was still there.

Smith's voice came from right beside him. "Turn on the headlights."

After the total darkness, the headlights were blinding, and when Gibson's eyes finally adjusted, he found that they were stationary in what appeared to be a large underground chamber, the walls of which were constructed from huge slabs of solid rock, each one larger than the car itself.

"The pyramid, I presume?"

Klein rested his hands on the steering wheel. He looked drained. Slowly he shook his head. "I guess we're going to have to get out and take a look around. Whatever the transfer mechanism is, it's going to be incredibly ancient, and we're going to have to teach ourselves to operate it."

French handed out flashlights, and the streamheat left the car, gingerly avoiding the residue of the strangely ineffective UFO weapons that was all over the exterior surfaces of the Caddy. They started a detailed examination of the walls and floor of the chamber, searching for the key to the dimension bridge. Gibson also climbed out, although, having no idea of what the others were hunting for, he took no part in the search. He looked slowly around the chamber. The air was cool and dry, and his boots kicked up a fine powdery dust as he walked. It was as if no intruder had entered the place in centuries. The walls were by no means as bare as they had first appeared. Large areas were covered in carved reliefs in a style that could have easily been the fountainhead of both Egyptian and Aztec art. Directly in front of the car there was a complicated circular sun symbol that, as far as Gibson could tell, seemed to contain stylized diagrams of the Solar system and a lot of other stuff that made no sense to him but looked equally impressive.

As Gibson approached the thing, Smith called out a warning. "Don't touch anything. We have no idea if this stuff is just decorative or if it has some practical control function."

Gibson walked back to the car. He was quite grateful to have nothing to do and was more than content to take the time to try and gather his wits. The madness in which he was embroiled was turning into his moment-by-moment normality at a speed that was shocking. It did seem to be true that the human mind could adapt to just about anything. Given the right combination of time and intensity, even pure terror could be unconsciously tuned down to little more than a constant background noise.

It was forty minutes before the streamheat, going over the stones of the chamber inch by inch with flashlights, like archeologists in Tut's tomb, came across the first clue to the operation of the transfer. It was Klein who made the discovery. He slowly straightened up with a satisfied sigh. His voice echoed hollowly, reinforcing the feeling that the chamber was a huge stone sepulcher. "I think I've found what we're looking for."

He placed the flat of his hand carefully on a spot on the wall about three feet above the floor, and a fine tracery of delicate, glowing lines that greatly resembled a highly elaborate printed circuit appeared on an area some six feet square. In rapid sequence, he touched a series of points on the tracery, and a section of the stone wall melted away, leaving a low doorway in the solid rock—a doorway that, according to the regular terrestrial rules of both life and physics, simply shouldn't exist. Gibson expected the streamheat to go through it immediately, and he had started toying with the idea of following them when he saw that Smith and French were waiting while Klein walked to where Gibson was standing by the car. His face was very serious.

"This is an ancient mechanism and it almost certainly will require an energizing procedure before it will work for us. The energizing techniques needed to make dimension crossing are the most closely guarded secrets of our people. We'll be going through them in the room beyond that doorway. We'd like you to stay in the car and not try to follow us or observe it in any way. Can I trust you to do that?"

Gibson nodded. "I get the feeling that if I don't say yes, Smith and French will have a few more drastic ideas for stopping me learning the secret."

Klein smiled wearily. "You got it."

"I probably wouldn't understand what I was seeing anyway."

"That's why they're letting me do it my way. Do I have your word that you'll stay in the car?"

Gibson nodded again. "I'll stay in the car."

Klein walked back to the others. For some time, Gibson had been noticing that Klein was a little different from the other two. Where Smith and French had a tendency to act like well-programmed automatons, Klein demonstrated a degree of wit, humor, and a certain lack of respect for authority. On the journey out of London, however, it had gone deeper than that. His handling of the car and his being the first one to get the chamber to give up its secrets seemed to indicate that he was the tech specialist of the trio. When the going got bizarre, Klein apparently got going. Gibson was growing to trust him, and he hoped the trust was justified.

The streamheat vanished through the doorway, and Gibson settled himself in the front seat of the car. He knew that the big one was almost upon him, the actual shift to another dimension, but he tried not to think about that. It actually wasn't easy to worry about something that he couldn't even visualize. Instead he concentrated on wondering what was going on in the room beyond the chamber.

The word "procedure" was so ambiguous that it could mean virtually anything, but, with the image of Windemere's energizing ritual so fresh in his mind, Gibson couldn't help wondering if what the streamheat were doing was anything along the same lines. They were such creatures of logic, programs, and systems that it was hard to imagine them in any kind of sexual context, but he couldn't stop himself from conjuring images of the variations that could be achieved by two men and one woman. He was very tempted to sneak a look into the other room, but the thought of how the trio might react held him back. He'd given his word to Klein, and even though the world had him pegged as a degenerate, his word was his word.

Whatever Smith, Klein, and French were doing in the side chamber, it took them just over half an hour by the dashboard clock in the Cadillac, and when they came out, it wasn't only Klein who looked drained. They were all showing signs of strain, and they appeared to be avoiding each other's eyes.

Gibson looked at them questioningly. "So what happens now? When do we make the move?"

French scowled at him. "Any moment now, so shut up."

Smith gestured to Klein. "Kill the headlights."

The Caddy's headlights went out and darkness was again total. And then things started to appear. Glowing silver tracery, more of the delicate circuitlike designs, spread quickly across the walls of the chamber, dancing from stone to stone like fine lines of living mercury, covering the interior of the room like geometric, speeded-up vines. It was as if they were inside some huge ancient computer that was rapidly powering up, section by section. The sun symbol at the end of the room also came to life, shining with a golden light. It slowly began to rotate, and the planetary-system diagrams contained inside it also turned on their axes. It quickly grew much brighter than the silver circuitry on the walls, a huge moving mandala, so magnificent that it had them staring open-mouthed.

It was about that time that the Cadillac became transparent.

They'd started out watching the spectacle that was unfolding inside the chamber through the windows of the car, but suddenly they could see it through the bodywork. It was as though the car had lost all substance. Gibson put out a hand. It still felt solid but there was nothing to see. Now the sun symbol was moving. Originally they had been looking at it head-on, through the windshield, but now, without any perceivable transition, it was above them. They were looking at it through the roof of the car, and it was rapidly expanding, becoming a ceiling and then a blazing sky, stretching to an impossible horizon that immediately started to drop downward, producing absolute disorientation. The gold sun seemed to be passing through them, and at the same time they were falling. Gibson felt sick. His body, the car, and everything around him was being impossibly stretched. He had no shape, and the signals from his nervous system made no sense at all. He was falling headfirst and fast. There was no sign of the others, and he couldn't even locate the car. All that surrounded him were sheets of golden flame. He was riding the flames but still falling. He was a streak of flashfire, a burning meteor. He was spiraling, leaving a trail of gold, a downward helix lighting up the void. He knew that it couldn't last. He was going to burn out. There was no travel to other dimensions. This was the end. He no longer had a body. He wasn't going out in a blaze of glory, he *was* a blaze of glory. The pain was monumental. The screaming in his ears shut out everything else. A black sea was beneath him and he was plunging toward it. He was falling and falling, down into the dark sea. Once he hit the water, it wouldn't matter anymore.

The White Room

THE IDEA OF escaping from the very exclusive clinic had been in the back of Joe Gibson's mind ever since he'd first been brought in, but he didn't really start thinking about practical ways of achieving it until he'd been there for about a month. It wasn't that he didn't want to get out of the place and back on the street to find out what had happened to his life, but it was complicated, and in those first weeks there had been only the briefest periods when the medication had left him in any mental shape to follow through even the simplest progression of logic. It was really his conversations with West that initially triggered his determination to figure a way to get out and stay out.

He realized almost immediately that it was impossible for him to follow West's advice and convince the staff that they were curing him. He increasingly suspected that it wouldn't be too hard to con Kooning into believing he was retrieving parts of his "real" life. Unfortunately the most perfunctory check would reveal the deception. He couldn't remember his "real" life because he had no "real" life to remember, and he couldn't be cured because there was nothing wrong with him. His only hope was a full-blown, go-for-broke escape.

The escape itself shouldn't be too difficult. Physical security in the place was fairly lax. The staff relied so heavily on drugs to keep the patients in line that they'd become lazy. They simply didn't expect a patient seriously to attempt a breakout. The hard part would be staying out. Once on the street, he was a man with no name. He had no ID, no money, and he didn't see himself taking up mugging or bank robbing to survive. The few days between his return to Earth and the freak-out that caused the cops to grab him and turn him over to the boys in the white coats had thoroughly convinced him that somehow all trace of

148

him had been wiped out. He'd even tried to contact Windemere, but he also seemed to have vanished without trace. During that first forty-eight hours at the clinic, he'd actually welcomed the drugs. There was only so much that a man could take.

He was well aware that his first move had to be a reduction of the medication that was constantly being pumped into him. Even if he didn't have a coherent plan, he knew that he had to cut down on the drugs just to have a chance of formulating one. It was impossible to do anything about the daily shots, but the pills that came three, sometimes four times a day were another matter. It was comparatively easy to fake swallowing a pill and then hide it in your mouth. Subsequently, getting rid of it was the hard part. Patients were always trying to lose, hide, or otherwise avoid their allotted medicines, and it was the major battle of wills between patients and staff; the staff had become very skilled at spotting those who were doing it and ferreting out their systems of disposal. A grid in the toilet bowls of the individual rooms even circumvented that obvious method.

After almost a week of thinking about it, Gibson decided that he'd come up with a new and, as far as he knew, original dodge that he might well get away with. He started dropping hints during the therapy sessions that, when he first woke up in the morning, he had fleeting memories of his real life but they were too mixed in with his dreams and, like the dreams, he quickly forgot them. He kept this up until, just as he'd hoped, Kooning suggested he keep a pencil and paper at his bedside to jot down these fragments while they were still fresh in his mind. This was exactly what he wanted. Writing materials were strictly controlled inside the clinic, and a patient had to be given the specific permission of a doctor before he could keep them in his cubicle. It was this permission that Gibson had been working toward and, within ten days of starting his campaign, it was this permission that Kooning gave, firmly believing that it was her own idea. He was taken to the administrative office, where he was issued two cheap Papermate ballpoint pens and a yellow legal pad. As he'd hoped, the pens were identical. He'd use one to write and the other, with the ink tube removed, as a receptacle for the pills that he didn't take.

From the moment he'd received them, he carried the pad and pens everywhere with him, and the staff quickly came to accept that it was his particular idiosyncrasy. Although he couldn't use West's principle of demonstrating that he was being cured as a means to get out, it was still useful to win himself a little slack. The staff thought that Gibson was making progress, and they didn't bother to watch him so closely. He was able to ditch the pills out of his hollow pen all over the clinic without anyone noticing him.

His covert reduction of his medication had the immediate effect of allowing him to think a great deal more clearly. He no longer stared mindlessly at *Ghostbusters* cartoons, the Chipmunks or reruns of *Mork and Mindy*. He began to make a careful, step-by-step analysis of his situation. One of his first thoughts in this new frame of mind was darkly hopeful. Why was he in this exclusive and expensive clinic at all? As far as anyone could tell in this world of so many changed details, he was an indigent bum. If that was the case, why the hell wasn't he locked up in Bellevue like any other penniless crazy? Someone had to be picking up a fairly major tab for his incarceration in this place, and it had to be safe to assume that whoever was doing this knew who he was, what he'd done, and that he wasn't raving mad when he swore that he'd just returned from another dimension. His newly reclaimed powers of reasoning led him to a single conclusion. There was someone out there who knew all about him and who was keeping him locked up here to insure his silence. If he could get out and find this person, there was at least the chance that he could beat the truth out of him about what had happened to his life.

Chapter
Seven

"DOES DRESDEN KNOW about him?"

Gibson didn't recognize the voice he was hearing as he swam up through the black sea, except that it had the officious, suspicious tone of a cop.

A second voice answered the question. "Of course Dresden knows about him. He's the replacement for Zwald."

Gibson knew the second voice. It belonged to Klein. He sounded tired. The cop voice was that of a man who couldn't leave it alone. "What happened? He's the wrong color."

Gibson knew that they couldn't be talking about him. How could he be the wrong color?

Klein's voice answered again. "The trans was rough, we had to use an unorthodox access point."

"How can he be a replacement for Zwald if he's the wrong color?"

The Klein voice started to sound impatient. "It really isn't my problem. We found him, we brought him, but something went wrong in the trans. Nothing can be done about it, so quit busting my balls."

"He's going to stick out like a sore thumb."

"I know he's going to stick out like a sore thumb, but that really isn't my problem. I've done my bit and the rest is up to Dresden."

Gibson was aware that he was lying on something hard. It felt like a concrete floor. He opened one eye and wished that he hadn't. Everyone around him was blue.

Klein's voice changed, urgent and warning. "Put a cover on it, it looks like he's coming round."

Gibson opened his other eye. He seemed to be in some kind of cavernous garage or workshop. A dozen or more people, both men and women, were moving around, and the majority of them were wearing the streamheat dark-blue jumpsuits with the same silver insignia at their throats. The disturbing part was that their skins were varying shades of the same blue.

Klein was standing over him, looking down. His skin was now tinted a soft aquamarine. "Are you okay?"

Gibson decided to play it traditional. "Where am I?"

"You're in Luxor."

"The car was on fire."

"That was a transition illusion."

Gibson struggled into a sitting position. His muscles ached. "How long was I out for?"

"About an hour."

Gibson stared down at his hands. They were also very pale blue, but much lighter than Klein's skin or anyone else's. "Why have we all changed color?"

Klein looked mystified. "What do you mean changed color?"

Gibson gestured at the other people in the place. "Everyone's blue. I'm blue, you're blue. Everyone's turned blue."

"You look a little strange but everything else seems normal."

Gibson started to get agitated. "Everyone's fucking blue."

"I think this might be a perception problem."

"You're telling me that I'm seeing things?"

Klein sighed. "Transition can produce some strange effects. Things become changed. You're in another dimension and what you're seeing is just a product of both your brain and the transition."

"My suit, too?"

The black suit in which Gibson had left London was now spotless white, as though it had been bleached. Klein shook his head. "No, the suit really did turn white."

"This is too weird for me."

"Just relax. You'll be okay."

Gibson started to take notice of his surroundings. He found that his first impression of a cavernous parking area fell well short of actuality. The place could have been an aircraft hangar, except that aircraft hangars weren't constructed from raw unfinished concrete and their roofs weren't supported by thick steel-reinforced pillars. It was hard to tell the true size of the underground installation beyond the basic impression that it was very large indeed. Brightly lit areas where intense beams of light blazed from overhead grilles alternated with pools of impenetrable shadow. In one of the nearest pools of light, a work detail in green rubber suits, filter masks, and protective goggles that made them look like invading Martians were hosing down a large white car, removing a gray film from its bodywork similar to the one that had coated the Cadillac after the UFO attack. It was no ordinary car wash. The hose they were using was made of jointed stainless steel, and the substance that gushed from it under high pressure seemed more like a gas than a liquid. Where it hit the car it splashed and smoked, and Gibson had a suspicion that it was causing the smell of ammonia in the air. The car wasn't a Cadillac, either; in fact, it wasn't like any car that Gibson had ever seen before, big and bulky like something out of the late forties or early fifties, a Tucker or maybe an overgrown De Soto, with fins and a radiator grille that belonged on a jet fighter.

"Is that our car?"

Klein nodded. "Changed a bit, huh?"

"Why couldn't it just stay a Cadillac?"

"Because it's also been through transition. It would be fairly pointless if it still looked like an Eldorado from your dimension."

"What is this place?"

"It our main base and access point in this dimension."

"You have something like this back on Earth?"

Klein shook his head. "We maintain a much larger presence here. The politics of this dimension are very unstable."

Other big baroque cars were parked in a group farther down the area as well as a handful of sinister black paramilitary vehicles like bulky Batmobiles with armor-plate, slit windows, and exterior-mounted heavy machine guns. A pair of cumbersome, old-fashioned helicopters also stood nearby, like ugly sleeping insects, with their rotors folded back and canvas covers over the Plexiglas cockpit canopies. Klein wasn't exaggerating when he said that the streamheat maintained a presence here.

A squad of armored men carrying automatic weapons marched past where Gibson was sitting. Their dark-blue body armor was made up of irregularly shaped plates of some thick porous material that protected their torsos, thighs, and upper arms. The helmets they wore were polished and cylindrical, with a stylized sunburst insignia on the front and vestigial metal crest at the back that might have had its roots in some sort of feathered headdress. Taken as a whole, the ensemble made them look not unlike high-tech Aztecs. As they tramped by in step with the measured stamp of steel-shod boots, Klein didn't pay them the slightest attention. Instead, he looked down at Gibson.

"You feel any better?"

Gibson nodded. "A little."

"Did you hallucinate a lot coming through?"

Gibson pushed his hair back with his fingers. "A lot? Yeah, I'd say a lot. I turned into a burning meteor and then I fell into a black sea."

"It can be rough the first time. Can you stand?"

"I don't know."

"You want to try?"

"Sure, why not."

Klein reached down and took Gibson's arm. Gibson tried standing and found that it wasn't too difficult. He momentarily wanted to vomit but that quickly passed.

"Where are Smith and French?"

"They've gone on ahead to report."

Gibson was startled by a shout from one of the cleanup crew working on the white car.

"Superior in proximity!"

A group of five people were coming toward Gibson and Klein at a brisk, businesslike pace. Two of them were what Gibson was already thinking of as regular streamheat, in the plain blue jumpsuits, and two were the military form, in the slab-honeycomb armor and pre-Columbian helmets. Gibson didn't have to be told that the fifth guy was some sort of officer. The extra gold on his collar, the cape thrown over his shoulders, and the arrogance of his bearing made it immediately obvious. If that hadn't been enough, the way that the cleanup crew came to attention and even Klein formally stiffened rammed the point home.

All through his life, Gibson had always experienced a problem with authority figures. When someone started telling him what to do, his natural reaction was surly hostility. Sometimes he believed this hostility had been one of the major forces in shaping his life, and if it hadn't been built into his personality by either nature or nurture, he might have become president instead of a rock 'n' roll degenerate. He saw that it wasn't going to be any different in a new dimension. While the streamheat officer was still twenty yards away, Gibson knew that they were going to inevitably clash.

Klein muttered quickly out of the corner of his mouth. "This

is Superior Dresden and he's the head of this section. Watch out
for him. He's hard as a diamond and cuts as deep.''

Superior Dresden was the kind of Nordic blond god that Hitler would have instantly used as a model for the Aryan super-
man. Why were all these streamheat so goddamned perfect? If
anything, Dresden was even more perfect than the lower ranks
like Smith, Klein, and French. Did they practice selective breeding back in the streamheat dimension? Even Dresden's attitude
came straight out of the SS academy. He looked Gibson up and
down as though he was an inferior piece of merchandise, and
Gibson responded by striking a pose of dumb insolence. After
the cursory inspection, Dresden turned his attention to Klein.

"Is this the one?"

"Yes, Superior Dresden, this is Joe Gibson."

"Why is he so pale?"

"There were some problems with the trans. He took it hard."

Dresden thought about this. "It will be best if he goes straight
to the apartment."

"Should I take him personally, Superior?"

Dresden nodded. "Yes, you take him, you've come this far
with him."

"What about my debriefing from the previous mission?"

"Smith and French are already covering that. You can turn
in your report later."

He looked Gibson up and down once more and still didn't
like what he saw. "He's not particularly impressive, is he?"

"He's something of a legend in his own dimension."

Dresden let out a short exhalation of breath that seemed to
indicate he would never cease to be amazed by what went on in
other dimensions, and Gibson, already sensitive to being talked
about as though he wasn't there, reached the limit of his toler-
ance.

"Listen, friend, you may have people jumping around here
like you were second cousin to God, but I'm not from around
here and I expect to be extended the common courtesies. You
know what I'm talking about?"

Dresden's face clearly demonstrated that he wasn't accustomed to being spoken to like that. He glared balefully at Gibson.

"Do you know who I am?"

Gibson grinned and looked Dresden straight in the eye, refusing to be intimidated.

"Yeah, I know who you are. Your name's Dresden and supposedly you're the big wheel round here. Trouble is, that doesn't do too much for me. I'm Joe Gibson and I didn't want to come here; I'm also not a part of your Boy Scout troop and wouldn't advise trying to treat me like I was. I've put up with a great deal in the last few days and I'm really in no mood to be pushed around."

Dresden held his gaze. "I don't like your manners, Gibson."

"That's funny, I was just thinking the same about yours."

"You may regret this." With a curt gesture of dismissal, Dresden turned back to Klein. "Take him directly to the apartment and then report back to me."

As Dresden and his escort marched away, Klein looked at Gibson and slowly shook his head. "You shouldn't have done that. Superior Dresden is vindictive and has a long memory. He won't let an insult like that pass."

Gibson stuck out his lower jaw. "I've dealt with power-crazed assholes before. I can take my chances."

Klein nodded. "You may well have to." He took Gibson by the arm and steered him down through the huge space of light and dark. They passed a gang of laborers humping large wooden packing cases from off the back of a big, old-fashioned semitrailer. The laborers, who wore baggy tan coveralls, were uniformly short and dark, with lank black hair and Prussian-blue skin. Maybe there really was something to this idea of the streamheat practicing selective breeding. If their society as a whole, back in their home dimension, was organized anything like their interdimensional secret police, it had to be a fascist anthill. It wasn't at all encouraging to think that he'd been forced to throw in his lot with a bunch of fascist ants. He couldn't dwell on the concept, however; some more immediate thoughts required his attention.

"What's this apartment Dresden was talking about?"

"We maintain a number of anonymous apartments throughout the city for the use of our people when they need to blend in with the native population. You're going to stay in one of them until your situation has been rationalized."

"Rationalized?"

"You'll be briefed when the time comes."

"And who'll do the briefing?"

Klein almost smiled.

"Superior Dresden."

Gibson's face fell.

"Oh, shit."

"Maybe that'll teach you to put a curb on your mouth."

They turned right at a point where a formidable chain-link and razor-wire fence cut off access to the rest of the area. Gibson couldn't read the red-and-white signs that were posted at regular intervals along the fence, as the text seemed to be in the same alien script that he had seen on the keyboard of the Cadillac's computer, but the red lightning bolts on each sign made the message pretty clear—the fence was electrified. Through it he could see figures, both tan and dark blue, moving around among rows of bulky, tarpaulin-shrouded shapes. For what was supposed to be a covert organization, the streamheat were amassing themselves quite a mess of matériel here in Luxor.

Gibson and Klein entered a tunnel or corridor, Gibson wasn't sure which; ever since he'd woken up from the transition, he'd had the feeling that he was underground, although he wasn't absolutely certain why. They seemed to be passing through the administrative hub of the base; the rooms and cubicles that opened onto the tunnel/corridor were filled with men and women in blue jumpsuits who were either shuffling papers or bent over computer monitors. In one large room, a line of operators stared at a hundred or more purple-and-white, postcard-size monitor screens that had to be a part of some Big Brother surveillance system. Gibson made a mental note of that—you never knew when the streamheat might be watching. It was also along this tunnel/corridor that Gibson caught sight of himself in a mirror. What he saw was enough of a shock to stop him dead in his tracks. His features and figure were much as he had last seen them, but practically everything else had changed. He was pale blue, a very pale blue. Even accepting the fact that he was temporarily seeing a world of people with blue faces, he had become extraordinarily pallid, not a healthy robust blue like Klein and Dresden and all of the others he'd seen since his arrival in Luxor, but a faded-unto-death, corpselike pastel. If anything shocked him more than the color of his skin, it was the way that his hair had changed: it had bleached out like his suit, white as the driven snow. It was also considerably shorter and brushed back into the pompadour of a fifties greaser.

"I'm fucking Eddie Cochran in negative!"

Klein looked a little guilty. "I was intending to tell you about that later when we got to the apartment."

"Tell me what exactly."

"You're extremely pale. You seem to have lost a lot of pigment in the transition."

"This isn't an illusion like the blue faces?"

"I'm afraid not."

Gibson's expression turned from shocked to suspicious. "What's that supposed to mean?"

Klein took a deep breath, as though steeling himself before delivering the bad news.

"You're pretty much an albino."

"An albino? I don't want to be an albino."

"There really isn't too much we can do about it."

"So much for blending in with the native population. I'm going to stand out like a sore thumb."

"In actual fact, you may not."

"The place is loaded with albinos?"

"Luxor has more than its fair share of strange people. Their development of nuclear energy was extremely sloppy and, on top of that, they've had three limited nuclear wars, so there are a lot of quite weird-looking folk walking around."

"So you think I won't be that noticeable."

"I'm hoping not."

"This is getting ridiculous."

The two of them waited at the door of an elevator. When they stepped inside and Klein pushed the buttons, they started going up.

"Where are we headed for?"

Klein glanced up at the ceiling. "Ground level."

Gibson nodded. He was pleased that his sense of being underground had been correct. It was good to know that one's instincts were functioning properly.

The entrance to the streamheat's underground base was concealed in a derelict warehouse in the middle of what seemed to be an abandoned industrial park. The sky was a metallic gray, and the smell of coming rain was carried by a brisk wind.

As they emerged into the daylight, Gibson looked around in disbelief. "This is another dimension? Shit, we could be back in Newark."

Klein smiled knowingly. "You'll find a lot of similarities."

A street ran past the front of the warehouse that looked as though it hadn't been used in years. The surface was cracked and littered with garbage that was breaking down into a uniform organic mulch that fertilized the rank grass growing up through the cracks.

Gibson looked up and down the street for some form of transportation but could see nothing. "So how do we get to civilization? I hope you don't think I'm going to walk."

Klein shook his head. "You won't have to walk. We're going to take a taxi."

Gibson looked surprised. After all they they'd been through, the idea of a cab ride seemed a little prosaic. "A taxi?"

"Sure, a taxi. Did it ever occur to you that cabs are an ideal means of transport?"

Gibson shrugged. "I'd never really thought about it. They certainly come in handy when you're drunk."

"We own one of the local cab companies. As well as giving us a line into some of the Luxor crime families, the cabs provide an inconspicuous way of moving around the city. Nobody ever looks twice at a cab."

Gibson scanned the street again. "So where is this cab?"

"One will be along in a moment to pick us up."

In confirmation of his words, a red-and-green vehicle appeared at the far end of the street, carefully steering around the heaps of debris and rusted-out shells of abandoned cars. Except for some minor details, it looked for all the world like a '52 Chevy. When Gibson got into it he found that the interior of the cab was the interior of a cab. He could have been back on Earth. The armored steel and Plexiglas between the driver and the passengers may have been a little more intense than the anti-theft screens in New York cabs, but not by much, and he wouldn't have thought too much of it if he'd climbed into the same vehicle on Fifty-seventh Street. If the protection that cabbies thought they needed was any indication, Luxor had a major problem with street crime. Gibson also discovered something that didn't make him happy at all. The back of the cab was plastered with the usual warning stickers and advertising signs, and these brought Gibson face-to-face with what seemed to be another and very serious failure of the transition.

"I can't read this stuff."

Klein's eyebrows shot up. "What?"

Gibson pointed to the various signs inside the cab. "It all looks like it's written in Martian. I can't read a word of it."

"That is a major problem."

"You're not kidding. I don't really relish the idea of being an illiterate. How can I even tell which is the men's room?"

Klein shook his head. "I don't know what to say. Transition is supposed to take care of things like basic reading skills."

"Is there anything that can be done?"

"I don't have a clue. I've never come across anything like this before. I guess you could try learning it the hard way."

Gibson was getting angry. "Give me a break, will you? I'm not about to learn to read all over again." A thought hit him like a thunderbolt. "Am I going to be able to speak the language?"

Klein looked worried. "I sure as hell hope so. All we can do is see what happens."

"Suppose I said something to the cabdriver?"

Klein shook his head. "He's one of us. He'd understand you anyway. You don't seem to have any problem with our language."

"You're talking your own language?"

"I have been ever since you woke."

"So what do we do?"

"We'll just have to wait until you're in among the natives."

"Might it not be a bit late by then?"

"That's a chance we're going to have to take."

"Fucking great."

"I'm sorry."

"Sorry really doesn't cut it in a situation like this."

Gibson turned and looked out the window. Driving into Luxor was depressingly like driving into any city anywhere. The cars that they passed were a little strange, and the design of the suburban homes was unlike anything he'd seen before. They were flat-roofed, ranch-style houses that might have come from some early-fifties, *Popular Mechanics* vision of the future. Those, however, were only details, and the drive was really no stranger than coming into, say, Moscow or Istanbul. At some point in the past, Luxor must have been extremely prosperous and indulged in a towering, skyscraper school of architecture that seemed to view the act of constructing a building as the creation of another monument to itself. The buildings that reared into the air, some for fifty and sixty stories, were loaded down with spires and gargoyles, flying buttresses, and heroic statues and reliefs. It was clear, however, that the good times were long gone. The imposing towers were filmed with soot and daubed with unreadable graffiti at street level, and the broad avenues were choked with traffic belching black unfiltered exhaust fumes probably thick with every toxin known to man. The monorail rapid-transit system that crisscrossed the streets at the third-floor level was in such a state of serious neglect and disrepair that its decay was obvious to Gibson at very first glance, and he resolved not to use it unless absolutely necessary.

It seemed that Luxor's population was growing too fast for the city to cope, and the groaning infrastructure was in the process of going down for the last time, drowning in a sea of humanity for which it had never been designed. The sidewalks were crowded with pedestrians, and although the bustle of busy city was still in evidence and well-dressed people were going about their business while new gleaming cars crawled through the near-gridlock, there were also ample numbers of those who clearly had nothing to do except lean or loiter or shuffle aimlessly and panhandle the passing stream of the more well heeled. Every couple of blocks, a drunk could be seen stretched out on the sidewalk or sleeping it off in a doorway, or a pair of winos would be huddled together, sharing a bottle in a paper bag. Many of the intersections they passed had their share of skittish hookers trying for the quick daytime trick, and, all in all, the newcomer was left in no doubt that Luxor had hit hard times.

If Luxor had economized on anything, it certainly wasn't law enforcement. One of the first things that Gibson noticed was the massive police presence. Although it seemed like a perfectly normal day with nothing special going on, there were cops everywhere. Foot patrols, pairs, and even trios of officers in helmets and flak jackets and with bulky submachine guns slung under their arms stood on street corners and prowled the sidewalks while the bums and hookers and guys selling stuff out of suitcases melted away at their approach. Even the more affluent citizens avoided looking straight into their hard, expressionless faces. The city's police cars were equally formidable—more of the slab-sided, huge black Batmobiles with the fins and the armor and the firepower, just like the ones that Gibson had seen parked underground in the streamheat base. As their cab inched along through the logjam of traffic, one of the black juggernauts slowly passed them.

Gibson glanced at Klein. "It can't be any picnic for criminals in this town."

Klein was also looking at the armored police cruiser. "They don't make a bad living, believe me."

Law enforcement wasn't confined merely to street level. Black helicopters buzzed overhead bearing what had to be police insignia, slowly circling, constantly observing the streets and rooftops below. They were bulky, slow-moving machines with round Plexiglas cabins like something out of the Korean War.

Klein offered a token explanation. "They're cop-crazy here."

"So you guys should fit right in."

Klein ignored him. "They have four separate police departments in this city alone, plus assorted unofficial thug squads."

Gibson continued to watch the police car as it pulled ahead. "You really brought me to a dandy vacation spot."

An architect had once told Gibson that when a city lost its pride, it covered itself in billboards. If the size and quantity of the ones in Luxor were anything to go by, the town had no pride left at all. Every piece of available space seemed to be given over to advertising. Billboards were everywhere, some of them a full block long. The techniques of selling in the United Kamerian Republics were by no means a fine art. Giant, scantily clad, garish women with big breasts and electric smiles held up various cans, bottles, and packages or else sprawled across cars, cookers, and TV sets without too much real relationship to whatever particular product they might be pitching. It appeared that in Luxor they believed that just about anything could be sold by sex. Gibson had never seen such expanses of blue skin in his life, and he wasn't sure how he felt about it. He was a little confused about having erotic responses to blue women. There was, however, one consolation. A good percentage of the blue bikini babes were offering packs of cigarettes.

"So they still smoke here in Luxor?"

Klein nodded. "Sure they do. Most of the natives have one going all the time. By pure dumb luck, they stumbled across a cure for cancer back in what, in your world, would have been the nineteen-thirties."

One of the main exceptions to the parade of blue bimbos was a set of billboards that featured huge black-and-white portraits of a good-looking man in his forties with brush-cut hair and a winning smile. Under the photograph there was a simple short slogan in red type that Gibson was, of course, unable to read.

After they'd passed five of the signs, Gibson pointed the next one out to Klein. "Who's that?"

"That's Lancer."

"Who's Lancer?"

"He's the president, Jaim Benson Lancer, the thirty-second President of the UKR."

"So why all the billboards? Is it election year?"

Klein shook his head. "They don't have real elections here anymore."

"So what's with all the advertising? The president's out selling beer in this dimension?"

"It's just an inspiration message to the people reminding them that JBL loves them and they love him."

"If they love him so much, what does he need all these cops for?"

"That's the weird thing about the United Republics. Lancer's been in power for ten years, and during that time, things have gone from bad to worse, but the more he screws things up, the more the population seems to adore and idolize him. Somehow, he's managed to completely detach himself from his disastrous administration."

They crossed a big intersection where a massive gilded statue of an idealized naked man with fountains dancing round his feet threatened to hurl a golden thunderbolt straight up the avenue and into one of the more affluent areas of the city that Gibson had so far seen. After five blocks however, the affluence dwindled to a neighborhood of genteel decay. The cab turned into a street of tall, reasonably well-kept apartment buildings and pulled up in front of one about halfway down the block.

Gibson glanced at Klein. "Is this it? Are we there?"

Klein nodded. "This is it."

They stepped out of the cab and Gibson looked up at the front of his new temporary home. It really wasn't all that different from his place on Central Park West, maybe a little down-market but basically the same kind of structure. A similar blue-and-white awning led up to the front door, and as he walked into the paneled lobby it was easy to picture Ramone, his New York doorman, standing there.

The streamheat apartment was on the fifteenth floor, and that was where the resemblance to his New York home ended. The place was small, dark, and dingy, with tiny cramped rooms and narrow slit windows, most of which looked out on a blank airshaft. It was also crowded with heavy, fifties-style furniture. Most of the space in the living room was taken up by a massive three-piece suite, upholstered in green leather that showed the marks of wear and even the scars of cigarette burns. Klein turned on a light, but it did nothing to improve the place's appearance. The walls were a dirty parchment yellow and the carpet an all-purpose excremental brown. Neither seemed to have been properly cleaned in the last decade.

"It's hardly the Plaza."

"It'll do for the moment."

Gibson sniffed. "You don't have to live here." Then he realized that he was only assuming this. "You won't be living here with me, will you?"

Klein shook his head. "No, I won't be living here. You'll be here on your own until other arrangements can be made."

Gibson raised an eyebrow. "Aren't you afraid that I might take a powder?"

The idea of Gibson walking out didn't seem to bother Klein at all. "Where would you go?"

Gibson nodded. "You have a point there."

They moved into the single bedroom. The double bed and a wardrobe like an upright coffin built for two hardly left enough floor space for the two men to stand in comfort.

"This is the kind of apartment where junkies come to die."

"It'll have to serve."

"Maybe if we got rid of some of the furniture?"

"I wouldn't bother thinking about redecorating. I doubt you'll be here long enough."

Gibson looked around. The place still seemed to be inhabited. There was certainly someone else's stuff strewn all around. "Who used to stay here?"

"Another agent. He was just transferred out."

There was a quality to Klein's voice that made Gibson suspect he was hiding something, but he decided that it was probably pointless to call him on it, and they returned to the living room. If Gibson had learned one thing during his acquaintance with the streamheat, it was that they were masters of keeping their mouths shut. He noticed a large TV set in the corner in a solid mahogany cabinet. Now what the hell was TV like in Luxor?

"So what happens now?"

"I have to return to the base and make my report."

"What about me?"

"This is your apartment for the moment. Relax, make yourself at home. I think you'll find there's everything you'll need."

This was all going a little swiftly for Gibson. "Wait a minute. You're just going to leave me here?"

"I don't have any orders to stay here and baby-sit you, if that's what you mean."

"What do I do about food and stuff?"

Klein shrugged. "The place is well stocked. I guess more will be sent in when you need it."

"Don't I get some kind of emergency number? Some way I can contact you people if there's a problem?"

"If there's a problem, we'll know about it."

Gibson remembered the bank of postcard-size monitor screens in the streamheat base. "You'll be watching me?"

Klein's face was blank. "I don't know what exact arrangements have been made for your security."

"So I just wait here and amuse myself?"

"You'll be contacted." Klein was at the door and on his way out. "I wouldn't recommend roaming the streets or anything, but otherwise you're free to do what you like. I believe alcohol has been provided."

Gibson's lip curled. "Then I'll be all right, won't I? I mean, that's all the poor old drunk needs, right?"

Klein ignored him. "Drop the deadbolt on the door after I've gone."

The door closed behind Klein, and Gibson was suddenly all alone. After about twenty seconds, the realization of this crashed in on him like a physical blow and he had to say it out loud to himself to make sure it was real.

"You're on your own in another dimension."

The idea was almost impossible to accept.

"You're on your own in another fucking dimension."

Suddenly something inside him crumpled. He no longer had Smith, Klein, and French hurrying him from one place to the next, or Windemere providing him with at least the illusion of protection. He now had nothing but his own resources, and that was frightening.

"Jesus Christ, boy, what have you gotten yourself into?"

He went into the kitchen of the apartment and found that, as Klein had said, the place had been fully stocked. The cupboards and refrigerator were full of brand-name goods that must have been brought through from his own dimension. Whoever planned his menu, though, had some strange ideas about what he ate. They seemed to assume he lived on a steady diet of Wonder Bread, peanut butter, Cap'n Crunch cereal, Dinty Moore beef stew, and Chef Boyardee ravioli. Although he wondered about the motivation and even the method that had brought him this bonanza of junk food from home, he was pleased to see it. He was in no shape to be struggling with unreadable cans of whatever they ate here in Luxor. He imagined he would come to that soon enough if the streamheat decided he was to stay in this dimension for a while, but in the meantime he'd do his best to chow down on what was there and not complain too much. He did wonder where the food might have come from. Did the

streamheat maintain supplies of cheap supermarket provisions
from a variety of dimensions for eventualities like this or had
the stuff been transed in specially for him? That scarcely seemed
possible considering the speed with which he'd been brought
there, unless, of course, they'd been planning to bring him long
before he'd known about it.

He was relieved to find that the promised alcohol had also
been provided. In the cupboard over the sink, he discovered
three fifths of Johnnie Walker Red Label, and there were also
two six-packs of Bud Light in the big, old-fashioned refrigerator. He opened a beer and poured himself a very large shot of
Scotch. He raised his glass to the empty air in a silent toast to
whomever might be watching and then set off on a detailed
exploration of the apartment and its contents. The previous ten-
ant appeared to have left in a great hurry: his clothes were still
there, along with a number of books in the local language, discarded magazines, and newspapers. Gibson even discovered a
clutch of local soft porn in which blue couples cavorted across
pages of implausibly cheap color printing. It wasn't long, however, before a certain uneasiness started to set in. The deeper
Gibson delved, the more he came to believe that the "other
agent" had not just moved out in a hurry—the signs seemed to
indicate that he had simply vanished. His razor, toilet articles,
and a selection of medications were still in the bathroom, and
there was even a signet ring on the edge of the sink, as though
a man had taken it off and placed it there while he was washing
his hands and then never put it back on again. Gibson inspected
the medicines with an experienced eye and found that one jar
contained some thirty or so yellow pills that looked uncommonly
like Valium. He was almost tempted to take a couple but decided
that it might be wiser to stick to Scotch for the moment.

On a table beside the bed he found a pile of what appeared to
be political leaflets, the kind of handbills that were printed up
and passed out on the street by radical and fringe groups trying
to make their point. They carried a less than flattering drawing
of President Lancer and a slogan in a loud, violent typeface.
Gibson sat down on the bed and studied the flyer. What had this
guy been, some kind of agent provocateur worming his way into
the confidence of local dissidents? Looking at the man's stuff,
Gibson couldn't believe that he'd been regular streamheat like
Klein or French. The man was too much of a slob. His shoes
lay on the floor were he had dropped them, and there was a half-
eaten plate of food in the refrigerator that he seemed to have

been saving. His very smell was still in the place, a mixture of dirty socks and cheap cologne that simply wasn't streamheat in any shape or form. Perhaps he'd been some hired-on local operative or maybe another unwilling import from another dimension.

The most disturbing find came as Gibson was taking a closer look at the TV. He spotted something down beside one of the carved legs of the baroque forty-inch set and went fishing for it. It turned out to be a wallet, and beside it, further under the TV, was a set of keys. Unease turned to outright spookiness. There was no way that any rational man left an apartment under his own steam without his wallet and keys. He flipped open the wallet and looked inside. This was the biggest shock yet. All it contained was a thick wad of the local currency and a single ID, and the picture on the ID showed a face that was close enough to Gibson's that it could have been his brother. His brother, that is, before the transition had turned him into an albino. Gibson closed the wallet and walked as calmly as he could to the kitchen and poured himself an even larger shot than the last one. As he drank, he looked around the ceiling wondering if the streamheat were watching him and had been all through the discovery of the wallet. Even as he looked, he knew that searching for the camera or whatever they might be using to spy on him was totally pointless. In his own dimension they had spy cameras so small that they were virtually indetectable, and at least the same had to be expected of the streamheat.

Once he calmed down from the initial shock, Gibson started to think seriously about what this new set of developments might mean. It could hardly be a coincidence that the last person to inhabit the apartment looked almost identical to him, so what the hell was going on? Was it some Prisoner of Zenda deal where he'd been shipped in to replace . . . and there that theory faltered. Without answers to questions like who and why, there was hardly any point in going on with it. Maybe if he could have read the print on the ID card, he might have learned something about his near double, if nothing more than the name he'd been using. Detective work was close to impossible when one was a functional illiterate. The only other theory that came close to holding water was that the streamheat were sticking it to him for some mysterious reason of their own, and that the wallet, the apartment, and everything else were the props in some weird, rat-maze, behavioral experiment in which he was the rat. The whiskey was starting to go to work, and some of his fear was turning into slit-eyed belligerence. He glared at the supposed cameras that might be looking down at him from the kitchen ceiling.

"What are you trying to do, you bastards, bust my balls or just drive me crazy?"

He turned to the fridge for another beer and noticed for the first time a package wrapped in greaseproof paper, way in the back of the vegetable crisper. More of the last guy's leftovers? He had a sudden urge to get rid of it, to throw out all the crap left behind by this mysterious look-alike. How would that grab any watching streamheat?

"Mark it down as symbolic cleansing of the new territory, you cocksuckers."

Hell, for all he knew, they might be broadcasting this as a nature show in the streamheat dimension. *Inferior Species Under Stress. Earth People Are Funny. Interdimensional Candid Camera*, even. Smile, Joe, you're on. How superior did those bastards really think they were?

His fingers closed around the package of what he thought were leftovers, but instead of encountering something that felt like semifrozen mush, they touched hard cold metal under the paper. He quickly tore off the wrapping and found to his amazement that he was holding a gun. Gibson's first reaction was to immediately put it down on the small kitchen table. The cold metal was burning his fingers. Was this another part of the game? If indeed the streamheat were running some game on him, it seemed like a dangerous play—or did they see him as such a weakling that even armed, he wouldn't be dangerous?

He gingerly picked up the gun again. As guns went, it was a nice piece. A Luxor model that was not unlike a Colt .45 automatic. He fumbled around the bottom of the butt until he found the release for the clip, and slid it out. The gun was fully loaded. Suddenly feeling cold sober, he clicked it back into place. Gibson had never had any luck with guns, and since the notorious incident with the roadie, he'd sworn them off altogether. He'd even refused the gift of a Saturday night special that Jerry Lee Lewis had tried to press on him at some drunken party following the Grammies, to the point where Lewis had started roaring that he was a worthless faggot. It took a certain kind of willpower to stand there and have Jerry Lee Lewis call you a faggot in front of the assembled music business, and Gibson had actually taken a warped pride in his own forbearance. Now here he was, in this filthy kitchen, clutching a big Mike Hammer automatic and wondering what he was going to do with it.

After about a minute, he decided that he wasn't going to do anything, at least not immediately. He poured himself a third drink and went back into the living room, taking the gun, the wallet, and the keys with him. For a long time he stared at the photo in the wallet but no inspiration came. It was only when he became convinced that the exercise was futile that he turned his attention to the bundle of cash. It would have been nice to know just how much it was worth, but, not even being able to read the numbers on the bills, it was impossible to tell. And then a thought struck him: he *could* read the numbers on the bills. A large brass sunburst clock hung right in front of him on the living room wall, flanked by two faded sepia prints of storms at sea. It was about as ugly as a clock could get but it had numerals that, as far as he could see, worked in exactly the same way as numbers worked back home, nine single characters and then ten, eleven, and twelve expressed as double digits. Even if there was some weird factor that he didn't know about, like the hours in Luxor were longer or shorter, it didn't matter. He knew the first rudiments of their numerical system. He suddenly felt incredibly pleased with himself and went to work figuring out the denominations of the various bills in the roll. It didn't take him very long to calculate that the bundle was just shy of two thousand of whatever unit passed as currency in Luxor. What he didn't know was whether this made him a rich man or would merely enable him to buy a cup of coffee and a sandwich.

The next thing to catch his attention was the TV. It occurred to Gibson that there was no need to go out mingling with the natives to find out if he understood the local language; all he had to do was switch on the set and watch for a while. Now he really was thinking for himself again, and it was like a breath of fresh air after having been told what to do for so long. He knelt down in front of the set, looking for the on/off switch. It turned out that Luxor could only manage two channels of black-and-white TV. One was showing a game show that, allowing for the natural culture shifts between dimensions, looked a hell of a lot like *Family Feud*. The main difference was that a comparatively normal family—albeit of ultramarine complexion—seemed to be competing against one composed of total freaks. He remembered how Klein had told him about the amount of radiation that was loose in this dimension. The genetic damage that must have been sustained by this family of four—Mom,

Pop, and two kids—was nothing less than awesome. Pop was a standard pinhead, tiny pointed skull balanced upon a beefy, overdeveloped body, while Mom was a circus fat lady of five hundred pounds or more who had also been liberally endowed with facial hair. One kid was a dwarf, twisted and misshapen with a face so filled with hate that he seemed on the perpetual verge of apoplexy; the second, a tall and gawky girl, had a face filled with nothing: two eyes and a rudimentary slit of a mouth were the only truly defined features in a blank blue moon of a face. The audience was howling its approval as the family of normals whupped the freaks hands down. It appeared that the humiliation of the handicapped was real big laughs in Luxor. In addition to this insight, the game show offered Gibson two other crucial pieces of information. He quickly found out that according to his perception, the citizens of Luxor spoke colloquial American English. Their accent was a little weird but it was nothing that Gibson couldn't handle. He wondered if they really did speak English here and all the stuff he'd been told about how transition gave you instant linguistic skills was bullshit and deliberate lies. He only had Klein's word for any of it.

"I mean, in a goddamned parallel dimension, why shouldn't the parallel people speak parallel English?"

It didn't explain, however, why he was unable to read their parallel writing, but he was learning very quickly that it was wise to stay away from these interdimensional brain twisters. They only confused him and ultimately made his head hurt. Better by far to stick to practical puzzles while he was on this mental roll, like the fact that the huge scoreboards at the far end of the game-show set not only showed the contestants' amassed winnings but also demonstrated the relationship between the cash prizes and the merchandise that was being given away. A car that looked not unlike a mid-fifties Studebaker was equated with a prize of ten thousand. That meant the two thousand sitting in the wallet wasn't a fortune but was quite enough juice to ease him out of trouble. He even learned the name of the currency. In Luxor, they wheeled and dealed and probably also lied and died for the almighty kudo.

The moment that he knew the value of the bundle of bills in the wallet, alarms started going off in Gibson's head. It could hardly be an oversight that the streamheat had set him up with an apartment in Luxor that came with an almost adequate fake ID, a decidedly adequate amount of walking money, a supply of booze, and a gun. In his experience, the streamheat didn't go in for oversights of this magnitude. So, if it wasn't an oversight, what was it? Were they hoping he would do something? Knowing the contempt in which they held him, he could only imagine that they expected him to take the money and the gun and go out and get drunk. It was crazy. Or was it? Maybe they expected him go to out and get drunk and then get arrested. That made a little more sense, and Luxor certainly had enough cops to bring him in if he were to cause a disturbance. The next question was why. By now, a theory was starting to develop. In the event of being arrested, he would almost certainly use the look-alike's ID, and that would mean an official report of some kind. Gibson frowned. Was he being set up as some sort of alibi for his double, creating the illusion that the man was in the local drunk-tank while, in reality, he was out doing something nefarious at the streamheat's bidding? Bringing Gibson across the dimensions seemed one hell of an elaborate way to set up an alibi unless, of course, it was going to be one hell of a crime.

Gibson poured himself another drink. Conjecture was making him weary. He realized that he was now at the point where he didn't believe anything that the streamheat had told him unless it was confirmed by another source. That meant doubting almost everything he'd heard about Luxor and challenging every supposition. He slowly sipped his Scotch and let the warmth course through him. The trouble with the intellectual rigor was that it was too much like hard work. He flipped the TV to the second channel to see if this might provide some new insight or inspiration, but all he got was an ugly and violent cop show in which, without too much benefit of plot, officers in heavy body armor blew away the bad guys with a selection of shotguns and automatic weapons. Gibson supposed that it was inevitable that this kind of show was popular in Luxor. Cultures that were big on law enforcement in reality were usually big on it as entertainment as well. He noticed that a large proportion of the bad guys in this show were genetic freaks, dramatically evil versions of the family on the game show. Gibson sighed. Was this how they siphoned off mass frustration, by turning up the hate against the atomic mutations?

"Jesus, this really is the fifties."

The cop show gave way to local news, and Gibson discovered that news presentation in Luxor was primitive, not unlike the old movie-house newsreels, with grainy photography, military band music, and a strident voice-over. The lead story was about the preparations for the president's forthcoming visit to the city, and it featured footage of Lancer riding in an open car, smiling and waving at a cheering crowd. Gibson instinctively didn't like Jaim Benson Lancer. The man was too handsome and too smooth, too many teeth and too much boyish hair. Gibson operated on the principle that anyone who looked so good just couldn't be trusted.

Gibson yawned. He had lost track of how much Scotch he'd poured into himself, and his eyelids were starting to droop. His sense of time was shot, but it was getting dark outside and the TV wasn't helping any. One channel was showing some grim movie about a bunch of chronically depressed peasants trying to eke out a living in some bleak, radiation-blasted rural hell, sort of *Little House on the Nuclear Wasteland*, and, on the other, an equally dour family drama, set in a apartment almost as wretched as the one that he was in, made him think of a version of the *Honeymooners* in which the humor had been replaced by raging angst and miserable screaming kids. He wondered if he ought to sleep or if he was in danger of psych attack in Luxor. Even though it meant taking the word of the streamheat, he had to assume that he was at least marginally secure. He couldn't spend the rest of his life staying awake because he was afraid of what might come at him out of his dreams. Whatever their ultimate intentions for him, he couldn't see that he would be much use to the streamheat either as a ringer or a rat in a maze with his brain fried by nightmares or crazy from exhaustion.

It was at some point around that thought that his eyes closed of their own accord and he went out into a merciful blackness without dreams, either good or bad.

The next thing he knew was that he was wide awake, and something was coming out of the TV at him.

The White Room

"IT'S INTERESTING THAT you always talk about this imaginary show-business career of yours as a failure."

"I fucked up at the end but it wasn't a total failure. There was a period when we were the biggest thing there was."

"So what went wrong."

"I guess we got too crazy."

"Can you be a bit more specific."

Gibson's face creased into a sly grin. "Does it really make that much difference? I mean, it's only a fantasy, right?"

"Why don't you tell me about it anyway?"

"What's the point?"

"Stay with it. The creation of an extremely vivid full-life fantasy such as this can frequently be a way in which we hide a very serious trauma."

Gibson was back in session with Dr. Kooning. Dr. Kooning had started treating him like her star patient. His hours with her had been increased. Instead of an hour a day, Monday through Friday, she'd bumped his hours up to a double deal on Mondays, Wednesdays, and Fridays, with the regular single on Tuesdays and Thursdays, a total of eight hours a week on the couch, although Gibson still refused to lie on the couch. Even though Gibson was doing his best to make nice and try to produce what would pass as a plausible recovery, the idea of lying on the couch still gave him the horrors. Eight hours a week of pouring out his soul to Kooning wasn't exactly appealing, either. He would much rather have spent the time talking to John West. Although West was definitely a couple of sandwiches short of a picnic, he had some paranoid conspiracy theories that were world-beaters. He was dropping hints that he was, in fact,

173

a top-rate intelligence operative who, after an attempt at resigning, had been confined in the clinic to be driven demonstrably mad so no one would believe him if he was ever in a position to tell what he knew. He was also the only person since Gibson's return who unreservedly accepted the story of his adventures in Luxor and the dimensions he'd fled to after the debacle there.

In the last few sessions, Kooning had been concentrating on the fine print of what she assumed was Gibson's elaborate, rockstar fantasy. Her strategy seemed to be that by getting Gibson to examine it in the minutest detail it would begin to reveal itself as not being his past at all but the creation of a very disturbed mind. To give her what she wanted to hear wasn't as simple as it sounded. The details came all too easily, too thick and fast, in fact. It was, after all, as far as he was concerned, the only memory that he had. When Kooning questioned him on a point, he was forced to go deeper and he worried that he was actually convincing her that the fantasy was even more complex than she'd first imagined. She was even thinking aloud about sessions in which he'd be medicated with chemical disinhibitors. As far as Gibson could figure it, a chemical disinhibitor was some sort of fancy designer hallucinogen that would almost certainly turn him into a babbling idiot. He had to do something about that. If it happened, he'd give away so much that Kooning would figure that he was worth a popular book and maybe even a Donahue show, and then he'd never get out of the clinic.

The previous three sessions, two doubles and a single, had been devoted to the early days on the glory road, when each new record sold more than the last one, and he and rest of the Holy Ghosts were gripped by a breathless excitement as everything went right, and the only fear was that they'd wake up and find that it was all a dream. At the start of this one, though, Kooning had switched focus and wanted to hear how it had all gone wrong.

"I'm not sure I'm ready to talk about that yet."

In this instance, the hesitation wasn't for effect. Gibson wasn't sure that he did want to talk about those final days, the nightmare days when he was watching everything fall apart and simultaneously losing his grip on his own sanity. Kooning fixed him with the blank expression that was neither compassion nor reproach but some neutral point between the two. It was a look that was supposed to prove that she cared but she wasn't involved.

"Please try. Perhaps there was one specific event—"

"There wasn't any single incident that did it. It was really a chain reaction of events that made things progressively worse. There'd be stress and then one of us, usually me, would flip out and do something really stupid and then, as a result, the stress would increase and there'd be another freak-out and the downward spiral would go through one more turn."

"What don't you tell me about some of these times that you feel you behaved so stupidly?"

Chapter
Eight

A PIERCING ELECTRONIC howl was filling the room as Gibson struggled desperately to recover his wits. He had been in such a deep sleep that, at first, he didn't even know where he was. Luxor? That's right. The apartment? He could remember that, but what was happening to the television? The glass of the screen seemed to have been transmuted into soft stretching plastic, and something was trying to push its way through it from inside. The raw energy blazing from the set was blinding, and it strobed back from the walls of the room like a short-circuiting psychedelic light show. Gibson raised an arm to shield his eyes, convinced that the picture tube itself was going to explode at any moment in a shower of glass. At that point he was still thinking in relatively normal terms like explosion or TV meltdown. He had yet to question why he was seeing flashes of dazzling color on a black-and-white set. It was only when something like an arm or a tentacle that seemed to be composed of swirling, multicolored interference extended out of the screen and into the room that he realized that he was still in the hostile world of the extraordinary. The thing was reaching around as though looking for a handhold, and it had formed indistinct fingers that blazed with red fire. It was like watching an electric lizard struggling out of its egg, except that as more of it emerged into the room it started to assume an increasingly humanoid form. Gibson watched transfixed as, with a final frenzied effort, it dragged its legs clear of the bulging screen and stepped to the floor, spilling cascades of sparks onto the dirty carpet, now only linked to the set by a glowing umbilical. It stood about six inches taller than Gibson, and he knew without being told that it meant him no good. When a black hole of a mouth opened the thing's approximation of a face, the electronic howl modulated as though it was trying to form words; then, without further preamble, it lunged for Gibson.

Gibson hurled himself out of the chair and rolled sideways. He was certain that if the thing touched him he'd be instantly fried. The thing didn't move particularly fast, and it seemed to have little sense of direction, but there was a flash of discharge and the stench of burning leather and horsehair as it hit the chair where he'd been sitting moments before. The whole room seemed to be filled with static, and Gibson could feel his hair standing on end and small shocks running up and down his spine.

The thing from the TV was turning and coming after him again. With no chance to get to his feet, Gibson scrambled backward across the floor like a terrified crab. It reached for him again, but he ducked under its arm. The gun! He had to get the gun. He didn't know whether it would do any good but it was all that he had. He could only go on ducking and weaving for so long. The gun was on the floor beside the chair where he'd been sleeping and, while the thing was turning again, he dived for it. Clint Eastwood would have been proud of the way that he came up off the floor with the automatic clutched in his fist. Doing his utmost to keep his hand steady, he squeezed the trigger. The gun bucked and the sound of the shot momentarily drowned out the electronic howl, but, to his dismay, the bullet went straight through the monster, and the only damage it did was blow a crater in the wall. A violet streak marked where the bullet had passed through the thing, but otherwise the only effect was to slow it up for a moment. The monster made what looked like a surprised gesture, as though it hadn't expected the bullet, but then it kept on coming.

A voice barked an order inside his head. "Shoot the TV!" It was as though an emergency area of his brain had assumed control. Gibson didn't think about it. The creature was almost on him and he could smell ozone. He fired twice. The TV exploded in a blue flash, and the thing vanished in the same instant. It was as though the TV set had not only been its means of entry to the room but also its source of energy, perhaps the source of its very being. He slowly lowered the gun. After the noise and confusion, the silence in the room was like a hollow void. The TV stood in the corner with a curl of blue smoke rising from the shattered screen. After thirty seconds of total, shocked paralysis, he stuffed the still warm gun into the waistband of his pants and ran for the Johnnie Walker in the kitchen. He didn't even bother to pour it into a glass; he went straight for the bottle.

Gibson knew he had to get out of there. It was a primal urge, not a logical decision. He didn't want to be in any place where things came at you out of the TV. Even though he'd killed the television, he had no reason to think that he was safe. For all he knew, there could be any number of other monsters waiting in the apartment to get him: in the fridge, the cooker, the electric toaster, even in the faucets in the bathroom. He wasn't waiting around for another attack; he'd rather take his chances on the streets of Luxor.

The one thing he wasn't going to do, however, was to go out wearing the suit that had been bleached out by the transition. He wanted to be as anonymous as possible out there, and an albino in a white suit was about as anonymous as Frosty the Snowman on the Fourth of July. He made a quick inventory of his double's wardrobe and picked out a baggy black suit, a dark-blue work shirt, and finally a white tie for just the slightest touch of flash. He dressed quickly, stowed the gun and wallet in the pockets of the borrowed suit, and, after a few moments' speculation whether the hostility to freaks that he'd seen on television extended to albinos, he completed the ensemble with a dark overcoat, a black fedora, and a pair of sunglasses he'd found in a drawer while he'd been going through the look-alike's stuff. After a final swift, hard belt of Scotch, he took a last look at the broken TV and let himself out of the apartment. As he was locking the door behind him, the blue face of a small balding man poked out of one of the apartments down the hall.

"What's going on? What's all the noise about."

"There's no noise."

"I heard shots."

Gibson pocketed his keys and started walking away. "I shot the TV because I didn't like the show. You never heard of that before?"

A fine drizzle was falling on the nighttime streets of Luxor as Gibson turned right out of the front door, pulled his hat down over his eyes, and started up the street at a brisk pace. He wanted to be as far away from the apartment building as fast as he could. There was always the chance that one of the neighbors had called the police. It didn't look to be the kind of building where gunshots were so commonplace that everyone ignored them. There was also the chance that if the streamheat had been monitoring the attack of the TV beast, they, too, might be on their way, if not to rescue him, at least to scrape his charred remains from the carpet. At the end of the block, he paused to listen, but he couldn't hear any sirens.

He was heading in the general direction of the big intersection with the golden statue that he'd seen on the ride in with Klein. Once there, though, which was about the limit of what he knew of the local geography, Gibson had little real idea of where he was going or what he was going to do. His flight from the apartment and its possible dangers had been so precipitate and so urgent that he hadn't bothered to stop and think through a plan. The best that he could come up with was to find a bar and use the breathing space to see what else he could learn about the ways of Luxor. After that, maybe a cheap hotel and a little time to think. He was screwed and he knew it, but the longer that he could put off accepting that unpleasant fact the better.

He turned the corner and kept on going. He could see the floodlit statue up ahead in the distance, and he continued in that direction. The traffic was fairly light in this largely residential area, and when he heard shouting and the gunning of car engines behind him, he reacted with the instincts of a paranoid and whirled round, his hand going toward the pistol in his pocket. He relaxed when he saw it was just a gang of teenagers in two convertibles, tops down despite the drizzle, drinking and hollering and generally carrying on. Then a beer can sailed past his head, bounced off the sidewalk, and was immediately followed by a torrent of abuse.

"Fuck you, albino bastard! You gonna die!"

"You gonna die, motherfucker freak!"

In unison the kids in both cars broke into a fast chant that drifted back to him as they accelerated on down the street.

"Die freak!"

"Die freak!"

"Die freak!"

It was only as they were speeding away that Gibson noticed the banner hanging out of the second car, a stylized purple eagle on a red background. So what were these juvenile idiots, junior normal nazis out for an evening of freak baiting? The problem appeared to be worse than he had imagined from just watching TV. Not only was he in another dimension and subject to electric-monster attack but he also seemed to have joined the ranks of the local "niggers." Gibson had been in Luxor for less than a day, and he was becoming rapidly convinced that it sucked.

After some more walking, he finally reached the intersection, and, as he stood wondering which way to go next, a police Batmobile came slowly round the statue, obviously making a routine inspection of anyone who was on the sidewalk. Gibson wanted to be the hell off the streets. The sooner he was in a warm, comfortable tavern with a drink in front of him the better. He'd seen a number of cabs cruising for fares but he'd hesitated over taking one. He still tended to believe Klein's statement that the streamheat operated one of the local cab lines, and the way his luck was running, he was quite likely to pick one of those and be right back in the frying pan again. On the other hand, though, he could wander around lost in the rain all night. It was time to take a chance and hail one and ask to be taken to the local equivalent of Times Square or whatever.

The first empty cab that he attempted to wave down went right past without stopping. At the last minute, he spotted a small purple-eagle sticker on the windshield, just like the teenagers' banner. Clearly this particular driver didn't stop for albinos. It was some minutes before another one came along, and Gibson spent the time becoming increasingly nervous. Fortunately this driver didn't share the prejudice against freaks. The cab pulled up beside Gibson and he climbed in.

"Where to?"

"I'm a stranger in town and I'm looking for a place to get drunk."

The driver didn't treat it as an at all unusual request. "You want it quiet or rowdy?"

Gibson grinned. "Oh, rowdy any time."

It wasn't just a matter of natural inclination. Gibson had decided rowdy would give him a good deal more natural cover. The driver set the cab in motion. "I'll drop you at the corner of Pomus and Schulman. That's pretty much the heart of the Strip."

Gibson nodded. "The Strip sounds good to me."

"Watch your money, though. The place is lousy with thieves."

"Isn't everywhere, these days?"

The driver nodded. "You said it, pal."

They passed yet another of the billboards with a giant picture of Jaim Lancer on it. Gibson wondered where the president stood on the matter of freak hatred. He suspected that the president was the kind that rode the fence, deploring it in public but tipping the wink to the local nazis in private. He had that kind of look about him.

Very soon they were passing through an area of gaudy neon

and busy sidewalks. Gibson felt a little more encouraged. This was more like it. The pulsing, rippling lights and their mirror images on the wet street were beacons of vibrant trashy humanity against a darkness that, from where Gibson was sitting, seemed increasingly cold, threatening, and polluted. Ever since he'd been a kid, Gibson had been drawn to the bright lights of big cities. They'd been both his strength and quite possibly a part of his downfall. Certainly they'd always been there, offering their comfort, winking and blinking and constantly renewing their tawdry promises, so no matter how many times he'd been stung or cheated or washed up and left for dead in the cold daylight, he always went back.

The driver turned in his seat. "You see anything you fancy in this sink of iniquity?"

Gibson stared out of the window at the passing show. "Yeah, a whole bunch of things."

What Gibson mainly saw were the crowds, and in their numbers he knew he had his best chance of safety. They moved along the sidewalks like the crowds in every red-light district he'd ever been in, strictly divided into two groups, the prey and the predators, the suckers and the players. The suckers always moved with a slow aimlessness, always looking for the forbidden thrills, always hoping and too stupid or too desperate to give up and go home, even when they must have realized that those thrills were just myth or imagined shadows. The predators only moved when they had to. With some, movement was a matter of open display, as with the prostitutes who swung their hips and lazily chewed their gum, or the corner cardsharps who flashed their cuffs and recited the soft come-on. Others merely waited in the shadows, like the smooth, watchful, well-fed pimps in their sharkskin and gold checking on their stables, or the nervous takeoff artists laying for the careless or the drunk and ready to melt away at the first approach of a cop. Streets like this were a beckoning refuge for anyone on the run or with a need to disappear. There were already so many criminals, marginals, and illegals living on them that an organic system of boltholes, hiding places, warnings, and alarms was firmly in place. Streets like the Luxor Strip might take no prisoners, but they also asked very few questions.

The driver pulled over to the curb. "I'll let you off here if that's okay."

Gibson squinted at the meter. If he was reading the numbers right, the fare was 3.75. Gibson had yet to learn the name of the smaller unit of UKR currency that was one-hundredth of a kudo. His reckoning must have been correct, because the driver seemed quite satisfied with his kudo-and-a-half tip.

As Gibson climbed out of the cab, the driver raised a hand. "You watch your ass now, you hear?"

Gibson grinned. "I will, don't worry." The driver didn't know just how carefully he would be watching his ass.

The first thing that Gibson heard was the sound of bebop: a tune that sounded uncannily like Charlie Parker's "C-Jam Blues" came bouncing from a nearby blue-lit doorway. Gibson's spirits immediately lifted. Luxor might be a fucked-up place, but if it had bebop, it couldn't all be bad. The temptation was to duck straight through the blue door and submerge himself in the music, but Gibson had a natural aversion to simply going into the first place he saw. He'd walk on down the block and check out more of what the Strip had to offer before he settled on somewhere; besides, a live band might well indicate that it was a nightclub behind the blue door, and Gibson had some serious thinking to do before he could let himself go. A friendly shot-and-beer joint would be more his speed, if indeed Luxor had such a thing. He suspected that they did, although he knew that he had to be prepared for friendliness to be just an illusion.

He couldn't read the neon signs, but the majority of their messages were loud and clear. Sex seemed once again to be the major selling point, and half the places that he passed featured some variation of striptease or girly show. On the other side of the street a blue neon woman with an hourglass figure and vibrant yellow hair towered three stories above the sidewalk, swinging her electric-light hips while her red bikini flashed on and off. When the bikini was in the off phase, pink nipples glowed in the center of her massive breasts. On the same sidewalk a gang of teenage boys shouldered their way through the slower-moving crowds with the nervous urgency of a gang on the prowl, obviously out of their own neighborhood but determined to play it tough in front of the more serious lowlifes who really operated on the Strip and called it home. In their black leather jackets, Hawaiian shirts, and black dungarees, they resembled the chorus from a revival of *West Side Story*. Gibson smiled to himself. What would they be getting next in this town, James Dean movies?

As he approached the next corner he spotted another group of people who seemed to be going against the general flow. A half-dozen hard-faced men in riding boots and field-green military-style uniforms were aggressively handing out leaflets, thrusting them into the hands of unwary passersby with intimidating looks that challenged the recipient to either refuse the flyer or try and hand it back if he dared. Gibson immediately recognized the emblem on their red arm bands. He was seeing altogether too much of the sinister purple eagle, and he quickly altered direction to give them the widest possible berth. A hooker in a red skirt slit to her thigh saw what he was doing and flashed him a fleeting smile of sympathy. Gibson had stopped believing in whores with hearts of gold a long time ago, but the smile gave him a moment of pause. Then he noticed that she, too, was wearing sunglasses after dark. Perhaps, under the thick pancake makeup, she was just a fellow albino expressing solidarity.

From the moment that he'd left the cab, Gibson had started noticing just how many genetic aberrations there were walking the streets of Luxor. Even allowing that there would be a higher proportion of freaks and misfits around a place like the Strip than maybe in other parts of the city, the numbers were startling. Gibson had spotted at least a dozen individuals with facial deformities in the space of two blocks, plus two more albinos and a beanpole of a man who had to be well over seven feet tall. The dwarfs were so numerous that they almost formed a second stratum on the sidewalk. The genetic damage in this dimension was completely out of control, and Gibson wished that the advocates of limited nuclear war back home could see what a bunch of dirty little bombs could do.

He came to a kiosk that sold newspapers, magazines, and tobacco, and he decided that it would be a good idea to stock up on cigarettes. The outside of the kiosk was protected from the weather by a layer of enameled tin signs, the kind that Gibson had seen in stores as a kid, and that they now sold in trendy antique boutiques to the kind of people who lived in apartments with exposed brick walls and Victorian furniture. It was the standard Luxor style of tits-and-ass advertising, and he probably wouldn't have given any of it a second glance, except that one of the well-developed and scantily clad blue babes was holding up a pack of Camels. Of course, the name was in the Luxor alphabet, but it was definitely a pack of Camels. The same tan, yellow, and brown pack, the same camel, and the same pair of pyramids and clump of palm trees in the background of the drawing. Gibson slowly shook his head: a different system of writing but an identical brand of smokes.

"I guess there's no telling with parallel worlds."

A fat man was taking his time over buying cigars, and Gibson had to wait. He glanced at the covers of the local tabloids. Luxor still had a lot of newspapers—as far as he could see, five in all. The headlines screamed unintelligibly, but Gibson could see from the pictures that, of the five papers on the rack, four had given their front pages over to a gruesome multiple murder. Huge color blowups of the bloody crime scene were positioned alongside smaller shots of a frightened pinhead being manhandled by police. A freak slaying appeared to be hot copy, and Gibson wondered why he hadn't seen the same story on TV. Was the press in Luxor so fast with its editions that the murder story had broken after he'd watched the news?

The fat man was through and it was Gibson's turn. "Three packs of Camel filters, please."

The man in the kiosk gave him a strange look. "Where you from, mister? Camel don't make a filter."

"So give me anything with a filter on it. I don't care."

The man treated him to a look like he was just one more crazy in a long day and tossed three packs of totally unfamiliar cigarettes onto the counter.

"Three kudos."

So a pack of cigarettes cost a kudo. That made life tidy.

Farther down the block, Gibson thought that he'd spotted his bar. The neon sign was elaborate, a foaming stein with suds running down the side, but as he turned into the entrance he ran straight into a burly bouncer in a black shirt and Tyrolean hat who made no attempt to get out of the way.

"You can't come in here."

Gibson still wasn't accustomed to being on the receiving end of a color bar.

"I just wanted a drink."

"So go down the street to the Radium Room. They serve your kind in there."

The Radium Room wasn't the most luxurious saloon that Gibson had ever been in, but for the moment it would suit his purpose. Nobody in the place seemed the kind to get inquisitive about a stranger who minded his own business. If he hadn't been told in front, he would have known immediately that the management had no reservations about serving mutations and also hiring them. The place was busy but not jammed, and at least a third of the clientele showed evidence of some kind of glitch in their genes. The bartender who asked him what he wanted had six fingers on each of her hands, and webs between the fingers.

It was then that Gibson made his second cultural error of the evening. "Scotch?"

"Huh?"

Clearly the term wasn't used in Luxor. He tried again. "Whiskey?"

"Why didn't you say so."

"I'm sorry. I'm from out of town. Could I get a beer back with that?"

"No problem."

Gibson pulled out the look-alike's wallet to pay for the drinks, and before he put it away, he took another look at the picture on the ID. A thought struck him. Could it be that the double was actually a parallel him? He didn't like the thought one bit and swallowed the shot of whiskey in one gulp.

"Jesus Christ!"

The bartender, who was still counting out his change, looked up sharply. "What's the trouble?"

"Nothing." He gestured to his now empty shot glass. "Why don't you do me again while you're still here?"

"You can put it away."

"It's been a rough day."

Gibson was wondering what, if indeed the double was his parallel in this dimension, would happen if the two of them met? Would they merely exchange pleasantries or would there be some hideous interface in which one or both of them were destroyed like matter and antimatter? Of course, the double wasn't an albino; maybe that would make a difference. A kind of sidebar idea jumped into his mind. If the streamheat's plan was really to swing some kind of substitution, the fact that he had come out of the transition as an albino may have seriously screwed things up. He sipped his second shot, hardly tasting it, and set the glass down on the bar. He took the whole parcel of thoughts that had been triggered by the picture in the wallet and, handling them with the mental equivalent of long tongs, consigned them to one of the deepest recesses of his mind. He should be concentrating on practical survival and concealing himself as far as he could in this red-light subworld of Luxor.

He took a deep breath to calm himself and clear his mind and then looked around the bar. He would probably be spending a lot of time in places like this over the next few days. The Radium Room appeared to be something of a pickup parlor. Gibson didn't know enough about the mores of Luxor to be able to tell if it was a swinging singles joint or a hooker bar, but he suspected the latter. He noticed that a woman a little way down the bar was looking in his direction. Taking the dim smoky light of the barroom into account, she actually didn't look too bad. Her close-cropped helmet of yellow-blond hair contrasted prettily with the blue of her skin, and her mouth, a slash of purple lipstick, pouted seductively. Gibson no longer had any doubts about how he'd handle getting close to a blue woman. To paraphrase Stephen Stills, love the color you're with.

The woman was coming through the crowd toward him. In her pencil skirt and low-cut blouse, she looked like a B-girl from some fifties gangster movies, and when she slid into the space at the bar beside him, he discovered that she had the matching, husky Lizbeth Scott voice.

"You wanna buy me a drink?"

Gibson smiled and signaled to the bartender. "Sure, anytime."

The woman's pout increased in provocation. "Are you alone?"

Gibson laughed. "You wouldn't believe how alone I am."

"My name's Zazsu."

Zazsu appeared to be a regular at the Radium Room. The bartender didn't bother to ask her what she was drinking, she simply set a green concoction in a conical glass in front of her and picked up some of Gibson's money. Zazsu sipped the green stuff through a clear plastic straw in a manner that seemed to be an open invitation to all manner of shadowy delights.

"Are you gonna tell me yours?"

"It's Joe."

Zazsu frowned. "Joe? That's a weird name. Are you from out of town?"

Gibson nodded. "Oh, yeah, I'm from out of town."

Zazsu came straight to the point.

"So I guess you don't know any girls in Luxor."

"Not a one."

"You looking for a good time?"

"I might be."

"I've got a place right near here. I could show you a real good time for a fifty."

"Is that a fact?"

Zazsu raised an eyebrow that seemed to indicate that time was money and he should make up his mind. "So, you wanna?"

Gibson hesitated. The offer was tempting, and even a little commercial creature comfort was preferable to the absolute isolation that he'd been feeling ever since Klein had left him alone in the apartment. As far as revealing his alien status, he was fairly confident he was on safe ground; the natives of Luxor seemed to believe that out-of-towners were capable of any gaucheness or stupidity. He was about to agree to Zazsu's offer when he happened to glance up. The smile froze on his face and the words stuck in his throat. Nephredana had just walked into the Radium Room and was heading directly for where he was standing. It was a somewhat different Nephredana from the first time he had seen her, with Yancey Slide outside Windemere's house in Ladbroke Grove, but there was no mistaking it was her. If nothing else, on high spike heels she was a head taller than most of the drinkers in the place. Back in London, she had been pure metal, the wet dream of any Megadeth fan; now she looked like a gun moll from some lost Robert Mitchum movie. As before, she was all in black, a sequined jacket like the skin of a vampire reptile over a sheath dress so tight that it gave no quarter, a wide-brimmed hat with a veil tilted at a piratical angle, and a pocket book over her shoulder big enough to hold a small arsenal of weapons. A hush fell and heads turned as she made her way determinedly through the crowd, and one dwarf actually dropped his drink.

She made short work of Zazsu. With a jerk of her thumb, and a rasp of that deep graveyard voice, she ordered the woman away. "Beat it, honey. This one's mine."

"Wait a minute . . ."

"I said beat it, bitch."

"I . . ."

"Now."

Nephredana raised the veil of her hat, and a pair of demon eyes exactly like Slide's were revealed. Zazsu immediately capitulated and moved quickly away, and Nephredana turned her attention to Gibson. Fortunately for him, she had dropped the veil again and the inhuman eyes were hidden.

"I would have thought you could have done better than that, Joe Gibson."

Gibson shrugged, trying his hardest to put on a careless, swashbuckling front even though on the inside he was on the verge of panic. "What can I say. I'm still getting orientated."

"Getting an orientation lesson from a twenty-kudo hooker?"

"She wanted fifty."

"Probably thought you were a rube."

Nephredana was the only person in the place who wasn't blue, but Gibson didn't think it was quite the moment to ask for an explanation. He glanced down the bar to where Zazsu appeared to be telling her troubles to a man wearing a silk suit with very wide shoulders whose long, straight hair was slicked back and tied in a ponytail. "The girl seems to be complaining to her pimp."

Nephredana also glanced down the bar. "I don't think we're going to have any trouble with him." She leaned across and said something to the bartender that Gibson didn't hear. Gibson, not quite convinced that there'd be no trouble, continued to keep one eye on the pimp while he tried to find out what Nephredana was doing there.

"I'm assuming that this isn't a chance meeting."

The bartender set two drinks in front of Nephredana. One looked like ouzo and the other crème de menthe. She poured one into the other, and the resulting cocktail came out resembling a glass of toxic waste. She drank half of it and then smiled at Gibson. "Of course it's not a chance meeting. Yancey figured it was time that you got out of the clutches of the streamheat."

"I may have already done that for myself."

"I wouldn't speak too soon."

"You think they're looking for me."

Nephredana swallowed the other half of the foul-looking drink and signaled to the bartender for the same again. "More likely they're waiting for you to come back dragging your tail behind you."

"And when I don't?"

"Then they'll come looking for you, if they still think you're useful to them."

"I hope I can manage to disappear before they get around to that. Unless of course Yancey Slide has other plans for me."

Nephredana mixed a second of the toxic concoctions. "Yancey doesn't have any plans for you. If you knew him better you'd be aware that Yancey doesn't exactly make plans, he just rides the flow. The only reason I'm here is because he wants you to come to a party."

Gibson blinked. This was the last thing that he had expected. "A party?"

"It's a very exclusive party. It's being given by one of the local power moguls."

"You want me to come right now?"

"Unless you want to stay here with the whores."

Gibson was becoming a little bemused. "No, no. I'll come to a party."

"You'll need a tux."

What the fuck was going on? "I don't have a tux. In fact, what you see is what I've got. I didn't exactly pack for this trip."

Nephredana started on her second industrial waste. "Actually, I took the liberty of picking one up for you. I think it'll fit."

Gibson shook his head. All this was a little overwhelming when added to the rest of the day.

"Okay, so let's go to this party."

It was while they were both finishing their drinks in preparation for leaving that Gibson noticed Zazsu's pimp coming through the crowd with a look of vindictive anticipation on his face. His hand was going to the breast pocket of the silk suit. It came out holding a straight-edge razor. Nephredana had her back to the man and saw nothing of this. Gibson opened his mouth to yell a warning but, in the same instant, she turned.

The pimp reached out to grab her arm. "I want to talk to you."

All Nephredana did was raise her right index finger. The man stopped dead in his tracks, and Gibson had never seen such an expression of pure terror as the one that came over the pimp's face. The razor dropped from his hand and clattered to the floor. He stood stock-still for a couple of seconds and then started to vibrate, as though in the grip of some violent palsy, all the time making small whimpering noises.

Nephredana glanced at Gibson. "In thirty seconds, he's going to have a fatal heart attack."

"You're going to kill him?"

"He pulled a razor on me, didn't he? Twenty seconds."

The pimp's face was going through progressively darkening shades of purple, and he was making noises as though he was about to swallow his tongue. The rest of the people in the bar stood silent and still, mesmerized by the spectacle of the vibrating pimp.

"Fifteen seconds."

Sweat was pouring down the pimp's face, and his eyes had rolled up into his head. One of his rings was shaken loose from his hand and bounced on the floor beside the razor.

"Ten seconds."

Somehow Zazsu seemed to break free from the spell that gripped the barroom. "Please! Don't kill him."

Nephredana looked at her pityingly. "Don't you whores ever learn? The asshole's probably better off dead. He's no use to you."

But she lowered her finger and the unfortunate pimp dropped to the floor like a puppet whose strings had been cut. The entire crowd in the barroom continued to stare as if hypnotized, except Zazsu, who crouched beside the man, sobbing and demanding that he speak to her.

Nephredana turned to Gibson. "Okay, let's get out of here."

Gibson had his hand in his pocket clutching the gun, but no one showed any signs of wanting to stop them from leaving. Indeed, the only sounds were the groans coming from the pimp on the floor and Zazsu's sobs. As he and Nephredana moved toward the door the customers stepped back like zombies opening a path for them.

The black Hudson was waiting at the curb outside the bar, gleaming with rain and reflected neon, apparently unchanged by its transition from dimension to dimension. A trio of punks were trying to peer in through the smoked windows but they scattered when Nephredana glared at them.

Gibson glanced back at the entrance to the Radium Room. "That was some trick you pulled in there."

Nephredana hurried round to the driver's door of the car. "You learn a few things over eighteen thousand years." She opened the door and slipped behind the wheel and leaned across to open the passenger door. "We shouldn't linger, though. The block I dropped on them will wear off in a minute or so."

Gibson climbed into the car and slammed the door. Nephredana eased the Hudson into gear and pulled away from the curb. Gibson took a last look at the Radium Room, half expecting an angry mob to come surging out of the door. "What did you do to that pimp anyway?"

Nephredana shrugged, concentrating on the traffic. "Just tweaked his nervous system."

"Was he really going to die?"

Nephredana nodded. "Oh, sure. In another five seconds if I hadn't stopped sticking it to him. The stupidity of prostitutes never ceases to amaze me. It's been the same since the invention of currency and it never changes. You'd think, after all this time, whores would come to realize that just because they're fucking for money, there's no need to give it all to a goddamned asshole of a man.''

Gibson made a mental note never to do anything that Nephredana didn't like. The idea of being vibrated into a heart attack didn't appeal to him at all.

Since there was no sign of either Slide or Yop Boy, Gibson could only assume that Nephredana had been sent with the wheels to fetch him to wherever the party was. He looked around the interior of the Hudson and discovered that there was something a little weird about it. It appeared to be a good deal larger than the outside of the car would warrant. Sure, it was a big, old-fashioned sedan, but on the inside it was about as spacious as a small RV. He surmised that it was a piece of demonic spatial trickery, and he was a little surprised at the ease with which he was coming to accept these things, things that just a few days earlier would have boggled his mind and maybe scared the hell out of him.

They seemed to be heading out of the city. After passing through the intersection with the gold statue, they took a broad avenue lined with soot-caked, leafless trees and equally dirty official-looking buildings. From the avenue, they came out onto a steel road and rail bridge across the river. This was the first that Gibson knew about Luxor having a river.

Nephredana turned on the radio and got something that sounded a lot like John Coltrane playing ''My Favorite Things.''

Gibson smiled. ''There's a lot of jazz in this town.''

Nephredana nodded. ''Luxor's a good town if you like saxophones.'' She pointed into the rear of the car. ''Your tux is back there, in the box on the seat; why don't you climb into it.''

''Right now, while we're driving?''

''Don't tell me you've never changed your clothes in a moving car.''

''Sure, but . . .''

''So get to it. You don't want to arrive with your party clothes under your arm.''

Gibson clambered into the back of the car and spent the next few minutes struggling into his evening suit and remembering how the back of a moving car is always a less than ideal dressing room. Now and then he glanced up to see if Nephredana was watching him in the rearview mirror. She didn't appear to be, and he could only imagine that after eighteen thousand years she had seen enough male nudity to be no longer interested. He managed to dress himself completely with the single exception of the tie. Gibson had never learned how to tie a formal bow.

Nephredana glanced back. "How are you doing?"

He scrambled back into the front passenger seat. "Okay, apart from the tie. I never was able to get the hang of these suckers."

Nephredana looked at him as though he were an idiot. "I'll do it for you when we get there. You'd better stash that gun of yours in the glove compartment. They may have metal detectors at the entrance to this bash and it'd be embarrassing if you were caught with a piece."

Gibson's hand went unconsciously to the pistol in the waistband of his tuxedo. He had transferred it from the pocket of the look-alike's suit while he'd been changing.

"How did you know I had a gun?"

"You telegraphed the fact when that pimp came at us in the bar, and I assumed that you'd keep it with you."

"No magic?"

"No magic."

"I'd be happier if I had it with me after all that's happened."

Nephredana treated him to a look that brooked no further argument. "Stash it."

Gibson caught the look and did as he was told.

They were now in the suburbs of Luxor, which proved to be quite a contrast to the inner city. Neat houses sat amid well-manicured gardens with the smug assurance of the safe and affluent, and Gibson suspected that genetic defectives probably didn't last too long around these neighborhoods.

Nephredana noticed him staring out of the window.

"So how do you like the Kamerian dream?"

"Looks like any well-heeled suburb. Same shit that I ran away from when I was a kid wanting to be Elvis Presley."

"It's much the same as what you have back in your dimension. They're just hanging on to appearances while they slowly sink into the mire. All the real money's being spent on the cold war with the Hind-Mancu with less and less left over for education or social programs. Even their consumer society is only sustained by impossibly massive deficit financing. Behind these facades, they're up to their necks in debt and stone terrified."

"Who are the Hind-Mancu?"

Nephredana raised an eyebrow. "How much did your stream-heat friends fill you in about Luxor, UKR, and this dimension in general?"

"Next to nothing, like with most everything else."

Nephredana sighed. "Seems like it might be a good idea if I ran down a little background to you before we get to this party. We can't have you looking and sounding like a complete idiot."

"I appreciate that."

Nephredana smiled. "Okay, so the first basic you have to grasp is that this dimension missed out on having World War II."

Gibson nodded. "That much they told me. Seems like it made quite a difference."

"Quite a difference is a hell of an understatement. Something like that can radically change the whole face of a twentieth-century parallel."

"It doesn't look so different to me."

"That's because the shit still has a long way to trickle; these divergences take time. You won't recognize this place in a hundred years, if indeed it survives that long. As late as 1900, your world and this one were running on pretty much the same tracks. Even the factors that brought about World War I were in place in both dimensions. Things only started to alter once the killing got started. Either they were crazier here or they had a higher threshold for exhaustion. Whichever it was, they didn't call it quits after four years. They really hung in and went on slaughtering each other until well into the twenties. And not only slaughtering each other on the battlefield, either. They started to get real sophisticated. By 1921, they'd learned how to bomb cities from the air and they'd even discovered how to set off firestorms. When they finally ran out of steam in 1926, the local equivalent of the European nations had wiped each other out, an entire generation of young men was gone and a good percentage of everyone else as well, and, if that wasn't bad enough, in the two years after the war, a series of epidemics decimated another third of the surviving population. National economies were shot to hell, and the Europe here was a thousand-mile strip of ruins, famine, and disease. No industry, no agriculture, colonial empires gone, precious little government; in fact, the very structures of whole societies and cultures had been ground down to nothing, nothing but grim, ragged-assed, exhausted anarchy."

Nephredana shifted gear and set the Hudson roaring past a slower-moving family car hogging the middle of the road. She drove with an assured contempt for other drivers that Gibson assumed was a result of having superior demon reflexes and also what had to be a superior car. When she'd completed the maneuver, she resumed her history lecture.

"With Europe effectively gone, the main centers of power became polarized between the League of Hind-Mancu, which you can think of as a combination of China and India, and the UKR, which is virtually the USA, Canada, and Mexico rolled into one. Neither of them had played more than a token role in the war and it was pretty much inevitable that these two superpowers should become natural adversaries."

"Inevitable?"

"You always find that, when a world is divided between two megastates, they have to start snarling at each other sooner or later. In this instance, the snarling went on for quite a while before they really got to it. Separated, as they were, by an ocean in one direction and the devastation of Europe in the other, overt hostilities didn't start immediately. Instead, they sank ponderously into a cold war of unbelievable rigidity and ignorance, like a pair of bull mammoths being swallowed by the muskeg, tusks locked and too stupid to disengage and scramble out. Every so often there would be an incident or proxy brush war, but the two superpowers were so cumbersome and inefficient that they tended, despite the crippling sums of money that both sides spent on weaponry, to keep it down to threats and posturing, and to avoid direct confrontation for three full decades. Then came June 5th, 1957."

"What happened on June 5th, 1957?"

"The Kamerians touched off their first A-bomb. Since then, there have been no less than five nuclear flurries. The last one was four years ago."

"How come there's any of this dimension left standing if they're so free with the nukes?"

Nephredana's expression indicated that she never ceased to marvel at the stupidity of human beings.

"Because they only invented small nuclear bombs. Just a dozen or so kilotons. They delivered them by primitive chemical-fuel rockets or turbo-prop bombers."

There was a new tune on the radio. Whoever was playing trumpet sounded a lot like Miles Davis.

Gibson stared through the windshield, noticing that the rain appeared to be stopping. "I guess they have the consolation that they were spared Hitler."

"Actually the Hind-Mancu managed to fill that slot. They're pretty nasty today, but they went for it real good back in the sixties under Govendar. They became highly efficient at exterminating minorities and political enemies and built camps that quite rivaled Auschwitz or anything created by the Khmer Rouge under Pol Pot.''

''What about this country, the UKR?''

''I guess the best thing you can say about the Kamerians is that they always stop short of going all the way. I wouldn't say that it's because they're intrinsically better people, it's more that they've got this hang-up about wanting to think of themselves as the good guys. Lancer has locked up a few million political prisoners, but they still think of him as the defender of freedom. Spying on each other and snitching to the authorities has become a way of life, and they call it patriotism. Right now they seem to be working up a full-scale hate against all the genetic freaks and mutations that have been appearing since they went nuclear.''

Gibson scowled. ''I already ran into some of that.''

Nephredana nodded. ''Oh, yeah, of course. I was forgetting, you're an albino here. Well, you can count on one thing, it'll get worse before it gets better.''

A thought struck Gibson. ''Did they ever invent rock 'n' roll in this dimension?''

Nephredana shook her head. ''Not that I know of. Why? Are you thinking of doing it for them?''

''If I'm stranded here, I'm going to have to make a living somehow.''

''So you're thinking of applying for a gig as Elvis?''

Gibson grinned. ''Why not? I could use the money.''

''I'm not sure the Kamerians are ready for an albino rock idol. It's a few years between Chuck Berry and Johnny Winter.''

Gibson deflated. ''I hadn't thought about that.''

''I think you ought to.''

Gibson did and realized that he didn't have a prayer with the levels of prejudice the way they were. It seemed that in this dimension he was fucked on every level. Outside the car, the overcast was breaking up into ragged cloud and the moon was showing through. The moonlight brought an intense sadness, and Gibson was stabbed by a sudden pang of desperation. He didn't want to be in this dimension, in a world of demon madness and dangerous TV sets. He wanted out of the whole freaking mess. Would he ever be home again among the safe and familiar? Even the IRS would seem comforting compared to all this.

After about forty-five minutes, they were in what appeared to be a private enclave of Luxor's most wealthy. They were driving along quiet, well-paved roads, past neat box hedges and high walls, and, at regular intervals along the road, they passed imposing gateways with high wrought-iron gates supported by granite pillars. By far the majority of these entrances were watched over at least by bulky, old-fashioned, closed-circuit TV cameras if not by actual armed, private security guards. A police Batmobile went past them going in the opposite direction, and the other cars that they saw were big and glossy. Beyond the walls and gates, Gibson was able to catch brief glimpses of solid stately mansions with grand porticos and warm lights shining out over immaculately tended grounds. If the economy of the UKR was in ruins, it didn't seem to be affecting this particular social stratum. When he mentioned this, Nephredana just shrugged.

"It's the same all over; the really rich stay rich, no matter what the situation."

"I take it that we're getting close to where we're going?"

"Pretty close."

"You think it might be an idea to fill me in on what this party's all about?"

Nephredana nodded. "It's being thrown by some local mogul. His name's Verdon Verster Raus and he's sixty-five years old and childless. He's been married seven times and his current wife of four months is a TV soap starlet called Immudia Deamorning, whose main claim to fame seems to be that she regularly drops out of her clothes on a show called *The Dexters*. She may not be around for too long, though. Current society gossip doesn't expect her to last out the year. This Raus is among the wealthiest and most powerful men in the UKR, and he owns a huge chunk of the country's media. According to current estimates, in addition to being the major stockholder in one of the two national TV networks, he also controls one hundred and twenty-seven newspapers and close to the same number of TV stations."

Gibson whistled softly. "You guys move in the big leagues."

Nephredana smiled wryly. "There aren't too many places where Yancey Slide can't get in."

"This Raus, what's he like? How does he use his power?"

"Raus? Oh, he's right in there pitching. When Jaim Lancer first became President, Raus was an ardent supporter. Then, four years ago, they had a falling-out."

"What happened?"

"There was something called the Gulf of Borg Incident where a Hind-Mancu naval cruiser shot down a Kamerian commercial airliner, claimed they thought it was a bomber. Lancer, with an uncharacteristic show of restraint, contented himself with tit for tat, taking out one of their aircraft carriers. It was probably the smartest thing to do under the circumstances, but Raus started screaming that Lancer was soft on the yellow devils and, since then, he's dedicated himself to doing everything he can to unseat the president."

"Raus sounds like Citizen Kane with a bad attitude."

They were approaching a pair of massive gates, and lights were visible beyond them. Nephredana began to slow the car.

"Yeah, he really fancies himself, but so far he hasn't achieved that much. Lancer is still in power, big as ever. In fact, this party is supposed to be a kind of show of strength by anti-Lancer forces. But we're there, so you'll have to figure out the rest for yourself."

Raus's mansion was by the far the most lavish of the homes that Gibson had seen on the ride out of town. The huge sprawling structure had been constructed in a bizarre cocktail of styles that was part *Gone with the Wind*, part Palace of Versailles, and part Castle Dracula. It seemed somehow fitting for the home of some latter-day robber baron. Sections of the building had been floodlit for the party, and these were reflected in the lake that ran along one side of the house, on which fountains played in the beams of more multicolored lights. Marquees of various sizes had been erected on the lawns in front of the main house, and the size of the crowds that were already moving among them indicated that when Verdon Raus entertained, he did it on a grandiose scale.

No less than a dozen burly men guarded the entrance to the Raus estate. Four large bouncers in shiny tuxedos checking the guests' invitations were backed up by eight uniformed security guards carrying the same kind of large-caliber weapons that were used by the police on the streets of downtown Luxor. Gibson smiled to himself. Whatever the dimension, it seemed that bouncers always looked the same.

He glanced at Nephredana. "You got the backstage passes?"

She looked at him, winked, and produced a pair of engraved invitations. "I've got everything."

She handed the invitations through the window to one of the bouncers. The invitations were checked against a list, and then the car was waved forward. As they drove down the long gravel driveway, they passed an area of less well-tended grass and scrubby bushes where, behind a deep moat and low retaining wall, a family of six gray rhinoceroses, two adults and two babies, stared balefully at the revelers. Gibson decided that a private herd of rhino, even a small one like this, had to be a pinnacle in displays of conspicuous wealth. At the head of the driveway, a carhop waved them down.

Nephredana stopped the car. She leaned over and deftly tied his bow tie. "This is it, Joe. Take a deep breath and smile nicely; we're going to mix it up with the jet set."

The White Room

DR. KOONING TOOK off her glasses, and for her it was a gesture of triumph. "So basically you wanted to sleep with Elvis Presley?"

Gibson shook his head wearily. "I never even met Elvis."

"But in your dreams you wanted him."

"I wanted to be him, I wanted to be Elvis Presley. That's a very different thing. You shrinks have sex on the brain."

Her gaze was level. "If it seems that way, it's probably just a reflection of the patients we treat."

Gibson glared. "I've really had enough of this shit."

"You seem unusually hostile today."

"I do?"

"Yes, you do."

"Maybe that's because I don't think you understand the motivations of an artist."

"An artist?"

Gibson lost his temper. "Yes, a fucking artist."

He'd promised himself that he wouldn't do it, no matter how much Kooning tried to provoke him, but he could feel his control slipping away.

Kooning smiled her irritating smile. "But you're not an artist, are you, Joe? You're only an artist in your fantasy. I think we've already established that."

Gibson silently cursed himself. He had run slap into the essential Catch-22 of his situation. He couldn't take the high ground on the strength of what he'd been because, as far as Kooning was concerned, he had never been anything.

She was leaning forward in her chair. "I think we should talk about this, don't you, Joe?"

Chapter Nine

YANCEY SLIDE WAS standing by himself at the bottom of the gentle grass slope that led down to the lake, smoking one of his thin black cheroots. But it was a somewhat different Yancey Slide from the individual that Gibson had seen in Ladbroke Grove. The gunslinger garb had been replaced by smooth, lounge-lizard evening dress, a white tuxedo jacket over black pants and a purple cummerbund, that made him look like a disreputable James Bond. Only the black sunglasses remained, concealing the frightening demon eyes. His hair was slicked back, and Gibson was amused to notice that his bow tie was undone, hanging loose. Maybe, even in eighteen thousand years, Slide hadn't learned to tie one, either. Slide also wasn't blue; like Nephredana, he had retained his white-boy demon pallor.

As Gibson and Nephredana approached, his back was toward them. He seemed to be staring thoughtfully out across the mirror-smooth water, but while they were still a few yards away, he appeared to sense them and turned. "So you brought him?"

Even though the demon eyes were hidden, Gibson still felt a definite chill when Slide looked at him. Nephredana made a sweeping gesture that seemed to present Gibson for Slide's approval. "He was already getting into trouble with the whores on the Strip."

It was happening again and Gibson wasn't having any. He wasn't prepared to be treated as a specimen any longer, and he quickly took a step forward. "Good evening, Mr. Slide."

Slide smiled and his dark glasses flashed with reflections of the party lights. He seemed to sense what Gibson was feeling. "Good evening, Mr. Gibson. It was nice of you to come at such short notice."

"It was nice of you to send the lady to fetch me."

Slide laughed. "Oh, the lady was very keen on the idea herself."

Gibson's eyebrows climbed. "She didn't mention that to me."

Nephredana shook her head. "Ignore him, Joe. He's just pushing your buttons."

Slide removed the cigar from his mouth. "I expect you could use a drink after your trip out here."

Gibson nodded cautiously. He trusted this affable new playboy version of Slide even less than the sinister longrider in Ladbroke Grove. "You're right, I could definitely use a drink."

Slide indicated a nearby floodlit marquee.

"Shall we walk?"

They started up the slope, away from the lakeside. Now it was Slide's turn to make a sweeping gesture. It took in all of the surrounding estate.

"So what do you think of Castle Raus, Joe?"

"I'm impressed, but I'm also wondering what I'm doing here."

Slide seemed to be working overtime at the demonic charm. "Doing here? You're my guest, Joe. I thought, after all that you'd been through, you deserved a little R and R."

"You won't take offense if, after all that I've been through, I don't absolutely buy that."

Slide shot him a sly look. "You don't believe that I could only want you to have a good time?"

"Why don't you just come right out and tell me what you really want with me."

"I hate to disappoint you, Gibson, but, right now, I don't want anything."

"You deny that there's something about me that interests you?"

"Well, sure you interest me. You got a whammy count on you higher than I ever seen on a human."

Gibson sighed. "An aura like a black cloud?"

Slide smiled and nodded. "Your mojo's rising so fast, boy, it should be making your head spin."

His whole accent had changed, switching from tuxedo velvet to the grate and rasp of all the way down and funky. Gibson was aware that he was being jived by a demon, but jive talk was better than no talk at all, and Gibson even had a strange feeling that Slide might be telling him the truth, albeit in a weirdly oblique manner.

"It's certainly making my head spin." He had to agree with that. "Trouble is, it seemed to me that any mojo I had was on a strictly down grade."

Slide looked at him knowingly. "That's because you're back-pedaling with it as fast as you can, hoping it'll go away, but it ain't gonna, so you'd best accept that you're on the rise and start taking bets on how high you'll go before the fall."

Gibson didn't like the sound of the word "fall." "You want to put any of that into plain English?"

Slide let out an impatient hiss. "That's as plain as it gets, boy. You want it any more plain, and I'll just have to assume you've been hanging with the streamheat for too long and you're beyond redemption. Why don't you just get drunk and enjoy the party? It'll all come to you in time."

They were almost at the entrance to the marquee and moving into the thick of Raus's guests. Despite the fact that everyone with the apparent exception of him, Nephredana, and Slide were rich shades of aqua and turquoise, and the styles of clothing, particularly among the women, were odd to the point of alien, the party was of a kind that Gibson instantly recognized. The guests had obviously gone to a lot of trouble to convince themselves that they were the cream of Luxor society. Back home, they'd confidently expect their pictures to appear in the next issues of *Vanity Fair*, *Interview*, or *New York* magazine. He found it strangely comforting to know that pretension hardly varied from dimension to dimension, and he discovered he didn't need a scorecard to help him spot the stereotypes. Society painters escorted politicians' wives; dress designers, hairdressers to the stars, TV actresses, and real-estate speculators ran in whooping packs; celebrity newscasters squired prominent lesbians; racecar drivers and teenage starlets carried out intimate investigations of each other in dark corners, as did fashion models and merchant bankers, while women who wrote sex novels avoided their lawyer husbands, and men and women with no claim to fame apart from an accident of birth making them heirs to legendary fortunes kept up a stream of inane chatter. Oh, yes, Gibson knew this bunch. The smart set had invaded too many of his dressing rooms and taken over too many parties thrown for him back in the old days. Even though he'd been a peripheral part of it for a while, Gibson had never understood and certainly never liked high society. He had never appreciated their absolute certainty that they had a right to be there, their condescension, their bland belief in themselves and their value systems. Above all, he loathed their arrogant stupidity. What was the old MC5 war cry from the sixties? "I see a lot of honkies sitting on a lot of money telling me they're the high society . . ." Among the lesser faux pas along the downward spiral of his career had been the times when, at the top of his not inconsiderable voice, he'd informed whole rooms full of the social crowd how he held them in total contempt and wished that they'd fuck off, stop drinking his booze, and leave him the fuck alone.

A woman walked by him in a dress that seemed to be a spiral of stiffened lace that followed a strategic track up her body. In one hand she held the leash of a small, white, poodlelike dog. On her other arm there was a short man in a purple-and-white striped suit, a dyed-pink Beatle haircut, and oversize, white-rimmed sunglasses. It seemed that, in this dimension, the parallel Andy Warhol was alive and well.

Inside the marquee, Slide made straight for the bar and Gibson followed close behind. White-coated waiters were pushing a sparkling white wine that was probably the local equivalent of champagne, but Slide steered Gibson past them. "Just leave it to me, that stuff's not fit to drink."

He caught a bartender's attention. "I'd like two doubles from Mr. Raus's private reserve."

The bartender gave Slide a look as though he had just spoken the most obscene blasphemy and implacably shook his head. "I'm not authorized to pour from Mr. Raus's private stock."

Slide slowly leaned across the bar. "Do you know who I am, kid?"

The bartender shook his head a second time. "No, sir, I don't know who you are, but I assure you it wouldn't make any difference. I have strict instructions not to serve anyone from Mr. Raus's private stock unless he personally orders it."

Slide lowered his sunglasses a fraction and treated the bartender to the briefest glimpse of what was behind them. "I think Mr. Raus would want us to drink his finest booze if he was here, don't you?"

The bartender turned pale, his eyes glazed over, and he answered with the dull monotone of a zombie. "I understand and I quite agree with you, sir."

Moving as though in a trance, he went to the back of the bar and returned with a bottle with a gold label that carried three initials, presumably the Raus monogram in the local script. He slowly and carefully poured Slide a double shot and then did the same for Gibson and Nephredana. Gibson took a first experimental sip, and his face broke into a blissful smile.

"Damn but that's good."

Slide also looked pleased. "Isn't it just?"

Nephredana, on the other hand, put herself above all this rapture. She turned disdainfully to the bartender. "Put a shot of yerlo in it, will you?"

Gibson watched in horror as the zoned-out bartender topped of Nephredana's glass with a clear spirit that turned cloudy as it hit the whiskey. He winced at the defiling of the whiskey. "Are you crazy?"

Slide grinned at Gibson. "She cultivates a terminal philistinism where booze is concerned. I think she does it to irritate me."

Nephredana tasted the mess and seemed satisfied. "You're irritated, therefore you are, Yancey."

Gibson tried not to think about Nephredana's drink as he tasted Raus's private stock a second time. It was whiskey, no mistake about that, but unlike any whiskey that Gibson had ever tasted in his own dimension. It was a kissing cousin to a single-malt Scotch but certainly not the same. All he knew for sure was that it was truly excellent, more than likely a quarter of a century in the cask excellent. Slide might have ulterior motives for befriending him, but he sure as hell knew how to show a stranger a good time.

A flashbulb went off nearby and momentarily distracted Gibson from the whiskey. There were a number of photographers cruising the crowd, no doubt looking for shots for tomorrow's society pages and gossip columns. He guessed paparazzi had to be expected at a party thrown by a media mogul. He was thankful that no photographer here would have any interest in him. His face meant nothing here in Luxor, and that was a welcome relief. More than once in the past he'd had problems with photographers. The worst incident had been the time when he'd been fined five hundred bucks after beating one up outside of the Roxy in LA. When they'd dragged him off the man, the LAPD hadn't been particularly gentle, and he wound up with seven stitches in his head and a much too intimate knowledge of the choke hold.

It surprised him that Slide didn't seem the least bit perturbed by the presence of cameras at the party. Gibson would have thought that a demon might object to being photographed. Maybe they didn't come out on film, like vampires didn't appear in mirrors.

Slide finished his drink and placed the glass on the bar. The bartender looked as though he wanted to refill it, but Slide shook his head and turned to the other two. "Let's move on to the main building. I think we're out with the B-list here."

They started walking toward where French windows opened out on a broad terrace that overlooked the lake. The crowds became even thicker as they approached the house itself, and Gibson started to realize just how big the party was. There had to be close to fifteen hundred people spread out around the estate.

Gibson glanced questioningly at Slide. "Are all these people actually against the president?"

Slide looked at him blankly. "What?"

Gibson realized that he wasn't explaining himself. "On the way out here, Nephredana told me that Raus was throwing this party as a kind of demonstration of support for his campaign to dump Lancer. I was just wondering if all these people could really want to get rid of the president."

Slide laughed and shook his head. "Hell, no, ninety percent of this bunch are just here for the party. Raus's newspapers and TV stations may claim different tomorrow, but most of these fools have come out for the booze and the food and to see and be seen and get drunk and get laid and all the other things people go to parties for. What you do have, though, is a serious gathering of the real anti-Lancer forces. They're probably up in some smoke-filled room right now plotting his downfall."

"Is that why you're here?"

Slide halted and looked hard at Gibson. "When are you going to stop believing that I'm a player in all this?"

Gibson also halted. He had seen what Slide and Nephredana could do to humans that annoyed them, and he was a little scared that he had gone too far.

"It's just hard to believe that, being what you are, you could avoid being a player."

"Did you ever think that, being what I am, I'd hardly want to be a player?"

That seemed to settle the matter for the moment, and the three of them walked on in silence, up the steps and in through the French windows.

Raus had clearly ordered his architects to go for breathtaking. Beyond the French windows, Gibson found himself in a huge cavernous hall. He imagined that he had been in other places that were as overbearingly impressive, but he couldn't think of one outside of the Vatican or Radio City. As with the exterior of the house, though, the hall suffered from wild clashes of style: rococo gold was positioned cheek by jowl with the smooth geometry of deco steel, and the quasi-Michaelangelo fresco that arched across the vaulted ceiling came into serious conflict with the stark lines of the postmodern staircase that led to the upper levels.

As they entered the hall, Slide and Nephredana paused to speak to a small Oriental man with a black patch covering one eye and a face crisscrossed by old dueling scars. Gibson wondered if he was a local or another kind of demon, but since Slide made no attempt at introductions, Gibson carried on by himself, expecting the other two to catch up with him when they were ready.

At one end of the grand hall, a trio was playing smooth lounge jazz and twenty or so couples were dancing. The singer/piano player sounded like Nat King Cole. It wasn't exactly Gibson's kind of music, but he moved closer for a better look. A waiter passed by with canapés on a tray. Gibson, realizing that he hadn't eaten in God knew how long, grabbed two or three. Forgetting to eat was one of the quickest ways to end the evening in a helpless alcoholic stupor. The trio didn't hold his attention for long. They were about as bland as one might expect at an event like this. Gibson started looking around the huge hall. Raus had by no means thrown all of the mansion open to his guests. Entrances to corridors were roped off and guarded by more tuxedoed bouncers and, on the staircase, another team of security vetted those who came and went. It seemed that you had to be a special super-VIP guest to make it to the upper levels.

Gibson glanced back at Slide and Nephredana, but they were still talking to the man with the eye patch. He wondered what had become of Yop Boy. Had he been left back in some other dimension, or was it simply that he didn't get to go to parties? Gibson knew it was a mistake to treat these *idimmu* lightly. He had only seen the mildest, sleight-of-hand displays of their power, and what they might be able to do when they really stretched out hardly bore thinking about. He had to resist being lulled by Slide's cowboy charm and Nephredana's aloof cool and keep on telling himself that these were two dangerous entities. Gibson took another look at the pair. What were they to each other, lovers, partners, running mates, master and concubine? Slide seemed to call the shots, but Nephredana's attitude was hardly subservient. Maybe it was a mistake to even attempt to judge them by human standards.

The train of thought was derailed by the whisper that quickly went round that Verdon Raus himself was coming down to mingle with the lesser mortals, and an outbreak of jockeying for position started at the foot of the stairs in front of the bouncers and the red velvet ropes.

To judge from the size of his escort and the care with which they guarded him, Raus might well have been the president. First down the stairs were a half-dozen security agents—slick, well-groomed young men carrying bulky walkie-talkies and presumably with guns under their dinner jackets. Raus followed, surrounded by a knot of people made up of beautiful young women and hard-faced, middle-aged men. The immaculate blond on his arm was presumably his current wife, the TV star, but there were seven or eight equally attractive and slightly younger women behind her who looked as though they'd be more than willing to step into her shoes the moment that she fell from favor. The men all had the assured veneer of accustomed power. Most were in dinner jackets, but there was also a sprinkling of military dress uniforms and one high-ranking police officer in blue and gold. Raus himself was one of those small Napoleonic men—squat, broad-shouldered, with splayed feet, the kind who walked leaning forward with his hands clasped behind his back and his jaw thrust out pugnaciously.

As the entourage made its way down into the hall, a sudden commotion erupted over on the other side of the stairs. Someone was yelling. "This is the palace of abominations!"

Nat King Cole faltered in the middle of a tune that sounded uncommonly like "Anything Goes," and half the room made ready to drop to the marble floor. A flurry of gunfire seemed to be expected at any second. Gibson tensed with the rest figuring this was the way they did things in Luxor. The yelling continued.

"Raus! You are the servant of Balg and you will die in hell!" Gibson blinked. Who the hell was Balg?

It was one of those slow-motion moments. Gibson could see the man who was doing the shouting. He was one of those nonentities who are never noticed in a crowd until the day they go ballistic. The downstairs bouncers were converging on him, hands outstretched in grimly professional desperation, getting to him before he could pull a gun. On the staircase, Raus's own bodyguards were turning, closing on him to protect him with their bodies. The man struggled to reach Raus.

"Abomination! Slave of Balg!"

Nephredana was beside Gibson and he quickly turned. "Who or what is Balg?"

Nephredana shook her head. "Later."

The bouncers were on the man and he was going down under a half-dozen of them. It seemed that, after all, he was a shouter rather than a shooter. The party on the staircase waited until the weirdo had been dragged away, and then they resumed their downward progress as though nothing had happened. Nat King Cole started up again. It was a slightly shaky start, but he, too, quickly resumed business as usual. It was around then that Gibson noticed that the man immediately behind Raus and slightly to his right looked exactly like Sebastian Rampton. Gibson stiffened. It had to be him—there was no mistaking the round Heinrich Himmler glasses, the stooped shoulders, and the thin, pale face. How in hell could the most suspect of the Nine be here in another dimension and apparently on intimate terms with one of its most powerful men?

Nephredana must have noticed his reaction. "What's wrong?"

Gibson answered without thinking. "I thought I saw someone I knew."

"Who?"

"Sebastian Rampton."

Nephredana turned and beckoned to Slide, who was still talking to the individual with the dueling scars. "You better hear this."

Slide detached himself from the conversation and came over to where they were standing. "Interesting guy, that. He's the Hind-Mancu ambassador. Made his name during the suppression of the Viet Minh back in the sixties."

Nephredana quickly interrupted him. "Gibson thinks he saw Sebastian Rampton in the group around Raus."

Yancey Slide adjusted his sunglasses. "No shit." He peered at Gibson. "Are you sure it was him and not a parallel from this dimension?"

For the life of him, Gibson didn't know why he'd blurted it out to Nephredana in the first place. Had she seen his reaction to seeing the man who looked like Rampton and hit him with some sort of influence? It was too late now, though; the damage was done and he could only go along. "I really can't be sure. I only had a fleeting glimpse but it certainly looked like him. Could the streamheat have maybe brought him here?''

Slide shrugged. ''It's possible. You can expect virtually anything from a people that had nuclear weapons in the early seventeenth century.''

This last remark took Gibson completely by surprise. ''Say what?''

Now Slide was looking surprised. ''Nobody told you the history of your traveling companions?''

Gibson was right off balance again. ''It seems that nobody tells me anything if they can possibly help it.''

Slide was thoughtful. ''Even if this Rampton you saw was a parallel from here, I still don't like the fact that he's so close to Raus. Anyone with his makeup is going to be up to no good.''

''You know Rampton?''

Slide nodded. ''Oh, yes, I know Rampton.'' He turned to Nephredana. ''Listen, I think I'm going to talk to Raus and see what all this is about.''

''What do you want me to do?''

''Stay with Gibson. You might fill him in about the streamheat. Let him know what kind of people he's been fucking with.''

Slide walked quickly away and disappeared into the crowd. Gibson looked expectantly at Nephredana.

She took a deep breath. ''Let's go and get a drink. I see I'm going to have to continue your education.''

They made their way to the nearest bar, and when they both had drinks in front of them, Nephredana started into the story.

''The people you call the streamheat come from a dimension where South and Central America, and not Europe, made the great leap forward. Up until the end of the fourteenth century, their history was running pretty much parallel to that of both your dimension and this one, but, from that point on, events began deviating fast. It all started in 1427 with the Emperor Izcoatl in Mexico. Izcoatl was something of a degenerate, even by the standards of Aztec royalty, but he had this thing about science, and driven by his relentless goading—and, believe me, Izcoatl could goad—his people not only managed to discover the wheel, but really went the distance in thinking through its possible applications. Just three years later, they stumbled across gunpowder and after that, they were off and running. During the next ten years, Izcoatl pushed his empire as far as Texas in the north and Rio de Janeiro in the south. Selective breeding of the northern bison gave him an effective substitute for the horse and, when iron-ore deposits were found in the equivalent of southeastern Brazil, and the Aztecs learned the trick of smelting, there was no stopping them. Izcoatl and his heirs were well on their way to becoming masters of all the Americas.''

Gibson was intrigued by the way Nephredana managed to make six-hundred-year-old events sound like they had happened just yesterday.

"Around 1500, the Europeans started showing up, but Montezuma, who was emperor by then, was ready for them, and they were never able to establish a beachhead on the continent. The threat from across the Atlantic, however, really galvanized Aztec science. In less than seventy years, they had electricity, the internal-combustion engine, and powered flight and were taking their first shots at splitting the atom.''

Gibson whistled. "You're putting me on?''

Nephredana shook her head. "Not a bit of it. You can't imagine what can be achieved in a state run by an absolute, life-and-death autocrat when the motivation's there. And remember something else: All this time they were still practicing the same sun-worshiping, human-sacrificing religion that they'd had when they were living in mud huts, only it had now grown to truly epic proportions. You should have seen the Great Solstice Festival of 1577. They snuffed a quarter of a million people at that four-day bash. Now that's what you call motivation.''

"You make it sound like you were there.''

Nephredana sighed. "I was. I was having an affair with a fighter pilot from Tenochtitlán at the time, but after that slayfest I had to dump him. Too much blood even for me.''

"So what happened next?''

"They let off their first experimental bomb in 1605 and then spent the next ten years perfecting a method for delivering a nuclear holocaust. The means wasn't all that spectacular—a big, clumsy, prop-driven bomber, all fuel and bombload—but it could make it across the Atlantic and that was all that mattered. The Aztecs weren't all that bothered about getting their aircrews home again.''

"Extra sacrifices?''

"Exactly.''

"So what did they want to do? Nuke Europe back to the stone age?''

"Precisely that. They knew that the Eurotrash in their sailing ships would keep on coming, and, more to the point, they would inevitably pilfer bits and pieces of Aztec advanced technology, upgrade their armaments, and begin posing a real threat. According to Aztec thinking, a preemptory strike was the only answer, and, as an added plus, it would be one fuck of a bonanza of souls for the Sun God. By 1615, the Aztec military industrial complex was in high gear, turning out an armada of planes for the raid on Northern Europe.''

"What stopped them?"

"Nothing stopped them."

"I don't understand."

"That's because you're still thinking in terms of your own dimension. Just because you've still got Europe intact, you assume that everyone else has."

Gibson blinked. "You mean they did it?"

"Damn right they did it. July 4, 1618, the Night of the Many Suns. They laid a strip of bombs from Lisbon to Warsaw, as far north as London and as far south as Naples. No more Europe in the streamheat dimension. Of course, all the dust and fallout and the rest of the crap went straight around the world. Russia and China took a beating and then it blew right across the Pacific and over the Aztec Empire, swamping them with cancer, birth defects, and sterility. Unfortunately it didn't kill them outright."

"Did it make them stronger?"

Nephredana nodded. "Stronger, meaner, and crazier. They now ruled the planet in their dimension, as much of it as they hadn't turned into an atomic wasteland, and it was a grim, nasty place.''

"They still went on with the human sacrifices?"

"Oh, yes, in fact they turned it into a science. They made inroads into death-moment energy physics that no normal culture would have imagined possible.''

"Death-moment energy physics?"

"You wouldn't want to know about it, except that's how they first got started in the interdimensional transit business."

"When did they start that?"

"They discovered the trick of dimension transfer about a hundred years ago, but even before that they had already left their impression on other dimensions. The attack on Europe produced massive print-throughs.''

"What are print-throughs?"

"When something as catastrophic as a nuclear attack occurs in one dimension, it can produce secondary effects in others nearby. In your dimension, the Night of the Many Suns and its aftermath was reflected as the Thirty Years' War and the plague. Eight million died in Germany alone.''

"Does it have to be a nuclear attack?''

"No, but they do produce the most noticeable effects. When they dropped the A-bombs on Osaka and Nagasaki in your dimension, a giant reptile thawed out of the Arctic ice and went on a rampage through a parallel Tokyo.''

Gibson was having a degree of trouble with some of this. "What about volcanos and natural explosions, do they cause print-through?''

Nephredana shook her head. "No, no, you're missing the point. It's not the crude energy release of the explosion that causes print-through, it's the cumulative effect of all the simultaneous death. When an entity dies there's a brief but massive release of psychic power and weird shit happens. Image that multiplied hundreds of thousands of times.''

Despite the booze, Gibson felt a chill clutch at his chest. "Death-moment energy physics.''

Nephredana raised her glass to him. "Now you're getting it, kid.''

"I'm not sure I want it. Let's get back to the streamheat; when did they start operating?''

Nephredana was looking around at the parade of passing guests, and she seemed to be getting bored with the lecture. "It's like I said, they made the breakthrough a hundred years ago, and by the late 1920s they'd started running all over, trying to reshape the whole fucking multidimensional universe in their own image. They apparently arrived in your dimension too late for the Russian revolution but in plenty of time for Hitler. Tried to get in with Mao Tse-tung as well, but Chairman Mao wasn't buying, and he had a bunch of them shot. He was smart enough to realize that the streamheat image was truly nasty. They called themselves the TSD at first, Time Stream Directorate, but it didn't catch on, they got the name streamheat from—well talk of the devil!''

Gibson stiffened. "What?''

Nephredana pointed across the grand hall. "Isn't that the bitch that brought you here?''

Gibson peered in the direction she was indicating, and there was Smith, wearing a severely cut, off-the-shoulder evening dress, in conversation with two men in dinner jackets. As far as Gibson could see, she hadn't spotted him, but he turned to Nephredana with a good deal of alarm. "You think she's looking for me?"

Nephredana shook her head. "Don't flatter yourself. This party is exactly the kind of environment in which the streamheat like to wheel and deal, but let's get out of here anyway. I don't think it'd be a good idea if she spotted you."

"So where to?"

"Let's go to the pistol gallery. I feel like shooting something."

"Pistol gallery?"

"Raus has a pistol gallery in a specially soundproofed corridor on the second floor. Raus has a lot of soundproofed areas in his mansion."

Gibson wasn't sure about the idea of pistol shooting. "I could use another drink after the history lesson."

Nephredana dismissed the implied objection. "We'll get one along the way."

"You've been here before?"

"Oh, yes."

She walked him in the direction of the postmodern staircase. The security men immediately lifted the ropes aside when they saw her coming. She didn't even have to say anything, and Gibson wondered if they knew her from previous experience or if they just recognized the look. Nephredana had a look and an attitude that could take her just about anywhere.

Beyond the red velvet ropes the party shifted into a whole other gear. They moved through a number of rooms, each of which had its own special attraction. In one, a dozen men and women were playing what looked like a version of high-stakes baccarat. A guest bedroom had been turned into an impromptu opium den where young men and women were, by turns, making themselves blissfully comatose by sucking on the multiple hoses of water pipe. The entertainment in some of the rooms was a little more perverse. In one that they passed through, couples sat round the shadowy walls, sipping cognac from balloon snifters as they watched a woman in a red leather cat suit administering electric shocks to a naked and kneeling young man. The large orchid house, which was an extension of the second floor under its own double-glazed dome, had been converted into a jungle room complete with parrots, Afro/Luxor drummers, highlife dancers, and a bar serving sticky cocktails with plastic snakes for swizzle sticks. Nephredana perversely decided that this would make an ideal pit stop. Gibson took one of the plastic-snake cocktails, wishing that he had a way to get some more of Raus's private stock, while Nephredana engaged the bartender—a muscular young man in a loincloth whose deep-blue skin had been oiled for the occasion—in lengthy conversation, obviously giving him the recipe for some fresh cocktail from hell.

When they finally reached the pistol gallery, a solitary woman in a purple sheath dress was shooting at targets with a tiny pearl-handled automatic. As Gibson and Nephredana came through the door, she smiled politely, daintily blew the smoke from the barrel of the gun, slipped it into her vanity bag, and left.

A well-stocked, glass-fronted gun cabinet ran along the back wall of the long narrow room. Gibson would have assumed that it would be kept locked, particularly during a party, but Nephredana went straight to it and opened one of the doors.

"What kind of piece do you want, Joe?"

"I'm not sure I really want to shoot; I'm on the way to being drunk, and I've gotten into trouble mixing guns and booze before now."

Nephredana smiled wickedly. "No roadies to shoot here, Joe."

Gibson caved in. "I don't know, I'm in your hands. What do you suggest?"

Nephredana grinned. "Take a big one, they're more satisfying."

"Okay, so give me the biggest motherfucker you can find, a damn, great, Clint Eastwood special."

Nephredana ran her eye along the racks of pistols like a browser selecting a book in the library. "Here we go, a Zeck & Dorf .45 Pacifier. Try this for size."

The forty-five was about the biggest revolver that Gibson had ever seen, with a seven-inch barrel, finished in burned chrome with ebony grips and a strip of fancy reinforcement running back from the front sight. As Nephredana handed it to him, she ran her forefinger sexily down the barrel. More than the gun itself, the gesture threw Gibson for a momentary loop. It wasn't that he didn't think of Nephredana as sexy; indeed, she surrounded herself with an air of sexuality that traveled with her like a purple cloud. It was just that he hadn't expected it ever to be focused on him. He'd assumed that they were on opposite sides of an alien gulf, beyond all possibility of coupling, and he'd never so much as fantasized about any carnal happening. Now that she was apparently bridging that gap, he had to take a couple of steps back and regroup. He doubted that Nephredana had missed his flash of confusion, but he covered himself by spinning the pistol on his index finger if for no other reason than that he felt it was probably expected of him.

"This is serious cannon."

Nephredana selected a piece for herself. It was an automatic, smaller than the forty-five but black and deadly. "You mind if I shoot first?"

Gibson bowed. "Go right ahead."

She loaded the automatic from a supply of ammunition on a shelf in the gun case and moved over to a control panel on the wall. "I'll set the targets."

She hit a number of switches on the wall panel. The target that the lady in purple had been shooting at flipped up into the ceiling. An electric sign came on.

READY.

Nephredana assumed the classic knees-bent, arms-extended firing position. A cutout figure flipped out from the wall. Nephredana fired, hitting the target squarely between the eyes. She was clearly no stranger to firearms. The first target withdrew and a second flipped up in a different position. She fired again. This target took it in the outlined heart. She shot four more targets before she paused. Every one of the cutouts was a photograph of the president, Jaim Lancer.

Nephredana noticed how Gibson was looking at them. "Raus's little joke." She took out two more targets and then stepped back. "It's your turn."

Gibson positioned himself. A target flipped out. He squeezed the trigger. The best he could do was to clip the shoulder of the presidential cutout. Nephredana looked him up and down.

"You're not exactly Wyatt Earp, are you?"

"I've only had TV sets to practice on."

He fired again. This time, he hit Lancer in the throat. As the echoes of the shot died away, he looked sideways at Nephredana. "I've been meaning to ask you, did you and Slide send that thing out of the TV set for me?"

Nephredana shook her head. "Not guilty, judge."

"But you knew about it?"

"Sure, we've been keeping an eye on you ever since you left the streamheat base. How do think I knew to find you in that bar?"

"You didn't know what happened inside the apartment, though?"

"What did happen in the apartment?"

"Some kind of humanoid electronic thing came crawling out of the TV. I think it was trying to kill me. When I blew away the TV, it vanished."

"That showed unusual presence of mind."

"And you've no idea who might have been behind it?"

Nephredana shook her head. "No idea at all; maybe the streamheat were trying to spook you."

"Maybe."

Gibson fired three more shots in quick succession. One missed; the other two hit the president in the chest. He shot once more, the last round in the gun, and blew away a section of head above the right ear.

Just as Gibson was shaking the empty shell casings out of the cylinder prior to reloading, the gallery door unexpectedly opened and a man with a bulky, old-fashioned press camera stepped into the pistol gallery. As Gibson and Nephredana turned, a flashbulb popped. Gibson lunged after the photographer but he was already out of the door and gone.

"Come back here, you!"

He dragged the heavy soundproofed door open, but there was no sign of either man or camera. He went back to Nephredana. "I lost him."

She didn't seem particularly concerned.

"I wouldn't worry about it. What's a picture one way or the other?"

"I hate fucking paparazzi."

Nephredana took him by the arm again. "I think you need a drink."

"Not in the jungle room, though, hey? I feel like a real drink."

She smiled. "Anything you say, Joe Gibson. Anything you say." And as though to emphasize the word "anything," she put a hand on the back of his neck and stroked his hair. "And after we've had a couple of drinks, we'll go and take a look at something that may well blow your mind."

Gibson had closed his eyes at the touch of her hand. It was very cold but not in the least unpleasant. Gibson smiled. He was starting to enjoy the sensation and wondering where it might lead. "It takes a lot to blow my mind."

"I think Balg may do it for you."

His eyes snapped open. "Balg?"

Nephredana's dark glasses were a couple of inches from his

face, and her lips were moist. "Balg." She spoke the word almost lovingly.

Gibson blinked. "The guy who did the shouting; he wasn't crazy? There really is a Balg?"

Nephredana stepped away from him. "You'll see."

They went back down the big staircase to the more public areas of the party. The jazz trio had been replaced by a large swing band that verged on the cacophonous. A lot more people were dancing and with a great deal more energy. The whole nature of the downstairs party had changed. People seemed more intent on enjoying themselves rather than just being seen, and it went without saying that the great majority of guests were now a good deal drunker and some appeared to be verging on doing things that they might later regret. Gibson and Nephredana went past the bandstand and started down the long corridor that linked the front and back of the house. Halfway along it, she quickly stepped over the velvet rope that was supposed to prevent guests from entering one of the side passages and indicated that Gibson should do the same.

It was about that time that a security man, on guard a little way down the corridor, spotted them. "I'm sorry, miss, you can't go in there."

He moved quickly, attempting to get to them before they went any farther. Nephredana made a fast pass with her right hand. The man stopped dead, then turned and went back to his post as though nothing had happened. She seemed to have blanked all awareness of them from the security guard's mind. Without waiting to see any further effects of her handiwork, she grabbed Gibson by the hand and pulled him over the rope.

"Come on! A zapper like that doesn't last very long."

Gibson followed her as she hurried down the passage. At the end of it there was a spiral flight of stone steps that led down, presumably into the cellars of the mansion. Nephredana plunged straight down them with her spike heels ringing on the stone. She reached the first level down and kept on going. It smelled like a wine cellar. The second level was different, colder and clammier, with a strange musty smell that Gibson didn't like at all. The third level was decidedly odd. The walls ran with condensation and the steps were slippery with a greenish slime. The musty smell was close to becoming a stench, and the few dim lights that there were created new threatening shadows with each turn of the stair.

"The foundations of this place are very old. Even though

Raus virtually rebuilt the house from the ground up, he kept the original roots. The roots were why he went to so much trouble to buy the property some ten years ago, right after Lancer came to power."

Gibson put a hand to his mouth. "What's making that smell?"

"You'll see."

"I'm not sure I want to."

"Chicken?"

"You're too fucking much."

The stairs ended and a door was in front of them. Although the door seemed to be constructed of dark, ancient wood reinforced with corroded iron bolts, the lock system was modern; preelectronic but very formidable. Nephredana hiked up her skirt. There was a small flat utility wallet made from some sort of ultra-soft leather strapped round her upper thigh like a garter. She extracted a small, silver cylinder, not unlike a very advanced dental drill, and pointed it at each lock in turn. The sound of the tumblers falling and the bolts pulling back was plainly audible.

Gibson looked on in admiration. This was one hell of a woman. "Useful thing, that."

Nephredana nodded. "My passkey. Help me push this door open."

The door opened on a small stone platform from which another set of steps led down, curving around the outside wall of a circular chamber that went even deeper into the earth, almost like a huge shaft or well. The word "bowels" sprang into Gibson's mind. This was the closest to the bowels of the Earth that he had ever been. The smell was definitely a stench now. Except that, once inside the door, there was a warm musky quality to it that almost seemed alive.

Gibson peered over the edge of the steps. He could see a light at the bottom of the shaft, a luridly poisonous green glow that also seemed to be the source of the stench. "What is that thing?"

"That's Balg."

"Balg's a bunch of glowing toxic radiation in the bottom of a pit?"

"I guess you'd call Balg an entity."

Gibson grunted. "Two entities in one day is at least one over my limit. Is it safe?"

"Not in the least."

"So what the fuck are we doing here?"

"It can't come out of the shaft. It's pretty well penned up."

"I have your word on that?"

"In the elder days, Balg was vanquished by Galmesh and bound outside of the time stream. Over the millennia, though, a small part of him began to intrude into this dimension. The original house on this sight was built around the intrusion. Subsequent owners have put in a lot of work attempting to set free Balg in his entirety. Verdon Raus is only the latest in a long line."

"You're telling me that Raus is trying to let this thing loose?"

"He believes that he can control it for his own ends."

"Can he?"

"He doesn't have a prayer."

Gibson held up a hand. "Wait a minute. Let's just back up here. I thought that this Raus dealt in newspapers and TV stations, was some kind of William Randolph Hearst." He nodded toward the glow in the pit. "You're telling me that, when he gets home from a hard day's moguling, he messes around with this H. P. Lovecraft shit?"

"Verdon Raus is a very complex individual. Shall we go a little closer?"

"Do we have to?"

Nephredana sighed. "Come on, Gibson. Live dangerously."

Gibson followed Nephredana down the stairs with serious trepidation. The stairs had no banister or safety railing on the outside, nothing but a long drop to Balg. Gibson didn't like heights at the best of times, and when they came with a dangerous glowing entity at the bottom, they were infinitely worse.

After descending for forty or fifty feet, with the glow of Balg becoming brighter by the foot, the steps terminated in a circular flag-stoned platform in the center of which was sunk the final shaft that contained Balg, or, at least, the portion of Balg that had made it into this dimension. Gibson noticed that a number of steel rings were set into the stonework right at the edge of this deepset well. Gibson glanced at them and then at Nephredana, whose face had taken on a ghoulish aspect now that it was lit green from below. "What are these for? The human sacrifices?"

Nephredana scarcely bothered to look. "Probably."

Gibson took a quick step back. "You're kidding me?"

Nephredana shook her head. "Balg feeds mainly on psychic energy, so I imagine a good few of those who've been messing with him over the years would have tried it. I've found that it never takes humans very long to get around to sacrificing their own kind. I guess it's the attraction of the ultimate.''

"Death-moment energy physics?"

"You got it."

There was a strange echoing noise from down inside the shaft and a sudden rush of the foul-smelling air. Gibson turned away. It was as though Balg had detected their presence. "Are you sure that thing can't climb out of the well?"

"Look down there."

"Must I?"

"Go ahead. It won't hurt you."

Gibson advanced cautiously to the edge and peered down. It was the act of looking into a green hell. His overwhelming instinct was to get away from Balg and out of his subterranean vault as fast as possible.

Nephredana was standing behind him. "What do you see?"

"Balg. Isn't that enough?"

"Be precise."

Gibson gritted his teeth. "A green glow that looks radioactive with a kind of white mist covering it."

"Look at the mist."

Gibson looked again. He could just make out lines of red light running through the mist. "Are those lasers?"

"Raus thinks it's his final defense against Balg."

"I didn't think they had lasers here. Shit, they don't even have color TV."

"They don't have lasers here. He's had a little outside help. I suspect your chums in the streamheat."

"Isn't that against the Prime Directive or something? Not giving advanced technology to a culture that it hasn't developed itself?"

Nephredana smiled. "Actually that's *Star Trek*, but the same principle applies."

Gibson looked back up the steps. "I think I've seen enough of this place. The stink is starting to get to me."

Nephredana nodded. "Balg isn't the most attractive of beings."

As they turned to leave, Gibson noticed that there was a small, dark alcove set beneath the curve of the steps where they rose from the platform. It appeared to contain racks of devices that, as far as he could see, had the sole common purpose of inflicting pain on various specific areas of the human body.

He quickly pointed the stuff out to Nephredana. "Is that what I think it is?"

Nephredana didn't seem particularly concerned. "What else would it be?"

"You mean he tortures his victims before he feeds them to Balg?"

"Once you get started in the sacrifice business, the rest pretty much follows."

Gibson didn't wait any longer. He was climbing the steps. "That's it, I'm out of here."

Nephredana followed without comment. Unfortunately, as they approached the door there were sounds from the other side.

Gibson looked round in alarm. "Christ, what do we do now?"

Nephredana was already out of her high heels and heading back down the stairs in silent stockinged feet.

She turned and hissed at Gibson. "Come on!"

"Where do we go?"

"The alcove, we can hide in there. It's probably Raus coming to show his pet to some selected guests."

There was the sound of keys in the door. Gibson gave thanks that Nephredana had had the foresight to relock the doors behind them. The alcove was small, and Gibson wasn't keen on taking refuge in a torturer's tool locker, but it was a case of needs must. It was far from being the ideal hiding place. There was hardly enough room for two people in among the various steel and leather appliances, and the glow from Balg was so intense on that level that they hardly had even the protection of darkness.

Gibson whispered urgently to Nephredana. "Can't you put some whammy on them so we can slip away?"

Nephredana shook her head. "Too risky with Balg just below us. Any influence could too easily backfire. Balg's all random surplus energy and no smarts. A hex could trigger all manner of ugly shit."

Gibson was about to protest that they were in all manner of ugly shit already when the sound of footsteps and voices came from the stairs above. Nephredana put a silent finger to her lips. Gibson suddenly recognized one of the voices. It was Smith.

". . . despite that, Verdon, this is still a very dangerous experiment. If that thing should get loose before we are able to control it . . ."

What in hell was she doing down here and what kind of deal was going down between Raus and the streamheat?

The voices and footsteps reached the platform, and Gibson's

horror was multiplied a hundredfold when he risked a peek around the edge of the alcove. Seven people had come through the door, and now they stood just a few yards from where he was hiding, black shapes against the green glow from the shaft. To his horror, he recognized four out of seven: in addition to Smith, the party included Raus, French, and the man who looked like Sebastian Rampton. If this was a parallel Rampton, it seemed that he was on a pretty much parallel trip. Two of Raus's tuxedoed goons brought up the rear. They were holding up a young woman who sagged between them, either helplessly drunk or drugged. Somewhere along the line, she had lost her dress, and she was now down to torn black lingerie that hadn't been too demure in the first place. Her head lolled, and every few seconds she was consumed by helpless giggles. In a moment of absolute, dark, crystal clarity, Gibson knew what was going to happen to the girl. He tensed but Nephredana put a restraining hand on his arm. It might be a grand gesture to leap out and try and save the girl, but it would also be suicidal. There was no point in sacrificing himself for some anonymous party girl. It was ultimately cold but wholly logical.

Rampton, at least, had the decency to raise a token objection. "Does this really need to be done?"

It was Raus who provided the rationalization. "The sacrifices have to be made. If they're not, Balg becomes violent. I doubt we could continue to contain it."

Rampton still seemed a little shocked by the proceedings.

"How many people do you have to feed to this thing?"

Raus's voice had an edge of cold, clinical pride, as though Balg was his hobby.

"Lately it's been taking about four a month to keep it quiet, approximately one a week."

"And nobody has wondered what you're doing here. There've been no rumors, no questions."

Raus sounded as if it was no problem. "When you control as much of the media as I do, rumors are easy to manipulate away. Besides, I'm very good to my people here. They understand and they keep their mouths shut. Also Balg doesn't leave any remains. There are no bodies to dispose of, and people vanish all the time."

Smith peered down into the shaft. "I think we'll have to talk about all this after the matter of Lancer has been resolved."

Raus seemed anxious to change the subject. "On the matter

of Lancer, has this man from another dimension been picked up, this double for Zwald?''

At this, Gibson's ears pricked up. Were they talking about him? He listened tensely.

French answered Raus's question. ''We don't have him but we're monitoring him. We can pick him up when we need him.''

Gibson's eyes narrowed. If they were talking about him, French didn't know half as much as he claimed. They weren't monitoring him so closely that they knew he was just a few feet from them.

Raus didn't seem entirely happy with French's answer. ''I'd rather we had him in a secure place. He's now crucial to the operation.''

''Don't worry, we'll pick him up in the morning.''

Raus continued to lean on the streamheat. ''I don't want any mistakes.''

Rampton also seemed to have misgivings. ''I certainly haven't made a dimension transition to attend a nonevent.''

Gibson was transfixed. Unless there were copies of Sebastian Rampton spread all over the multidimensional universe, it had to be the Rampton from New York, the one that he had met, and they had to be talking about him.

French was doing his best to be reassuring. ''There's no problem, Gibson is too stupid to be a problem.''

While Gibson had to fight to control himself, Smith was at her most efficient and reassuring as she backed up French. ''There won't be any problem. We can handle Gibson.''

Gibson's jaws clenched in silent fury. Handle me, can you, you bastards? We'll see about that.

Raus signaled to the two black-tie goons, indicating that he thought it was time to feed the bimbo to the entity. As the two men moved the girl toward the edge of the shaft, her legs suddenly sagged, as though she'd lost control of them. She burst out in another fit of giggles. Gibson found that there was something particularly hideous about the sound, about her total unawareness of what was about to happen to her. Then, somehow, awareness cut through whatever they'd given her or whatever she'd taken. She let out one long awful scream before they pushed her over the edge and then a second, even longer one as she fell that reverberated with echoes. There were sobs and sucking noises from the bottom of the shaft and finally a single obscenely satisfied belch. Gibson closed his eyes and bit down on the knuckle of his index finger. When he looked again, Raus and his party, now only six in number, were going back up the steps. A few seconds later, the door closed and there was the sound of it being locked from the outside.

Gibson let out a sigh from the heart. "Jesus Christ."

Nephredana stepped out of the alcove. "Them's the breaks."

"I don't know how you can take something like that so calmly."

"It wasn't my first human sacrifice."

"I guess not."

"I'm very, very old, Joe. Don't be attributing any phony innocence to me. I've truly seen it all."

"This isn't easy."

He had probably never said a truer word. He walked over to the edge of the well and looked down. He didn't have a clue what to think. In the bottom of the well there seemed to be a new smug quality to the green glow. Nephredana came and stood beside him. She also looked down into the shaft. "One day we're going to destroy that thing."

"I sure as hell hope so. Did you hear what those bastards were talking about?"

"They were talking about you."

"They seem to have plans for me. The word they used was 'crucial.' You think they can get me?"

Nephredana shrugged. "It depends on how crucial it is to you to stay away from them. You seem to be doing okay so far."

"I've only been away from them for a few hours."

"For the fugitive, it's one hour at a time."

Gibson knelt down and touched one of the steel rings in the stonework. "How many people do you think have died here?"

"Probably hundreds. Maybe thousands over the years. Balg has been here for a very long time."

Gibson shook his head. "Balg? What's next? Necrom?"

Fury flashed across Nephredana's face, and she grabbed him angrily by the lapels of his tuxedo jacket and pulled his face close to hers. She was very strong.

"Don't even say that name. Not here, not ever. You don't have the faintest idea what you're talking about."

Her fingers were in his hair. He could feel her long nails against his scalp. She hissed into his face. "Never say that name. You humans are so ignorant that you're dangerous."

Then she kissed him. The kiss was electric. His whole body trembled, and it was some moments before he could break away. "Surely not here?"

Gibson couldn't tell whether the force in her whisper was anger or passion. "Yes, right here. There are a lot of ways to fight the power."

She was holding his face between her hands, her nails were digging into the skin of his cheeks, and her hands were icy. He was revolted by the idea of making love in this place, but he knew that he could never find the strength to resist. A slow, languid smile spread over Nephredana's face.

"I'm going to hurt you, Joe Gibson . . . and you're going to love me for it."

The White Room

THE CHARADE OF appearing to recover when there was, in reality, nothing from which to recover was proving harder than he had first imagined, and the sessions with Dr. Kooning were becoming a strain. Too much real anger was churning inside him, anger that boiled up despite the drugs and despite all his efforts to convince Kooning that he was emerging from what she considered to be fantasy and returning to the real. He constantly ran into the basic stumbling block of his deception. He had no existence and no history in this world, and if he let go of the "fantasy," all that remained was a blank slate. To Kooning, this was even more fascinating than a patient who was in the grip of a delusion. In psychiatry, the deluded were ten a penny; the real blank slate was rare and exotic. Gibson was now fully convinced that there was no way he was ever going to obtain any legitimate release from the clinic and that the only way out for him was going to be a breakout. The conviction was particularly strong on the days when Kooning took it into her head to probe him on the fine print of his paranoia.

"You claim, although apparently either living or wishing to live in the world of rock 'n' roll music, you've never heard of the Rolling Stones?"

Gibson nodded. He felt weighed down by the seeming contradictions that were built into his story. Only a certain dogged stubbornness kept him from curling up on the couch and refusing to answer. "Where I came from, there was no band called the Rolling Stones."

"Doesn't that tell you something."

Only the drugs stopped Gibson snarling. "It tells me that I have come back to a world that's been radically altered, altered to the extent that I no longer exist."

226

Kooning regarded him gravely. "That's a very interesting statement."

"Isn't it just?"

"Could it be that because of some crisis in your life, perhaps what you perceived as a failure to win the level of success and recognition that you thought you deserved in music, you fixed on one very successful group and decided that they had usurped what was rightfully yours?"

They must have been round this point a dozen times in previous sessions, and Gibson could see what was coming a mile off.

"You're telling me that the only way I could get what was rightfully mine was by blanking out this band, creating the illusion that they didn't exist."

Kooning smiled and nodded. "It does make a lot of sense, doesn't it?"

"It would, except that it isn't the case here."

"So how do you feel when I make such a suggestion?"

Gibson didn't bother to pretend. "I get scared. If I give up what you call my fantasy, what do I have left? There doesn't seem to be anything else. Without it, I'm quite literally nothing."

"Don't you think this is something we are going to have to work on?"

Chapter
Ten

GIBSON WOKE FROM a hideous dream into an almost as hideous reality. In the dream, the well that contained Balg had given up its dead. One by one, and then in increasing numbers, an army of slow-moving, crawling luminous corpses had scrambled painfully over the rim of the shaft, dragged themselves across the flagstones, and started clawing their way up the stairs on their hands and knees while Gibson watched in horror. He had spotted Lancer, the president, in among the crowd, along with a host of friends and faces from his past: Gideon Windemere and Christobelle; Rob Tyler, the bass player from the Holy Ghosts who'd been the most bitter about the breakup of the band; even Desiree and the woman who'd been at his apartment the day that Casillas had come calling were part of this legion of the living dead.

He only recognized the woman that he'd seen seen sacrificed by the torn black lingerie still clinging to her green, decaying flesh. Instead of crawling to the stairs like all the others, she made straight for Gibson, giggling as she dragged herself toward him, the same mindless, stoned-out, space-case giggle that he'd heard the previous night, as she had swayed on the edge of the pit, staring uncomprehendingly at her death. Her black fingernails scraped on the granite flags, and her eyes had the vacancy of madness. He wanted desperately to get away from her but he found that he couldn't move. He was flat on his back, naked, exposed, and helpless, chained by the wrists and ankles to the iron rings set in the flagstones. He twisted and struggled until his wrists were raw and bleeding, but he couldn't free himself. He also didn't seem able to close his eyes, and he was compelled to watch as she agonizingly inched nearer, leaving a slime trail like a slug or snail.

The giggle and the scrape of the nails was close to deafening, and her hands were reaching out for him. "I'm going to hurt you, Joe Gibson . . . and you're going to love me for it."

His screams were still ringing around the circular chamber when his mind lurched back into the real world, but he experienced none of the grateful sense of relief that usually comes after waking from a nightmare and realizing that it was all just a bad dream. To his horror, he found that he was still in the underground chamber, Balg was still in his pit, and very little was right with the world. No corpses were crawling from the well shaft and he wasn't chained to the flagstones, but he was naked, frozen and stiff and hung over. There were scars across his chest as though he'd been raked by talons, and Nephredana had vanished. He couldn't believe that he had fallen asleep in this hellish place. How the fuck had he managed that? He hadn't even been particularly drunk. The only mercy was that he was alone in the awful place, unless he counted Balg.

His clothes were scattered all around, and Gibson started hastily gathering them up, at the same time praying that Nephredana hadn't locked the door at the top of the stairs, if indeed she had left by the door at all. He didn't want to spend another moment in the green glow of Balg and was already frightened about what ugly long-term effects he might have racked up in his mind or body by sleeping in such close proximity to the monstrous entity. He saw it as the psychic equivalent to bedding down in a nuclear reactor. As he wriggled into his pants, he held off from wondering about what might have possibly happened to cause Nephredana to disappear, leaving him alone in a place like this.

Without bothering to slip into his tux jacket or tuck in the tails to his dress shirt, he started up the steps that led out of the chamber, taking them two at a time and not looking back. To his infinite relief the door opened when he tugged at it. Up to that point, his only motivation had been to get away from Balg. As soon as he was through the door, however, a whole new set of problems dropped on him with lead boots. He was not only in Raus's mansion with no readily available means to get away, but he was also deep beneath the mansion in an area that had to be fatally off limits to strangers like himself. He took the next flight of stairs slower and with a great deal more caution. The very last thing he wanted was to run into a couple of Raus's minions bringing Balg his breakfast. Gibson had no doubt that such an encounter would almost certainly result in his being included on the menu.

Fortunately, he seemed to be blessed with the kind of after-the-fact luck that allows one to crawl away intact following a disaster. The mansion was very quiet. The only noises were what he might expect from an early-morning cleanup crew, plus somewhere in the main hall someone was playing a slow walking-bass figure that was almost rock 'n' roll.

Gibson started down the main corridor in the direction of the grand hall, doing his best to look like a drunk who had woken up in a dark corner somewhere and was now trying to retrieve his bearings and get home. It hardly required any award-winning feat of acting to create the illusion.

The grand hall smelled of smoke and stale booze, and the floor was a sea of debris that was being slowly swept into more manageable piles by four men in gray overalls pushing wide industrial brooms. One of them glanced up as Gibson came across the empty dance floor.

"Where did you come from?"

Gibson rubbed his eyes and looked bleary. "That's a good question."

"You just wake up?"

Gibson nodded. "Sure did."

The man pushed the garbage in front of his broom for a few more feet. "Some party, huh?"

"What I remember of it."

"They're serving coffee in one of the marquees by the lake for stragglers like you."

Gibson slipped on his jacket. "I could use some coffee."

He glanced up at the stage, where a figure in a tuxedo was standing by himself on the empty bandstand with his back to the room, plucking thoughtfully at the strings of a standup bass. Gibson watched him for a few moments and then shrugged. Some people never stopped. He started toward the coffee and whatever his next move might be. He had just realized that he had no money. His wallet was still in the borrowed suit in Slide's Hudson. This upset him more than anything since Balg. He seemed to be moving toward a dependency on the kindness of strangers, and this wasn't a pleasing prospect in a place where albinos appeared to be high on the list of targets for prejudice.

The voice that stopped him in his tracks echoed across the grand hall just as he was approaching the French windows that opened on the lake.

"Wait up there, I'll come with you."

There was no mistaking the millennia-old rasp. Gibson spun round. "Yancey Slide?"

The figure on the stage was carefully setting the bass on its side. "I've been waiting for you."

"I didn't know you were a musician."

"You learn a lot of things by the time you're as old as I am."

Slide jumped down from the bandstand and walked briskly toward Gibson, who stood waiting for him.

"You ready for some breakfast?"

"Where's Nephredana?"

Slide made an unconcerned gesture. "She's around somewhere."

"Why did she leave me alone with Balg?"

"You'll have to ask her about that. Nephredana can be a little strange at times." He glanced quickly around. "I also wouldn't go shouting about Balg around here, someone might hear you."

Outside, a gray dawn did little to raise Gibson's spirits. A waist-deep white ground mist was rolling off the lake, lending everything a sad and sinister unreality that was heightened by the handful of leftover guests who wandered aimlessly like lost souls in disheveled evening dress. Crews were already pulling down the marquees, and the one that was left standing, a red-and-white island in the mist, was presumably the one where coffee and breakfast was being dispensed. Gibson never made it there, however. With Slide beside him, he had walked down the steps from the terrace and into the mist until, once again, his quest for creature comforts was interrupted by a voice from behind.

"Stand where you are, Gibson. We want to talk to you."

The four people Gibson most wanted not to see in this world or any other were standing on the terrace looking down at him. Smith, French, Raus, and Rampton had arranged themselves between the statues on the terrace, the classic marbles of gods and heroes, like a quartet of avenging angels, posed dramatically in the dawn against the facade of the mansion. Gibson's first thought was that it was a setup and his instinct was to run like hell, but logic quickly reasserted itself and pointed out that the running would most likely get him shot. Smith, French, Raus, and Rampton weren't alone; behind them, a four-man backup lurked like threatening shadows. Two uniformed streamheat toted their distinctive weapons, and two of Raus's goons, maybe the selfsame ones who had fed the girl in the black lingerie to

Balg, were armed with heavy, old-fashioned machine guns that looked very like Thompsons, right down to the fifty-shot drum clips. The pretending seemed to have stopped. The gloves were off, and Gibson wondered how long it would be before someone started hitting him.

He glanced quickly at Slide. "Any way you can get me out of this?"

Slide shook his head and moved a few steps away from him. "Sorry, kid, I have a strict policy of nonintervention."

"You bastard! Did you set me up for them?"

Smith spoke from the top of the steps that led up to the terrace. "Don't blame Slide, Joe. We could have picked you up anytime. We just thought we'd let you run around and have some fun until we needed you. Allow you the illusion that you'd escaped."

Gibson's lip curled. "Oh, yeah? If you were so fucking clever, how come you didn't know that I was hiding in the chamber last night when you were all watching Balg get fed?"

Beside him, Slide groaned. "You've got a big mouth, kid."

Just how big became immediately evident. Raus rounded angrily on Smith. "He's seen Balg."

Smith didn't show the slightest concern. "It hardly matters."

Raus, however, thought differently and wasn't about to let it go. "He has to die. It's the rule by which I live. I've not remained the master of this thing for as long as I have by breaking that rule."

Slide guffawed. "You really believe that you're the master of Balg, do you, Raus? Are you really that stupid?"

Smith snapped at him. "Keep out of this, Slide." She turned to Raus. "Gibson can't be killed. We have to have him."

Gibson felt decidedly relieved, but it was short-lived. Smith looked straight at him. "We have to keep him alive until after the Lancer project is completed. After that, we have no more interest in him."

Relief deflated like a punctured tire. Gibson made one last appeal to Slide. "Can't you do anything? They're going to kill me."

"I'm sorry, kid, it's nothing personal. I just can't get involved."

There was the sound of a car engine and Gibson turned to see the Hudson coming across the lawn, bouncing through the mist like a battleship in a heavy sea. Gibson experienced an irrational moment of hope that it was Nephredana coming to the rescue.

The group on the terrace must have thought the same thing, because both the streamheat and Raus's goons raised their weapons and trained them on the car. Slide moved quickly toward the steps. "Hold it! Hold it! It's nothing to worry about, it's just my ride coming to pick me up."

Gibson was drifting into a state of total unreality. The thing from the TV, Balg, Nephredana's unbelievable lovemaking and then the dreams, and now standing, up to his waist, in horror-movie mist while this latest drama unfolded all added up to a feeling that his world was being governed by the laws of surrealism. He also had the impression that some kind of influence was being used. Despite the obvious drama that was taking place in the area between the terrace and the lake, there were no curious bystanders hanging around. Even the small residue of party guests had melted away, and the cleanup crews went on with their work as though nothing was happening.

The Hudson came to a stop beside Gibson and Slide. On the terrace, they still didn't look terribly happy about the arrival of the car, but they weren't about to start shooting. The driver's door opened and Nephredana stepped out. Her image had completely changed from that of the night before. Now she had her hair scraped back into a bun and was dressed in a black leather version of a ninja suit, with decorative chrome shoulder guards. The black sunglasses had been replaced by a diamante creation with flyaway wings. Even her voice had altered. She talked out of the side of her mouth like some B-movie Chicago gun moll.

"Okay, Yance, ya ready to blow?"

Slide began to walk to the car, and Nephredana beckoned to Gibson. "Ya wanna get the shit that ya left in the car?"

Smith started down the steps of the terrace with the two uniformed streamheat behind her. "Don't try anything, Gibson."

Nephredana stepped into Smith's path. "He isn't gonna try nothing. If he does, I'll break him in half. I just want him to get his stuff out of the car."

Gibson didn't know what the hell was going on, but it seemed like the best idea for the moment was to bow to the superior firepower.

He faced Smith. "Is it a problem to get my things out of the car? I can't live in a tuxedo for the rest of my life, no matter how short you think it may be."

Smith nodded. "Get your stuff, but no tricks."

Gibson moved to the Hudson, and Nephredana opened the

back door. He leaned inside and started gathering up the look-alike's clothes.

He glanced back at Nephredana, who was standing watching him. "Thanks for leaving me with Balg."

She moved closer to him and spoke in a low voice. "Don't panic yet, Joe. It ain't over until it's over." It was her normal voice and all trace of the gun moll had gone.

"And what's that supposed to mean?"

She ignored the question. The gun moll was back. "Ya want what ya left in the glove compartment?"

Gibson thought of the gun in the glove compartment and then of weapons that were ranged against him and shook his head. "No, I think I'll leave it where it is."

Nephredana nodded. It was the old voice again. "Wise move, Joe. They'd cut you down before you could get off a shot. Remember, I've seen you shoot a pistol."

Gibson stepped away from the car with the bundle of clothes in his arms. Nephredana reached into the backseat, pulled out Gibson's hat, which he'd left behind, and stuck it on his head; then she and Slide climbed into the car. The doors slammed, the engine revved, and the Hudson backed up, made a fast turn, and drove away into the mist. Gibson watched it go and then, feeling totally abandoned, braced himself to face whatever fate had in store for him.

"Okay, what are you going to do to me?"

Smith gestured to the pair of uniforms who followed at her heels. "Take him."

Raus was coming down the steps after her, still protesting, "I think you're making a big mistake."

Smith regarded him coldly as the two streamheat seized Gibson. "What do you want me to do? Cancel the entire Lancer project?"

Rampton caught up with them. "Be sensible, Raus. There's no way that we can bring it off without Gibson."

"But suppose he talks?"

Rampton blinked impatiently behind the Himmler glasses. "And who would believe him? Who would believe that one of this country's most successful entrepreneurs kept a supernatural monster in his cellar?"

While the argument was going on, Gibson's arms were being pulled behind him and handcuffs clamped on his wrists. It was the final confirmation that the streamheat's pretense of protecting him or attempting to obtain his cooperation was now history. He was their prisoner, pure and simple.

Meanwhile, Raus seemed to be finally caving in. "There must be no mistakes."

Smith was all but showing her contempt for the Kamerian power broker. "There will be no mistakes."

"And I want it on record that my choice was dispose of him here and now."

"Your position has been noted. Can we go now?"

Raus couldn't forgo a final burst of huffing and puffing. "I still don't like it."

Smith ignored him and signaled to French. "You'd better bring the car around."

When French arrived with the car, a large black sedan that looked a lot like a Packard, Gibson was unceremoniously bundled into the back with a uniform on either side of him.

"Since I seem to be under arrest, do I get to call my lawyer?"

Smith glared at him from the front seat. "Shut up, Gibson. I don't want to hear from you."

"I thought I was crucial to the plan?"

Smith eyes were steely and dangerous. "We have a use for you, Gibson, but don't let that go to your head. You can fulfill your function with any number of minor bones broken. Burroughs and Wellcome here, the gentlemen on either side of you, are experts at causing pain without doing serious damage."

This was enough of a warning for Gibson. He leaned back in the seat, closed his eyes, and did his best to make himself as comfortable as possible with his arms pinned behind his back. An old-time criminal had once told him, "When you're really in the shit and there's nothing you can do about it, rest up. You may need your strength later." Gibson didn't say a word for the rest of the drive.

Their destination turned out to be an apartment building back in the city, in much the same neighborhood as the last one. The apartment, however, was much larger, with a big living room that looked more like a temporary command post than a home, and three, maybe four bedrooms. Gibson didn't have much time to look around as he was hustled through, but he did see a large chart table with a model of a city square set up on it, a lot of sleek electronic equipment that was too advanced for Luxor and had to be all streamheat. Maps and photographs were pinned to the walls, and a selection of small arms that were a mixture of local and streamheat designs were stacked in a makeshift rack.

Wellcome and Burroughs took Gibson directly to a small windowless bedroom at the far end of a corridor from the living room and threw him inside. There was nothing in the room except a narrow, military-style cot and a bucket that he assumed was for emergency waste.

"Are you going to take these damned handcuffs off?"

Wellcome and Burroughs ignored him and left the room, locking the door behind them. In a sudden flash of rage, Gibson was across the room, kicking on the door and screaming after them. "Fuck you, you bastards! My hands are getting numb."

His anger, however, was short-lived. It had been a rough night and he quickly ran out of steam. With no response forthcoming, Gibson sat down on the bed and stared at the opposite wall. He was past the point of self-pity or asking why him or what had he done to deserve any of this. It didn't even help to wail that he was deeper in the shit than he had ever been. All he could do was to sit and wait and maybe pray that some kind of way out would present itself and that he'd have the presence of mind and the resources to take it. He wasn't exactly optimistic about his chances.

He sat like that for maybe forty-five minutes with the pain in his hands worsening with every one of them before a key rattled in the lock. It turned out to be Klein with an amiable smile on his face that Gibson didn't buy for a moment.

"I brought some cigarettes."

Gibson gazed at him with a look of solid dislike. "How am I supposed to smoke them with my hands chained behind my back?"

"Nobody took your cuffs off?"

Gibson scowled. "Full marks for observation, nobody took my cuffs off and my hands are swelling up."

Klein raised a hand. "I'll see to it straight away."

He quickly left the room and was back in less than a minute with a key. He freed Gibson's hands, stepped back and handed him a pack of the Luxor-style Camels. "Are you hungry?"

Gibson didn't answer right away. He massaged his wrists until there was circulation in his hands again; then he shook a cigarette from the pack and stuck it in his mouth. "Could I get a light for this?"

Klein lit his cigarette, leaving the matches on the cot, and repeated the question. Gibson exhaled and nodded. "Yes, I'm hungry, and I could kill for a drink."

Klein smiled. "I don't know about the drink, but I'm sure I can rustle up some food for you."

Klein's whole act was irritating Gibson, and he found the implied chumminess in the word "rustle" really offensive. "Listen, Klein, if you're trying to Mutt and Jeff me, forget it. I'm too far gone for any good-cop, bad-cop routine."

Klein had the gall to actually look hurt. "I was only trying to make you a little more comfortable."

"Bullshit. Smith probably sent you in here to soften me up, but it ain't going to work. You want something from me and once you've got it you're going to kill me. For my part, I'm going to do my best to stay alive by any means possible. That's the relationship and pretending it's anything else is garbage. Do I make myself clear?"

Klein stood up with an expression of guarded neutrality. "I'll see about the food."

"You do that."

Once again there was the sound of the door being locked. Allowing that he was probably incapable of feeling any worse, Gibson's mood had actually improved after his clash with Klein. He'd had a chance to vent some of his hostility, and also the fact that Klein had come in there to try and get on his side indicated that whatever they wanted him to do required some measure of his cooperation. It wasn't exactly a break, but it might prove to be the source of some slack and he was certain that slack was the only thing that was going to save his ass.

Klein was back in fifteen minutes with a plate of eggs and beans and bottle of local Luxor beer. "I managed to find you a beer."

Gibson looked dourly at the food. "You even managed to make something like prison food."

"It's what we all eat."

"You ought to complain."

Klein seemed to realize that it was pointless arguing with Gibson. "Is there anything else that you want?"

Gibson nodded. "Yeah, I want to go home."

"You know that isn't possible."

"So fuck off and leave me alone to eat this mess."

Gibson did his best to make the food last as long as possible; eating was something that kept him occupied and let him avoid thinking. After a couple of forkfuls, though, he realized just how hungry he was and wolfed down the rest of the eggs and beans in double time. He took a little longer over the beer and longer still over his second cigarette. When that was done, there was nothing to do but sit and wait. After Klein's departure, he had expected to be left alone until the streamheat felt like feeding him again. Thus it came as something of a surprise when, after only a half hour, the door was being unlocked again. This time the visitor was Smith, and she was making no attempt to make nice.

"Klein tells me you're acting belligerent."

Gibson's face twisted into a sneer. "What was I supposed to be? Grateful?"

"You're suddenly acting uncharacteristically tough."

"Maybe all the things that haven't killed me lately have made me stronger."

Smith clearly didn't like this new attitude of Gibson's. "You're really in no position to be paraphrasing Nietzsche at me."

Gibson's sneer broadened. "Oh, yeah? It seems to me that I'm in a position to do pretty much what I want. Or, more to the point, not to do what I don't want. I mean, what can you do? You already told Raus that you're going to kill me when I've done whatever it is you want. You've kind of closed off your options."

"Pain can be a great motivator."

Gibson met her gaze. "Burroughs and Wellcome."

"They're just outside."

"You know something? I really don't think you're going to torture me."

Smith raised an eyebrow. "You don't?"

"I think whatever you want from me has something to do with the look-alike."

"The look-alike?"

"My double. The guy who was living in that appartment before you put me there. The guy whose wallet and ID I found."

"Leh Zwald."

"Is that his name?"

Smith nodded. "What about him?"

"I figure that the reason you brought me here was to use me as a ringer of some kind, a substitute. I don't think I'm going to be any use as a ringer if I'm too busted and messed up to walk or talk."

Smith looked amused. "You've changed, Gibson."

"Probably because I've been fucked with and lied to a little too consistently."

"You think we've been lying to you?"

"I know you've been lying to me. You've been lying to me since you picked me up in Jersey. All that bullshit about looking after me and protecting me, that's all it was, bullshit. The way I see it, you had a plan for me from the get-go."

Smith's eyes were hard slits. "That's what you think?"

"I've been hearing all about you people and a few things are starting to make sense."

"You've been hearing about us?"

"All about you."

Smith sniffed. "You've been talking to those ridiculous *idimmu.*"

"They filled in some of the blanks."

"I suppose they gave you the usual human-sacrifice nonsense and how we're bent on conquering the universe."

"That was touched on."

It was Smith's turn to sneer. "And you, of course, believed them."

"It all seemed pretty plausible."

"That's the word for it, plausible. Not necessarily the truth, though."

Gibson lit a cigarette, with the matches that Klein had left for him. It seemed the streamheat weren't worried that he'd set fire to the bed. "I still tend to believe it."

"Your demon friends weren't much help to you this morning."

Gibson had to concede this. "You have a point there."

Smith changed the subject. "You want to tell me the point of this tough guy talk, Gibson? What are you hoping to achieve by it?"

Gibson dragged on the Camel before he answered. He felt that he was near to playing the only card that he had. "I'm trying to save my ass."

"That's understandable, although, from where I'm standing, you don't seem to have much bargaining power."

"I could cooperate. Fully."

Smith smiled nastily. "Believe me, Gibson, you'll cooperate."

"I think the saying goes 'One volunteer is worth ten pressed men.' "

"And what would you want in return for this full cooperation?"

"Just that I'd walk away once whatever it turns out to be is all over. You shoot me back to my own dimension and I keep my mouth shut.''

Smith actually laughed. "It certainly is an intriguing proposition.''

"So you want to deal?''

Smith shook her head. "I don't know. I'll have to think about it and discuss it with my colleagues. I promised Raus that I'd have you eliminated.''

"How would Raus know, if I was in another dimension?''

Smith continued to shake her head. "I really have to think this one through. There are a couple of things that you ought to know, however.''

"What's that?''

"Leh Zwald isn't just your double. He's actually the parallel of you in this dimension.''

Gibson's jaw dropped. He didn't quite know what to do with this bombshell. "Jesus.''

Smith was obviously enjoying this part. "There's something else.''

"There is?''

"Leh Zwald is planning to assassinate the president of the UKR.''

While Gibson was dealing with that one, Smith turned and let herself out of the bedroom. "I'll give you my decision later.''

Gibson flopped back on the bed, totally drained. He had given it his best shot and then had it handed back to him in spades. Assassinate the president? There was almost a bizarre logic in that. He'd made his mark in his dimension, and it seemed that this Zwald was trying to make a truly indelible mark on his. Indentical personalities, presumably with the same primal drives and desires, are shaped by two very different societies, and one turns out to be an entertainer while the other strives to carve a niche in history by killing the leader of a country. Just to complicate the matter, the streamheat had organized it so both individuals were now in the same dimension and participating in the same killing. Gibson pulled his feet off the floor and lay on his back. He was actually surprised at his own calm and a little curious why he wasn't in the throes of a life-threatening anxiety attack. The big question was the same one that had been hovering over him ever since this thing had started. What exactly did the streamheat want with him? Some of the periphery of the puzzle had been filled in, but the essential core was still a frustrating blank.

As far as he could estimate, two hours passed before he got any further answers, although it was hard to gauge the passage of time in the locked bedroom. The only thing he knew for sure was that he had smoked five more cigarettes before he once again heard the sound of the door being unlocked.

This time it was Klein, who held the door wide and beckoned to Gibson. "Come with me, will you?"

Klein seemed less than friendly. Perhaps he was miffed at Gibson's negative response to his providing him with beer, butts, and breakfast. Gibson followed Klein down the corridor into the living room. The first thing that he noticed was that the model on the chart table had been covered over with a white sheet. Presuming that it was a miniature of the planned assassination scene, they plainly didn't want him looking at it. Smith, French, and Rampton were waiting for him, and, to Gibson's great relief, there was no sign of Burroughs and Wellcome.

Smith came straight to the point. "You'll be pleased to hear that we have provisionally decided to take you up on your offer."

Gibson nodded. "If I cooperate, you'll let me live?"

"That's the gist of it."

"Well, I'm very pleased to hear that. What are the provisions?"

Smith smiled. "Really there's only one. If you try to double-cross us, we'll shoot you out of hand."

"That's direct and to the point."

"It is, of course, a somewhat strange agreement since we don't trust you and I imagine you have equally little faith in us."

Gibson thought about this. "What you might call a conspiracy of mistrust."

Rampton seemed to like this. "There are times, Gibson, when you put things very well."

Gibson looked round the room. A number of the photographs on the walls were different views of the same building. It was a square, seven-story industrial building, either a factory or warehouse, but there was something oddly familiar about it and he couldn't for the life of him put a finger on what it was or where he might have seen it before.

Giving up on the puzzle, he faced Smith. "Since we seem to have the basis of an agreement, shall we get down to business? I'm a little anxious to know what's expected of me. I take it, since you're so friendly with Raus, that you're on the side of the assassins in this plot."

"That's not strictly true."

Gibson raised his eyebrows. "You mean that you're going to try to save the president?"

Smith sighed. "No, we're not doing that either."

"So what's the deal?"

"Essentially we are monitoring events in Luxor. There's no real debate that the administration of Jaim Lancer has been a complete disaster for this country, but this is an internal matter of the UKR, and contrary to popular opinion, we don't actually go around interfering in the domestic affairs of sovereign states in other dimensions. The most that we can do is to nudge events in the direction that we believe will lead to maximum stability in the region."

"And I'm to be a part of this nudging process?"

"In fact you may only be a backup. The assassination will be carried out by Zwald and three other unnamed shooters. Behind them are Raus and a number of other powerful men in the country. Although the mantle of power will naturally fall on Raus and his friends, there will also be a major public outcry following the president's death. Lancer enjoys a totally irrational popularity among the people of the UKR, and there's bound to be a massive outcry following the assassination and probably the need for a scapegoat."

A chill ran up Gibson's spine. "I hope you don't have me cast in that role?"

"It was considered at first but rejected as impractical."

"So who will take the fall?"

"Zwald."

"While Raus gets crowned king?"

Smith's expression was that of the world-weary professional. "Isn't that the way these things are done?"

Gibson went to the window and looked out. Many floors below, people were walking on the sidewalks and traffic was moving up and down the street. The overcast was breaking up, and patches of watery blue sky were showing through. It was a normal day in any big city. "No honor among conspirators?"

"Would you expect any?"

Gibson nodded in slow agreement. "So what do I have to do?"

"Basically, it's very simple. We move you around various locations in the city to confuse witnesses and generally promote the idea of Zwald being a lone-nut assassin."

"Trying for the lone-gunman theory?"

"That's what Raus is looking for."

"And you?"

"We would prefer the most massive conspiracy paranoia that is possible without Raus's position actually being compromised."

"This sounds a hell of a lot like the Kennedy assassination."

"That was one of the models we used for reference."

"And does Raus know about the Kennedy assassination?"

Smith shook her head. "Of course not."

Rampton seemed to feel a sudden need to show off his knowledge. "There's something called the bottleneck theory that puts forward the proposition that certain events are, for all practical purposes, preordained, racked up in the time stream like a bottleneck that has to be passed before the culture of that dimension can move on."

Smith and French exchanged swift angry glances. It was plain that, as far as they were concerned, Rampton had said too much. Smith went into spin control. "I wouldn't worry about the bottleneck theory, Gibson. Many of us don't subscribe to it."

Gibson, however, was a lot more interested in Rampton than he was in the theory. "While all this explaining is going on, how about someone explaining to me what exactly Rampton is doing here?"

Rampton looked at Gibson coldly. "I don't see what concern it is of yours, Gibson."

Smith still didn't seem particularly pleased with Rampton. "Rampton is simply here to observe."

"Like observing the sacrifice to Balg?"

"He's here to study our methods."

Gibson smiled in disbelief. "That seems about as plausible as the CIA taking along a Boy Scout to show him how they work. What did they promise you, Sebastian? To make you king of the hill back in our dimension once they're finished with this one?"

Rampton only kept his temper under control with some difficulty. "At least I'm not begging for my life."

"Don't speak too soon, Jack. You may be yet."

Smith had had quite enough of this. "Really, Gibson, the reasons for Rampton's being here don't concern you."

Rampton's face broke into a faint sneer. "Ever heard the phrase 'need to know,' Joe?"

"The only thing that I need to know is that he isn't going to be coming up behind me at some crucial moment."

Smith put a final stop to the exchange. "You have our assurance on that."

"I seem to be getting a lot of assurances."

Rampton laughed. "What did you call it, Gibson? A conspiracy of mistrust?"

For the next three days, the streamheat were as good as their word. Gibson was taken by car to various locations in the city and expected to perform simple tasks under the watchful eyes of either French, Burroughs, or Wellcome. He was sent to walk down a specific block, or through the lobby of a building. On one occasion, he had to walk into the offices of a bank and exchange briefcases with a man in a dark suit. Gibson assumed that all this was probably being filmed or photographed or at least watched by a third party who might serve as a witness at some point in the future. Gibson knew that these actions were probably digging him deep and that he was setting up a lot of stuff that could backfire on him if anything went sour. This was an eventuality, however, that he tried not to dwell on. For the moment, he was alive and functioning and that was what counted when you were living on a one-day-at-a-time basis. The fact that he didn't have a solitary clue regarding the relevance of any of the things that he was doing was something else that he preferred not to ponder.

Before the first of these excursions, Gibson had created a fuss about how exactly they expected an albino to impersonate a normal man, no matter how much alike they might look in every other respect. Fortunately, this problem had been anticipated. A makeup artist was brought in, an attractive Luxor native who looked a little like Elizabeth Taylor, who spent a half hour transforming him but didn't seem too pleased that she was hired to help some dirty albino pass as blue.

While all this was going on, Gibson was totally insulated from the outside world. The streamheat made sure that nothing came to him except through them. He saw no television, and, even when he passed a newsstand, the knowledge that Smith, Burroughs, or Wellcome probably had a gun on him didn't encourage him to pause to even look at the banner front pages of the newspapers. Thus it came as something of a surprise to be told, as he was returning from an afternoon of posing for photographs in front of a brick wall at some abandoned industrial site, holding a rifle and looking belligerent, that the assassination would take place in the morning.

"As soon as that? I thought it wasn't for a week or more."

Gibson had no tangible facts on which to base this assumption. He had just been hoping.

French had smiled one of his contemptuous smiles. "What's the matter, don't you feel ready for it?"

Gibson had scowled. "I don't know what I'm ready for. Shouldn't I be briefed for this? It'd be nice if I knew what I was doing."

"In fact, you won't be briefed until the last moment."

"Security or just keeping old Gibson in the dark as usual?"

"Neither, actually. The truth is that we aren't even sure if we'll need to use you at all. If things go smoothly, we won't."

"That's good news."

"I thought it might be."

Despite French's words, though, a clawing tension built inside Gibson all through the evening. He was no longer locked in the small bedroom, and the streamheat had gone so far as to allow him a couple of beers, but that was it, and it hardly made a dent. Unable to read and without a TV to distract him, Gibson found that there was nothing to do except pace, chain-smoke, and stare down at the lights of the cars in the street below. It had gone beyond the level of thinking about it. He wasn't asking himself how or why or what-if any longer; anxiety was a fist-size knot in his stomach, and he had a fist-clenching need to be constantly on the move. The robot state of just doing what he was told, by which he'd been surviving since he'd agreed to cooperate, was a trick that had been used from the dawn of time by those who only stand and wait, but there was a limit to how long he could turn it. He'd reached the point, this final evening, when he simply couldn't pretend anymore, or keep on shifting the fear along with the responsibility. In the morning, he'd be involved in the killing of a president, and that was all she was going to write. His life had become so terrifyingly fragmented that nothing remained on which a hold could be maintained. Mindless motion was the only thing stopping him from coming apart. Finally, even Smith realized that he couldn't go on building up this kind of pressure without something blowing.

"Gibson, do you want a tranquilizer?"

"I'd rather have a bottle of Scotch."

"We can't have you hung over in the morning."

Down on the street, a black police cruiser was scanning doorways with a spotlight. Gibson watched until it was gone. "I thought you weren't expecting to have to use me."

"Nothing's settled yet."

"Suppose the local cops have a line on us?"

"They don't. They've been taken care of."

Gibson turned away from the window and paced across the living room. "This shit is starting to get to me. I need a fucking drink."

"Let me give you a shot."

"Will it put me out?"

"It should. You probably won't even dream."

She was already reaching in a drawer for a syringe, a foil-wrapped needle, and a bottle of colorless fluid. "Roll your sleeve up."

Gibson didn't like the idea of being shot up by Smith, but it was worth it if it stopped him twitching. He bared his arm without a word. Doing what he was told seemed to have become habitual.

The drug put Gibson out almost immediately, and he only just made it to the small bedroom before his eyes stopped focusing and their lids began to droop. It didn't stop him dreaming, though, and sleep became an ordeal as his subconscious disgorged a fearful invasion of violent newsreel images, stampeding crowds, screaming mouths, terrified faces, and helpless, ineffectual gestures as flesh tried to ward off bullets.

The images came on relentlessly: huge black cars with Secret Service men swarming all over them, a woman in a pink wool suit crawling back over the trunk of one of them, hand reaching out. Brown hair, a head haloed in the pink spray of its own brains going forward and back, forward and back. Knives slashing, a machete-wielding figure being clubbed to the ground by riot police. Another figure, a wild-eyed, tubercular kid, running alongside an open, horse-drawn carriage. A dead man's pistol shot, and the kid was cut down by the sabers of the hussars, blood spurting, head going backward and forward, backward and forward. And more pistols in the night, pistols in the light of the TV cameras and more shots and more blood, blood matting more brown hair and more hands reaching out, bloodstained white uniforms, and blood running in the gutter, white shirts, dark suits, clubs and sabers swinging, fists hurting, faces blank with shock, screaming. "Get him! Get him!"

And each time he was the assassin. He was always the assassin. Eternal, now and forever, world without end, universe of pain.

"Amen."

"Get him!" "Get him!"

Twice Gibson woke sweating, fearing psych attack but knowing that the nightmares were only the creations of the terror in the black bilges of his own mind.

And then it was morning and Klein was sitting on the bed, holding out a cup of coffee. "Are you okay, Joe? You were screaming during the night."

Gibson struggled and sat up.

"Yeah, yeah. I guess so. I've been having nightmares ever since this thing got started."

He took the coffee and sipped it tentatively.

"What time is it?"

"Six A.M."

"What's happening?"

"I'm afraid I have some bad news."

Gibson lowered the coffee with a sinking feeling in his stomach. "What?"

"Zwald is dead."

"Huh?"

"He tried to back out at the last minute."

"Back out of the assassination?"

"Right."

"I know how he felt."

"Raus's people killed him."

"What did they do? Feed him to Balg?"

Klein shook his head. "I believe they shot him."

Gibson beamed as though the sun had just come up in a blaze of glory and a great weight had slipped from his shoulders. "I don't want to come on like I'm self-obsessed or anything, and I'm sure it's real bad news for the late Leh Zwald, but what does this mean for me? The assassination is canceled, right? So you don't need me anymore, right?"

Klein wasn't smiling. "The assassination hasn't been canceled, Joe."

The sun went out and the weight crashed back onto Gibson like a cement overcoat. "What?"

"The assassination is still on. There are two other shooters, don't forget."

"What happens to me?"

"I'm afraid you're going to have to play the assassin."

Gibson felt sick. "I can't do that. I'll never hold together."

"All you have to do is to walk through the moves that Zwald

was going to make. It's no different from what you've been doing already, and you'll be covered every inch of the way."

Gibson started slowly, shaking his head. He felt as though he was going into shock. "No."

"It's very simple. All you have to do is walk into a building, ride up in the elevator, wait awhile, then ride back down again and leave. Once you're clear of the immediate area you'll be pulled out, and Zwald's body produced as that of the lone assassin. All you have to do is allow yourself to be spotted by a few witnesses and that's it."

"That's it? Aren't you forgetting the fact that the president of the country will be shot between this going in and coming out? Won't that make this getaway a little difficult, particularly if I'm pretending to be the assassin?"

"It'll be a total chaos right after the shooting. No one will imagine you're the assassin until well after the fact. Remember that Raus controls most of the news media. He'll make sure that everything is pinned on the late Leh Zwald. Besides, French will be with you every step of the way."

French's voice came from the doorway. "Doesn't that fill you with confidence, Gibson, that I'll be right beside you?"

Gibson was shaking his head again. "I'm not doing this."

French leaned against the doorjamb. He was wearing dirty tan workman's coveralls and holding another set, which he tossed onto the bed in front of Gibson. "Put those on and cut out the dramatics."

"I'm telling you, I'm not doing this."

French straightened up and put one hand in his pocket. "I'm going to keep this real simple, Joe." He pulled out a large revolver of local design, not unlike the one that Gibson had fired in Raus's shooting gallery, and pointed it at Gibson. "You see this gun, Joe? Regular pistol, no fancy technology, straight bullet in the brain, right? Well, that's exactly what you're going to get if you're not out of that bed and into those coveralls in the next thirty seconds. You understand me?"

Gibson sighed. "I understand you."

Watched by French and Klein, Gibson crawled from the bed and began pulling on the coveralls. His only thought was that it was a sorry set of clothes in which to die.

French hadn't finished with him. "I'm going to have the same gun all the way through the operation, and if I have the slightest feeling that you're trying to screw things up, I use it on you. You understand that?"

Anger came to Gibson's rescue. "Yes, I understand it. Death is real easy to grasp."

French nodded and then looked at Klein. "Okay, give him his shot."

"Shot? What shot?"

"A stimulant, to help you through."

"Not more goddamned speed?"

Klein was preparing the needle. "No, something of ours. It has a long complicated name, but usually it's called hero serum."

The needle went into his arm, and within seconds Gibson was feeling a whole lot better, light-headed and reckless. Rolling down the sleeve of his coveralls, he followed French into the living room. He was seeing things from a detached, insulated point of view that had to be an effect of the drug. He noticed a line of local script, presumably the name of a company, was stenciled across the back of French's coveralls, and Gibson presumed that his carried the same name and that they'd be posing as workmen.

Beyond the living room windows, the first gray dawn was creeping over the city and the sky was streaked with high pink clouds. It looked as though it was going to be a fine day. What was the Indian saying, "It's a fine day to die." Lights were burning in some of the apartment buildings nearby, others rising early or nighthawks not yet ready to give up and go to bed. It was all so damned normal. He wanted thunder in the distance and portents of doom. His mind wandered further. Somewhere out there, the president was sipping his coffee or talking on the phone, maybe dressing, maybe, at that very moment, splashing water on his face and blinking at his reflection in a bathroom mirror, readying himself for the parade through Luxor and unknowingly readying himself for death.

French, briskly getting down to business, put a stop to Gibson's speculations. "Do you want to eat?"

Gibson quickly shook his head. "No."

"I didn't think you would. The hero serum tends to suppress the appetite." He pointed to a small collection of objects that had been placed on a side table: two packs of cigarettes, Leh Zwald's wallet, some loose change, and a couple of packs of matches.

"Put that stuff in your pockets."

"What's this, my junior assassin's kit?"

French ignored the remark. "Is there anything else that you want?"

"I want a drink."

French didn't argue and called out to Klein. "Get Gibson a large shot of whiskey."

Gibson flipped open the wallet. It contained Leh Zwald's ID and a bundle of notes. Gibson didn't count it, as at that moment Klein had come into the room with a generous measure of booze in a tumbler. Gibson took the glass gratefully and downed its contents in two swallows. When he spoke, the words came out as a hoarse gasp. "Damn but that's better."

He glanced at French. "What about my makeup?"

"The woman will be here momentarily."

The makeup woman was as good as French's word. In a matter of minutes, the door buzzer sounded and Klein let her in. She quickly rendered Gibson blue and left again. After she'd left, Gibson was thoughtful. "Aren't you running a risk using her? I mean, she could talk. She knows that I'm an albino."

French didn't look in the least perturbed. "She won't talk."

"She won't?"

"As we speak, she's being picked up by Raus's people on her way out of the building."

"What's going to happen to her?"

French was putting things in his own pockets. "That's none of your concern."

"Are you saying that she's going to be killed? Christ, she was an attractive young woman and has nothing to do with any of this."

"She was a drug addict, deliberately selected because of that. No one cares what happens to them."

Gibson's expression was grim. "Oh, of course. No one cares about drug addicts, do they?"

French gestured to the door. "Shall we go?"

"Where are we going?"

"I'll explain in the car."

On the way down to the street, another question came up.

"Where are Smith and Rampton?"

"Smith has duties elsewhere. I don't know what Rampton might be up to."

"How come he isn't along on this little junket? Shouldn't he be observing or something?"

French scowled. For once, he seemed to agree with Gibson's sentiments. "I don't think Rampton does field work."

A beat-up blue car that was completely in keeping with the two men's blue-collar image was parked at the curb. French got behind the wheel, and they pulled out into the stream of traffic. French talked as he drove. "We are heading for a warehouse building across town. It belongs to the Crown Electrical Company, and the reason that we're going there is that it overlooks the point where Lancer's motorcade will pass through Craven Plaza."

Gibson nodded. "This is the building that Zwald was going to shoot from?"

"Exactly. It was arranged some four weeks ago that Zwald would go to work there. We're going to park the car in the employees' lot and go into the building just like two regular guys on their way to work. From the moment that you enter the building, you will be Zwald. Fortunately, he kept very much to himself and it's unlikely that anyone will engage you in anything but the briefest conversation."

"What if they do?"

"Make an excuse, say that you're busy and have to be somewhere."

"Wouldn't that appear a little weird?"

"Not for Zwald, believe me. He was weird, you can take my word for that."

"So what do I do once I'm inside the building?"

"You punch in just like anyone else. I know you can't read but I'll indicate which card to use. After you've punched in, we take the elevator up to the sixth floor. Turn right out of the elevator and the fourth door along the corridor will be that of a large, empty storeroom. We go inside and wait."

"That's it?"

"That's it."

"And you'll be with me?"

French smiled nastily. "I'll be right behind you, Gibson. There's no way you'll be able to give me the slip."

Gibson sighed. "I think you've made that point."

"So, is there anything else you need to know?"

"There is one thing. What's your cover story when we get to Crown Electrical? I mean, do you have a job there or are you just going to wing it on the strength of wearing the work clothes?"

"I have a job there. I'm due to start this morning."

"Isn't that asking for trouble? Surely the local equivalent of the FBI or whatever are going to be checking on all newly hired employees and stuff like that.''

This time French's smile was grim. "By the time they start doing that kind of checking, I'll be a long way away.''

They drove across town for about fifteen minutes, but Gibson, not having even the foggiest idea of the geography of Luxor, had no idea where they were going. They left the residential neighborhood and passed through an area of industrial buildings. All along the route there were the signs of a city waking up and starting the day. Lines of gray-faced workers waited for buses while others thronged the roads in their own almost uniformly run-down cars. For anything but the closest examination, Gibson and French fitted right in with nothing to make them stand out from the crowd. During the last five minutes of the trip, they were diverted by a number of police sawhorse barriers and temporary detour signs. They were obviously near an area that was being kept clear for the presidential motorcade.

The Crown Electrical building was a square brick structure and, apart from the fact that it overlooked the open space of Craven Plaza, was totally unremarkable. There were probably a thousand commercial buildings just like it in the city. French parked and locked the car, and he and Gibson walked to the staff entrance just like any other poor bastards on their way to work. The act of punching in went without a hitch, even though Gibson hadn't punched a clock since sometime in the sixties when, as a struggling rock 'n' roller, he'd worked in a bakery before the advent of fame and fortune.

He and French rode up in the elevator together with two other characters in the same tan overalls. One of the characters nodded in a routine way to Gibson. "How you doing, Zwald? Heard you went out sick.''

Gibson fought down panic and nodded back. "I must have ate something that didn't agree with me.''

"That's a bitch, ain't it. You still look a bit under the weather. You want to take it easy.''

Gibson grinned. "I'll sure do that.''

To Gibson's relief, the two men got out on four and he and French continued to the sixth floor on their own. As soon as the elevator door closed, Gibson let out a long sigh. "I could have done without that.''

"You're doing fine, just hold it together.''

Gibson blinked. As far as he could remember, it was the first time that he'd ever heard French utter an encouraging word.

They emerged from the elevator, turned right, and went through the fourth door they came to. As French had predicted, there was nothing behind it apart from a large dusty storeroom containing a half-dozen or so empty boxes. French immediately went to the window and looked out; then, apparently satisfied that all was as it should be, he turned to Gibson and pointed at the radiator against the wall. "Look down behind that radiator and see what you can find."

"The radiator?"

"Just do it."

Gibson gingerly reached down the back of the radiator. He had once heard a story about how, in Australia, they had something called the funnel web spider whose bite could kill a grown man in a matter of seconds. Since the coming of modern civilization, the funnel web had taken to living behind radiators in hotels, factories, and apartment buildings. He hoped there was nothing similar in Luxor. His fingers touched wrapping paper. A package of some kind was hidden down there, long and narrow. When he lifted it out, he could feel its hard metallic contents: it contained either curtain rods or a broken-down rifle.

"Is this Zwald's gun?"

French nodded. "It's been hidden there for over a week."

"You want me to unwrap it?"

"No, come and help me with these boxes."

French was walking a packing case over to the window. As Gibson brought more, he arranged them into a low wall in front of the window so they formed a perfect sniper's nest. Gibson scratched his head. He didn't know if it was a side effect of the hero serum but the modest exertion had made him sweat. "Did we really need to do that?"

French was pushing up the window. "Got to make it look right."

Gibson moved over to the window and looked out. Crowds of spectators were already lining the motorcade route where it passed through the square of sooty green that was called Craven Plaza. On the right-hand side of the square, there was a low rise dotted with scrawny trees and, at the far end, a bridge that carried the monorail tracks over the streets. Motorcycle cops formed knots on every corner, and patrolmen on foot were strung out all along the route. The sinister, black, armored police cruisers were prowling up and down like grim headwaiters making final adjustments to the place settings before a banquet. Gibson gave thanks for the hero serum, which was keeping him from imagining every law-enforcement officer that he could see storming up to the sixth floor of Crown Electric to get him.

French was tearing the wrapping from the rifle. It came in five basic parts, clean, brand new, and covered in a thin film of gun oil. He quickly snapped together the barrel, the trigger mechanism, and the skeleton stock. He'd fitted the scope sight and banged in the clip with a final flourish, and then, to Gibson's horror, he knelt in the firing position and experimentally sighted the rifle out of the window.

"For Christ's sake don't do that, someone will see you."

French shrugged and lowered the gun. He placed it on a packing case beside him. "You worry too much."

Gibson shook his head as though he couldn't quite believe French. "Damn straight, I worry. How long do we have to wait here?"

French took the pistol out of the pocket of his overalls and placed it on the packing case beside the rifle. Now both weapons were handy for use.

"Lancer isn't due for another hour."

"Jesus. What if someone comes up here?"

"I locked the door behind us."

Gibson's mouth was very dry. "I think maybe this hero juice is wearing off, I'm starting to feel a little jumpy."

"I'll give you another shot in about forty-five minutes so you don't falter when the moment comes."

Gibson lit a cigarette. "It's going to be a long hour."

While Gibson chain-smoked, French sat cross-legged on the floor in front of the window with one hand on the rifle. There was something almost Zen about his level of calm, as if he had the ability to just turn himself off until he was needed.

In the plaza below, the crowds were growing larger and the cops had completely closed off the streets along which the motorcade would pass and those feeding into them. A loud metallic clack made Gibson start. French had jacked a round into the breech of the rifle.

Gibson dropped his latest cigarette onto the floor and ground it out with his heel. "What do you need to do that for?"

"Just force of habit."

"Now I'm so far in, how about explaining something to me?"

"What's that?"

"How does all this, the plot against Lancer and everything, fit into the battle against Necrom? How does it help?"

"It's a matter of stability."

Gibson was quite surprised that French was willing to talk to him. He supposed that with all the preparation complete, there was nothing to lose. "Stability?"

"The waking of Necrom will produce an era of violent chaos across the dimensions. Our only hope is to maintain the maximum areas of stability that we can sustain. Behind the combination of Lancer and the current oligarchy in Hind-Mancu, this dimension is already drifting toward chaos."

"So Lancer has to go."

"It would seem so."

"Will Raus be any better?"

French shook his head. "I doubt he'll even weather the scandal of the assassination. A junta composed of police and military officers will be in power inside of two months. Then we'll have some stability."

"The Kamerians aren't going to like that too much, are they?"

"That's hardly the point, is it?"

This seemed to end the conversation, and Gibson turned back to the window. Something about the plaza below had started to bother him, a nagging feeling that somehow it seemed familiar. After worrying it around for a while, he dismissed the thought. It was probably the effect of the drug. Wasn't it time for another shot? He put this to French, and the streamheat produced a small junkie kit in a flat stainless-steel box. Gibson normally hated needles but in this case he would make an exception. The hero serum really did make the fear go away. French filled the syringe and indicated that Gibson should roll up his sleeve. "You know that this stuff can be highly addictive if used for an extended period?"

Gibson sighed. "All I need is a brand-new drug habit."

French smiled. "I wouldn't worry about it. After today, you won't be able to get any more, so you can crave all you want but it won't be more than a wistful memory."

French's tone led Gibson to suspect that he was speaking from personal experience.

Gibson lit yet another cigarette. The first of the two packs was almost empty. "Shouldn't Lancer be here by now?"

French nodded. "He's late. Lancer's famous for being late. He'll probably be late for his own funeral."

French was sighting the rifle again, resting it flat along the stacked-up packing cases. Gibson couldn't see the point of this. It seemed like such a needless risk. "I wish to hell you wouldn't do that."

French looked at him as though he clearly thought that Gibson was an old woman. "Relax, will you? Don't you know people never look up?"

"Cops look up on a gig like this."

"Let it go."

Gibson couldn't let it go. "Anyone would think you were going to do the thing for real."

There was the sound of cheering, out of sight, away down on one of the side streets.

"He's coming!"

French tensed, hunching into the rifle.

Gibson knew that something wasn't right.

The motorcade came round the corner. Four motorcycle policemen led the way on bikes as big as the biggest Harley Davidsons back on Earth. They were followed by two LPD cruisers, and a closed black car not unlike a Cadillac Coupe de Ville of the early sixties. After that came the president, riding in the back of a long, black, open-topped limo with Secret Service men or the equivalent riding the running boards. More motorcycles roared alongside the cars in low gear, belching black, unburned fuel. President Lancer was waving, acknowledging the cheers of the crowd. He was slim with an easy debonair stance and a shock of light-brown hair. His wife was beside him; she was wearing a pink dress. The motorcade was taking the curved road that ran diagonally across the plaza and on down to the underpass at the far end.

The pink dress did it. Gibson knew what wasn't right.

French was aiming the rifle.

The plaza was so familiar because he'd seen it all back on Earth. He'd seen it in newspapers, in newsreels, and on TV. The Zapruder film. It hadn't been in Luxor, it had been in Texas. It wasn't indentical but it was damned close. The motorcade had made it complete. The underpass, the grassy knoll to the right. Dealey Plaza.

"Stop!"

Gibson made a grab for French's pistol.

"Stop!"

French fired. "There are certain events contained in the time stream that cannot be avoided. The bottleneck theory."

Parallel worlds and parallel events.

"Stop!"

Inevitable.

French worked the bolt and fired again.

The president jerked forward.

Unshakable destiny.

Simultaneously there were more gunshots that seemed to come from the grassy knoll.

A pink halo briefly surrounded the president's head.

How many shooters were there on this thing?

The president jerked back.

French fired a third time.

Gibson had the pistol. He knew and was consumed by rage. The streamheat were still lying to him. He was set up. He was the dumb bastard who could be conned twice. He was the fall guy and they were going to turn him into Lee Oswald!

"I'm going to kill you, you motherfucker!"

French turned. The rifle was pointed at Gibson.

The White Room

WHEN GIBSON HAD first been brought to the clinic, the medical staff had seemed determined to bury his so-called rock-star fantasy beneath an impenetrable layer of mind-numbing drugs and mental dislocation. Now, as the weeks turned into months, Dr. Kooning appeared determined to dig it all up again. She was particularly fascinated by the incidents that had destroyed his career. One day, hardly able to disguise her glee, she had let slip that she believed he was experiencing autodestructive delusions of grandeur. From her excitement, he gathered that she believed that this was some big deal.

The pattern for the sessions was normally set by the first question. First, Kooning would read her notes, then remove her glasses and look at him. Gibson didn't like it that she wore the same round Himmler glasses as Rampton.

"You talk about a chain reaction of events that put an end to your career . . ."

Gibson was not in a particularly good mood. He was beginning to believe that his wholesale avoidance of the prescribed pills was setting up a serious psychochemical imbalance in his metabolism. The problem was that the shots continued, which meant he was actually only getting one half of the intended medication, and God only knew what that was doing to him over the long term. He'd found that he was waking up feeling increasingly ratty. He was also heartily sick of the sessions with Kooning. There had to be some finite limits on how much you could talk about yourself, especially when you had long since ceased to be your favorite topic of conversation. Escape was more and more on his mind.

"I thought we'd agreed that the whole thing was just a neurotic fantasy."

"I'd still like to hear about it."

"The downfall?"

"It seems to be the thing that you're least willing to talk about."

"Is that really surprising?"

"It might prove to be a lot easier than you think."

"There isn't really that much to it. I fucked up. I fucked up by abusing the audience and walking off the stage at the Garden. I fucked up on the Letterman show by being drunk out of my mind. I went on the Woody Allen Show after doing coke and mescaline and took it into my head to mouth off about how I was the reincarnation of Ivan the Terrible and what the country needed was a good, old-fashioned autocratic tyranny, which was obviously the gig for me because there was absolutely nothing that I couldn't excel at if I put my mind to it, and how I'd end up ruling the world and the inner planets. I've seen the tape; my last words to Woody before they dragged me off were 'I'm Joe fucking Gibson, Master of the Universe, and don't you forget it.' "

Kooning's eyebrows had shot up like a pair of twin tilt signals on a pinball machine. "Woody? The Woody Allen Show?"

"In my reality, he was a talk-show host."

In fact this wasn't true but he was so tired of talking to Kooning that he had started slipping in selected pieces of fiction. As far as he knew, Woody Allen was the same in the reality he was in as in the one he'd come from. In fact, it had been Oprah Winfrey who'd borne the brunt of that piece of lunacy.

"Did you really believe that you were the reincarnation of Ivan the Terrible?"

"Of course not. I was just trying to upset people by being perverse. And attract attention, too, I guess."

"And did it work?"

Gibson nodded. "Oh, sure. I was banned from over two hundred radio stations and MTV."

"So you wanted to be a victim?"

"Shit, I didn't know what I wanted. In fact, what I wanted hardly came into the picture."

"You felt you had no control over what you did?"

Gibson sighed. He was weary of even thinking about it. "Listen, what was really going on was that I had this job. The Holy Ghosts in general and me in particular had landed this job. Aside from the music, which at times became almost incidental in the minds of some of the fans and most of the media, we were expected to go out to the edge and come back and tell the world what it was like. We were professional pushers of the envelope. We gave the world a window on the weird. In the beginning, the world was titillated and gave us loads of money and drugs and sex. They liked it while it was all fun and frolic and nobody was getting hurt, but when we started showing them what it was really all about they didn't like that. When we publicly got the horrors, they started looking a bit askance.''

Kooning was looking a bit askance herself, and Gibson became a little alarmed. Dear God, had he overdone it? He couldn't imagine what might happen to him if she started believing what he was telling her.

Chapter Eleven

GIBSON FIRED FIRST. French staggered backward but didn't go down or even drop the rifle. They must have been made of sterner stuff in his dimension, maybe more selective breeding. There was no mistaking that the heavy-caliber slug was hurting him. His face was contorted, and his whole body cringed around the point of impact as though trying to contain and blanket the excruciating pain. It wasn't stopping him, however, even though purple blood was now seeping from the entry wound and Gibson could only guess at the mess that had been made of his back where the bullet exited. French was bringing up the rifle again. Gibson fired a second time. French dropped to his knees but still struggled to stand, and might even have made it if Gibson hadn't put a third bullet into him. This time he dropped the rifle. He was clawing inside his coveralls, pulling out a miniature version of the multibarreled streamheat weapon. Gibson hesitated. What was French doing? Why would he bother to zap him when he could have killed him the old-fashioned way with the rifle?

Before Gibson could react, French turned the weapon on himself. He placed the barrel in his mouth and pulled the trigger. There were twin flashes and French vanished as Gibson watched dumbstruck. The streamheat weapon clattered to the floor when the hand that was holding it ceased to exist in that dimension.

For the first time, Gibson was aware of the pandemonium in the square below, a cacophony of massed sirens and the sounds of people screaming, a lot of people screaming. He resisted the temptation to run to the window and look out. He had to clear his mind and think. If he didn't think it through and think it through right, he would be dead within minutes, shot by the police or torn apart by a raging crowd. His first thoughts were the simple ones: Go, run, hide, find a hole and crawl into it, then pull the hole down on top of him. Unfortunately any hole that might offer protection had, by definition, to be well away from Crown Electrical and Craven Plaza.

His instincts said flee, and since he couldn't think of any better plan on the spur of the moment, he followed them. He fled. With a last look at the rifle, the pool of French's purple blood, the spent shell casings and the streamheat weapon lying on the floor, he stuffed the pistol into the pocket of his coveralls and was out of the room and hurrying down the corridor. Next question—the stairs or the elevator? The elevator would probably be quicker but the stairs were less claustrophobic. He opted for speed and pressed the elevator's call button. To his surprise, the door immediately opened on an empty car. Maybe he did still have some luck left. He pushed the button for the second floor. There could be all manner of problems in the lobby, and he'd decided that the second floor would provide a little early warning. As he stepped out on two, he found that his caution had been justified. There was the sound of heavy, almost certainly cop, boots coming up the emergency stairs immediately beside the elevator shaft. He stepped back into an open doorway and found that he was in the small lunchroom. It was empty. He turned and right in front of him was a soft-drink vending machine.

Do something. Demonstrate a reason for being there. He felt for the change in his pocket and started feeding it into the machine. It was the only way that he could think of to cover himself if anyone came into the room. A twelve-ounce bottle of carbonated brown liquid rattled into the vending slot at the bottom. Gibson was just in the process of opening it when a fat red-faced cop in full riot gear, visor up and clutching an assault rifle, came panting through the door.

"You see anyone come out of the elevator?"

Gibson kept his cool and shook his head. "What's going on?"

"You don't know? They shot the president, goddamn it. That's what's going on."

With that he was gone and Gibson let out his breath. Too close, much too close. His mouth was dry and he took a drink of the soda. It tasted a lot like Pepsi or maybe RC Cola. Suddenly he choked and he couldn't stop soda from bubbling out of his nose.

"Oh, Christ. Oh, Jesus." A memory had come out of nowhere and poleaxed him. Lee Oswald had been seen by a cop at the vending machine in the lunchroom of the Texas Book Depository right after the assassination. Panic. He was locked into some historical parallel. They'd made him Oswald and he had no free will. Leh Zwald? Even the fucking name was nothing more than an echo. Had there ever been a Leh Zwald or was he just a streamheat invention? Had it all been supposed to go this way from the start? These were questions that would lead to madness. Ignore them. "Get a grip, kid. Don't go mystic." This was a time of survival, not Shirley MacLaine.

Still clutching the soda bottle, he walked hurriedly down the emergency stairs doing his best to look like a worker who had just heard the terrible news and was coming down to see what was going on. More cops came charging up the stairs, pushing past Gibson and almost knocking him over in their blind headlong rush but at the same time not giving him a second glance. They obviously thought that the assassin was still somewhere on the upper floors. Had that been the plan? That French was to somehow incapacitate him and leave him to be captured? Gibson could just see him babbling to a roomful of ugly, angry Luxor cops as the hero serum wore off, telling them how he'd been instructed to pose as a presidential assassin by some characters from another dimension. They would have him pegged straight away as a lone nut, and that was probably exactly what Raus and his cohorts wanted. Or maybe the plan had been a whole lot simpler than that. Maybe they would have simply killed him and made it look like a suicide. Either way, he'd been taken for a sucker, all the way down the line.

The lobby of the building was in the grip of madness. Cops milled around while bemused and hysterical Crown Electrical workers got under their feet. He made his way to the main door, and found that the street was a hundred times worse. Police cruisers screamed up and down with their lights flashing and sirens wide open while more cops on motorcycles buzzed in between them like angry banshees. Uniformed officers and plainclothesmen with their badges out on display hollered orders, although it was debatable whether anyone was paying very much attention. All over, people stumbled around in blind shock, apparently unsure of what to do or where to go while patrolmen on foot attempted, without too much success, to create some kind of order out of the confusion at the same time as their colleagues confiscated cameras and tried to detain potential witnesses.

Gibson stood for a couple of moments on the steps of Crown Electrical before he moved down onto the sidewalk and let the crowd swallow him up. He eased his way through the milling, weeping people, avoiding the police and doing his best not to make it obvious that he was attempting to put as much distance between himself and the scene of the shooting as he could. While he walked, he hunted through the disorganized junkroom of his memory for some clue as to a feasible escape plan. What did Oswald do next? He wasn't that well up on his Kennedy Assassination trivia. Robo the bass player had been the band's conspiracy expert. As far as he could remember, Oswald had left the Texas Book Depository on foot and gone back to the rooming house where he was staying to get a gun. Gibson already had his gun and that in itself was a break with the pattern. A theory was starting to coalesce. If history had some sort of lock on him, maybe each time that he made a decision on his own, and didn't simply mirror the actions of Lee Oswald, he was increasing his chances of survival and moving away from an inevitable death that mirrored the events in Dallas three decades earlier and a bunch of dimensions away.

He reached the end of the block and turned left on a side street. It was a great deal quieter there, and Gibson was glad to be away from the concentration of police on the plaza. He realized that he was pretty much walking blindly, but he still lacked a definite plan of action. He'd only walked a half block on the side street when the sound of an engine behind him caused him to look down. To his dismay he found that a police cruiser appeared to be not only following him but was actually slowing down. Even the hero serum didn't stop the cold chill from clutching at his stomach like a physical pain.

The black bulk of the police car came to a halt beside him. There were mesh screens down over the windows and it was impossible to see inside. A hand reached out and lifted the screen that was covering the front window on the driver's side, and Gibson, whose own hand was moving surreptitiously toward the gun in his pocket, heard a familiar voice.

"Joe, quick, get in. I'm going to take you out of here."

It was Klein, dressed in full LPD uniform. Gibson stood his ground and shook his head. "I'm not going anywhere with you."

"Just get in the car, Joe. We don't have time to argue."

"I'm not arguing. You people have tried to nail me once, and I'm damned if I'm going to give you the chance for a second shot."

"Everything can be explained, Joe, but not here. You must get in the car. I have to get you to a safe place."

The car door started to open. Klein was coming out to get him. Gibson's fingers touched the butt of the pistol. Without even thinking he pulled it out and pointed it at Klein.

Klein looked up at the gun in amazement. "You don't understand . . ."

"Oh, yes I do."

He pulled the trigger once. The bullet took Klein in the forehead. Blood, brains, and bone were splattered across the roof of the car. Klein jerked back and then fell forward. It seemed that a forty-five slug in the head was enough to stop even a streamheat. Klein lay half in and half out of the car with his shattered head in the gutter. The purple blood formed a miniature river, flowing toward the first open drain. As the echoes of the shot died away, the car's radio crackled into life.

"This is to all cars. This is to all cars. President Lancer was pronounced dead three minutes ago at Memorial Hospital. I say again, President Lancer was pronounced dead three minutes ago at Memorial Hospital. This is now a homicide investigation. All officers will stand by for an updated description of the suspect."

Gibson didn't wait to hear any more. He quickly turned and started down the street. As he hit his stride, he saw that there was an old lady standing in the doorway of one of the nearby buildings, a tiny woman with white hair and a pale-blue, heavily lined face. Their eyes met but she didn't look away. She returned his stare without the slightest trace of fear. Thoroughly unnerved, he turned and ran. After the first corner he slowed to a walking pace, and tried to look as normal as possible. Down the block, on the other side of the street, he spotted the red-and-blue neon sign of what had to be a movie theatre. He couldn't read the title of the movie on the marquee but he had to assume that it was some kind of parallel-dimension Rambo flick. The poster showed a muscular, stripped-to-the-waist figure in ragged fatigue pants brandishing a huge phallic machine gun. The temptation to slip inside and hide himself in the darkness was overwhelming, but that would be following the pattern with a vengeance. Oswald had lammed out on foot and so had he. Kennedy had died on the operating table and so had Lancer. Oswald had killed a cop and Gibson had shot Klein, who was disguised as a cop. Now here was the movie house and the Dallas cops had taken Oswald when he'd tried to hide in a movie house. Was it all really inevitable?

A police car screamed through the intersection at the other end of the block, and Gibson knew that he had to get off the street. Screw the pattern. If he continued walking aimlessly, there wasn't a doubt that he'd be picked up inside of an hour. The movie house would at least give him a chance to sit and think his way out of this mess. He was now level with the theater, and he quickly looked up and down the street. There was no one around. He hurried across the street and up to the box office. A teenage kid was selling tickets.

Gibson pulled out his money and slapped down a twenty. "Has the movie started yet?"

"It's about halfway through."

"That's okay, I'll pick it up."

The kid punched the buttons on the old-fashioned ticket machine, and a single ticket popped out of the slot. Was it Gibson's imagination or was the kid looking at him a little strangely? He had a portable radio in the booth with him that was playing muted martial music. Had the police started circulating descriptions of a suspect to the media?

The ticket taker tore his ticket in half and handed him the stub. Gibson passed through into the darkness. On the screen, the naked-to-the-waist figure from the poster in front of the theater was engaged in wholesale slaughter of small blue soldiers with narrow Oriental eyes. It seemed quite in keeping with the Cold War mind-set of this dimension. Gibson dropped into a seat about three rows from the front and cast a quick precautionary glance around the darkened theater. He found little difference between a lunchtime movie audience in this dimension and one back in his own. It was largely empty except for a sprinkling of old people, a couple of solitary men, and three teenagers sitting together, probably cutting school, unless they had been given the day off for the president's visit. None of them paid him the slightest attention. He realized that if the movie had been running for a while, these people might not even know what had just gone down in the plaza only a few blocks away. Or had they interrupted the movie?

Gibson sat and stared uncomprehendingly at the screen. The Rambo character had taken a break from slaughtering Orientals and was talking to a very beautiful woman who was wearing very few clothes. It was clearly a preamble to going to bed with her.

The ideal thing would be to get out of the city except that he doubted it would be possible. They probably had the airport and the bus and train stations completely sealed. What the hell was he going to do?

Gibson had just decided that he'd see the movie around two or three times and wait until the streets were dark before he reemerged, and the Rambo character on the screen was in bed with the beautiful woman, when the film abruptly stopped. It was as though the projector's plug had been pulled. The visual images flickered and then the screen went black. The audio plunged to a sub-bass grumble and then there was silence. The houselights went up. Suddenly cops were pouring into the theater. Black uniforms coming down the aisle, guns out, badges flashing. The other patrons looked round in alarm. The kid from the ticket booth was with the police and pointing at Gibson. "That's him!"

The kid's voice was high with excitement. He'd probably tell the story for the rest of his life. Gibson was on his feet, reaching for the gun, with no clear idea of what he intended to do with it.

One of the cops was shouting. "Watch it! He's got a gun!"

And then the cops were on him, punching and hitting. One had him by the hair; then the gun was gone from his hand and someone was yelling obscenities in his ear. The cop who had him by the hair abruptly jerked his head down, smashing it into the arm of the seat. He could feel blood on his forehead. He was being picked up bodily. A fist struck him on the upper thigh, probably a blow intended for his balls. His head was smashed into the seat arm for a second time, and it felt as though his hair was being torn out by the roots. There was more shouting. Someone seemed to be trying to pull the cops off him. "For Christ's sake don't kill him! We want him alive. He can't go on TV if he's too messed up."

That seemed to say it all. He couldn't go on TV if he was too messed up. Now that they had him, they planned to exhibit him. He was on his feet again. His arms were being forced behind him and handcuffs snapped around his wrists. They were far too tight and started hurting almost immediately. Before he could protest, they were hustling him up the aisle. He could even hear himself yelling to the other people in the cinema.

"Remember me! I'm being set up here! If I wind up dead, remember me!"

It hardly seemed that the voice belonged to him. It was as though he was hearing someone else yelling, the voice of a hysterical stranger.

One of the cops holding him punched him hard in the stomach. "Shut the fuck up."

He doubled over with the wind driven out of him. He wanted to vomit but there was no time. He was helpless, being half dragged and half carried toward the back of the theater. Then he was in the lobby, propelled quickly through it by a lot of hands. A small crowd had gathered and they were being held back by even more cops.

He heard someone telling someone else, "He's the one, he killed the president."

Gibson tried to struggle. "I didn't do it. I didn't kill anyone. I'm being set up."

They were pushing him into a police cruiser. An officer put a hand on his head to stop him smashing it on the doorframe. Inside the car, the cop sitting next to him thrust his face into Gibson's. "I'd like to get you alone in an empty room for just ten minutes. I'd show you what we think of people who kill presidents."

Gibson, with nothing left to lose, sneered back at him. "Yeah, but you ain't going to get the chance. I'm too fucking important. You've all got to keep me in one piece for the TV cameras."

For a moment, Gibson thought that he'd gone too far and the cop was going to smash his fist into his face. The man controlled himself, however, and had to be content with a simple snarl. "Yeah, but I'll be the one laughing when they strap you into the crusher."

Gibson shook his head. "That's never going to happen."

Although Gibson had no idea what was going to happen to him, he had a strangely absolute certainty that trial and execution weren't in his future. He realized that he didn't even know how they executed people in Luxor, although the crusher sounded particularly cruel and unusual. He turned and looked out of the window as the police car roared through the city, being given a complete right-of-way through the early-afternoon traffic. He knew that this might be the last moment of calm that he would be allowed for a very long time.

Before Gibson could think about it too much or start hoping too hard, they arrived at police headquarters and turned into a long sloping tunnel that led down to an underground lot in the bowels of the building. The circus that was waiting for him there was nothing short of pandemonium. There were wall-to-wall cops, maybe two hundred in all, so far in excess of the manpower that might be needed to either prevent him escaping or protect his safety that he could only assume the majority had come down from other parts of the building just to watch the arrival of the man who had killed the president. In addition to the cops there was a large crowd of reporters complete with cameras, lights, and bulky tape recorders. As the car slowed to a halt, they broke through the line of cops that was supposed to be holding them back and swarmed all over the car, elbowing each other and struggling for the best position, peering in the windows of the cruiser and bellowing questions at the tops of their voices. The place was disturbingly like the underground police garage where Jack Ruby had shot Oswald, and Gibson had to remind himself that Oswald was being taken out and not brought in, although the thought provided little comfort. If it wasn't today, it could just as easily be tomorrow or the next day, if events continued to conform to the JFK-Oswald pattern.

Gibson and his escort sat in the car for a full five minutes, waiting for some kind of order to be restored. Finally one of the officers in the front of the car produced a blanket and threw it back to the cop sitting beside Gibson. "Put that over his head."

Gibson immediately protested. "I don't want a fucking blanket over my head."

"You'll do what we say, boy. You're in no position to be arguing about anything anymore."

"Why do I have to hide under a goddamned blanket? I haven't done anything to be ashamed of."

"We don't want pictures of you in circulation until we're good and ready."

"Maybe you don't want pictures of me looking like I just went ten rounds with the heavyweight champ."

The cop didn't seem to be prepared to argue any more. He just tossed the blanket over Gibson's head and the world was black. With his hands cuffed behind his back, there also wasn't a damn thing that he could do about it. As they helped him out of the car, the press started hollering again.

"Did you do it?"

"Did you kill the president?"

"Who are you working for?"

"The Hind-Mancu?"

"Were you the only one?"

"Why did you do it?"

Gibson wasn't given any chance to answer the questions, although he was certain he'd be asked a lot more of the same once he got inside. He was hustled from the car and into an elevator. In some respects, it was almost like arriving for a concert at Madison Square Garden or London's Wembley Stadium when the Holy Ghosts were at the peak of their fame, except that he'd never done the run from the car to the stage door with a blanket over his head before. He grimly told himself that he'd always liked to be the center of attention and now he was undisputedly just that.

In the elevator, beyond the range of the photographers and TV cameras, they took the blanket off his head. Gibson and his escort rode the elevator up to the third floor, where a smaller circus waited for them. Up there, it was all cops. The media was mercifully missing, as was the pandemonium of the basement, and there was no elbowing, jostling, or shouted questions. The massed cops watched him in hostile silence and stepped aside as he was brought through. Doubtless, just about every one of them would have been more than happy to tear his head off on the spot, but discipline kept them in check, and he was taken to a secure interview room without incident.

The interview room was like something out of a forties gangster movie. A single hardwood chair was set up in the center of the small room. A metal floor lamp was positioned so it would shine directly into the face of whoever was sitting in the chair. His escort was now down to the three original uniformed officers who had been in the car with him. They removed his handcuffs and, without giving him a chance to massage the circulation back into his hands and wrists, had him empty his pockets out onto a table against the wall. The officers poked perfunctorily through the few odds and ends that the streamheat had allowed him to bring to the Crown building. About the only thing that held their attention was the wallet with Leh Zwald's ID in it, and they passed that from one to the other. The largest of the cops, the one who'd been sitting in the back of the car with him, pointed to the chair under the light.

"Sit."

"Can I have a cigarette?"

"Later. Sit."

Gibson seemed to have no option but to do as he was told. He sat and continued to sit, with the officers leaning against the wall, watching him in silence. After about ten minutes, a policewoman came in with a portable fingerprint kit and took a set of prints from him. She was fast and businesslike but avoided looking him straight in the eye and wasn't quite able to disguise her distaste when she had to take hold of his hands to roll the balls of his fingers and thumbs across the ink pad. The next visitor was a police photographer who showed up with a bulky flash camera and proceeded to take head shots of him from a dozen different angles. A new set of problems was unveiled with the arrival of the photographer. He set his camera down, looked at the cops, and then pointed to Gibson. "He's going to have to be cleaned up before I can do anything with him."

The largest of the policemen scowled. "Cleaned up?"

"I can't photograph him looking like that."

Gibson, who hadn't seen himself in a mirror since he'd been arrested, wondered just how bad he did look.

One of the officers left the room and returned with a bowl of water and a sponge. As he went to work, none too gently wiping off Gibson's face, the truth quickly became apparent.

"He's a fucking albino."

The three other men gathered around him, peering at the white skin that had been revealed under the makeup.

"Dirty freak."

The big cop clenched his fists. "I ought to show you what we think about your kind, you bastard."

One of his partners put a restraining hand on his arm. "Leave him for the brass. It's your ass if you mess him up before they get here."

The big cop spat on the floor. "I hate fucking freaks. They disgust me."

Gibson sat very quiet, anxious not to do anything that might cause the big cop to break through his tenuous restraint.

The brass arrived about twenty minutes after the photographer was through with his business. Initially there were three of them. A short, fat individual in gray suit and white hat appeared to be in command. Flanking him was a tall thickset man in the uniform of a high-ranking police officer that was heavily decorated with medal ribbons and gold braid, and a worn-looking man in a rumpled suit who had the kind of deceptively lazy eyes that, while seemingly half-asleep, actually missed nothing. There were no formal introductions, but along the line Gibson discovered that the one in the hat was Luxor Police Commissioner Layen Schubb; the uniform belonged to Assistant Commissioner Lar Boveen, the head of the city's uniformed force; and the individual with the eyes was Chief of Detectives Revlich Valgrave. Gibson was certainly getting the full treatment. These three men ran the entire civil police force of Luxor, and they had come down to personally supervise his interrogation. As far as they were concerned, the crime of the century had been committed in their city and they weren't going to entrust the investigation to subordinates or turn it over to any of the half-dozen paramilitary national agencies. For almost a minute, they stood looking at him as though inspecting something so low and disgusting that it was beyond even their experience.

Finally Schubb pushed back his hat and shook his head. "You've really done it, haven't you, boy?"

Gibson avoided looking directly at Luxor's top cop. He stared down at the floor trying not to think about what might be going to happen next. "I really don't have anything to say."

Schubb walked slowly around Gibson's chair. "That's not a good attitude, boy. You've just shot the president of the UKR and a lot of people are going to want to hear what you've got to say for yourself and, I have to tell you, some of them are not going to be as patient as I am."

This time Gibson looked up at him. "I don't expect you to believe me, but I didn't shoot the president."

Valgrave stepped forward and turned on the light. Gibson closed his eyes, temporarily blinded. The lamp was a powerful photoflood, and it was only a matter of inches from his face. The three ranking officers and the patrolmen in the background were nothing more than indistinct shadows.

Valgrave's voice came out of the darkness beyond the light. "Let's start with some basic details. Your name is Leh Zwald, right?"

Gibson squinted into the light and shook his head. "No."

"It's not?"

"It's not."

"That's what it says in this wallet."

"I'm not Leh Zwald."

"So who are you?"

"My name is Joe Gibson."

"Jogibson? What kind of name is that?"

"You wouldn't believe me if I told you."

"Try me."

Gibson took a deep breath. He might as well tell them in front; it was going to come out eventually. "It's a name from another dimension."

Schubb broke into the exchange between Gibson and Valgrave. "What are you talking about, boy? If you think you can worm your way out of this by acting crazy, you can forget it. Nobody's going to go along with that."

"I said that you wouldn't believe it."

Boveen took a turn. "You don't know how lucky you are, son."

"You could have fooled me."

Schubb stabbed a finger at him. "Don't get smart, boy. We don't have much time."

Boveen resumed. "You don't know how lucky you are being held by us. The Luxor Police Department, unlike some of the national law-enforcement agencies, don't use torture as a routine technique in the interrogation of suspects."

Gibson took another deep breath. There was no answer to that.

Schubb nodded. "Not so cocky now, huh, boy? The mention of torture usually takes the wind out of the sails of little shits like you."

Boveen was looking at his watch. "The way I figure it, we have maybe ten minutes before delegations from State Security, the Treasury Police, and the Presidential Guard will be all over us demanding we give up custody to them. They want you badly, and every last one of them will be quite prepared to do their worst to get a confession out of you."

"And will you give me to them?"

"We don't want to. Right now you're in our jurisdiction. The president was shot in Luxor, and we want to be the ones who crack the case. The trouble is that you can't fight politics. Unless you've given us something to work on we may not be able to keep you. It's as simple as that."

Gibson nodded. Either the commissioner was telling the truth or it was one of the most elaborate Mutt and Jeff setups that he'd ever heard. "I see."

"You understand our position?"

It might be a Mutt and Jeff play but Gibson was still thoroughly intimidated. "I do."

"So shall we start again?"

"I'll tell you what I can."

Valgrave took over. "Name?"

"Joe Gibson."

Valgrave sighed disappointedly. "I thought you understood your position."

Gibson was starting to get a little desperate. "Believe me, I'm trying to cooperate. I'm not Leh Zwald. My name is Joe Gibson. Joe, first name, Gibson, second name. Leh Zwald was originally supposed to shoot the president but he tried to back out and was killed. I was forced to take his place.

"Who killed this Leh Zwald?"

Gibson shook his head. "I don't know for sure. I do know who ordered it, though."

"Who ordered it?"

"Verdon Raus."

Valgrave's eyebrows slowly went up. "Are you serious?"

"Perfectly serious."

Boveen sharply sucked in his breath. "That's some name, boy. Are you sure you're not just using it to buy some time for yourself?"

"Verdon Raus was at the head of the whole conspiracy."

Schubb's eyes were narrow piggy slits. "Even assuming that there was such a conspiracy, why should a man like Verdon Raus use a piece of garbage like you to do his work for him?"

"I've already told you, I wasn't the assassin."

Valgrave tried the kid gloves again. "So why were you selected to replace this Zwald?"

"Because I look exactly like him."

Schubb had the expression of a man who thinks he's just uncovered a conspiracy of mutants. "Zwald was another albino?"

"No."

"Then how could you look exactly like him?"

"We were identical apart from our color. That was the only difference."

Schubb rubbed his chin. "That's quite a big difference, boy."

Valgrave eased back into the interrogation. "Explain your role in this, how you replaced Zwald."

"They told me that I was going to be a decoy. I was to go through the motions of pretending to be the assassin. I was led to believe that our purpose was to stop the shooting. It was only when I was actually inside the Crown building, I found that I'd been lied to. I found that I was being set up as the fall guy."

Even the low-key Valgrave couldn't keep a certain mild excitement out of his voice. "You admit that you were in the Crown building?"

Gibson nodded. "I was beside French when he shot at Lancer."

"French?"

"This is where it becomes difficult."

Up to that point, Gibson had been feeling that Valgrave might be buying his story. Then Commissioner Schubb stepped back in.

"Don't be telling me tales of other dimensions, boy. That would make me very unhappy."

"Maybe I should get a lawyer."

"You'd be better off with a priest if you start lying to me."

"If I tell the truth, you're just not going to believe me."

Valgrave stroked his chin. "I believe we've reached an impasse."

Schubb wasn't having any. "I believe we're dealing with a lying piece of shit who's trying to convince us that he's crazy."

Gibson tried a desperation play. "French wasn't the only shooter."

Now he had their attention. "What?"

"There was one, maybe two more."

Valgrave was leaning close to him. The chief of detectives' breath smelled of garlic. "In the Crown building?"

"No."

"Where?"

"I'm not sure, somewhere else on the square. Maybe the grassy knoll at the far end."

There was a long silence. Gibson had the impression that they might finally be taking him seriously. Valgrave walked over to the table where the contents of Gibson's pockets were still laid out. He picked up one of the packs of Luxor Camels.

He came back and held out the pack to Gibson. "Cigarette?" Gibson took one. "Thank you."

Valgrave took one for himself. He put it in his mouth and lit it, and then he lit Gibson's with the same flame. "How many?"

Gibson was confused. "How many what?"

"How many other shooters?"

"I don't know. At least one more, maybe two."

"You know who they were?"

Gibson shook his head. "No."

Before Gibson could elaborate, there was an urgent rapping on the door of the interview room. One of the patrolmen opened it and looked out. After a couple of seconds, he closed it again and faced Schubb. "There are some men out there who want to speak to you."

"Did you tell them that I was interrogating a prisoner?"

"They seemed pretty fired up about talking to you. The word they used was imperative."

Schubb nodded. "Imperative, huh? That's what I hate about

those college-boy, national-agency assholes. They've always got to use some big-ticket word when a simple one would do.'' He looked at Valgrave and Boveen. "You keep at our boy and I'll go talk to the assholes.''

In fact, while Schubb was out of the room, the other two didn't keep at him. Valgrave smoked in silence, and Boveen watched the door. The cigarette smoke drifted lazily through the lamplight.

Valgrave smiled wearily at Gibson. "Better hope that the commissioner's feeling really feisty. He's going to have his work cut out keeping State Security and the rest of them off of you.''

There was the sound of raised voices outside the door, and Schubb's was one of the loudest. After about three minutes, the door flew open and Schubb stormed back in again, slamming it behind him. "Goddamn it to hell!" He ducked into the lamplight and glared at Gibson. "You better be giving me everything you've got and no more crazy shit, you understand me? I've gone out on a limb to hold on to you, and there's three national agencies trying to saw it off right now.''

Gibson looked straight back at the commissioner with a strangely detached terror. "I can only tell you what I know.''

"So tell me. Start at the beginning.''

"But you aren't going to believe me. I'll get to the part about the streamheat and you're going to get crazy and call me a fucking liar and hand me over to State Security.''

"I'm trying to avoid that, but you aren't making it any easier.''

Boveen glanced at Schubb. "We could turn him over to a couple of my boys for a half hour to loosen him up a bit.''

The three patrolmen at the back of the room looked as though they were ready to volunteer. Schubb thought about this. He stared hard at Gibson. "What's it going to be, boy?''

Gibson was desperate. "I'm trying to help you, believe me.''

Valgrave motioned to Schubb that he wanted to take over the questioning. Schubb deferred to the detective and stepped back.

Valgrave looked almost sympathetic. "What are the streamheat, Joe?''

"They're the ones who got me into this mess. They're the ones who set me up.''

"But what exactly are they?''

Gibson shot a nervous glance at Schubb. "They're . . . from another dimension.''

Schubb didn't say anything but he appeared to be keeping his temper with some degree of difficulty. Valgrave went on. His voice was soft and calm.

"What do you mean by another dimension, Joe?"

Gibson nodded to Schubb. "He's going to kill me if I tell you."

To his surprise, Boveen came to his rescue. "Forget this crap about other dimensions for the moment. Tell me about how you came to kill one of my patrolmen."

Gibson swallowed hard. He had been hoping against hope that, since they hadn't so far mentioned the murder of Klein, they hadn't tied him in with that killing.

He heard his voice come out as a blurt. "It was self-defense. He was going to kill me. He was a part of it."

"Part of what?"

"Part of the conspiracy, part of the setup that put me here."

Boveen's face hardened. "Are you telling me that one of my men was in on this?"

"He wasn't one of your men."

"What?"

"He was streamheat. He was one of the ones who brought me here. He was only dressed as a cop. God knows where he got the car from."

Schubb looked as though he was going to work Gibson over himself. "You're starting with that shit again."

Gibson did his best to defend himself. "You must have the body in the morgue. Fingerprint it, run an autopsy. You'll find out that it isn't one of your men."

Schubb started to steam. "Don't tell us how to do our jobs."

Valgrave and Boveen, however, exchanged significant glances, but before anything else could be said there was a second knocking on the door of the interview room. Once again one of the patrolmen opened it, and a man in a dark civilian suit came in. Although Gibson was able to see past the blinding light a little better than when it had first been turned on, he still had to squint to make out any details of this new arrival. He didn't have to squint too long, however, before it became plain that the newcomer was a lawyer of some kind. He and Schubb fell into immediate head-to-head discussion, the gist of which was that they had troubles.

"I can't see any way that we can go on refusing to hand him over."

Schubb removed his hat and ran a handkerchief across his bald head. "I'm damned if I'm going to turn him over to those glamour boys in State Security. We caught him in our city and our jurisdiction and we're going to hold on to him.''

The lawyer, who, Gibson was to discover later, held the office of city solicitor, the Luxor equivalent of the DA, shook his head. "You can't do that. They've been to a judge and obtained an order. They'll serve it by force if need be.''

"They're that steamed?''

"They just lost a president and they want someone to hang it on personally.''

"So what do I do?''

"You're going to have to hand him over.''

Gibson didn't like the sound of this one little bit, but then Valgrave, who appeared to be by far the smartest of the three top cops, seemed to have an idea. "I take it that the order only refers to the murder of the president.''

The city solicitor blinked. "I only scanned the order and then came straight over here, but I believe that's basically correct.''

"So there's no reference to the killing of the police officer?''

"None.''

"Then we can go on holding him. Gibson has already confessed to that killing.

The city solicitor looked sharply at Gibson. "Is this true? You've made a confession?''

"I told them I shot him, but he wasn't a police officer and I shot him in self-defense . . .''

The lawyer held up a hand. "That doesn't matter for the moment. You admit that it was you that fired the shot?''

Gibson nodded. "I already said that.''

The city solicitor looked triumphantly at Schubb. "In that case, he's still ours, at least until he's had a preliminary hearing on the charge of killing the officer.''

Schubb smiled at the lawyer. "So why don't you go and politely tell our State Security friends to take their judge's order and roll it into a cylinder. I imagine they can guess the rest.''

The city solicitor grinned at the commissioner. "It'll be a pleasure.''

Schubb turned and looked at Gibson.

"I think it's time to consolidate what we've got. Let's give the media a good look at you.''

Gibson sighed. He seemed to remember that, at one point, the Dallas sheriff had exhibited Oswald to the assembled press. "And what am I supposed to tell them?''

Schubb's eyes narrowed and he smiled nastily at Gibson.

"Oh, you aren't going to tell them anything. This is going to be strictly a photo opportunity. You can act as crazy as you want because, from now on, until a better idea presents itself, you're going to be the lone-nut gunman."

Gibson exhaled hard. The Kennedy pattern was still holding. Now he was the lone assassin.

While the press was assembled in a large conference room on the second floor of the police headquarters building, Gibson was put in a holding cell with two patrolmen acting as suicide watch. He remained there for over an hour. When he was finally brought in, the press conference appeared to have been in full swing for some time. Schubb was standing on a raised platform behind a lectern on which there was a battery of a couple of dozen microphones. He was flanked by Boveen and Valgrave and four other men that Gibson hadn't seen before. Two were in LPD uniforms, but the other two wore dark suits in the manner of national-agency men. Once again, icy fingers grabbed for Gibson's gut. Had some kind of deal been struck regarding his custody while he'd been locked up in a holding cell? Not that he was left with any time for conjecture. His entrance was the signal for an outbreak of complete bedlam. Gibson had been clearly held back as Schubb's pièce de résistance. Boveen was displaying the rifle. The media had been told whatever official story Schubb had decided to go with, they'd been shown the weapon, and now, as the grand finale, here was the killer. The press conference had obviously started as a fairly well-organized affair. The heavy, old-fashioned TV cameras and the batteries of lights that went with them had been positioned in the rear of the room, while the print reporters and still photographers were given free range of the area in front of the speaker's podium. With Gibson's entry, however, all the organization went to hell in a basket. The reporters rushed at him in a solid mass while the TV cameramen became tangled in each others' leads as they tried to swing round for the shot. Flashbulbs went off in his face and everyone was yelling at once.

"Hey, Zwald! Did you kill the president?"

"Zwald! Were you on your own?"

"Hey, Zwald, look over here!"

"Over here!"

"Smile for the camera, you bastard!"

"Why d'yer do it, Zwald?"

"Are you working for the Hind-Mancu?"

Gibson could imagine how he would look when the photos

were printed and the pictures went out on the air, scared, blinded, and dazed, handcuffed and helpless, not knowing where to look. A saint would look like a psycho killer in the face of that kind of mob. Mercifully, though, the madness was of short duration. He couldn't have been in the conference room for more than two minutes, although it seemed like an hour while it was going on. Schubb was as good as his word. It was strictly a photo opportunity. Even if Gibson had tried to answer their questions, the reporters were yelling so loud that they wouldn't have heard him anyway. All he could do was repeat the same thing over and over.

"I didn't kill anyone. That's all I have to say. I didn't kill anyone."

He doubted that there would be a person in the entire country who'd believe him. One reporter in the front row was holding up a 10x8, black-and-white glossy that showed Gibson posing with a rifle, one of the photographs that the streamheat had taken the day before the assassination. "Is this you, Zwald?"

"I didn't kill anyone. That's all I have to say."

He wondered if the reporter worked for one of Raus's newspapers. The odds were that he did. Obviously, the media campaign to make Gibson the fall guy had gone into full swing while he'd been in the hands of the cops.

It came as a welcome relief when the patrolmen escorting him turned him around and started to move him out of the room, while a flying wedge of cops fended off the reporters and photographers. Gibson was more than willing to go, but then he saw something out of the corner of his eye, a white face and the flash of round Himmler glasses. Rampton! What in hell was Rampton doing in police headquarters? Where did he get the gall from? Something inside Gibson snapped.

He turned quickly before his guards could grab him and started yelling at the reporters. "If you want to know who killed President Lancer, ask him! Ask that man over there in the corner! His name's Sebastian Rampton! The one in the glasses! Ask him! Ask Rampton!"

And then the cops were on him, dragging him to the door. Gibson didn't resist. He knew if he did, they'd only beat him up when they got him outside. The moment had passed.

As they led him away down the corridor, one of his escorts leaned close to him. "What was that last bit all about?"

"There's a guy in there who knows much more about all this than I do."

The cop obviously didn't believe a word of it. "Yeah, right."

"I'm not kidding."

"So tell it to the chief. All I have to do is stop you from cutting your own throat or hanging yourself. I'm not required to listen to no crazy bullshit."

"Whatever you say."

"You just remember that and we'll get along fine."

For a long time, Gibson was left to wait in an isolated holding cell. He wasn't quite sure for how long because it turned out that telling him the time was something else that the cops who were keeping suicide watch on him weren't required to do. Somewhere along the line, though, a patrolman brought him the evening editions of the city newspapers.

"So you made the front page."

Beneath screaming banner headlines that Gibson, of course, couldn't read was a large, black-bordered picture of Jaim Lancer. Inset at the bottom was a much smaller picture of himself, taken earlier at the press conference. His eyes were staring, bugged out like those of a violent lunatic, and his mouth was half-open, frozen in a silent scream. It was no exaggeration to liken him to a cornered animal. Gibson didn't imagine for a moment that the newspapers were just a compassionate gesture on the part of a passing patrolman. They had probably been sent down on Schubb's instructions, probably hoping that the shock of reading the reports might shake something loose. Unfortunately, Schubb didn't know that Gibson was a functional illiterate in this dimension and all he'd be able to do would be to look at the pictures.

There were more pictures on the inside, a very grainy amateur snap of Lancer in the act of slumping forward in the car, moments after the bullets had hit him, and several other pictures of Gibson at the press conference, along with a shot of Boveen holding up the rifle. Page three carried a very strange shot showing a surprised-looking Gibson, standing in Verdon Raus's target gallery holding a pistol. Nephredana should have been standing beside him but either she'd been edited out by a very skilled photo retoucher or *idimmu* really didn't come out in photographs. Now he was cursing the fouled-up dimension transfer that had left him unable to read. He would have dearly liked to know what was being said about him.

As he folded up the paper, one of the suicide watch grinned at him. "How does it feel to be the center of attention?"

"You think I'll get a book deal?"

The cop's grin widened at Gibson's remark. "Think you'll live long enough to enjoy it?"

His partner guffawed. After that, Gibson shut up.

The time dragged on and nobody came to see him, which both surprised and disturbed him. He thought Schubb would have had investigators working on him around the clock. The suicide watch changed shift, but apart from that nobody came near him. He began to imagine the kinds of power politics being played out in other parts of the building and then wished that he hadn't made the effort. None of the scenarios that he could conjure up had anything like a happy ending for him.

As far as Gibson could estimate, it must have been around midnight when they finally came for him. "On your feet, you're being moved."

Along with Schubb and his usual entourage was a tall burly man in a dark suit. Schubb didn't introduce this new addition, and Gibson experienced a moment of panic. Had Schubb given up the jurisdiction fight and turned him over to State Security or one of the other national law-enforcement agencies? "Where are you taking me?"

"You'll find out when you get there."

Gibson was handcuffed for the third time, and this time a chain was put round his waist and attached to the cuffs so he couldn't raise his hands more than a few inches. With no further explanation, he was marched to the elevators. His mind was racing. It seemed that, if events were continuing to conform to the Kennedy-assassination pattern, he was rapidly approaching the point where Oswald was killed by Jack Ruby, and there wasn't a damn thing that he could do to prevent it.

As they were riding down in the elevator, Schubb leaned close to him. "You look sick."

"I feel sick."

"How is it that you neglected to tell me that you also had a try for Verdon Raus?"

"I don't know what you're talking about."

"There's a report in the late editions of the papers that you went to the Raus Mansion intending to kill him but you chickened out. Didn't you read the papers I sent you?"

Gibson shook his head. "I just looked at the pictures."

"There was even a picture of you, boy, inside the mansion, waving a gun around."

"I was a guest at a party and the picture was taken in Raus's private shooting gallery."

"I wish you'd leveled with me."

Before the exchange could go any further, the elevator came to a stop. The doors opened on the same parking garage through which he'd entered police headquarters. A number of people were standing around, uniforms and plainclothes. There were even a couple of TV cameras. As he looked out into the garage, Gibson's stomach cramped and his legs threatened to give out on him. A patrolman pushed him forward, propelling him out of the elevator. He looked round desperately. Which one was going to turn out to be Ruby? Which one had the gun under his coat and was pulling his courage together to go for the shot? A man in a black hat was coming through the crowd. Gibson hung back. The cop behind him thought that he was just being difficult and forcibly pushed him forward, directly at the man in the black hat.

The man in the hat had a hand under his coat, but as far as Gibson could see he was the only one who had noticed. The gun came out in a slow-motion movement, and then the world froze as tires, screaming straight from hell, came down the ramp from the street. A 1951 Hudson—Yancey Slide's Hudson—howled into the parking garage, trailing sparks from its muffler and flame from its exhaust as it bounced onto the level floor of the garage. Cops were turning and guns were coming out. The man in the black hat was turning right along with them. The near-side rear door of the Hudson swung open. Yop Boy was out and running. He swung up the fancy assault rifle that Gibson had seen in London and sprayed the cops around Gibson. They were instantly scattering in every direction. One was hit and went down with a look of dumb, outraged surprised on his face. Gibson stood and stared. He was in shock, but then he heard Yop Boy yelling.

"Get into the car, goddamn it! We're rescuing you."

The White Room

GIBSON DECIDED THAT he was getting nowhere with Kooning. If anything, he was digging himself in deeper. She had him talking too much about his previous "fantasy" life and the weird anomalies between "his" world and the world in which he found himself. At the same time, he knew that the regime of drugs and therapy, far from "curing" him, would eventually drive him truly and irrevocably nuts. Within the limits of his meager resources, he activated the first phase of his escape plan. He embarked on a painstaking study of the routines of the clinic. When doors might be left unlocked or the nurses away from their stations. He began to keep copious notes in a code that he'd invented for himself. The notes were obviously reported to Kooning, and when she asked him about them he told her quite frankly that he was conducting a study of the clinic's operation with a view to escaping. She found that extremely interesting and began talking about the motivation behind the compulsive gathering of data. He also attempted to discuss the idea with John West and to his surprise received a very similar response. He had toyed with the idea of taking a partner along, and West had been the ideal choice, but when he broached the idea he found it received with an amused disdain. In fact, West treated him as though he was endearingly crazy and a little stupid.

"Oh, yes, old boy, crashing out of the joint? I believe that's how they described it in the old Hollywood big-house movies. Have you carved a gun out of soap yet?"

Having only trusted the man after a good deal of soul-searching, Gibson was understandably miffed.

"I've been making a study of the routines in this place. I'm going to figure out a way of walking out of here."

"Oh, do give it up. They call it compulsive data gathering and they give you a whole lot of new and different drugs on top of what you're taking already."

Gibson persevered but only with great difficulty. "If I was to find a way out of here, would you come with me?"

West shook his head as though the answer was self-evident. "Oh, no, quite out of the question. I couldn't survive out there. They wouldn't let me."

Chapter
Twelve

GIBSON WAS HALF thrown into the back of the Hudson. He went sprawling on his knees as Yop Boy dived in behind him, still spraying the Luxor Police Department with machine-gun bullets. Nephredana was lounging unconcernedly in the backseat. Slide was behind the wheel, sitting hunched in the driver's custom bucket seat, pumping the gas pedal, with his hat pulled down over his eyes and the collar of his duster coat turned up. The red and green displays of the car's complex and definitely non-1951 control panel bathed his face with a decidedly satanic light in the otherwise darkened interior. The moment everyone was safely aboard, he popped the clutch and sent the car rocketing toward the exit ramp. Gibson was tossed onto his side by the acceleration. Using his manacled hands, he tried to push himself into a sitting position.

"I thought you had a nonintervention policy?"

Slide laughed. "That was then, this is now. What's the matter, ain't you grateful?"

"I'm grateful, but you cut it pretty fine."

Nephredana shrugged. "Cutting it fine is the spice of life."

They were on the street hurtling straight at the traffic. Yop Boy, dressed for combat in his own outsize version of ninja fighting threads, had swung into the passenger seat, riding shotgun beside Slide, with his assault rifle pushed through the open window. A cab crossed an intersection, and the bewildered driver, seeing the Hudson coming at him like some avenging Detroit angel, stopped dead, right in their path. Slide only avoided it by mounting the sidewalk, sending a group of pedestrians diving for safety. Slide appeared to drive with a total disregard for the fate of innocent bystanders.

Fortunately the streets around police headquarters were comparatively empty in the small hours of the morning, and the innocent bystanders were down to a minimum. As they hurtled through the night, with Slide concentrating on the driving and Yop Boy playing defense, Nephredana pulled the electronic lock pick from her leather utility garter.

She pointed to Gibson's handcuffs. "Let's get those things off you."

She aimed the small cylinder at the handcuffs and they opened with a soft double click. A moment later, the padlock on the chain had opened and the whole deal had dropped to the floor of the car. Gibson eased himself into the seat, rubbing his wrists. "Damn, but it's good to be out of those things."

Nephredana crossed her legs. "You were in a lot of trouble back there."

"Tell me about it. I think I was just a fraction of a second away from being gunned down by the local Jack Ruby."

Yancey Slide turned in his seat. He seemed quite able to drive with one hand and without looking at the road.

"At last we've broken up that fucking pattern. I hope for good and all."

"You mean the Kennedy pattern?"

"I could have probably stopped the one in your dimension if I hadn't let Howard Hughes sidetrack me, the paranoid piece of shit."

"You knew Howard Hughes?"

"You have to deal with all kinds of assholes in my business. If Hughes hadn't faked me out by pretending that he knew more about the conspiracy than he really did, I might have had a chance to talk with Jack Kennedy before he went down to Dallas."

Gibson was getting a little off balance from all of Slide's name-dropping. He guessed that if you had lived for some twenty thousand years, you did get to meet a lot of people. Whether, though, you should retain a need to ostentatiously boast about it was something else again.

"You knew Kennedy, too?"

"Jack Kennedy wasn't an asshole. Except maybe for his need to jump on anything that breathed. That was neurotic behavior."

Nephredana snorted derisively. "That's kind of rich coming from you."

Slide flashed his sinister snaggletoothed grin, and his inhuman slit eyes blazed with a brief humor. "I'm a demon. I've got an image to maintain."

He turned back to the road. They were now running on a fairly empty highway that led out of the downtown district of government buildings and big business and possibly out of the city altogether. The Hudson was humming along at a speed that, from the way the streetlights flashed by outside the windows, must have exceeded 150 miles an hour, but its motion had a deceptive, almost dreamlike quality, a lack of vibration that made it feel as if they were in some sort of simulator rather than a real nuts-and-bolts vehicle.

Gibson leaned forward and asked the obvious question. "So what happens now? Are we going someplace or are we just on the run like Bonnie and Clyde?"

Gibson half expected Slide to launch into a detailed account of how he ran with the Barrow Gang and helped Bonnie with the poems that she sent to the newspapers. In this case, Slide either resisted the temptation or he had never met the gangster twosome, because he actually came up with a straight answer.

"We're getting out of this fucked-up dimension while the getting's still good."

Gibson glanced nervously out of the rear window. They might be going fast enough to outrun a police car, but the LPD also had helicopters.

"The cops are going to be looking for us in the worst possible way."

Slide dismissed this with a shrug. "There's a whammy on this car that's going to make it very difficult to find."

"Are you sure about that?"

"Listen, kid. The cops are the least of our worries. In a matter of a few hours, this city is going to be one great big radioactive parking lot. Although the UKR doesn't know it yet, the Hind-Mancus have decided to use the confusion created by Lancer's murder to launch a sneak nuclear attack. Fifty of their flying wing atom bombers are coming up hard on their failsafe points right now."

Gibson had a good deal of trouble adjusting to this new piece of news. "You're putting me on?"

"The hell I am. I'm not just getting out of this dimension for the sake of your health. This whole place is going to blow."

"Unbelievable."

Slide shook his head. "Not really. The same thing nearly happened in your dimension. I know for a fact that some of the politburo wanted to do exactly the same thing except that Khrushchev put his foot down."

"Are the Kamerians so blown away by the assassination that they can't defend themselves? Can't they stop the bombers?"

Slide grimaced. "Sure, they'll have fighters in the air and their SAM batteries will be on full red alert. The League's going to lose most of its bombers but some are going to get through. Some always do, and some are quite enough."

Nephredana was unwrapping a stick of gum.

"So where are we going to be when the shit hits the fan?"

"Back at the Hole in the Void."

Nephredana rolled her eyes. "The Hole in the Void? Does that mean you're going to go on another hundred-day drunk?"

Even Gibson, with his record of wretched excess and current bemused state, couldn't help but stand awed by a being who could routinely contemplate a three-month, nonstop binge. Slide, however, was shaking his head. "No hundred-day drunk this time round. Things are so delicately balanced right now that we're all going to have to stay on top of it."

Nephredana frowned. "It's really that bad?"

Slide nodded. "It's really that bad."

Gibson was starting to come out of shock and move back into confusion. "I'm grateful for being rescued and everything, but I really could use a certain amount of filling in as to what's going on. I mean, I seem to have just come out of an assassination conspiracy that I still don't fully understand, and now you're telling me a nuclear war is going to break out and we're going to someplace called the Hole in the Void. You've got to realize that I'm feeling a little ragged at the edges after all this."

Slide turned away from the road again and gave Gibson a hard look. "So I not only have to save your sorry ass, I also have to explain what's going on because you're too dumb to figure it out for yourself?"

"I wouldn't put it quite that way but . . . ."

"But you'd like to know what the deal is."

"I'd feel a lot better."

"I wouldn't count on that."

"I was afraid you'd say that."

"So where do want me to start?"

"This nuclear attack is quite inevitable?"

Slide nodded. "Quite inevitable. Accept that and then put it out of your mind. This isn't your city or your country or even your dimension. You may find the death of all these people regrettable, but there isn't a damn thing you can do about it. Regret it and move on. Screw this dimension, in fact. What can you do with a place that has a supermarket chain called Hitler's? There's plenty ahead for you to worry about.''

"That's not so easy to do.''

Slide made a take-it-or-leave-it gesture. "You don't have time for the luxury of guilt or trauma. Concentrate on what happens next.''

"The Hole in the Void?''

"The Hole in the Void.''

"What is this Hole in the Void?''

"It's a bolthole, a refuge for us demons, an anomalous place in a fold between the dimensions. A few of us old boys created a safe hideout there, a place to go when the regular time stream gets too hairy. It'll give us a breathing space, you dig?''

Gibson shook his head. "Not really, but I expect I'll find out when I get there. I assume the present situation qualifies as hairy.''

"Megahairy.''

"How do we get there?''

"Right now, I'm looking for a soft spot where we can trans through.''

Gibson could only assume that a soft spot was something akin to the transition point at Glastonbury that he and the streamheat had used to get to Luxor. Slide and his gang seemed to have a much more casual attitude toward moving from one dimension to another than anyone else he'd encountered on his travels.

"So what about the conspiracy? Why did the streamheat want to get rid of Lancer?''

Slide winked and tapped the side of his nose confidingly.

"You're making the mistake that everyone else makes. Conspiracies are hatched in the shadows and, like anything else in the shadows, they frighten people. The temptation is to imagine that they are much bigger and better organized than they really are. Most of the conspiracies I've ever become involved in have been a mess. They're usually uneasy alliances of individuals with a lot of different goals and motivations. Nobody tells the truth, and the internal fighting usually starts well before the deed's been done. Nothing I've seen of this one has caused me to think that it was any exception to the general rule. The way I figure it, the Luxor natives who were in on it were pretty straight ahead in just wanting to off the president and seize power. Their mistake was that they were too greedy. They only had their eyes on the prize and they didn't pause to wonder how Hind-Mancu, the big rival superpower, might react.''

"This is Raus's bunch?"

Slide nodded. He was looking at the road again, driving with one hand and taking a cheeroot from the pocket of his duster coat with the other. He lit it with the same snap of his fingers that he'd demonstrated for Gibson and Windemere in Ladbroke Grove.

"I don't think Raus himself was the same as all the rest. Anyone who keeps Balg penned up in his basement probably has a much more complicated game plan. When the dust settled, though, he probably expected to be crowned king."

"And the streamheat?"

"Those bastards? That's the hard one. The one thing you can count on is that they're lying ninety percent of the time, with a dime of truth to keep you off balance."

"So what's the truth in this instance?"

"The truth? It's probably some floating crap game or movable feast; it usually is around the streamheat. What's their euphemism for getting their faces into other folks' business? Constrainment of chaos? A poke here, a prod there, a dirty little deal in a back alley or a banana skin on a crucial sidewalk, the odd cosmic manhole cover removed, and they think they're playing fucking God, but all they're really doing is screwing things up worse than they're screwed up already. The thing you gotta remember about the streamheat, kid, is that they're basically a bunch of semisavage sons of bitches whose physics peaked too early. A whole bunch of us, the ones who knew what was what back then, should have gone in there in 1427 and wiped out the lot of them. A culture that stumbles across atomic weapons while it's still making sacrifices to the Sun God needs to be nuked themselves, right back into the Stone Age. But no, don't interfere, we all said. Let them work out their destiny. Well, no more, kid, total the swine and work out the destiny later. The problem with the streamheat is that, despite all the crap they give out about interzone cooperation, they're really the tool of a culture that's still as mad as hell that it can't predict the future. That's why they always try to pretend that they can. All their computers, their logic engines, their behavioral projections, societal convection rolls, Lorenz's butterfly, and all the other paraphernalia, it's all just chicken entrails and burned goat bones when you get down to it. All their efforts really only prove that they don't have a plan, they don't have an overall strategy. They run around in a frenzy being personally offended by the chaotic unpredictability of the universe and trying to fix it so it'll be the way they like it. When they fail, as they almost always do, they become even more hysterically convinced that they are fighting some kind of holy war against the forces of havoc, randomness, and disorder. It makes about as much real sense as human sacrifices to the Sun God.''

Gibson blinked. This whole new assessment of the streamheat took a little digesting. ''What did they really hope to achieve in Luxor by killing Lancer and pinning it on me?''

''They probably thought that they could install Raus as the head of a puppet government and have the UKR under their control, although I do wonder how they expected to control someone who kept Balg in his basement. Anyway, that's what the lower ranks seem to have believed, the ones you were dealing with like Smith and Klein. The fact that it now looks like the whole of the UKR is going to get dixie-fried as a result of the assassination puts a slightly different complexion on things.''

''You actually think the streamheat engineered this nuclear attack that's coming?''

Slide nodded. ''Sure do. They've got the UKR so heavily infiltrated it'd be kinda dumb not to assume that they've done much the same thing to the Hind-Mancu on the other side. They probably suggested the sneak attack in the first place.''

Gibson was at a loss. ''But why? What would they have to gain from nuclear devastation?''

Slide took his hand off the wheel and jerked a thumb in the direction of Nephredana. ''Didn't she explain death-moment energy physics to you?''

''Sure, but . . .''

''So work it out for yourself. Think about all that death.''

''A huge burst of energy?''

''Right on the money, a huge energy bonanza. Which, in light of recent reports that they have the means to catch and store DME, seems to make a lot of sense from their point of view. Plus they have the added bonus of a lot of random print-through in other dimensions that they probably think they can exploit to their own ends.''

''And you figure that Smith and the others didn't know about this?''

''Never tell the minions what they don't need to know.''

''I've been getting more than my fair share of that.''

''What did you expect?''

''That's the problem. I didn't expect anything. I didn't ask to be a part of this in the first place. What is it with me?''

Slide laughed. "What is it with you? You want me to tell you?"

Gibson was becoming a little unnerved by the way that Slide kept turning his head away from the road to talk to him. At speeds around a hundred and a half, it seemed to verge on the suicidal unless Slide was driving by some kind of telepathy.

"I'd be delighted if you'd tell me."

Slide grinned. "You, Gibson? Hell, you're a very special person. You're a veritable crossroads of coincidence, a repository for untapped mischief, a catalyst for confusion."

"I am?"

Nephredana popped her gum. "Lighten up on him, Yancey. He's had a hard day."

"He asked."

Gibson nodded. "That's right, I asked."

Slide started counting off Gibson's problems on the five fingers of his free hand. "First there's all this business of your opposite number in Luxor being a potential presidential assassin."

"You believe that? Couldn't that have just been something else that the streamheat cooked up?"

Slide shook his head. "I tend to doubt that. I think it falls within the ten percent of truth. If it didn't, why would they mess with you at all?"

"You think they pointed Casillas and the Nine at me in the first place?"

"I'm sure they did. That's why I came to London to check you out."

"So what about this massive aura that I'm supposed to have?"

"You could say that it kinda falls into chicken-and-egg territory, so to speak. Does shit happen to you because you've got the aura or do you have the aura because shit happens to you? There's also the point that the streamheat may well have been hedging their bets over your filling the Four Requirements of the Prophecy of Anu Enlil."

Gibson had the sinking feeling that the cosmic opener was busy on yet another can of worms. "What the hell is the Prophecy of Anu Enlil?"

"Nobody told you? I'd have thought Abigail Voud would have filled you in. She's big on stuff like that."

Gibson sadly shook his head. "No, nobody told me. So what else is new?"

Slide turned to Nephredana. "How does the text go?"

Nephredana recited from memory. " 'And a man shall come among them, a man who was a leader of men but who fell from the favor of his followers, a man who crossed the great divide and, arriving in the country beyond, took up arms and slew the king of that country.' Those are the Four Requirements, you want me to go on?"

Slide nodded. "Yeah, get on to the part about entering the Realm of Gods."

Nephredana picked up the thread. " 'And, taking flight, he came with companions to the place between worlds where the Portal was made known to him and he entered the Realm of Gods where the Sleeper lay and he spoke with the Sleeper of the time that He might wake.' "

Gibson frowned. "That's all very fancy, but how does it apply to me?"

"Leader of men, right?"

Gibson laughed in amazement. "The last thing that I've ever been is a leader of men."

"Anyone one who can fill Madison Square Garden has to be a leader of some kind. Young men all over the world were copying your clothes and your walk, your haircut and your sneer, even your brand of sunglasses. Think you weren't a leader? And you certainly fell from favor, you can't deny that. You've moved from one dimension to another, and as for killing the king . . ."

At that moment, Yop Boy cut in with a warning. "Lights up ahead, boss."

Yop Boy must have had extraordinary eyes, because Gibson couldn't see a thing. Slide, too, who nodded in reply. "I got 'em."

Yop Boy was still peering into the darkness. "Looks like a cop roadblock. I guess they must have penetrated the whammy."

Slide grinned back at Gibson. "Watch this, kid."

Slide seemed to find an extra surge of power somewhere inside the car. Up ahead, four police cruisers were drawn across the highway, completely blocking the four lanes. Uniformed figures were clustered around the cars, and Gibson could imagine the tension and the weapons clutched tightly in their hands. The Hudson was charging straight at them. It no longer felt as though they were riding in a simulator. The car was vibrating wildly.

Slide glanced at Yop Boy. "We got a power window?"

Yop Boy nodded. "Anything we want. Full banshee halo if we need it."

Slide's grin was truly demonic. "Ha!"

He hit a number of buttons on the car's control panel, and the Hudson was immediately enveloped in orange flame. At the same time, there was a hideous howling from outside the car.

Gibson looked round in alarm. "Are we on fire?"

Nephredana shook her head. "Just scaring the hell out of these cops."

It was certainly working. Through the flame envelope in front of the windshield, Gibson could see the cops leaving the cars that were blocking the road and running for their lives. The cars remained, however, and it looked as though the Hudson was going to plow into them and total itself. Then, as Gibson watched in complete amazement, an unseen force lifted first one car and then a second clear into the air and threw them violently aside. It was as though they were the toys of a giant, invisible, and very petulant child who had hurled them away in a fit of pique. One landed on its roof about twenty yards on down the road while the other arced straight up, turned over, took a nosedive into the hard shoulder, and folded up like a concertina. The Hudson raced through the gap that had been left in the roadblock, and, as they flashed past the police cruiser that was lying on its crushed roof, its gas tank exploded and it burst into flame. The fire envelope that surrounded the Hudson was suddenly gone.

Slide was chortling. "Did you see those guys run?" He glanced at Gibson. "Do you know what that was, kid?"

Gibson shook his head. "Never seen anything like it."

"Threw a banshee halo round the car."

"Was that difficult?"

Slide made a dismissive gesture. "Piece of cake. Unpotentialized psychic power. All you gotta do is focus it and it'll do what you want. There's always plenty of loose spook energy around. Most of it's too stupid to do anything for itself except maybe condense into a half-assed apparition and make a few moaning noises, but if you give it a focus, it'll go the whole nine yards for you. Nothing spook energy likes better than to be given something violent to do."

Gibson slipped down in his seat and closed his eyes. Slide, on the other hand, seemed to treat running a police roadblock as no big thing. He went back to the previous conversation as though nothing had happened.

"So you see how you qualify for the Four Requirements of Anu Enlil."

Gibson took a deep breath. "It all seems a little farfetched. For one thing, I didn't kill the king. I only took the rap for it."

"Everybody thinks you did and that may be enough for the prophecy. A lot of prophecies are really just a matter of perception."

Gibson started shaking his head as if by doing it he could ward off this new idea. "If it's all the same to everyone, I really don't think I want to have anything to do with this Anu Enlil business. I gave at the office."

Nephredana took out a compact and, still chewing gum, checked her makeup. "You may not have much choice in the matter."

Gibson scowled. "Why didn't I guess that? So what happens to me if I qualify for the prophecy, do I get taken out and burnt at the stake or what?"

Slide grinned. "Hell, no. You do okay on this one. When He wakes and returns, you become the Master of Humans in your dimension."

"He?"

Slide's grin faded. "Don't make me say his name."

"You mean Necrom?"

Slide winced. "I wish you wouldn't do that."

Gibson blinked. "I'm not sure I want to be Master of Humans in my dimension."

Apparently satisfied with her face, Nephredana put away her compact. "It sure beats living as a bond slave, or, worse still, culled out with the excess."

Gibson frowned. "Culled out with the excess."

"When He walks again, the numbers of your species will be appreciably thinned out."

Gibson swallowed hard. "Thinned out."

"Well, you have been rather overbreeding for the last few centuries."

Gibson couldn't believe what he was hearing. "Thinned out? Just like that?"

"What did you humans expect? To go on breeding exponentially until you'd filled up the known universe?"

Gibson leaned forward and clasped his head in his hands. It was starting to hurt. "I wish someone would offer me a drink."

Nephredana produced a flat, one-pint, sterling-silver flask and handed it to Gibson. "Why didn't you ask?"

Gibson took a grateful pull on the flask, and fire exploded in his throat, than roared through his head and chest. He coughed and his eyes watered. "What the hell was that?"

"I call it a sheer drop."

"No kidding."

He remembered the frightening cocktails that Nephredana had ordered in the bar and at Raus's party and was thankful that he couldn't see what he had just drunk. Damn, but he wished that he had some more of the streamheat's hero serum. Being pitch-forked from police headquarters into a car full of mad demons who proceeded to inform him that it was the eve of destruction and that the cause of all his troubles might well be because he was the subject of some ancient prophecy was taking a sorry toll on his nerves, and he needed something to dull the edge. Despite the taste, he took a second hit from Nephredana's silver flask, and after the rerun explosion had rippled through his nervous system, he let loose a long sigh. "You know, all I really want is for the world to leave me alone for a while."

Nephredana's smile was brittle and impatient. "Didn't you hear, Joe? You can't always get what you want."

Gibson nodded. "I imagine there's also a catch to all this prophecy business."

Slide quoted in a low voice. " 'And qualifying according to the prophecy, the man shall pass the Portal and, entering the Realm of Gods, shall look upon the Sleeper in the act of wak-ing.' "

Again, Gibson shook his head. "I really don't think so. I don't want to pass any portals and look on any sleepers, and, even if it's inevitable, I'm still going to go kicking and scream-ing."

Nephredana laughed delightedly. "That's my Joe Gibson."

Any further protests from Gibson were cut short by Yop Boy pointing at a light that had started flashing on the control panel. "Looks like we got a soft spot, boss."

Slide pushed back his hat. "It sure does. With luck, we'll be out of here momentarily."

"I'm not too sure about that, boss." "

Slide glanced at Yop Boy. "What now?"

"More lights out there."

"Another roadblock?"

Yop Boy shook his head.

"I don't think so. This is something weird."

Now Gibson was scanning the road up ahead. So far he couldn't see anything, and he didn't really want to imagine what

Yop Boy might define as weird. It was a couple of minutes before he saw it, a pale-gold light, way off in the distance. Slide didn't slacken speed, and as they came closer Gibson could see that the light was some sort of beam coming from an object that appeared to be hovering above a point on down the highway.

"Helicopter?"

Yop Boy cursed under his breath. "That's no helicopter. In fact, you're not going to like this, boss."

"I'm not."

"I think we've got a saucer up ahead. As far as I can tell, it's sitting on top of the the soft spot just like it was guarding the trans point."

Slide pursed his lips. "Goddamn it to hell. I hate those fucking things."

Gibson leaned forward. "What are they?"

Slide snarled at the beam of light. "I don't know, that's why I hate them. I've never, in all my days, ever got a satisfactory explanation of those things." He began to slow the Hudson until it was only moving forward at a crawl. "I don't take any chances with those things. I don't trust them."

"You think they're alien spacecraft?"

Slide shook his head. "I gave up that bullshit theory a long time ago. Never could believe that aliens could act so weird. If they were aliens, there would have been some kind of contact by now. Aliens wouldn't keep up the same terminal skittishness century after century."

Gibson was leaning forward on the back of Yop Boy's seat, staring through the windshield. "I heard a theory once that UFOs were really time machines from some point in the future."

Slide nodded. "I heard that idea a few times myself, and I have to admit that it's one that best fits with the facts. It certainly accounts for the lack of contact. I imagine time travelers would be real hung up on not causing random time displacements and what have you. You must have heard about all that stuff? Tread on the wrong beetle and, a million years down the pike, a whole civilization vanishes without trace. I gave up on that theory, too, though. I just didn't like to think about it. There are enough contemporary problems without bastards coming back from the future to fuck with you. I don't think about these things anymore. I just hate the sight of goddamn saucers."

It was now possible to make out details of the craft, and Gibson's heart sank as he recognized the configuration of the thing, the gray metal superstructure like a giant hubcap with portholes ringing the top turret and the three large hemispheres on the underside.

"It's an Adamski saucer."

Slide turned and looked at Gibson as though he was surprised that he knew about such things. "Adamski was a fucking liar. He claimed that he went for rides in one of these things with tall handsome guys from Venus. Take my word for it, there are no guys from Venus, handsome or otherwise."

Nephredana snorted. "He was just making it up to sweeten his book deal."

Gibson continued to stare at the saucer. It was fascinating to see one close up. It must have beeen about forty feet across and was hovering at about its own diameter above the roadway. The single wide beam of golden light streamed down from a source that Gibson couldn't see, somewhere on the underside, at a central point between the three spheres. It formed a circular pool of gold on the roadway that was like a spotlight on the stage at a Vegas casino. It only needed Frank Sinatra standing there singing "My Way" to complete the picture.

"I've seen saucers like this before."

Slide dismissed Gibson with a slight wave of his hand. "Yeah, I know, one buzzed your plane while you were on the way to London. It was a lot different from this one."

Gibson was angry at the curt dismissal. "I'm not talking about that one, I mean saucers exactly like this."

Three heads turned in unison.

"Where? When? What happened?"

"It was on the way to Luxor. After we'd left Gideon Windemere's house in Ladbroke Grove and taken a conventional road out of town."

Nephredana interrupted him. "We know that, we were following you."

"That's right, you were. Anyway, out in the country, near some ducky English village, we hooked into the laylines."

This time it was Slide who interrupted. "So that's where you vanished to."

"So we're lost in the ozone in this kind of layline fairyland and suddenly these UFO's started strafing us."

"Ones like that?"

Gibson shook his head. "No, it was another kind that were attacking us, ones that looked like white glowing disks with a kind of blue aura around them. I thought that we were going to be blown all to hell by these red fireballs they kept shooting at us, and then these other guys showed up like the goddamn cavalry, ones exactly like that one, and ran off the first bunch, seemingly saved our ass.''

Slide was giving him a decidedly squint-eyed, Clint Eastwood look of suspicion. "They helped you and the streamheat?''

"Right.''

"So they might have been saving you or they might have just been saving the streamheat.''

"I guess so.''

"Or they may have just been having a beef among themselves.''

"I guess that's possible, too.''

"It still sounds too much like they're getting into our business.''

They were now just fifty yards from the silently floating craft, and Slide brought the car to a halt.

"If that thing doesn't get out of our way and fast, we're in a lot of trouble.''

Nephredana blew a quick bubble and snapped the gum back into her mouth again. "Can't we go looking for an alternative soft spot?''

Yop Boy shook his head. "No time.''

Slide opened the driver's door. "There's no point in sitting here like a bunch of idiots. I'm going to take a look at that thing.''

Slide started walking toward the saucer. Gibson opened his door to follow but Nephredana quickly put a hand on his arm. "Don't be ridiculous. Anything could happen with that thing.''

"Slide's going out there.''

"He's Yancey Slide.''

Gibson grinned at her as he slid out of the car. "Yeah, and I'm Joe Gibson. Don't forget that.''

Yop Boy didn't say a word. He just climbed out of the car and followed with the ever-present assault rifle at the ready.

Nephredana's voice rasped after the three of them. "Damn you, you macho morons, wait for me!''

They walked until they were thirty feet or so from the saucer and then they stopped, standing side by side, well back from the pool of light. The saucer hung above them like a silent floating enigma. No hatches opening, no ladders extending to the ground, no octapoids rushing out to carry off Nephredana and no zapping death ray.

The other three stood and watched while Slide fumed. "At

the very least the bastards could take the trouble to explain what they want.''

Nephredana produced the silver flask. "I've never seen you too keen to explain yourself to strangers."

"That's not the point."

Nephredana spat out her gum, took a long pull on the flask and then passed it to Gibson. Gibson took a hit, wondering if the stuff could make a man go blind, and handed the flask to Yop Boy, but Yop Boy didn't drink any and passed it straight to Slide. Slide didn't hesitate. He put the flask to his mouth and tilted his head back, seemingly draining it. When he was through, he let out a satisfied gasp and looked up at the saucer.

"I'm going to have to do something about you. The question is what."

At that moment a flight of jets roared across the sky heading east. It was too dark to make out anything but the faint flare of their exhausts. Whatever the jets were and wherever they had come from, they were traveling without navigation lights.

Gibson looked at the dark sky in alarm. "Are those the enemy bombers?"

Slide was also looking at the sky. "Kamerian interceptors, but the Hind-Mancu wings can't be far away. We have to do something about this fucking saucer or we're going to find ourselves caught out in the firestorm."

Nephredana retrieved the flask and upended it. Slide had finished off the booze. "So what do you do about a flying saucer?"

Slide paced round in a small frustrated circle three times before he halted and slapped his fist into his palm.

"That's it, I can't fuck around any longer." He gestured to Yop Boy. "Fetch the doombeam."

Yop Boy looked at him doubtfully. "Are you sure about this, boss?"

"Just get the damned thing."

Yop Boy started back toward the car. Nephredana was also staring dubiously at Slide. She didn't even have to say anything for him to snarl angrily. "Don't you start."

"The last time you tried to use the doombeam you blew away half of that Mexican village and all but discorporated yourself."

"You have a better idea?"

Nephredana shook her head. "I'm not sure that the doombeam is an idea at all. What do you hope to do to the saucer with that thing? Blow it up?"

"At the very least, I'll annoy it."

Nephredana shook her head in disbelief. "Now we're annoying flying saucers."

Further argument was halted by the arrival of Yop Boy with the doombeam. Gibson could hardly believe what he was seeing. The thing looked like an antique, art-deco vacuum cleaner mounted on a telescopic steel tripod. It resembled something that might have been pressed into service as a prop in a 1930s Flash Gordon serial.

"Where the hell did you get that thing?"

"Don't ask."

Nephredana supplied the answer. "He built it. Yancey always wanted a genuine raygun. Some of it's made from stuff that the AEC had locked up in a vault at Oak Ridge until Yancey and some of his friends broke in and stole it. He matched that up with some black-market streamheat components and a few odds and ends that he got from this weird dimension where reptiles developed a civilization and eventually he created a weapon that's probably too dangerous to be fired."

Slide ignored her. He was bending over the tripod, carefully sighting the device. When he was satisfied, he stepped back. "You'd better all take cover."

Nephredana started walking quickly away.

"I'm taking cover all the way back to the car."

Yop Boy remained beside Slide, but Gibson turned and followed Nephredana. Being one of the boys was okay, but there were limits. The two of them had no sooner reached the car than a massive and blinding fireball filled the space beneath the saucer. At the same time a thunderclap of an explosion almost deafened them. Gibson's jaw dropped.

"Sweet Jesus Christ!"

It seemed impossible for Slide and Yop Boy to have survived the blast and conflagration. The doombeam had the desired effect, however, and the saucer flipped up as though it had been given a hot foot. The gold light narrowed down to a tight pencil beam and skittered over the ground as though it was searching for who or what was responsible, then the saucer went straight up and zigzagged away at high speed.

Gibson looked on in horror: the actual surface of the road was burning. "There's no way that they're going to walk out of that."

Nephredana was surprisingly unconcerned. "I know I tend to bait Yancey but you shouldn't underestimate him. He's virtually indestructible."

In confirmation, two figures came walking out of the flames. Their clothes were trailing ribbons of smoke, and the right sleeve of Yop Boy's ninja suit was actually burning. Despite a certain charring of his duster, Slide was grinning like a maniac. "I said I'd annoy them."

Nephredana yawned. "My hero."

Slide rubbed his hands together. "Okay, let's all get in the car and get going."

In the moment that he spoke, the sky behind the car became brilliant, blinding white. It was as though a star had exploded just beyond the horizon, and Gibson, even the three demons, cringed away from it. A brief moment of the most terrible silence made the world seem as though all sound had been drained away and replaced by light, a hideous killing light that rapidly condensed into a single brilliant fireball, blazing over the city of Luxor like a new sun, while evil smoke roiled up around it, beginning to form into the familiar mushroom cloud.

Even Slide stood awed. "One of their bombers made it through early."

Then the spell broke and he was galvanized into action. "Get going! Get into the car!"

The shock wave hit moments after they were all inside. Slide's hands flew over the control panel as the Hudson bucked and shuddered on its springs in the grip of an instant hurricane and debris slammed into the car's windows and bodywork. The engine caught and it roared forward, accelerating like a dragster for fifty yards as nuclear hell howled all around. When he reached the spot over where the saucer had been hovering, Slide slammed on the brakes. He worked on the panel again and then sat back.

"Okay, here we go. Leaving town one jump ahead of the holocaust."

Gibson braced himself for the same kind of mind-wrenching hallucinations that had accompanied his previous transfer from dimension to dimension. To his surprise, nothing happened except that the Hudson sank smoothly into the ground.

The White Room

GIBSON HAD IT figured. After three weeks of intensively studying the minutest workings of the small and very exclusive clinic, the theft of an old discarded raincoat that had been left behind by a crew of workmen who were repainting the clinic's dayroom, and a trade of his accumulated candy ration with another inmate in return for a blue Mets baseball cap, he believed that he was ready to go. He'd discovered that there was a loophole that happened every day during the lunch period. For over two months, Gibson had been taking his lunch in the dayroom with the other patients who were trusted to eat outside their rooms. It was supposed to be an advanced level in patient interaction. Gibson had initially hated this communal lunching and would have much preferred to have gone on eating in his room. Most of his mealtime companions were doped to the eyeballs and had trouble finding their mouths, and, since the lunches served at the clinic uniformly consisted of various flavors of semiliquid goop, it was always a messy and unsightly affair. Even John West, who was an urbane sophisticate by inmate standards, occasionally missed his mouth with a plastic spoonful of creamed spinach or strained beats, and some of the others looked like ambulatory Jackson Pollacks by the time they had made it through to dessert.

Lunch became considerably more attractive after Gibson noticed that, toward the end of the meal, if it had gone without incident, the three burly male nurses who supervised them while they were eating made a habit of vanishing two at a time into the storeroom in back of the glassed-in nurses' station by the door. While one remained in the station to watch the inmates, the other two were in back, probably smoking a joint or snorting coke. Gibson, having clandestinely curtailed his own medication, was a much more skilled eater than most of the other inmates, and consequently finished much sooner than the rest. After he was done, he made a practice of going to the bathroom that was down the hall from the dayroom at exactly the same time as the nurses were getting high. According to the rules, a nurse was supposed to go with him, but Gibson had become so trusted that the one who was looking out while the other two were taking their turn in the storeroom just waved him through, unlocking the door from inside the station.

Gibson tried this five times before he decided that it was the route for the great escape. He had already stashed the raincoat and the Mets cap in the bottom of a cupboard in the bathroom that was used for mops and buckets and toilet paper, and nobody seemed to have noticed them. Once he was in the bathroom, it was a simple matter to slip into the coat and hat and walk down to the final checkpoint at the front door. He'd gleaned from the conversations of the painters that security on the front door was also fairly lax. The reception desk in the lobby was manned by rent-a-cops and not clinic nurses, and they paid more attention to who was coming in rather than who was going out unless it was obviously a patient. The rent-a-cops wouldn't be familiar with his face, and his only real problem was his white hospital pants and slippers. He was hoping the coat and hat would do it and if they noticed his pants at all they'd assume that he was a painter on his break.

On the day that he picked for the escape, Gibson found that he was almost too nervous to force down his food. The chipped beef and mashed potatoes, at the best of times, turned into wallpaper paste in his mouth, but on this day they threatened to choke him. He couldn't even contemplate the lime jello. As soon as the nurses had retired to their station and the storeroom, Gibson stood up and started for the bathroom. The nurse waved him through without a second glance. A swift walk along the corridor and he was in the bathroom. On with the raincoat and the Mets cap. They didn't install mirrors in the patients' bathrooms, so there was no way of checking his appearance or reassuring himself that he could bluff his way past the front desk. Down the rest of the corridor. An orderly was mopping the floor, but the man didn't give him a second glance as he walked by. Down the stairs and on to the final obstacle. Just a single rent-a-cop was on duty, and he was deep in conversation with a pretty occupational therapist. Gibson mumbled something about going out for coffee and doughnuts. The rent-a-cop nodded. He was too busy trying to peer down the occupational therapist's uniform. Gibson walked out of the main door, doing his best not to run. Suddenly he was out, out in the roar of New York traffic heading for the corner of 28th Street and Third Avenue.

Chapter
Thirteen

YANCEY SLIDE LIT yet another cheroot. "It was a magic age, I've got to tell you that, boy. I know everyone is getting twisted about His coming again, but, when He was in the world before, I personally had the best time of my whole, extremely long life, up until the end, that is, when things went a little wrong. Hell, I doubt you could even imagine it. We were lords of creation, cruising round in our aircars and living in the lap of luxury. I kid you not, the Great City between the Twin Rivers was a wonder to behold, what with the waterways, the flame groves, the floating gardens, and the whole system of streets and avenues on ten different levels, and the dreaming needle spires and the white stones of the piazzas in the blazing sun, and the great ziggurat towering over everything, close to half a mile high and black as the ace of spades, devouring energy and in total control of all who looked upon it. You should have seen that place, Joe Gibson, power entities coming and going like a bright shimmer across the sky that could stretch back to the horizon, and the *ilalassu* and the eagles and the little flying cars skipping in and out of the force skeins of their being and soaring in the backwash, so the air was as alive as the ground. And the nights, boy, the wine-dark nights and the women, heavy heat, and dangerous perfume on the wind off the sand, dark-eyed beauties with soft words and wicked mouths, and you couldn't even tell if they were djinn or human, and you were damned if you cared. It was an age of magic, boy, make no mistake about that."

Slide nodded to himself, and it was the first time that Gibson had ever seen him look wistful. Gibson took a pull from the jug, and the *idimmu* corn spirit warmed him through to the deep of his soul. It was hard to pin down time in the Hole of the Void,

307

but Gibson was certain that he'd been warming his soul for at
least three straight days with the result that his speech was slurred
and objective reality was becoming elusive. "It sounds idyllic."

Slide continued to nod. "You're fucking right about that,
boy. It was idyllic." He paused to swat at one of the tiny cartoon
things that flittered through the air like miniature bats or maybe
large leather butterflies. Failing to hit it, he lay back, staring up
at the constantly changing sky.

"Of course, there were times when it wasn't quite so perfect.
I mean, there were bloody nearly ten thousand years of it. That's
probably something else that you can't imagine. In a period of
that length, you've got to expect a few ups and downs."

"That's understandable."

"When He was on a jag, things could become downright
dangerous."

Slide lay reflecting on this for so long that Gibson was forced
to nudge him back to speech.

"How dangerous?"

"You should have seen the armies go out at the start of the
Five Thousand Day War, banners streaming, armor flashing,
and the lightleak from their weapons hanging above them like a
snow cloud of silver. Or the endgame Battle of Kia Mass when
Suhgurim sent in the trolls of his own breeding to massacre the
demahim with their knives and electric clubs and might even
have held the day if the stormcrows hadn't dropped on them like
avenging vultures, ripping and tearing the trolls' weird flesh
with their steel claws. Damn it, boy, you've never seen so much
blood, I swear we were wading in it up to our knees."

Gibson and Slide had taken themselves and their jug of corn
to the crest of one of the low hills that overlooked the valley and
the bizarre, ill-assorted collection of buildings that were the heart
of the Hole in the Void. Gibson had been grateful for his introduction to the *idimmu* corn liquor; even though the transition
from Luxor had been quite painless, coming down from the hero
serum had been making him feel quite ill. It had the effect of
numbing him against the irrational fears and constant dull ache
that seemed to be the aftermath of the streamheat instant courage.

Slide had never satisfactorily explained the Hole in the Void
to Gibson, and Gibson had some doubts that the demon really
understood it himself. When he tried, he came out with little
more than vague analogies. "Think of it as a glitch, something

that shouldn't be there, a twist in the fabric of whatever makes up the space between dimensions.''

When Gibson pressed him, he simply retreated into anger. "Think of it as a cancer cell on the sunburned ass of time if it makes you any happier.''

Certainly it was the strangest place that Gibson had ever been, making him feel, in fact, that he was as good as on another planet. As a kid, he always wanted to go to another planet—that was, until he discovered that other planets, at least those that might be accessible to him during his lifetime, were essentially boring. When he found out that Mars was without either Martians or even a system of canals, that Venus had no exotic tropical jungles and wasn't ruled over by the Treens, and that Jupiter was just plain impossible, it came as more of a shock than finding out there was no Santa Claus, whom he'd always found a little implausible at the best of times. He had decided that he wasn't going to be an astronaut after all and concentrated on rock 'n' roll.

The ground on which he and Slide had stretched out was a weird, bright orange-porous substance, and Gibson wouldn't have taken bets that it was even a mineral. Here and there, it appeared to sweat, exuding a sticky yellow liquid that first hardened and crystalized and then, after a few hours, crumbled to dust and blew away. The sky above them was without a sun and, for all the world, looked like a huge cathode screen in the blazing grip of wild interference. Juddering snags of white light blipped across psychedelic washes of color and line patterns that waved and contorted like the encephalograph of a madman, always rolling from east to west like someone had been screwing around with cosmic vertical hold. The Hole in the Void was far from being a restful place.

The buildings seemed to have been picked up at random from a variety of places in space and time for no other reason than because individual denizens of the Hole in the Void had taken a fancy to them, and then dropped willy-nilly, without thought or design, into an untidy cluster at one end of the valley. The overall impression was that it could be the deeply surreal back lot at some insane movie studio. In the loose approximation of a main street, an oak-beamed English tavern called the Rearing Eagle, that might have come from seventeenth-century London, stood between a crumbling adobe and a phallic pink glass tower with circular Lucite balconies that could have been a set for *The Jetsons*. At the top of one of the nearby hills, surrounded by its own grove of oaks, heavy with Spanish moss and dark shadows, an antebellum mansion from the Old South kept itself to itself and, in the periods of darkness when the sky went out, ghostly lights moved from window to window.

Even day and night in the Hole in the Void were a matter of apparent anarchy. Although the settlement experienced approximately equal measures of each, they appeared to occur with little rhyme or reason. With maybe only the brief preamble of the sky streaking into a parody of a tropical sunset, the lights would go out and might not return for six or seven hours, but could also come right back on inside of five minutes. This chaos made slightly more sense when Gibson discovered that by far the majority of the demons were quite able to see in the dark, and some that couldn't actually glowed themselves, but, coupled with drunkenness and a drug comedown, it was a gross irregularity that had the effect of shooting his body clock all to hell, and he had no idea if he was ever going to sleep normally again. He had virtually given up the struggle for orientation and abandoned himself to a constant state of confusion.

The inhabitants of the Hole in the Void were more than a match in strangeness for the landscape and the architecture through which they moved, and the erratic cycles of light and dark that they appeared to take in their stride. Although the majority were humanoid in form, if fanciful in style and costume, like Slide, Nephredana, and Yop Boy, others were blessed or cursed, depending on one's point of view, with far more outlandish figures and forms. Gibson had seen creatures whose bodies were unholy combinations of man, beast, and mythology, while others totally defied description by being little more than changing forms of light energy, or gaseous apparitions that seemed only partially to occupy even the same reality as Gibson. With some, it was hard to tell if they were actually inhabitants of the place or merely decorative native fauna. On first arrival, as Gibson had left the Hudson with his head spinning from the first shock of this new world, he had walked straight into two massive insects like giant roaches, more than four feet long, with compound eyes, waving antennae and body carapaces lavishly decorated with inlaid jewels and metalwork. Even the size of the Hole's inhabitants failed to conform to any set pattern, with the inhabitants ranging from those who seemed to have the need to be giants, arrogant striding colossi over twenty feet tall, down to eighteen-inch munchkins who chattered about their munchkin business like characters from a Beatrix Potter nightmare.

"There's something that I don't get."

Slide sat up, looked at Gibson, took a pull on the jug and spat into the dust. "There seem to be a hell of a lot of things that you don't get."

"Sometimes you make it sound as if all these characters here, the *idimmu*, have been here forever, and there are other times when you refer to you all as being created by the superbeings."

Slide laughed. "Of course, boy. We were all created. The Old Ones, what you call the superbeings, made all of the *idimmu* and a bunch more other beings who didn't survive that last great exit. That's why we only have legends of the last time that He awoke. None of us was around to see it. He made us because He needed an intermediary being who could act as a go-between, bridging the gap that separated Him from the humans who were already living in the dimensions."

Gibson shook his head. "You look so human."

Slide shrugged and grunted as though it was obvious. "That's because we are partially human, to a greater or lesser extent, depending on the individual. We're the product of crossbreeding humans with a number of ancient discorporate entities."

Gibson had to consider that for a while. It was hard to get a grip on the idea of superbeings who could, with apparent ease, create an entire new species to do their bidding. "Does that make Him a god?"

Yancey Slide shook the jug beside his ear to see what was left in it. "It depends on what you mean by a god."

"How did you fall out with Him? What was the trouble at the end?"

Slide shook his head. "I'm not ready to talk about that yet, not with you. Suffice to say that things got a little out of hand when the time came for Him to pull out of the multidimensional universe and go back to the place of dormancy."

"What did you do? Lead some kind of revolt?"

Slide snarled at Gibson. "I told you, kid, I'm not ready to talk about it."

Gibson was left with the feeling that he had maybe hit a little too close to the truth for Slide's comfort, and then, as if to add dramatic effect to what Slide had just said, the light decided to go out. The sky disintegrated into purple streaks and then quickly faded to black. The Hole in the Void instantly became a place of a thousand points of light, flames and fireflies, and St. Elmo's fire dancing over the crystalline rocks that, here and there, projected through the orange ground material.

Slide got slowly to his feet. "There's nothing left in this jug so I guess it's time to head back to the tavern. You given any more thought about what you're going to do?"

Ever since they had arrived in the Hole in the Void, Slide had been putting a good deal of none too subtle pressure on Gibson to make some kind of decision regarding himself and the Prophecy of Anu Enlil. "You'd be a hell of a lot wiser to go through the preparation rituals and then go to the Portal and see whether or not it opens for you than just to let it all just fall down on you without warning when He starts to move."

Gibson, who felt quite justified in opting to keep out of all embroilments in epic events for the time being, was decidedly reluctant to agree to any of the stuff that Slide seemed to be proposing. He wasn't even completely sure that he understood the whole business of the Prophecy and the waking of Necrom.

"Let me get this straight: according to this here ancient prophecy, when Necrom starts to wake . . ."

Even in the dark, Gibson could see Slide's pained look. "Yeah, yeah, I know, don't speak his name out loud. Okay. When He starts to wake, some unfortunate human has to go through this portal to aid the whole waking process."

Slide, who seemed to be rapidly shifting into an increasingly foul mood, grunted angrily. "I already explained that to you."

Gibson, who wasn't in the best of humors himself, snapped back. "Yeah, well maybe you ain't been explaining it too clearly. I still don't see the point of all this. Why the hell would something that, according to what you've been telling me, is close to being a god need some poor bloody human to help Him get up? It doesn't make any sense."

"You don't try and make sense out of what He does. You just obey and hope that you get out alive."

"That's where I have trouble with this whole deal. I've been spending too damn much of my time of late doing nothing but trying to get out alive. I'm also wondering why you're so all-fired keen to have me do this. What's in it for you, Yancey?"

Slide, who was walking down the hillside a little ahead of Gibson, suddenly whirled round with his eyes blazing dangerously.

"I'm getting real tired of your bullshit, Gibson. Maybe I should have left you to die in Luxor."

"You might as well have if I'm just being set up as the sacrificial lamb again."

It seemed that one of the side effects of the local corn was rapid negative mood swings. Slide was actually pushing back his duster coat, exposing the heavy-caliber revolver that was strapped to his hip. "I'm getting really fucking tired of you, Gibson."

Gibson slowly spread his hands. Familiarity must have bred a measure of contempt, because it was only at that moment he realized that he was actually dealing with an out-of-control demon. He forced himself to be as calm as he could.

"I don't have a weapon, Yancey. And, even if I did, I don't want to fight with you."

Slide's only reply was an animal growl. Gibson could feel himself start to sweat. "This is crazy, man. We're both drunk and things are getting twisted."

Slide held the threatening gunfighter pose for a few more seconds, and then he let it out with a short rasping laugh. "Damn it to hell, kid, will you look at me. The booze in this place is fucking poisonous."

Gibson eased the tension in his shoulders. "But I guess we're going to drink some more of it."

Slide nodded. "That's the truth."

They continued down the hill in the direction of the Rearing Eagle.

As they walked into the main room of the tavern, Gibson realized with some trepidation that he was the only human in the place. It occurred to him that he might actually be the only human in the whole of the Hole in the Void. This wasn't exactly an encouraging thought. When he'd just come as close as he had to being shot by Yancey Slide, whom he thought of as, if not a friend, at least a solid drinking companion, he didn't exactly relish the prospect of hanging out with a bunch of strange, hard-drinking *idimmu* who might turn out to be even more evil-tempered in their cups than Slide had proved to be.

The Rearing Eagle was crowded and there was noticeable tension in the air. As Slide and Gibson had earlier sat drinking on the hillside, Gibson had noticed that a major influx seemed to be taking place, with large numbers of demons coming to the refuge from the dimensions beyond. Every few minutes, a new vehicle and even individuals on foot would materialize in the soft spot at the opposite end of the valley from the collection of buildings.

It didn't take long to find out why the *idimmu* were coming
to this place in such large numbers. Even as they made their
way up to the bar for yet another jug, Gibson caught snatches
of conversation that seemed to indicate things were bad all over.
He didn't know whether the upheavals that were being experienced in numerous dimensions were a result of the print-throughs
caused by the nuclear attack on Luxor or merely unrelated events,
but it did seem that large areas of the multidimensional universe
were going to hell on the high-speed elevator. He caught a number of conversations that placed the blame for the current troubles squarely on the streamheat.

"I'm telling you, those bastards are out to get rid of the whole
bunch of us. When I got to Xodd, they were all over the goddamned town, thicker than flies on fresh shit. I ain't kidding—
they were practically running the fucking City Senate. They
had the local cops toss me in jail as a political undesirable. I
mean, do I look undesirable? I didn't have no alternative, I
blew a hole in the wall of the jail and lammed it out of there
and back here as fast as I could. Without a word of a lie,
they think they're lowering the net on us and no mistake."

The speaker was a short, squat *idimmu*, dark-skinned and
wearing a stained leather jerkin, and although to Gibson's eye
he looked pretty undesirable, he was nothing unusual by the
standards of the Rearing Eagle. When he had finished talking
there was a lot of nodded agreement. Clearly, his was no
isolated case.

Gibson and Slide gratefully made it through the crowd to the
bar and, armed with a fresh jug, retired to a booth beside the big
open fireplace. Despite the strangeness of its location, the
Rearing Eagle was actually quite a comforting, cozy place, with
its low, smoke-blackened, wood-beamed ceiling, roaring fire,
and dense boozy atmosphere, and Gibson could see why, out of
all the gin joints in all the dimensions, so many *idimmu* should
look on it as the watering hole of last resort. It really only existed
because of the burly, red-faced landlord, Long Tom Enni-Ya,
who ran the place much more for his own satisfaction than as a
service to his fellow demons. Like Slide, he cultivated a strong
human image, and his fantasy of choice seemed to be to live the
life of some Dickensian publican. It was only his glowing demon eyes that revealed that he was something more than the
bluff affable host of an English country inn.

Once installed in the booth with a drink in front of him, Gib-

son had a chance to look around the place. Most of the tables
were taken and groups of demons sat hunched in muted conversation over jugs of corn and earthenware pots of Tom Enni-Ya's
beer. The group that stood clustered around the bar was arguing,
sometimes passionately, about the current political situation, the
inroads that were being made into what they saw as the traditional *idimmu* freedoms, and what needed to be done about them.
A number of the suggested solutions were spectacularly violent.

A swarthy woman with gold earrings and a leather coat
was hunched over an instrument akin to a guitar, playing something that might have had its start in Delta blues but had gone a
long way in a direction that Gibson had never heard or experienced. Long and drawn-out notes echoed mournfully around the
room, calling to the ghosts of Robert Johnson and Jimi Hendrix.

Gibson wasn't sure it was the music or just the general atmosphere but he had a sudden insight into the *idimmu*. Despite
their swagger, their bizarre looks and bravado, they were an
old and frightened race. They didn't really live, just existed on
the periphery of the real world. They had been around for thousands of years, but only as parasites on the stream of history.
They had been made almost indestructible but they were also
sterile, eternal but without offspring or progress. A wave of truly
maudlin sadness washed over Gibson until he caught himself.
He was being ridiculous. Sympathy for the demons? Feeling
sorry for the *idimmu* because they didn't have any kids was
about on a level with feeling sorry for Attila the Hun because
his daddy had never taken him fishing.

The similarities between the world of the *idimmu* and that of
Attila the Hun were forcibly brought back when, partway through
the arbitrary evening, a figure came into the place who stopped
conversation dead. He was one of the *idimmu* who looked part
man, part beast, having the bumpy armored skin of an alligator
and the same flat shovel head, the mouthful of exaggerated teeth,
and small cunning eyes that blazed like the glowing coals in the
fireplace. The fearsome pair of long, single saber-shape antlers
that protruded from the top of his head lent him a close resemblance to the traditional devil of the Middle Ages, although these
later turned out to be a part of a strange iron headdress rather
than an integral part of his skull. As he came through the door,
backed up by a gang of five others, who, although not as fearsome as their leader, still looked like some of the baddest de-

mons in the place, Gibson went through an instant of primitive devil shock. Then he saw that the figure was headed straight for the booth where he and Slide were sitting, ducking his head to avoid hitting it on the low ceiling beams, and supernatural dread gave way to a much more instant and rational fear.

Slide had also spotted the man-beast coming toward them through the crowd, and he cursed under his breath. "Shit, Rayx."

"Who's Rayx?"

"You'll find out."

The creature halted in front of their booth and leered down at Slide. "Well, well, well, look who we have here. I thought you'd gotten yourself nuked to hell inside of Luxor. How did you get out of there, Yancey my love? Still got that knack for running away."

The thing's voice was a mixture of croaking rasp and hissing sibilance.

Slide regarded him calmly. "You still here, Rayx?"

"Where else should I be, Yancey?"

"Thought you might have crept off to play Prince of Darkness in some dimension where the inhabitants are real dumb and gullible."

Rayx picked at his teeth with a talon. "You know I gave up that shit eons ago. These days I just lay back and amuse myself. How about you?"

Slide shrugged. "I get by."

Rayx turned his attention to Gibson. "Is this the human?"

Slide nodded. "That's him."

"He don't look like much. You sure he fits the Four Requirements?"

"He seems to."

Rayx was shaking his head. "He sure don't look like much. You tried him at the Portal yet?"

"He ain't sure if he wants to get involved."

Rayx looked at Slide in amazement and wisps of steam issued from his cavernous nostrils. "He ain't sure if he wants to get involved? Since when did a human have a choice in the matter, Yancey Slide? Put him at the damn Portal and see if it takes him, and if he doesn't want to go, drag him there. We got too much riding on this to let the whim of some goddamned human get in the way."

Gibson raised a hand. "Does anyone mind if the goddamned human has something to say about this?"

Rayx snorted and the wisps of steam turned to twin billows. "Feisty little fuck, isn't he?"

Gibson was becoming exceedingly angry. He thought he had moved on from situations where people talked about him as though he was an object with no free will of his own. "That's right, he's a feisty little fuck, and he isn't about to allow himself to be dragged off to any portal against his will without putting up one hell of a fight." He turned to Slide. "And what is it that you all have riding on this?"

Slide gave Gibson a warning look. "Stay out of this, kid. You don't know what you're dealing with. You're drunk."

"So are you."

"Stay out of it, kid."

Gibson, however, was feeling restless. He took a hit on his jug of corn. "How am I supposed to stay out of this when I'm in it up to my fucking neck?" Slide was right, he was drunk. "And another thing, I'm getting tired of being called 'kid.' You may be older than the rocks on which you sit, but you still don't have to address me as 'kid.' "

Rayx pointed a talon-tipped finger at Slide. "You want to get your little human under control, Yancey, or people are going to start talking."

Gibson had the bit between his teeth and he glared at Rayx. "I'm not his little human. I'm my own man and maybe you better get used to that."

This was too much for Rayx; he lunged for Gibson, grabbed him by the front of his jacket, and half dragged him out of his seat. "Someone needs to teach you some manners, little man."

Slide's voice was hard and cold. "Put him down, Rayx."

Gibson, who by this point was terrified out of his mind but determined not to show it, caught a blast of Rayx's breath full in the face. The demon had the foulest breath imaginable, and he almost gagged. Rayx continued to hold on to him and truculently faced Slide. "Do you intend making me?"

Gibson twisted his head around and looked at Slide. His hands had vanished beneath the table, and Gibson wondered if he had surreptitiously pulled out his gun. Slide was sitting very still and very calm. "Put him down, Rayx, or you'll answer to me."

Gibson was aware that the confrontation was no longer over him but was just the latest twist in some long-term rivalry between the two *idimmu*. There was almost a ritual to the facedown that told of a long history to the hostility.

Rayx lowered Gibson into his seat again and took a step back.

His eyes flashed. "You think you're ready for me, do you, Slide?"

"I'm always ready for you."

"Why don't you can the bullshit and just get to it?"

Slide's face was impassive. "So take your best shot."

Something silver had appeared in Rayx's hand, but before he could use it the table in front of Slide exploded in a flash of blue flame, smoke, and wood splinters. Rayx tottered back with an angry scream. "You bastard, you had a piece under the table."

Green blood was streaming from the man-beast's right shoulder, and the silver weapon had dropped from his hand. Slide was on his feet. The smoking pistol that he was holding looked exactly like a Civil War Navy Colt, except that Gibson had never seen a Colt that could spout blue fire.

Rayx was down on his knees, trying to stop the flow of blood from his shoulder. Gibson was also on his feet. "Is he going to die?"

Slide shook his head. "No, he'll live. It takes a lot to kill something like Rayx. I just hope that he'll think twice before he fucks with me again." The remark was made as much for the man-beast's benefit as it was for Gibson's. When it was clear that Rayx wasn't going to continue the fight, Slide looked around at the demons who had come in with him. "Why don't you get him out of here before he bleeds all over everything?"

Rayx's gang of five helped the wounded leader out of the barroom, but it was immediately plain that the incident was far from over. A group of *idimmu*, including Tom Enni-Ya, gathered around Slide with the attitude of people who wanted answers. The landlord of the Rearing Eagle became the spokesman for the group with the weary tone of a man who doesn't want to take control but knows that he has to. "Okay, Yancey, the fun's over. We all know that Rayx is a loudmouthed blowhard who frequently deserves shooting, but, this time round, he did have a point. What do you intend to do with the human?"

Slide holstered his pistol and sat down again. "I need a drink."

Tom Enni-Ya signaled to one of the serving women, and a fresh jug was placed in front of Slide; then the innkeeper put the question again. "What about the human, Yancey? Is he the one?"

Slide shrugged. "What can I tell you? He seems to fit the Requirements but we won't know for sure until he goes to the Portal."

"And when's that going to be? We may not have too much time. Every day more folks come in here with more stories of the changes going down. Since Luxor, it can only get worse. I hear tell there's print-throughs fucking things up everywhere. There are even rumors of a couple of serious continuity disruptions. Shit like that can't help but speed His waking process, and if we don't make our move pretty damn fast, it could well be too late."

Slide pointed to Gibson. "You heard what he said. He's his own man. It's his decision whether he goes or not."

At this, a number of the *idimmu* growled, and the demon whom Gibson had overheard telling the story of his run-in with the streamheat in the town called Xodd took it upon himself to voice the feelings of the others. "Maybe Rayx had the right idea. We can't let our whole future get hung up on the whim of one human. Maybe we ought to drag him to the Portal whether he likes it or not."

Now every eye in the place was on Gibson, and he knew it was time to make some moves on his own behalf. "Before everyone gets carried away, do I get to say something?"

Tom Enni-Ya nodded. "Sure, say your piece."

Gibson took a deep breath. "I haven't agreed to go to this portal and find out if I really am the one in the prophecy, but I also haven't refused."

The demon from Xodd looked round at the others. "He's got a point there."

Gibson continued. "I might be more willing to go along with this thing if I knew a bit more about it and had a better idea of what my chances of survival might be."

Again the demon from Xodd faced the crowd. "Seems to me that he can't say fairer than that."

Gibson was pleased that at least one person in the Rearing Eagle was taking his part; then one of the eighteen-inch munchkins piped up." Ah, screw it, why are we dicking around with one dumb human. I say drag him to the Portal and be done with it."

The general approval with which this was received was hardly encouraging. Gibson glanced at Slide. "You have anything to say about this?"

Slide shook his head. "Not a word, kid. You're on your own here. You told us that you're your own man."

Gibson sighed and turned back to the crowd. "I might be able to make a decision if I knew why my going to this portal was so goddamned important.''

The mass attention immediately shifted to Slide, and the munchkin, who had been all for dragging Gibson to the Portal by force, climbed up on the shattered table and glared into Slide's face. "You didn't tell him?"

Slide looked more uncomfortable than Gibson had ever seen him. "I didn't think the time was right yet."

Now Gibson was not only terrified but also furious. "The time wasn't right for what? There was sure as hell enough time to bore the shit out of me with all your drunken stories of the Battle of Kia Mess and all the rest of the ancient history."

"It was the Battle of Kia Mass."

"Whatever."

The munchkin turned round to face Gibson. "He didn't tell you that us *idimmu* were counting on the Prophecy of Anu Enlil to save our collective ass when He wakes?"

Gibson looked at Slide and shook his head. "He left out that part."

Tom Enni-Ya growled in his throat. "Fuck it, Yancey, have you always got to be so goddamned devious?"

Slide avoided the landlord's eyes. "Ain't you kind of forgetting that my devious behavior is responsible for us all being here today, drinking it up in this here tavern instead of having been blown to our component atoms fifteen thousand years ago?"

The munchkin turned angrily on Slide. "Yeah, right. We're all real grateful. It don't give you the leeway to be screwing around with the Prophecy, though."

Tom Enni-Ya was glaring at Slide. "Are you going to tell him or am I?"

Slide glowered back at the crowd of demons. "I'll tell him, goddamn it."

Gibson sat down again and leaned back. "So tell me."

Slide sighed. "It was like this. Fifteen thousand years ago, we all knew that His time in the dimensions of Earth was coming to an end, and we were getting worried about what was going to happen to us. The humans were gone already, some of us had even taken part in the exterminations."

Gibson looked outraged. "You exterminated the humans?"

Slide at least had the decency to look shamefaced. "Hell, we left enough of you guys alive to carry on the species and even that was taking a risk. We had orders."

The munchkin was nodding. "When He gave an order, you didn't screw around."

Gibson was getting bemused. Once again he'd asked for information, and more was being thrown at him than he could ever absorb in one sitting. "So you'd wiped out the humans. What happened then? You started getting worried about your own future?"

Slide nodded. "Pretty much. A bunch of us, most of the people here in fact, were ordered to the twin cities, Sadan-Gomrah, out on the plain. The last of the civilized humans, except for the few we'd let slip away to the hills, were gathered there. The idea was to level the place with a couple of nukes."

"This is a charming story."

Slides eyes flashed. "Fuck you, Gibson. I'd like to see what you'd do in the same situation."

"Just go on with the story."

"Okay, so we get to Sadan-Gomrah and start setting up for the destruction of the place. We'd tipped off one of the Patriarchs, though, that the shit was going to go down, so he was able to sneak a bunch of his people out of there . . ."

Gibson's lip curled. "You really are all heart."

This time Slide ignored the remark. "All the time, though, we're thinking that we might be next, since it was obvious that He was going for a full-scale scorched-earth policy, no traces left when he went dormant."

"So what did you do?"

"I organized this scam whereby we armed the bombs but set them to go off earlier than planned, so it'd look as though we'd fucked up and blown ourselves to hell. Just before the explosion, we all took off, spreading out across the dimensions so, as He was already slowing down for the dormancy state, He most probably wouldn't find us."

"And you got away with it?"

Slide nodded. "Sure did. A few were caught, but only a few."

"What happened to them?"

"You don't want to know."

Gibson shook his head. "I do want to know and I'm asking."

The demon from Xodd supplied the answer. "Can you imagine a thousand years of relentless pain or being buried alive in the heart of a mountain?"

"I don't think I can."

Slide smiled nastily. "That's why you don't want to know."

"So what happened next?"

This time the munchkin answered. "He slept and we survived."

"And now he's waking, you're worried that he's going to come after you."

Slide nodded. "His wrath is something else you don't want to screw around with."

"And where does this prophecy fit in?"

"We hope to appease Him through making sure the Prophecy is fulfilled."

Gibson frowned. "That doesn't make any sense. If he wakes up mad, how is one sorry human going to tip the balance in your favor?"

"When the Prophecy of Anu Enlil was told to us, we took it as an order that had been left behind. It has always been interpreted as a chance to redeem ourselves for the previous deception."

"Why not just go on hiding out?"

Slide sadly shook his head. "There'll be no hiding from Him when He wakes. He'll be strong, and He'll sense us wherever we are. We're His creatures, He'll be able to draw us to Him. We'll go to Him whether we want to or not, because that's what His power is all about."

Gibson took a long deep drink from the jug. He was beginning to sense what was coming, but he was determined to stave it off for as long as possible. "I still don't see how my going through the portal is going to save you all from the wrath of Necrom."

A shudder ran through the parlor of the Rearing Eagle, and Slide actually winced. "How many times do I have to tell you not to do that?"

Gibson was only now becoming aware of just how terrified the *idimmu* were of what might happen to them when Necrom woke. Slide had to be the most frightened of all. "I guess he's going to take a special interest in you, seeing how you were the leader of the mutiny and all."

Slide nodded. "He'll be looking for me."

"So what happens to me after I pass through the Portal?"

"I don't know. We only have the Prophecy."

"But I'll be a part of the waking process?"

"That's our guess. When a massive mind like that comes back on line, it has to be a complex process. Maybe He'll draw something from you, some energy, or maybe He'll use the mem-

ories in your brain to somehow orientate a part of Himself. I
truly don't know for sure.''

"And will I come out the other side intact. Do you know that
for a fact or is that just more guesswork?''

Slide spread his hands, and Gibson had the feeling that the
demon was telling the truth, trying his hardest to overcome his
previous reputation as a pragmatic liar. "It's written in the
Prophecy, the very last verse, 'and he shall return and become
the Master of Men.' ''

"That's a lot to hang my life on. I mean, you're asking me
to drop in on this being, and you're all too scared to even say
his name.''

Tom Enni-Ya pushed his way to the front of the crowd.
''That's exactly what we are asking you.''

Gibson nodded. "And you want an answer.''

He knew that there was no way out. There hadn't been a way
out since Slide had shot Rayx. Slide had saved him from being
summarily dragged off by the man-beast, but it had been more
of a case of saving his face rather than saving his skin. Slide had
really only bought him the time to agree to go voluntarily.

"Okay, I'll do it. What else can I say.''

A pandemonium of applause and relief filled the Rearing Eagle. The munchkin was pumping his hand and some other demon was slapping him on the back. Tom Enni-Ya was clapping
his hands for the serving women and announcing drinks on the
house. A load had obviously been taken off the minds of the
idimmu and placed squarely on Gibson. For the moment, though,
working on the principle that you might as well enjoy yourself
while you can, he allowed himself to be carried along by the
general euphoria. While an all but naked demon woman was
kissing him, and, in the process, smearing Day-Glo green body
paint all over his clothes, a full jug of corn was set in front of
him along with a jar of ale with which to wash it down. It was
almost like being a rock star all over again. He did, however,
wonder how long all this was going to last, how long he would
be the hero of the hour before they'd expect him to go and face
the waking Necrom.

He glanced round to Slide. "So when am I . . .''

He found that Slide had gone and that he was talking to an
empty seat. He looked at the munchkin. "What happened to
Yancey Slide?''

"He left. He didn't look too happy.''

Gibson was immediately alarmed. Why had Slide suddenly

vanished when he'd just got what he wanted? Was there something more that he wasn't telling? Gibson disengaged himself
from the woman in the Day-Glo body paint and moved quickly
to the door. A few of the demons, thinking that he was running
out on the party, called after him, but he hurried on. Outside on
the street, it continued to be dark. Slide stood by himself, head
thrown back, staring up at the pseudo night sky.

Gibson halted, suddenly unwilling to approach him. "Yancey, are you all right?"

Slide didn't appear to either see or hear him. His mouth suddenly opened and a stream of words came out. *"Eli ameri-ia
amru-usanaku! Imdkula salalu musha urra!"* It was like the cry
of a wounded animal, plaintive and desperate.

Gibson moved quickly toward him, but, before he reached
where Slide was standing, Yop Boy stepped out of the shadows.
"Leave him be, Gibson."

"What's wrong with him?"

"He's just contemplating his fate, his mortality."

"But I thought that everything was settled. I agreed to go
through the Portal."

"That may not be enough to save him. Remember that he
was the leader of the escape. He may not be forgiven for that,
whatever you do."

The terrible cry came again. *"Eli ameri-ia amru-usanaku!
Imdkula salalu musha urra!"*

"Is there anything we can do for him?"

Yop Boy shook his head. "Just leave him alone. Go back
inside and leave him alone."

"But . . ."

"Just go back inside."

Gibson took a last look at Yancey Slide and then did as he
was told.

Back inside the Rearing Eagle, the party was still in full swing,
and no one else seemed to be suffering the same soul torture as
Slide. The booth where Gibson had been sitting had been taken
over by other revelers, so he made his way to the bar, where he
was greeted like a long-lost friend even though he had only been
gone for a couple of minutes. Once again he was congratulated
for his courage in deciding to brave the Portal, more drinks were
pressed on him, and women smiled into his face. Borne along
by a company who, at least for that night, seemed to be determined to adore him, he found that it was all too easy to turn his
back on Yancey Slide's angst and bask in his own moment of

glory. Over in the corner, the woman with the guitarlike instrument had struck up a lively dance tune and was singing in a husky voice.

> *"Ssalmani-ia ana pagri tapqida duppira*
> *Ssalmani-ia ana pagri taxira duppira*
> *Ssalmani-ia iti pagri tushni-illa duppira*
> *Ssalmani ini ishdi pagri tushni-illa duppira.*

Slide was speared by a pang of guilt. The words of the song sounded very close to the same language in which Slide had been screaming, the same hissing sibilants and guttural vowel sounds.

> *"Ssalmani qimax pagri taqbira duppira*
> *Ssalmani ana qulqullati tapqida duppira*
> *Ssalmani ina igari tapxa-a duppira*
> *Ssalmani ina askuppati Tushni-illa duppira."*

He couldn't, however, make Slide his problem. Slide had Yop Boy to look after him, and Gibson was essentially on his own.

As it turned out, though, he wasn't alone for very long. A woman moved along the bar and stood next to him. She was dressed tough, in stained leather jeans and a loose white, Greek-cut shirt with embroidery on the collar and cuffs. A belt of silver chain was slung around her hips, and a dagger hung from it in an ornamental scabbard. A brooch in the shape of a small green lizard, decorated with rubies, was pinned to the shoulder of her shirt, or that's what Gibson thought until the brooch turned its head and looked at him, at which point he realized that it was an extraordinarily tame ornamental pet. The woman's skin was deathly pale, and her tawny Nordic hair hung dead straight, clear to her waist. Even though there were some demon beauties in the tavern, this one was something special, a cool blond warrior maiden who probably gave no quarter.

"I'm Thief Lanier."

"I'm Joe Gibson."

"I know that."

Gibson, well aware that the *idimmu* tended to take a superior attitude around humans, ignored her somewhat snotty tone and continued to play it pleasant. "Thief is a strange name."

"It's what I do."

"Oh, yeah? And what do you steal?"

She suddenly laughed. "Practically anything that isn't nailed down. Do you know I saw you perform once?"

"I hope you liked it."

"You were okay." Her tone seemed to indicate that she considered she was doing him a favor by even attending one of his shows.

Gibson didn't have much to say after that shutdown so he went for the obvious. "Would you like a drink?"

Thief Lanier nodded. "Yes, but none of that god-awful corn that you're swilling." She gestured to Tom Enni-Ya. "Hey, Tom. Get out one of my private bottles, will you?"

The private bottle carried no label and was thick with dust. Thief Lanier blew the worst of the dust from it and removed the cork herself. When she poured her first drink, Gibson saw that it was a pale-golden liquid that actually seemed to shimmer and move in the glass.

"What is that stuff?"

Thief Lanier swallowed the first glass in one gulp and closed her eyes for a moment as though in ecstasy. "Very rare."

"Could I try some?"

Thief Lanier shook her head. "Not now. Maybe later, though. You wouldn't feel it after all that rotgut corn you've been pouring down your throat."

"What happens later?"

Thief Lanier smiled. "I figured that I'd take you off somewhere. There's something about a man who knows he's only got a few hours."

Gibson blinked. "What?"

"I said that there's something about a man who's only got a few hours."

Gibson was alarmed. "Who said I only had a few hours?"

"You're going to the Portal as soon as the celebrating stops. Even if you come back this way, you're going to be changed by the experience. It's your last hours as you are now."

"I'm not sure I like the idea of changing."

"You're so perfect as you are?"

"No, but I've grown accustomed to myself."

"Well, there ain't a damned thing you can do about it, but why worry? You humans change all the time, so you ought to be used to it. It's because you're so short-lived. You have a lot to get in."

Gibson was more concerned with the idea of his last few

hours. "I also didn't realize that I was going to the Portal so soon."

"Nobody here wants to wait around."

"I wouldn't mind."

"Having second thoughts?"

"Of course."

"It's too late now."

"I'm well aware of that."

"So, are you coming with me?"

Gibson, aware of his new celebrity status, decided to play it a little hard to get. "Coming where?"

"To where I live."

Gibson looked around the Rearing Eagle. The party had reached that stage where it had taken on a life of its own, and it could get on very well without him. Gibson smiled nicely at Thief Lanier. "I'd be very happy to come to where you live."

As it turned out, Thief Lanier lived in the phallic pink glass tower with the circular Lucite balconies that stood right beside the Rearing Eagle. To be precise, she lived, or at least entertained, on the third level of the phallic pink glass tower. They entered the building by a circular door that faced the street and operated like the iris diaphragm of a camera, and then climbed a transparent spiral staircase. The third level was one large round room with a diffused rose-colored light coming from the walls. A huge circular bed with a red satin cover was positioned in the exact center of the room, and the ceiling overhead was one huge mirror. Thief Lanier obviously took her entertaining very seriously.

The space was surprisingly bare. Gibson had half expected that an *idimmu*'s home, if indeed the *idimmu* had homes as he knew them, would be filled with the booty of countless lifetimes. Not so in the case of Thief Lanier. A suit of armor in black-and-red lacquer that must have come from sixteenth-century Japan stood against the wall like a mute guardian, and a small white bird of prey, maybe an albino falcon, sat quietly on its perch secured by a thin silver chain and with a leather hood over its eyes. A silver pitcher and two matching chalices stood on a small Moorish table that was inlaid with mother-of-pearl. Thief Lanier placed a hand on the pitcher.

"I think you're ready to try my private stock?"

Gibson nodded. "Why not?"

She poured golden liquid into each of the chalices and handed one to Gibson. He looked into the glass. The liquid actually seemed to be shimmering, squirming almost.

"What is this and why does it move like that?"

"It's the wine of a very weird dimension."

Gibson took a first sip. The wine was aggressively cold and vibrated and bubbled on his tongue like a very dry champagne that had somehow acquired a life of its own, and, to his surprise, it actually seemed to clear his head. He had heard of people drinking themselves sober but he had never really believed in it. The wine had to be some kind of stimulant that he had never encountered before. As he took a second sip he noticed that a straightedge razor lay on the Moorish table beside the chalice.

"What's that?"

"I like to have a weapon to hand."

Gibson felt a little uneasy. "I hope you don't intend to use it on me."

Thief Lanier flashed him a fast smile. "You're perfectly safe as long as you behave yourself."

She took hold of his hand and and gave it a slight, brief squeeze. "I'm going to leave you for a moment. Don't go away."

She ran up the next flight of stairs to the level above, and Gibson was alone in the round room. He looked at the hooded bird and then walked over to the suit of armor and inspected it more closely. It seemed as though it might have been made for Thief herself, certainly for a woman, which was damned unique. What was the story, had she actually ridden with samurai?

Gibson was a little nervous. His only previous sexual encounter with a female demon had been the one with Nephredana, and that had left him close to shell-shocked. He guessed the only thing he could count on was that she wouldn't do him any permanent damage. They must want him intact to go to the Portal.

The sound of heels on the transparent stairs heralded Thief Lanier's return. As Gibson had imagined, she had slipped into something a little more comfortable, although when he saw her, he had to admit that comfortable was closer to magnificent. Her hair was piled up on her head and fastened with a gold chaplet, and the jeans and shirt had been replaced by by a flame-colored negligee that, when coupled with the rose glow of the walls and the scarlet of the bed, made the space look like a whorehouse in some high-tech hell. The garment was fastened at her shoulder with a gold pin so one breast was exposed and a revealing vent ran the length of her body, from ankle to armpit. The material was so sheer that she might as well have been naked anyway, and it also appeared to ripple and dance in a similar manner to the wine, as though it really was woven from living flame. Gibson could only imagine that the fabric also came from a very weird dimension.

"You look beautiful."

She moved past him, going to the bed and standing beside it, idly stroking the satin with her fingertips. "Come here."

Gibson put down his drink and went to her. For a second time, he was entering the strange landscape of demon lovemaking. After he had woken in Balg's lair to find Nephredana gone, it had seemed to him she had been able to cast a spell that rendered him incapable of remembering individual moments or specific details. All that remained was a series of peaks that had taken him to a frantic, spine-snapping, mind-wrenching euphoria. It seemed that Thief Lanier had a similar ability to cloud his mind. It was as if she didn't have to touch his skin, but was able to reach right inside him and stroke his actual nerve endings. Pain and pleasure blended and blurred into a single cresting frenzy that had him pleading that he couldn't stand it and yet, at the same time, begging for more. There was really only one coherent image that stood clear of the screaming erotic background noise, and, in many respects, Gibson wished that it, too, had been lost in the roiling erotic mists. At the peak of what seemed like the hundredth climax, Thief Lanier had left him, standing over him for a moment as he shuddered and spasmed on the bed, and then disappearing from his sight. In seconds, she had returned with the falcon on her wrist. In her other hand was the straightedge razor, and she spun it between her fingers. He saw the razor with the alarming clarity of sudden unthinking fear. It had a pearl handle and along the gleaming blade was the maker's logo—Charleston Bluesteel. The blade flashed blood-red as she sliced at and through the neck of the bird. The falcon, still being hooded, didn't see the blade coming and didn't so much as flinch. Thief Lanier stood over Gibson, straddling his prone body and holding the twitching headless body of the falcon by the wings that had stretched out in death. The blood dripped onto his chest, burning like acid and sending waves of shock coursing through him while his back arched so only his head and heels were touching the bed. Above him, every action, every contortion of his white body against the red satin was repeated in the ceiling-size mirror, and then red flame took over his vision and his whole body seemed to be sucked into a rent in the tissue of reality and then slowly ejected into a gradually cooling limbo.

Gibson lay for a long time, relearning how to breathe and feel. After what seemed like an eternity of recovering, he reached out to touch her but she was nowhere on the bed. His mouth was now so dry that he was quite unable to speak, and he rolled over, reaching for his wine. The first thing that he saw was the falcon, standing on its perch, intact and seemingly unharmed. Thief Lanier was bending over it, stroking its feathers and whispering small cooing noises to the creature.

Despite the wine, which had lost none of its unnatural chill or sparkle, his voice was little more than a croak. "I don't understand . . . the bird . . . I swear I saw . . ."

Thief Lanier smiled wickedly. "And was it good for you, too, darling?"

Gibson shook his head and fell back on the bed. He knew that questions were pointless.

She finally took pity on him. "Don't try to work it out, Joe Gibson. You, if anyone, should know, by now, not to be dictated to by your senses. Just tell me I was better than Nephredana."

The White Room

THEY CAUGHT HIM at the corner of Nineteenth and Third. He had been heading for the East Village, hoping to find natural cover among the other crazies. An unmarked white truck pulled up beside him and three nurses jumped out.

"Decide to take a little walk, did we, Joe? We can't have that. You could get hurt out here."

When they grabbed him, he put up only a token resistance. He knew all three of them. They were burly ones from the nursing staff, well trained in the art of subduing patients. They threw him bodily into the truck, climbed in after him, and slammed the doors behind them; then they had the straitjacket on him and started beating the crap out of him. One of them had a leather-covered blackjack that hurt like hell.

Chapter
Fourteen

"OKAY, GIBSON, IT'S time for you to stop your drinking and whoring, we've come to prepare you for the Portal."

Nephredana and the two women who were with her had come up the spiral stairs to the circular chamber on the third level without either Gibson or apparently Thief Lanier hearing them. Gibson had been drowsing, basking in the warm weariness and the soft, rose glow of the walls. Gibson sat up with a start, and the falcon let out a high-pitched angry squawk. Thief Lanier, on the other hand, hardly reacted at all. She had been lying spread and naked, looking at herself in the overhead mirror, with the tiny ornamental lizard curled above her left breast. At the sound of Nephredana's voice, she languidly rolled over onto her stomach while the lizard scuttled for cover in a fold of the red satin bedcover.

"Have you come to take him from me?"

Nephredana looked round the room, taking in the whole aftermath of the debauch. The spark of rivalry between the two women was plain. "You've had him long enough, haven't you?"

Thief Lanier propped herself up on one elbow. "I suppose I have. Where are you going to make Preparation?"

"Right here, if you have no objection."

Thief Lanier shook her head. "No objection at all. Do I need to assist you?"

Nephredana smiled. "I think you've done your part. You're welcome to watch, though."

"Then I think I'll put some clothes on."

Thief Lanier started gathering up her jewelry and what was left of the flame negligee, and Gibson also made moves preparatory to getting up, but Nephredana waved him back again. "Don't move, Gibson, you're just as we want you."

"Shouldn't I put some clothes on, too?"

Nephredana shook her head. "You're exactly as we want you."

Gibson rubbed the drowse out of his eyes and took his first good look at Nephredana and her two companions. They were like a trio of Valkyries come to carry him to Valhalla. Nephredana herself was wearing full plate body armor that was burnished to a deep, rich shine. From the way she moved, the armor was either extremely light or she was much stronger than he had ever imagined. Gibson recognized the woman on her left as the one who'd been drunkenly kissing him in the Rearing Eagle before Thief Lanier had picked him up, only now the Day-Glo green paint had been replaced by a somber cowl and long robe. The third woman was equally serious in her attire, if a little more up-to-date, clad as she was in a very tight black leather motorcycle suit with all of the obligatory zippers and chains and a red dragon on the back of the jacket. In another time and place they would have made a great set of backup singers. The thought jumped into Gibson's mind uninvited, but he quickly pushed it aside as unworthy of such a weighty occasion.

Nephredana positioned herself at the foot of the bed. "Are you ready, Joe?"

"I guess as ready as I'll ever be. What is this preparation? Some kind of ritual?"

Nephredana's voice was surprisingly gentle. "Don't ask any questions, Joe. Just do exactly as you're told. First, I want you to lay flat on your back with your arms extended and your legs together."

Gibson did as he was told even though he was a little surprised that the Preparation for the Portal was turning out to be so physically elaborate. He'd expected a few incantations to be muttered over him and that would be that.

Gibson stared up at his own reflection. "I look like I'm ready to be crucified."

The woman from the Rearing Eagle spoke reprovingly. "Please don't speak, Joe."

Nephredana seemed to be in command of the ceremony. "First the bowl, the oil, and the coins."

A gold bowl, about eight inches in diameter, was placed on Gibson's chest and then filled with a pungently scented oil.

"Remain very still, Joe. Don't try and move or we'll have to tie you down."

A gold coin about the size of a silver dollar was placed on the palm of each of Gibson's hands. He saw in the mirror above him that Thief Lanier, now dressed in her jeans and shirt, was watching from the transparent stairs.

Nephredana spoke again. "Now the book."

The woman in the biker leathers handed her a thick, leather-bound volume in which a number of places in the text had been marked by black ribbons. She opened it to the first passage and started reading from it in a low voice.

> *"Isa ya! Isa ya! Ri ega! Ri ega!*
> *Bi esha bi esha! Xiyilqua! Xiyilqua!*
> *Limuttikunu kima qutri litilli shami ye*
> *Ina zumri ya isa ya*
> *Ina zumri ya ri ega*
> *Ina zumri ya bi esha*
> *Ina zumri ya xiyilqua."*

As she read aloud, the rose glow of the walls seemed to dim and deepen like a sinister sunset, and Gibson could feel sweat forming on his body. The temptation to move was very strong, to jump up and ruin the whole Preparation, anything to buy him a respite or a bit more time. Unfortunately, if he did make a run for it, it would probably only buy enough time for an angry mob of *idimmu* to either stuff him bodily into the Portal or hang him from the nearest approximation of a tree.

Nephredana spoke in English again. "Now the wafer."

The woman from the Rearing Eagle held up a round, flat, white wafer about the size of a half-dollar. "Extend your tongue, Joe."

Gibson stuck out his tongue, and the woman placed the wafer on it. All feeling immediately left his mouth, and a rapid numbness spread through his whole body. What were they trying to do, turn him into a zombie? Maybe it would be the best thing. At least he'd feel no pain. Nephredana turned to the next marked passage in the leather-bound book. For this reading, her voice was louder and more forceful.

> *"Zi dingir anna kanpa!*
> *Zi dingir kia kanpa!*
> *Zi dingir uruki kanpa!*

Zi dingir nebo kanpa!
Zi dingir nergal kanpu!
Zi dingir ninib kanpu!
Zi dingir annunna dingir galgallaenege kanpu!
Kakammu!''

Gibson's body was now completely without feeling, and as he stared transfixed at his reflection, his own eyes seemed to be boring back into his brain. Nephredana's voice came from a long way away.

"The flame."

The woman in leather snapped her gloved fingers and blue fire appeared at their tips. She held her burning hand above her head and then plunged it into the bowl on Gibson's chest. A column of blue flame leaped almost to the mirror on the ceiling. Gibson felt nothing. Either it was the effect of whatever drug had been in the wafer or the blue flames were a cold fire. Nephredana started reading again.

"Ia! Ia! Zi azag!
Ia! Ia! Zi azkak!
Ia! Ia! Kutulu zi kur!
Ia!''

With the last word the flames went out as though a switch had been thrown or a tap turned off, no dying down or gradual dwindling, just poof, out. All that remained was a thin haze of smoke, hanging in the air.

"The blood."

Gibson didn't like the sound of this and he said so. "Whose blood are we talking about?"

Nephredana held up a hand. "Do not speak, Joe, or you will have to be gagged. We are going to take a very small amount of your blood. It won't hurt you." She turned to the woman in leather. "The dagger?"

Thief Lanier came down the stairs. "Use the razor. It will be better."

She was holding out the Charleston Bluesteel, but Nephredana hesitated before taking it. "You performed the illusion of the hawk?"

Thief Lanier nodded. "I did."

"And it was good?"

"It was good."

Nephredana nodded. "Then you're right, we will use the razor."

She took the Charleston Bluesteel from Thief Lanier and passed it to the woman in leather; then she removed the coin from the palm of Gibson's left hand. The woman in leather opened the blade out with a flick that showed she was well accustomed to straightedge razors and at the same time picked up Gibson's left wrist. *"Barra ante malda! Barra ange ge yene!"*

The woman in leather recited this part from memory. Nephredana opened the book again. *"Namtar galra zibi mu unna te!"*

The woman in leather sliced a nick out of the tip of Gibson's little finger and a red bead of blood appeared. She moved Gibson's arm so his hand was over the bowl on his chest. Drops of blood fell into the bowl, mingling with the oil.

"GAGGAMANNU!"

The single word from Nephredana caused a ball of flame, this time green, to explode from the bowl and hang in the air above Gibson until it dissipated after a few seconds.

"And now the anointing."

The woman in leather closed the razor and handed it back to Thief Lanier; then she leaned over Gibson and lifted the bowl from his chest. When she stepped back, he could see in the mirrored ceiling that the bottom of the bowl had left a mark like a brand where it had rested on his chest, a broken pentacle contained in a circle.

Gibson couldn't hold back a cry of protest. "You've marked me, damn it."

Nephredana's eyes flashed. "I won't tell you again to be quiet."

Gibson bit off his complaints. He didn't particularly want to be gagged and helpless. The ceremony continued. Nephredana and the woman in leather stood one on either side of the woman from the Rearing Eagle in the robe and cowl. The woman in leather held the bowl while Nephredana removed the gauntlets of her suit of armor. She placed them on the bed beside the book and then turned to face the woman in the robe and cowl.

"Are you ready?"

The woman nodded. "I'm ready."

Nephredana pushed back the cowl and slipped the robe from her shoulders. It dropped to the floor behind her, revealing

that the woman from the Rearing Eagle was naked beneath them
apart from a web of silver chains around her hips. Even preoc-
cupied as he was, Gibson couldn't help being reminded that she
had a magnificent body.

Nephredana put the ritual question a second time. "I ask you
again, are you ready?"

The woman nodded a second time. "I'm ready."

Nephredana dipped her hands into the bowl and began to
smear the mixture of oil and blood all over the front of the
woman's body. As Nephredana's hands moved over her breasts,
the woman let out a long shuddering groan. *"Ssarati
sha!"*

Nephredana replied in a soft voice. *"Sha limnuti!"*

When the woman's torso and thighs were covered in the mixture of oil and blood, Nephredana stepped back, wiped her hands
on a white towel handed to her by the woman in leather; then
she picked up the book again and opened it.

> *"Epu-ush salam kashshapi-ia u kashapti-ia
> Sha epishia u mushtepishti-ia."*

The woman from the Rearing Eagle climbed onto the bed and
approached Gibson on all fours.

> *"Qu-u imtana-allu-u pi-ia!
> Upu unti pi-ia iprusu!"*

Now she was on top of him, squirming against his body,
rubbing the oily mess from her skin onto his. If he hadn't been
so numbed out, it probably would have been a memorable erotic
experience, too, but drugged as he was since the administration
of the wafer, it was about as exciting as a rubdown with a hali-
but. His loss, however, seemed to be the woman's gain. As she
moved against him, her breath came in short ecstatic gasps.
". . . o Kakos Theos . . . o Kakos Dasimon . . . uh . . . o
Daimon . . ."

And all the while, Nephredana's voice provided a steady
counterpoint.

> *"Sha ipushu u mushtepishti-ia!
> Kal amatusha malla-a sseri!
> Alsi bararitum qablitum u namaritum!"*

The woman from the Rearing Eagle let out a last climactic groan, and Nephredana's voice rose, in seeming sympathy, to a final shout. *"TUSTE YESH SHIR ILLANI U MA YALKI!"*

Somewhere outside the glass tower, something crashed like thunder, and the light from the walls strobed and flickered, agitating from red to purple and back to red again. The woman from the Rearing Eagle rolled off Gibson and away from him, lying sprawled on the bed, facedown and seemingly unconscious, while both Nephredana and the woman in leather sank to their knees as though exhausted by their efforts. Only Thief Lanier remained standing, and even she had the look of someone on the verge of going into shock. For a long time, none of them moved or spoke, and then, little by little, the disturbance in the light diminished and things returned more or less to normal, at least as normal as anything could be in the Hole in the Void.

Slowly, Nephredana got to her feet. There was a great weariness in her face and voice. "Rise, Joe Gibson, we have done all that can be done for you."

Gibson's whole body felt as though it belonged to someone else. "I'm not sure I can move."

"Try. You can move."

He turned his head and saw the gold coin that remained on the palm of his right hand. He closed his fingers around it and held it up. "What do I do with this?"

"Keep it. It may prove to be a talisman."

"And I need all the help that I can get?"

"You said that."

Gibson attempted to sit up and found that it was possible even though his muscles protested and, at the same time, his mind and body felt strangely detached one from the other. "What did you people do to me back there?"

"It was a basic purification and an infusion of energy, plus a number of protections against any third-entity intrusion."

"I don't feel like I've been infused, more like the energy has been drained out of me."

"You'll feel like that for a while, but then you'll start to grow stronger."

"How can you know any of it will work? I mean, you can't have done this before, right?"

"It is all in the footnotes to the Prophecy."

"And what happens now?"

"We dress you and then take you to the Portal." Nephredana

turned and gestured to the woman in leather. "Bring the clothes."

Gibson swung his legs over the side of the bed and then paused before attempting to stand. "So this is it?"

Nephredana nodded. "This is it."

They dressed him in white: white suit, white shirt, white patent shoes. He guessed that it was symbolic of his new purification, although the suit leaned a little too much toward *Saturday Night Fever* for his taste, with overwide lapels and slightly flared pants, but he figured that he couldn't be too picky in a place like the Hole in the Void. He was probably lucky that they hadn't given him a toga.

When they came out of the pink glass tower a small, silent crowd was waiting for them. Yancey Slide was there, as were Long Tom Enni-Ya, the aggressive munchkin, the demon from Xodd, and a dozen or more other faces from the Rearing Eagle. Even Rayx stood in back of the gathering with a bandaged shoulder and a sour expression. It had to be a moment of truth for the *idimmu* as well as for Gibson. They were pinning a lot of hope on the Prophecy of Anu Enlil and his being the one, and very soon they would see if that hope was going to pay off.

A strange little procession started out of the valley of the Hole in the Void, away from the cluster of buildings and along a fold between two of the orange hills. Nephredana led the way, immediately followed by Gibson, while the other three women who had taken part in the preparation walked behind him, side by side. Gibson had half expected that Yancey Slide would assume some sort of major role in all this, but it seemed that the women were in complete charge of his being offered to the Portal.

Overhead, the sky was going insane, as if responding to the events that were taking place on the ground, and the air was alive with wild bursts of random energy. Jagged swaths of black raced from horizon to horizon like angry electronic clouds against a juddering background of purple and magenta pixels that careened and danced in spectacular swirls and eddies as if in the grip of some huge and complexly shifting magnetic field, and although there were regular explosions of dazzling brightness, for the most part the Hole in the Void was cloaked in a dim semi-twilight, which, at least as far as Gibson was concerned, was a more than fitting background for a man going to a fate at which he could only guess.

The route of the procession took them past the gates of the antebellum mansion that was almost completely hidden in its grove of oaks. Three pale, black-clothed, vampiric figures stood just inside those gates, apparently waiting for the procession to come by.

As Nephredana drew level with them, one of them called out to her in a high hissing voice. "Are you taking him to the Portal?"

"We are."

"Is he the one?"

"We hope so."

As they crested the hill behind the mansion and Gibson took one final backward look at the buildings that constituted such civilization as could be found in the Hole in the Void, he had the feeling that he was walking back in time, away from the technology and the intrigues of the world in which he'd been born and raised and back across a hundred centuries or more into a pagan past, where men had mattered little and power had been in the truly demonic hands of the *idimmu* and their unimaginable master. Maybe it had been the ritual, or maybe it had been the drugs, but he knew that he had reached a place beyond fear where all will was gone and everything was inevitable.

In some respects, the Portal itself was something of an anticlimax after all the buildup. Gibson was too far gone at that point, and had been through too much, to be overawed by a ring of megaliths, no matter how ancient or how large. He had seen Stonehenge and the Great Pyramid and the ruins at Nazca, and his only thought on approaching this stone circle on the orange hillside was the mundane cliche: When you'd seen one, you'd seen them all.

The procession halted, and Nephredana turned to face him. "From here, you go on alone."

Gibson hesitated. He might be beyond fear, but that didn't mean he was about to rush into whatever foolish shit was going to present itself. In many respects, it was like going on stage. At that instant when he went to step into the lights, it had always been the very last place in all the world that he wanted to be, and yet he was in such a transcendental position of no turning back there was no choice but to go on. On the stage, though, the adrenaline pumped and the crowd howled and the show started and the orgone high came along and carried you away with it. There among the tall blue-gray megaliths, he didn't know what was going to come along and carry him away.

He looked back at Nephredana. "What am I supposed to do now?"

"Just walk forward to the center of the circle."

"On my own?"

"This is as far as we go."

Gibson drew two, quick breaths, sighed, shrugged, and then marched smartly forward, talking to himself like whistling past the graveyard. "What the fuck, let's get to it."

When he reached the center of the circle, the worst possible thing happened. Exactly nothing. Zip. Sweet fuck-all.

"Fucking great. Now start jerking me around. I guess that's a god for you."

Gibson had a sneaking feeling, however, that it wouldn't stay nothing for very long, and, in around twenty seconds, he was proved right. The world started to revolve. Like a broken wheel, with him at the hub, the huge, hundred-ton stone columns began to move as one, spinning the hillside around him. He looked for the small crowd of *idimmu* but they had vanished. The megaliths were now moving faster, circling him at a gathering speed that was already turning them into a blur. It occurred to Gibson that perhaps he was being a little subjective about it all and that it was actually him doing the spinning. He should have felt dizzy but he didn't. For one thing, he was too busy watching the ground at his feet become transparent. He hadn't experienced anything like it since the time back in the seventies when he'd accidentally OD'd on PCP by mistaking it for cocaine and making a pig of himself.

He seemed to be floating very slowly down into a long spiral shaft, a virtual kaleidoscope of light, that extended deep into the unnatural bowels of the Hole in the Void. It was as if George Lucas had made a deluxe, no-expense-spared version of *The Time Tunnel*. Dark loops of crackling energy revolved around him, and beyond them, the wall of the shaft danced with multicolored patterns and images. The air was filled with bizarre snatches of sound, voices and music and sounds that Gibson couldn't begin to identify melted and blended as though all the broadcasts in a hundred dimensions were trying to crowd onto the same single wavelength. The deeper he sank, the louder the sound became. At first it had been an easily ignorable background buzz, but it rapidly increased both in volume and intensity until he felt as if he was being impaled on a column of white noise.

And then it all stopped, and he was alone in total darkness, with his ears ringing and his eyes straining for dancing afterimages, and he realized that he was falling. He opened his mouth to scream but the void snatched away the sound. Points of red light flashed up past him, and they made the sensation of falling even worse. How the hell did astronauts ever get accustomed to free-fall? Of course, astronauts knew, at least intellectually, that the ground wasn't going to come up and smash them to pulp at any second. Gibson had no such consolation.

And then the red lights were coming up more slowly, as though he was slowing down. Could he be dropping to a soft landing? He hit before he even expected it, no bump, just a cessation of the falling sensation and the world expanding laterally in two ripples of light.

And then he was in the landscape, a place of hanging mist and rocky spires, pristine uneroded geology and billowing vapors. He was standing on a flat tabletop mesa of white crystalline rock, looking across a wide valley to a horizon that was shrouded in cloud, breathing deeply of the seashore smell of ozone that was carried on the wind. At regular intervals, somewhere deep within the clouds, flashes of gold fire would briefly erupt, like infant volcanoes venting their heat and infusing the layers of mist with bright luminous refractions. With each gout of flame, the faint reek of sulfur wafted past Gibson, and he had the distinct feeling that he was in a place where time was just beginning, a world that was before protozoa, let alone dinosaurs.

"This must be the world when it was young."

"Apt, don't you think?"

"What?" Gibson spun round but there was very little to see, although something was definitely there, a disturbance, a wavering of the air about four feet from him across the flat, decklike top of the mesa.

"I remarked how apt it was, a newborn world waiting for the second birth."

Gibson took a step back; his mind was suddenly bristling with feral animal fear. Something that had been keeping him calm had released its grip, and he was poised to run blindly with no thought of the consequences. "Who or what are you?"

"That's not an easy question."

Gibson swallowed hard. "Are you Necrom?"

The infant volcanoes all went off at once, and sheet lightning flashed across the sky with a single clap of thunder.

The voice came again. It was a male voice and hardly godlike. "Am I Necrom? Now, that is a truly impossible question, particularly when so much still sleeps. Am I a separate entity or merely a detachment of the whole? I would imagine that question could be pondered by generations of philosophers without their coming to a satisfactory conclusion. Such is the complexity of Gods. Look on me as a messenger, if it makes it any easier. A herald, an angel, if you like.''

Even Gibson wasn't buying this. ''One of Necrom's angels?''

''Hark the herald angels sing.''

''I'm getting the feeling that I'm being fucked with.''

''Perhaps I should slip in a mortal form so you don't start being difficult.''

The figure that appeared looked like a young debonaire Cab Calloway in a white tailsuit, white tie, and fistful of diamond rings. A small white table appeared right beside the figure, on which was an ice bucket that contained a chilling bottle of champagne. The figure lifted the bottle from the ice.

''Drink?''

Gibson realized that there was going to be no way to short-circuit the foolishness and all he could do was to go with it.

''Delighted.''

Cab Calloway plucked a glass out of the air, filled it, and handed it to Gibson. ''Your health.''

''Drinking champagne in hell?''

''What makes you think this is hell?''

''I was sent by demons, wasn't I?''

''If you'd prefer it . . .'' Cab Calloway snapped his fingers. The two lateral ripples of light came again, and, in the blink of an eye, Gibson was in a fourteenth-century hell. The terrain was much the same—he and Necrom's messenger still stood side by side at the top of a rocky promontory, looking out across a wide valley—but now, instead of mist and crystalline rock formations, it was a bubbling cauldron of red fire, hot slag, and belching black smoke that made Gibson gag. All through this blast furnace of a nightmare, miserable snaking columns of pleading naked people were being herded by fearsome misshapen devils armed with pikes, pitchforks, and a whole array of spiked devices for which there were probably no names. The heat was unbearable and the continuous sound of screaming rolled around Gibson and the messenger like a hot howling gale. The messenger had become one of the devils, no longer Cab Calloway but a classic Beelzebub, towering over Gibson, horns, goat legs, shaggy red fur, reptile skin, and glowing feline eyes. ''Now you really are drinking champagne in hell.''

Gibson looked down at the glass in his hand: the champagne was coming to a boil. That was too bad, it had tasted like a good vintage. Horny fingers snapped again and slavering fanged mouth curved into a grin. "Or maybe this would be closer to your taste . . ."

The lights rippled outward, and Gibson was in an art-deco Hollywood heaven where mirrored pillars rose from a bed of fleecy clouds and a glass staircase was draped with blond Busby Berkley angels in diaphanous shifts who wore tinsel wings and sang elevator harmonies into a sky of truly monotonous blue.

"Okay, okay, I get the point. Everything is just an illusion."

Snap, flash, everything changed.

They were back in the primal valley of mist and crystal, and Cab Calloway was laughing at him. "Even illusion is a very inexact word. If you accept the idea of illusion you also have to accept the counterconcept that somewhere there exists a solid reality and you, if anyone, really ought to know by now that is not the case. How would you feel about another glass of champagne?"

Gibson nodded, going with the flow. "I'd like another glass of champagne."

"Even though it's only an illusion."

"I've already told you you'd made your point."

Necrom's messenger refilled Gibson's glass. "You seem to be getting a little impatient."

"I thought I'd been brought here for a purpose."

"Indeed you have."

"All I've seen so far are party tricks."

"That's because my function is to keep you amused."

"I don't understand."

The messenger produced a second glass out of the air and poured himself a drink. "I know that you're in a place that you're absolutely incapable of understanding, and very frightened, and the preparation you went through for this probably led you to expect the worst. Believe me, I understand your fears and I must compliment you on how well you're standing up to them."

"Are you going to tell me what you have in store for me, or just leave me hanging?"

"That's the terrible secret, Joe. Nothing is going to happen to you. At least, not in the way you imagine it. No fiery pits, no laser dissection, you're not going to be impaled on a shaft of burning chrome. To be truly precise, what's going to happen to you is already happening."

Gibson turned, looking around helplessly at the mist-shrouded illusion world. "This is it?"

"You are a specimen, Joe, a sample if you like. Maskim Xul was motivated to bring you here."

"Who the hell is Maskim Xul?"

The messenger made a small, apologetic bow. "I'm sorry. You know him by his new name. You know him as Yancey Slide."

"So it was Slide pulling the strings? He was behind it all?"

The messenger shook his head. "Slide was only a part of a very complex selection process."

Gibson blinked. "I was selected for all this? Right from the start?"

"A great deal of care was taken in designing the test program that made sure you were the right one."

Gibson felt himself starting to lose it. "Test program?"

"A progressive filter system that, in the end, came up with you."

Events had come full circle and Gibson had returned to the perpetual unanswered question. "But why me?"

"In the beginning, you attracted attention because your behavior, your musical career had made you stand out from the rest of your kind."

"I didn't stand out that much. I wasn't president or anything."

"In that respect, you were just plain unlucky."

Inside the clouds, an infant volcano spouted golden flame. "Unlucky?"

"You stood out from the crowd, but you had also put yourself in a position where you wouldn't be particularly missed if you were taken to another dimension or, as you are now, to a place beyond the multidimensional universe. As with so many things in the affairs of your species, the root cause of the chain of events was really a matter of happenstance."

Gibson paused to sip his champagne. He needed time to think, to make sense out of what was going on. He wasn't too optimistic about his chances, however. "I thought it was the stream-heat who first latched on to me."

"They were allowed to believe that and, indeed, they did play a very useful part after they'd been panicked into believing that you were somehow crucial to their so-called war against

Us, and they involved you in that ludicrous conspiracy in Luxor with your dimensional counterpart.''

"A whole country got itself nuked to hell on account of that.''

"That's why We had to motivate Yancey Slide very quickly to get you out of there. Such a catalyst potential had to be examined.''

"And how did you motivate Slide?''

"Slide believed that he was following the Prophecy of Anu Enlil, but, in fact, he was actually running the tests on you to determine if you were in fact the specimen we required. The *idimmu* are easy to control. They are, after all, Our creatures.''

"What about all the people who died?''

"Your species spends half its time dying. It's really no concern of Ours.''

Gibson slowly shook his head. "This is all too much.''

The messenger's voice was very quiet. "It's only a tiny part of it.''

A faint flush of silent lightning flashed across the sky, and Gibson stared silently across the valley. The messenger took a step toward him. His voice was almost sympathetic. "I wouldn't try to comprehend it, Joe. You can't. You're no longer in the reality of men and it's really no disgrace not to understand.''

"You still haven't told me what's being done to me.''

"What happens to a specimen, to a sampling? You're being tested, analyzed, typed, recorded, and inspected. Right now, we are making an evaluation of everything from the mutating microorganisms that infest your body to the conditioned responses of your subconscious. Everything about you is being absorbed and considered. We know your childhood memories and your DNA codings, the weaknesses in your immune system, and the capacity of your paranoia.''

Gibson was starting to become alarmed. "I don't feel anything.''

"There's no need for you to feel anything. Would you rather you were stretched out on a cold steel table with tubes up your nose and electrodes in your brain?''

"No, but . . .''

"And stop all the self-pitying nonsense about why me, why me. It's you and them were the breaks. Things could be a lot worse. And also don't flatter yourself, there are thousands of you from as many dimensions being tested in the same way. Much has changed in the time We've been dormant and there is much that We have to know before We can plan Our waking behavior.''

''You make it sound like I'm being fed into a giant computer.''

The messenger shrugged. ''Think of it as market research of the gods if it helps you accept your situation.''

''Who says that you're gods? All this god talk only started just recently. Before that, everyone called you a superior being.''

''Isn't a superior being a god to the inferior being? Go ask your dog.''

Gibson was gripped by the flash of heady, self-destructive rebellion. ''Yeah? Well I ain't no dog and I don't see you as a god.''

The messenger's eyes hardened, and Gibson realized that his rebellion may have been a very bad idea. This was confirmed when lightning lanced across the clouds, chased by an extended and deafening clap of thunder, and even the ground trembled. The messenger's voice deepened and intensified to one much closer to Gibson's expectations of Necrom, the kind of voice that biblical prophets must have heard when they went one-on-one with Jehovah.

''WHAT'S THE MATTER, LITTLE MAN? DON'T WE MEASURE UP TO YOUR EXPECTATIONS OF A GOD?''

Gibson was so afraid that he responded by blurting out the absolute truth. ''I never heard of a god who went to sleep for fifteen thousand years.''

The messenger's voice instantly returned to the way it had been. ''That is a weakness.''

Gibson realized that he had possibly spotted another weakness. Necrom, or at least this part of Necrom that he was being allowed to experience, could get angry, could come near to letting go of its control. He had a strong feeling that it had come close to blasting him. How was that possible? It shouldn't be possible for him, Joe Gibson, alcoholic and washed-up rock star, to spot a weakness in a being that was so powerful that it could alter his reality on a whim. It was only then that another, even more terrifying thought struck him. If it could read his mind . . .

''Of course We can read your mind, and that is an avenue of thought that We would advise you to avoid.''

A long silence passed before the messenger finally offered the bottle of champagne again. ''Refill?''

Gibson held out his glass. The champagne bottle appeared to remain perpetually full, and, as the messenger poured, Gibson asked a question. "You keep referring to yourself as 'We,' as though you were some kind of composite being."

"We are, for the moment. Only when the waking is complete will we achieve Our Full Singular Wholeness."

"And what will happen when you are fully awake?"

The messenger winked. "That's something you will have to wait and see."

"Yancey Slide seemed to think . . ."

"The *idimmu* are tough and cunning but they suffer from a great narrowness of vision. They believe that our return will make things as they were fifteen thousand years ago. I can guarantee that this will not be the case."

"Can I ask one more question?"

"It hasn't stopped you so far."

"What's going to happen to me?"

"You will eventually be returned to your dimension of origin. It may be necessary for you to remain here for a while until an unobtrusive reentry cover can be devised, so you're not seen to simply appear out of nowhere. We assure you that, in the meantime, you will be quite comfortable."

"How long will I have to stay here?"

"It shouldn't be more than a couple of weeks, as you perceive time."

Gibson nodded. "I guess I can handle that."

The thought occurred to him that, if he was placed in the right illusion, it might even constitute a well-earned rest. The messenger winked. "Look on it as a rest, Joe."

"I wish you wouldn't read my mind."

"It's unavoidable."

"Then just don't read it back to me."

The messenger sighed. "If it makes you happier to pretend."

"I take it that I'm not going to get to be the Master of Men out of all this?"

"You want that?"

Gibson grinned and shoved his thumbs into the pockets of his white pants in a decidedly hoodlum gesture. "Maybe I could handle that."

The messenger shook his head. "I'm afraid that's *idimmu* romance. Things will be a good deal more complicated this time around."

"So I just drop back into my old life?"

The messenger laughed. "Your old life has gone. You've seen far too much to return to the way you were. Of course, the memories of what you've been through, particularly this current episode, will become blurred and indistinct."

Gibson was outraged. "I'm going to forget all this?"

"Temporarily."

"More drugs?"

"Your own mind will do it. You're not going to rest easily with the memory of talking to a superior being. You're going to suppress and mythologize all of this, and turn it into some symbolic peyote vision, something that you'll be able to handle more easily."

"You said I'd forget temporarily."

"When the time comes for Us to enter your world, We may need you to serve Us. When that time comes, your memories will return."

Gibson looked sideways at the messenger. "I'm going to be your servant?"

"We always reward Our servants, and if it's power you want, We can easily give you power."

"I've really never been that keen on power."

"You make that obvious in your behavior. It may be one of your redeeming features."

An abrupt flash of crimson stained the clouds across the valley. It seemed as though one of the volcanoes was burning red rather than gold. A second volcano belched red flame and purple smoke that spread like a stain across the clouds.

Gibson looked sharply at the messenger. "What is that? Is something wrong?"

The messenger didn't answer right away. He stood staring out across the valley at the angry red intrusion, as though listening to instructions inside his head. "We have been made aware that the Hole in the Void is under attack."

"What?"

"Streamheat forces are attacking the Hole in the Void. They have transported aircraft and heavy weapons across the dimensions and seem to be bent on wiping out the *idimmu*."

Gibson looked around as though he expected them to come bursting through the cloud cover. "Thank God I'm here and not there."

The messenger was shaking his head. "You cannot remain here. You have to return immediately to the Hole in the Void."

"What the hell would I want to do that for? The streamheat

don't like me any more than they like the *idimmu*. I could be killed."

"You will die for sure if you remain here."

"But you told me . . ."

"This attack has changed everything. The Hole in the Void is your link. It is the route by which you are connected to your dimension of origin. If that link is broken or that route is severed, you will become a wraith and you will simply wither to nothing."

"I can't stay here?"

"Go, Joe."

The landscape vanished and the Messenger of Necrom along with it. For a fleeting instant, Gibson seemed to be in some gray, indistinct limbo, a place of fog and gloom and visual distortion. He sensed that there were other beings crowded around him, but beings who were not completely there, insubstantial and ghostly, a whisper on his senses rather than something fully real.

And then he was standing on an orange hillside above the valley of the Hole in the Void, right in the middle of a full-blown and very real firefight.

The White Room

BACK AT THE clinic, in the days that immediately followed his short-lived escape bid, they kept him submerged in a sea of pills and injections. It was almost as if they were trying to medicate the will for freedom out of him. He was so doped that he didn't even dream, merely drifted through a gray fog of nonfunctioning responses and dull frustration. Only a handful of what could be classed as clear memories came through that period. He could remember passing John West as they dragged him down a corridor bundled up in a straitjacket. West had been sitting in a wheelchair, and he had treated Gibson to a sad salute. "I told you you shouldn't have tried it."

He also remembered Kooning coming to look at him, staring down at his bed with a look of outraged betrayal.

The worst of the lasting memories was the nasty smile on the face of one of the male nurses who had recaptured him; he suspected it was the one who had used the blackjack on his kidneys while they were in the van. The man had leaned so close to him that Gibson had been able to smell the spearmint gum on his breath. "You were lucky they didn't dust off the ECT for you. Back in the old days they used to cook your brain if you broke out."

It was a constant reminder of the helplessness of anyone who got themselves labeled as a mental patient.

Chapter
Fifteen

GIBSON, WHO HAD never in his life been in combat, instantly discovered that it wasn't in the least like the movies or even the TV news. Combat happened all at once, and so fast there wasn't enough time to take it in or even to be specifically frightened, just a dry-mouthed, unfocused terror and a gasping, sobbing need to scramble away, out of the line of fire. Beneath him, in the inhabited valley of the Hole in the Void, buildings and vehicles were burning. As far as he could tell, one of the structures on fire was the Rearing Eagle.

"Bastards."

The sky was a dull gunmetal-blue streaked with rushing parallel lines of gray interference that provided little light by which to see. Two large aircraft, black shapes above the glare of the fires, hovered over the valley, filling it with the high-pitched siren wail of their engines. They were like big helicopter gunships, but without rotors, and of a design unlike anything Gibson had ever seen in his own world. They were pouring fire into the village, both conventional tracer and the jagged beam of some advanced energy weapon. Small dark figures were moving around among the flames, and Gibson could make out the repeated pinpoint muzzle flashes of weapons. He wasn't, however, allowed the luxury of wondering what was going on in the valley. Other dark figures were coming over the crest of the hill above him. To his relief, he spotted Nephredana, still in her armor, among their number, and he realized that they had to be a group of defenders. The bad news was that they were in full retreat.

Gibson yelled and waved his arms, even though he realized the gesture was probably pointless in the gloom. "Hey, over here!"

Nephredana spotted him. "Gibson?"

She hurried to where he was standing. There were scorch-marks on her armor and her face was streaked with dirt. She smelled of smoke and sweat. "Where the hell did you spring from? What happened?"

"He heard about the attack and sent me back here."

He realized that he wasn't saying the name Necrom any longer.

Nephredana glanced over her shoulder. "We've got to get out of here. They're coming up the other side of the hill."

Her voice was momentarily drowned out by the nearby chatter of automatic weapons. "They Pearl-Harbored us right out of nowhere. We never had a chance to get organized. They've got these fucking weapons . . ."

In the next second, he was able to see these fucking weapons firsthand. A horde of what Gibson instantly recognized as streamheat assault troops from their helmets and uniforms poured over the top of the hill. A number of them seemed to be armed with what looked a great deal like World War II flamethrowers. Tubes were attached by hoses to heavy backpacks. When they opened fire, though, they proved to be flamethrowers from some future hell. Streams of dazzling light danced and shimmered, now spasming along the ground, now juddering through the air, jumping and twitching like a set of random lines in a flick book. When they reached an obstacle they either arced over it or skit-tered around. Each streamheat trooper appeared to control the lines of energy flowing from his weapon by means of a twist grip behind the trigger mechanism.

Gibson stared open-mouthed until Nephredana grabbed him and dragged him to the ground. "Get down, you idiot!"

They pressed themselves flat as one of the streams of light cracked over their heads. "Holy shit! What are those things?"

"The swine have come up with something that can finish us *idimmu*."

"Kill you?"

Nephredana shook her head. "It can't terminate us, only the Maker or a direct ground-zero nuclear blast can do that, but they can fuck us up good."

"What will they do to me?"

"Turn you into a fucking grease spot."

A defender was caught by the blazing lines of energy, a hulk-ing brute not unlike Rayx. He screamed horribly, became one with the energy stream, retaining his own basic shape as a burning outline for a few seconds and then vanishing.

Nephredana's eyes were an iceburn. "It's some beefed-up version of the regular streamheat return-gun. It's capable of burying each of us at the fucking heart of nickel-iron planetoid and we'd never get out." She was now looking anxiously for an escape route. "We're in deep shit here."

Gibson could only assume that what Nephredana called a streamheat return-gun was the original weapon that he'd seen Smith, Klein, and French use all the way back on the Jersey waterfront, the same one French had turned on himself in Luxor.

The weapons swallowed a second and third of the defenders and Nephredana was off at a crouching run, ducking and dodging the energy streams as they slashed across the hillside like electric whips. Gibson didn't hesitate; he was right behind her. A gully ran down the hillside a little to their left, and Nephredana dived into it, taking advantage of the momentary shelter. Gibson all but rolled in on top of her. He now had orange stains on his white suit and was gasping for breath.

"Where's Slide?"

Nephredana shook her head. "Don't know. We were separated."

She quickly fumbled in a pouch at her belt and pulled out a small metallic object. "Quickly, take this!"

It looked like a small pistol.

"What is it?"

"Don't you recognize it?"

Gibson looked at the multibarreled configuration and realized that it was a pocket version of one of the streamheat return-guns. "What am I supposed to do with it?"

"Use it on yourself."

"I thought these things could bring you out five miles up in the air or a mile under Mont Blanc."

"That's a chance you take. If you stay here you'll be killed for sure, or taken alive and that would be even worse."

Gibson looked at the thing in his hand as though it were a poisonous snake. "I can't do that."

"Do it, damn you. You have to get out of here, you've been to Him."

Gibson was shaking his head. "I can't do it."

Energy streams danced along the edge of the gully.

"There's no time! Use it!"

"I can't."

"Then give it back to me, damn it, and I'll use it on you."

"What about you and the others?"

"We'll take our chances. Now give me the damned weapon."

Gibson passed the gun back. Nephredana went into her pouch again and tossed something else to him. "These may help."

It was a small leather pouch. He found that it was heavy. "What . . . ?"

A third gunship came over the hill, laying fire. Tracers flashed along a section of the gulley. Nephredana pointed the small streamheat weapon at Gibson and fired.

He was running down a long white corridor. It was tilted over on one side and he had trouble keeping his feet. There was fire behind him and a golden light ahead of him. He had to reach the golden light to be safe, but the white corridor was very long and he was very tired. He wanted to lie down and rest, but, if he did, he would be consumed by the fire. It was then that the thought struck him. A white corridor, a golden light. He looked down at himself and found that he seemed to have vacated his body. If he'd had a physical form to groan with, he would have groaned out loud.

"Don't tell me I'm fucking dead!"

The inward groan seemed to trigger something. His body came back with a vengeance. He was falling. He fell about twelve feet, hit the ground, and blacked out.

He opened his eyes but he had no idea where he was. He had been dreaming, a long, intense, and complicated dream, a terrible dream in which he'd constantly been running, a dream full of demons and monsters and death and pain. He had only woken from the dream because he imagined that he was dying. He shivered, he was cold. Had he taken something? What the hell had he taken? He couldn't remember. All he knew was that he was glad to be back in his own bed.

Except, although it was dark, he wasn't in his own bed.

He was sprawled on hard, muddy, cold ground that was littered with garbage and dead leaves, and he could see the lights of what looked like apartment buildings beyond the branches of sooty trees. Rain was falling on him and, worst of all, he was naked. Groggily he raised his head. The question was no longer what the hell had he taken but what the hell had he done? He'd never woken up in a state like this before. A bundle was lying beside him. He reached out. It was his clothes. The moment he touched the sleeve of his jacket, it all came back to him: Nephredana, Yancey Slide, and the saucers. And, before that, Gideon Windemere; Christobelle; Smith, Klein, and French; and the Nine. It hadn't been a dream. It had been an insane reality, and it was still going on. Instantly he was up. Mercifully his suit and shirt had turned black in the trans. It saved him from the added absurdity of running around in the dark dressed like John Travolta. Trying to get into his pants in a half crouch before someone spotted him, and not to get too much mud on them while he was doing it, was no easy trick, but he struggled. The last thing he needed was to be arrested for public lewdness. There were too many questions that he couldn't satisfactorily answer for himself, let alone for a bunch of suspicious cops. Besides, he had seen quite enough of cops in Luxor.

As he slipped on his jacket, something heavy in the pocket bumped against his hip. It was the leather pouch that Nephredana had given him. He pulled it out, loosened the drawstring that held it closed, and shook some of the contents into his palm. He could scarcely believe what he was seeing. The pouch was full of large gold coins.

"Fucking Krugerrands."

Nephredana really had taken care of him, if indeed gold had any value where he'd landed. The first problem was to find out exactly where that was. If the streamheat had been telling him the truth back in Jersey, he ought to be in his own dimension. That was supposed to be the function of the weapon and why the *idimmu* called them return-guns. To his surprise, he accomplished the task of orientation by simply standing up. He instantly recognized where he was. He was back in New York, in Manhattan, back where he'd started or, to be exact, a ten-dollar cab ride from where he'd started. Unless he was badly mistaken, he had fallen out of the void and into the Lower East Side. He'd emerged into the world in, of all places, Tompkins Square Park, behind the bandshell. In some ways it wasn't too bad a place to materialize at random from another dimension. If any of the denizens of the ravaged little park had noticed him suddenly appearing out of thin air and dropping to the ground, they'd probably only have shaken their heads and wondered about the quality-to-quantity ratio of the stuff they were drinking, smoking, or shooting up. On the other hand, it was a bad place to be lying around unconscious. He was damned lucky that someone hadn't stolen his boots, the rest of his clothes, and the bag of Krugerrands. It would have been a cool score for a junkie.

Gibson straightened up and slowly looked around. From the

lack of activity in the park, he guessed it had to be four or five in the morning. The homeless were stretched out on the benches or sleeping in makeshift cardboard shelters. Somewhere someone was playing rap music on a boom box. The bars on Avenue A were closed, and he had to assume that it couldn't be all that long till dawn. Even though he wouldn't have chosen the manner of his arrival, it was good to be back somewhere familiar and, by the standards of his recent adventures, relatively normal.

The question was what he should do next. His instinct was to go back to Central Park West, to the seclusion of his apartment to fix himself a drink, take a hot bath, and sleep for three or four days. The kind of prudence that he'd learned in recent days stopped him, however. Maybe he should go to a hotel. He couldn't be sure that there wasn't something unpleasant waiting for him at home. It would be better to hang on until daylight before investigating the apartment, and even then it would pay to be a little circumspect. He started walking toward Avenue A, but after the first couple of steps, he had to stop and stand very still to prevent himself throwing up. His system had taken such a beating in the last couple of dozen hours that it was now in open revolt. Gibson badly wanted a cigarette, but a search of his pockets revealed that he didn't have any. The lack of cigarettes brought his first problem home to him. He might have a pocketful of gold but he didn't actually have any American money. He couldn't very well walk into the Warwick or the St. Regis without even an overnight bag, slap a couple of Krugerrands on the desk, and expect them to give him a room. He doubted that he could even try a stunt like that at the Chelsea. Damn it, the way things were, he couldn't so much as hail a cab.

There were at least six all-night bodegas within easy reach of the park and, in the second of these, he was able, after a great deal of very suspicious negotiating, to sell one of the coins to the Lebanese behind the counter for fifty bucks. He knew that this was only a fraction of its real value, but his need for a little operating cash made it more than worthwhile. As soon as the stores were open he'd make his way over to the jewelry strip in Chinatown and sell the rest of the coins for a much more realistic rate. Now all that remained was to decide what to do for the rest of the night. Fifty bucks was by no means enough to get him a room in anything but the most raunchy of flophouses or hot-sheet hotels, and that was almost worse than staying awake. He knew an after-hours joint on Third Avenue just by Fourteenth Street that went by the name of the Candy Box. He'd go there.

With a couple of drinks inside him, he might feel a whole lot different about the world.

As soon as the cab he hailed on the corner of Avenue A and Sixth Street hit Third Avenue, he knew that there was a problem. The traffic on Third Avenue was going the wrong way. When he'd left, Third Avenue had been one-way uptown, and now it was running in completely the opposite direction. He couldn't imagine how, in the comparatively short time that he'd been in London and in other dimensions, the City of New York might have been able to completely reverse its whole Manhattan grid system. Just to be sure, he checked the street signs. They were tired and rusted and looked as though they'd been there since the fifties. It made no sense except to worry the hell out of him.

To his infinite relief, the Candy Box was still there, and open to him, subject to a little bargaining with the gorilla on the door. He realized that he didn't look like much: his suit was rumpled and covered in purple stains, probably the translation of the orange stains that he'd got on it during the hillside firefight in the Hole in the Void. The Candy Box was filled with a typically representative cross section of those who couldn't find a reason to go home that particular night. Drunken rock 'n' roll musicians rubbed studded-leather shoulders with the silk suits of off-shift dope dealers, while nervous coke whores chain-smoked Marlboro Lights and waited for their next invitation to the bathroom. Wired leftovers from downtown discos, and alcoholics who hadn't quite drunk themselves into zombiehood, tried to keep the party alive long after all the vital signs had ceased. Gibson put away two cognacs in quick succession and felt considerably better. He even made a trip of his own to the bathroom to buy a beat quarter of a gram from a tall black man who went by the name of Elk. He told himself that the cocaine was purely for medicinal purposes. He needed something to keep him going until he'd completed all that he had to accomplish. He was a little surprised to see that there was no one he knew in the place, and even more surprised that no one even recognized him. He told himself that it didn't really matter. His ego could take a backseat for one night. He was more than happy to sit on a bar stool with a drink in front of him and his elbows propped up on the bar. The last things he needed were recognition or conversation.

Nine o'clock the next morning saw Gibson on the corner of Canal and Mulberry, waiting for a Chinese jewelry store to open. The owner, after a good deal of haggling, offered him two hundred an ounce for the coins, and Gibson accepted. The net weight was close to seven ounces, and although he suspected that the Krugerrands were probably worth close to twice that, it was a comforting sum to have in his pocket. Outside on the street, he flagged down the first cab that he saw and rode it uptown, having it stop a block short of his building on Central Park West. He stood for a full five minutes, observing the comings and goings to and from the building, satisfying himself that there was no one keeping watch on the place, before he risked approaching the main entrance. To his relief he saw that Ramone was the doorman on duty. A large weight fell from his shoulders. He was all but home free.

He grinned at Ramone, as he walked in the direction of the elevator. "How you doing, Ramone? What's been going on while I've been away?"

He knew in an instant that something wasn't right. Ramone's face was a semihostile mask. It was the expression reserved for the most dubious visitors. "Can I help you with something?"

Gibson blinked. Ramone didn't seem to know him. Admittedly, there had been times when he'd come home roaring drunk and acting up, and Ramone had been needed to coax him into the elevator, but he'd always tipped the man very well after these incidents and Ramone had never been the kind to hold a grudge after money had changed hands.

"Hey, Ramone, what's going on here. Don't you know me?"

Ramone's eyes were narrowed and he looked at Gibson with practiced suspicion. "You sure you have the right building, my friend?"

Gibson wished that he had a mirror in which he could check himself. Had there been some weird change in his appearance during the transition back to Earth? "Ramone, don't you know me? It's Joe Gibson. I live in 10-E. What's going on here? Did the IRS put a padlock on the place or something?"

Ramone positioned himself between Gibson and the elevator. "I don't know what your problem is, pal, but I think you'd better get out of here."

Ramone was talking to him as though he was some crazy who'd wandered in off the street, and panic was rising in Gibson's chest like a flood. "I'm Joe Gibson, damn it. I live in this building, in apartment 10-E."

"I never heard of any Gibson. Dr. Cohen lives in 10-E. I think you'd better go now. We don't want any trouble, do we?"

Gibson made a desperate lunge for the elevator. "I want to get to my apartment, okay? I live here."

Ramone headed him off, ready to get physical if need be. Gibson knew for a fact that Ramone carried a blackjack in the hip pocket of his uniform pants. "You got keys for this apartment of yours?"

Gibson shook his head. It was getting worse and worse. This was like fucking Kafka. "No, I had a bit of trouble . . ."

That did it for Ramone. "Piss off, okay? Just piss off before I call the police."

Out on the street again, Gibson hailed a second cab. "Twenty-third and Seventh. Chelsea Hotel."

At the Chelsea, they didn't want to know anything about his business except that he had the money for the room and a deposit for the phone, and the phone was the first thing he headed for when he was through the scant formalities of checking in. His first call was to Tommy Ramos. Back in the seventies, Ramos had been in the punk band Grim Death, and he and Gibson had been firm friends for longer than either of them, now they were in the nineties, cared to remember. The number rang four times and then an answering machine picked up. "Hi, this is Wilson . . ."

". . . and this is Kimberly . . ."

". . . and we can't come to the phone right now but, if you leave a message after the tone, we'll get back to you as soon as we can."

It sounded like a pair of goddamned yuppies. What the hell were yuppies doing at Tommy's number? Tommy lived in a cheap, rent-controlled apartment on Seventeenth Street that he'd had since Sid Vicious was alive and stumbling. It was full of as much junk as Gibson's place, and there was no way that Tommy was going to give it up. He tried the number again to make sure that he hadn't misdialed, but all he got was the same annoyingly cheery message for a second time. Could Tommy have had his number changed? He tried 411.

"I'm sorry, we have no listing in that name."

First Ramone didn't know him, and now Tommy Ramos seemed to have vanished off the face of the Earth. He called the desk. "Could someone get me a couple of drinks from the bar."

He tried three more numbers that he had committed to memory. None of them answered. Fear of the unfathomable was starting to gnaw at his brain. One more number remained that, if anything was weird when he called it, he'd know for sure that he and the world were seriously out of whack. He was reluctant to use it, however. He'd only talked to Desiree maybe a half-dozen times since she'd walked out on him, and all of those conversations had finished on notes of petty and wretched acrimony. By this point, however, he was sufficiently disturbed to resort to his ex-girlfriend. At that moment, though, the drinks arrived, giving him the chance to delay the call for a few moments. He'd ordered two double Scotches and four bottles of Amstel Light and the porter looked round for the other person.

Gibson grinned. "There's only me. I came a long way and I was thirsty."

The porter nodded. "Been thirsty myself a few times."

Gibson drank one of the Scotches and half of the first beer, and then he picked up the phone again and dialed Desiree's number. Desiree was now living with an entertainment lawyer whom Gibson considered to be one of the worst examples of primordial slime that ever walked on legs. She answered on the second ring. "Hello."

At least she hadn't vanished into limbo.

"Desiree?"

She sounded puzzled. "Who is this?"

"It's me, Joe."

"I'm sorry, Joe who?"

Gibson didn't like this at all. "How quickly they forget. "

Puzzled changed to nervous. "Who is this?"

"We only lived together for two and a half years."

"I think you have the wrong number."

"For Christ's sake, Desiree. It's me, Joe—Joe Gibson."

"I think you have the wrong Desiree."

Gibson felt himself losing his temper. "What the fuck do I have to do, repeat intimate details of our sex life?"

Nervous was replaced by angry. "Listen, you sicko creep, I don't need this shit. I'm hanging up right now."

New York women knew how to hang up a phone. Gibson sat holding the thing until it made the reproachful beeping of a receiver off the hook. It was only then that he hung it up and reached for the second Scotch. What the hell had gone down? It was as though he'd become some Orwellian nonperson, expunged from record and even memory. His mind started searching through some of the available options. The first to present itself was that he had really died when Nephredana had shot him with the streamheat return-gun, and now he was in some custom-tailored hell. He put that to one side as too absolute and went on to the next. The idea that he was still in the region of Necrom, and all this was just one more illusion, maybe some grandiose, rat-maze psychology test, just didn't hold water. When he'd been in the primal world with Necrom's messenger, a certain disconnection and detachment had prevailed, making him aware that his surroundings weren't strictly real. It wasn't the case now. All this was too damn real.

After a lot of thought, he narrowed the field down to a pair of theories in which he couldn't find any truly gaping holes. The first was that there had been some glitch in the transition and he wasn't in his own dimension at all. Instead, he'd landed in one that was incredibly close to his own, separated by only the smallest of details, like the one-way streets of New York going in the wrong direction and the fact that he'd never been born. The second theory was a little more complicated. He was actually back in his own dimension, but, since he had been gone, some subtle but deeply weird change had taken place, maybe because of a print-through from the nuking of Luxor. His only problem was that he hadn't been here to go through the change along with everyone and everything else. He was less successful at thinking up ways to confirm or refute these theories, and inspiration was a long time coming.

"In times of crisis, turn on the TV."

He turned on the TV and flipped round the dial. It looked like perfectly normal afternoon programming: the regular soaps, Donahue doing a piece on women who married Satanists, Oprah sobbing along with the mothers of child prostitutes. There were kids' cartoons on channels five and eleven and a rerun of *Cannon* on nine. Nothing amiss on the tube. It was only him that was out of place. Maybe Phil or Geraldo should do a show on him: "Men Who Never Were."

Since the TV was of no help, he returned to the phone. There was one very obvious call that he could make. He dialed the desk to get the correct time. It was 3:45, and that meant that it was just before midnight in London,. He was back on the phone again getting UK information.

"I'm sorry, sir. There is no listing in the Greater London area under that name."

Damn it to hell.

"Are you sure about that? It's not just an unlisted number?"

"I'm quite sure, sir. I have no listing under the name Gideon Windemere."

The booze seemed to be loosening up his brain, because a

new idea immediately presented itself. Maybe he should have another shot at trying to find Tony Ramos. Even if his memory had somehow been expunged from Tony's brain, Ramos was quite crazy enough to at least listen to his story. Ramos had a longtime, on-again and off-again girlfriend, Cupcake Di-Maggio, a short, feisty, and very unpredictable little spitfire of a woman with a beehive hairdo straight out of the Shangri-Las and a tattoo of a black panther licking its paws on her left shoulder. If anyone knew what had become of Tony Ramos, it would be Cupcake.

Back to 411. "Do you have a listing for a Lois DiMaggio?"

The computer came on the line. "The number is 718-555-5678. The number is 718-555-5678."

Gibson dialed the number.

"Yeah?" It was Cupcake.

"I don't know if you remember me, my name is Joe Gibson."

Cupcake was suspicious and hostile, her regular demeanor with strangers, except Gibson had known her as long as he had known Tony. "I don't remember you. Should I?"

"I was a friend of Tony Ramos."

"Is this some kind of fucking joke?"

"I'm just trying to get ahold of him."

Now Cupcake was angry. "What are you, pal? Some kinda ghoul? All of Tony's friends know that Tony died eight months ago. So unless you've been out of town or something . . . "

Gibson felt ill. "Yes, yes, I've been away. What the hell happened?"

"The asshole OD'd on dope."

Gibson could see why her voice was so full of anger and bitterness. Cupcake had never made any secret of how much she loved Tony Ramos. It was one of those Sid-and-Nancy things. "I'm sorry."

"So am I, pal."

Gibson called for another Scotch. He needed it. Tony had always gone in for bouts of dopefiending, and, eight months ago, Tony Ramos had indeed OD'd, except that he had OD'd at Gibson's apartment, and Gibson had called the paramedics and Tony had pulled through. In this new world, where Gibson didn't seem to exist, he hadn't been there when Tony had scored the ultra-pure, miraculously uncut China White that had fucked him up, and Tony Ramos had died. Gibson couldn't shake the sick feeling that somehow he was responsible.

The porter came by with more booze. "You're drinking heavy."

Gibson nodded. "Yeah, I got problems."

"Take it easy, okay?"

Gibson nodded again and tipped the man. "I'll do my best."

He had to get out of there. The hotel room was getting claustrophobic, and he knew he wasn't going to learn anything more or come up with any solution by just sitting on the bed, drinking, watching TV, and making phone calls to people who couldn't remember him.

Out on the street, he took it into his head to walk down to Tower Records. The record store should show if any trace of his music remained. He started down Twenty-Third Street until he reached the Flatiron Building; then he turned south, heading downtown. He also stopped at a couple of taverns on the way. He realized that he was building to a full-scale drunk and that might not be such a smart idea, but a certain recklessness had come into the picture. What did he expect from himself? He'd lost his past, his history, his home, and he had found out that one of his best friends was dead, and he certainly had reason enough to get as disgustingly drunk as his mood indicated and damn the torpedoes.

It was with much the same attitude that he entered Tower Records. The uniformed security guard just inside the front door gave him a hard look, but Gibson walked the walk with such stunning arrogance that, despite the fact he looked like some ten-day drunk out of a Charlie Bukowski story, the man backed off. Gibson went straight to the Rock H section and found, with the feeling of a drowning man who can't even find a straw, that there was no subsection for the Holy Ghosts and not even any of their recordings in H General rack. That did it. He was beginning to lose it. His music was gone and that was too much. When he'd set out, he hadn't imagined he would feel it so strongly. The controls were snapping and slipping away. The newly acquired strength that had been maintaining him intact since Slide had pulled him out of Luxor was draining out of him. He wasn't even aware that his fists were clenched so hard that his nails were cutting into the skin of his palms and he was muttering to himself under his breath.

"I don't fucking exist. I don't fucking exist."

Shoppers around him were beginning to tense. In New York City, the individual who talked to himself was treated like an unexploded bomb in a crowded store.

He moved on for one final try. His solo albums had sold nothing like the numbers of the ones with the band, but it was worth checking. There was nothing under G, either. Gibson looked around the store. Some of the names were comfortably familiar: Lou Reed, Miles Davis, Cher, Bruce Springsteen, Elvis, The Who, and The Clash. They were all there, just as they should be. There were others, however, that meant nothing to him. Who the hell were Belinda Carlisle, Stevie Nicks, or Page Seven? None of them had existed when he'd left for Luxor, and now they seemed to be established stars with long careers behind them.

"Now it's me that doesn't exist."

He was most upset by a band called the Rolling Stones. Before all this, there hadn't been any Rolling Stones. He went to their bin and found that they had dozens of records on sale, records going back to the early sixties. It was insane. They had taken his slot in history. The look, the image, the attitude, it was pure Holy Ghosts. The only difference seemed to be that the Rolling Stones had kept it together while the Holy Ghosts had fucked up.

It was while he was looking through the Rolling Stones records that the tilt sign lit up in his brain. He had no clear memories of what happened next. He knew that he had started screaming and people had stampeded away from him.

He screamed at a blond girl behind the checkout. "Where are my fucking records? What happened to my fucking music?"

The security guard had attempted to subdue him and Gibson slugged him. At some point he'd also been throwing records and CDs around. "What happened to my fucking music?"

Along the line, the police showed up, and he could vividly remember the firm hand on his head, stopping him hitting it on the doorframe as they lowered him into the blue-and-white.

They put him in a holding cell on his own. This was probably because he'd had over a thousand dollars in cash on him, which separated him from the average, run-of-the-mill drunk. He sat in the corner on the floor, feeling completely drained and mindless. The sooner they took him across to Bellevue the better.

A lot later, an NYPD detective came to talk to him. "Do you realize that you don't exist?"

Gibson, who had recovered a little by that time, looked up, slack-faced. "That's what I was trying to tell them in the store. I'm not even history anymore."

"You're not in anyone's files, either. We've run you through both local and federal. You don't show up anywhere. You care to comment on that?''

Gibson shook his head. ''Not really.''

''Have you ever been fingerprinted?''

''Dozens of times.''

''So why is it that they aren't on record anywhere? Do you have a driver's license?''

''Haven't had a driver's license in years. I used to be driven everywhere.''

''That must have been nice.''

''You get used to it.''

''So life was good for you?''

Gibson nodded. ''Sure, life was good. I was a big-ass fucking rock star.''

''So how come no one has ever heard of you?''

''You wouldn't believe me if I told you.''

''Try me.''

''I went off to another dimension and when I came back things were different. Not very different, but different enough that I didn't exist.''

The detective's face didn't even flicker. ''And what did you do in this other dimension, Joe? It is Joe, isn't it?''

''Yeah, it's Joe.''

''You want to tell me what you did there?''

Gibson's voice was flat. ''I shot the president, narrowly avoided a nuclear war, and talked to a god.''

''It's sounds like you had quite a time.''

''It was actually very stressful.''

''You take drugs, Joe?''

Gibson nodded. ''Sure, all the time.''

''What kind of drugs, Joe?''

''What've you got?''

''You want to tell me about the money you had on you?''

''It's legit, my money.''

''Where did you get it?''

''A friend gave it to me.''

''This friend have a name?''

''Her name's Nephredana. She's an *idimmu*, a minor demon.''

She looked at him long and hard. ''You're a weird one, Joe. You ever kill anyone?''

Gibson shook his head. ''Not in this dimension. Not yet.''

He threw in the ''not yet'' as bait. He was quite ready to go to Bellevue. They'd knock him out there and he'd be able to sleep. The detective didn't rise to it, however, and just kept on asking routine questions, mainly about the money and what drugs he'd been taking.

Finally she stood up. "You're lucky you have rich friends."

"I don't have any friends, rich or otherwise."

"You may not know it but you do. They're paying to put you in this private clinic."

Alarms went off in Gibson's head. "I'm not going to any private clinic. I want to go to Bellevue."

"You don't have any choice in the matter. Your friends went in front of a judge and got a temporary order on you."

She tapped on the inside of the cell door for it to be opened. When it swung back, she beckoned to two burly men in hospital whites. "Okay, guys, he's all yours."

Gibson didn't resist as the two male nurses put white canvas restraints on him and led him through the precinct house and out to a private ambulance. He didn't resist because he was through. All the fight had gone out of him. He was burned-out. The drive was a short one, and inside of a half hour Nurse Lopez was shooting him up with his first cocktail of tranquilizers.

The White Room

HIS FIRST SESSION with Kooning after the escape bid was a wretched hour of recrimination.

"I'm very disappointed in you, Joe."

"I only wanted to try it on the outside. I would have thought that you'd be pleased with my progress toward recovery."

"I'm not pleased at all, Joe. I think your behavior was willful and childish. Did you really think that you could survive out there?"

"I was going to give it a shot."

"What did you think you were going to do?"

"I was going to be a wino on Forty-second Street."

"Please don't be flippant."

"Is it flippant to want to be free?"

"Here at the clinic, we have a responsibility to keep you from doing yourself harm."

"So freedom's harmful?"

"You are a very sick man, Joe, sicker than you realize. Your freedom was only removed from you because you were a danger to yourself."

"So freedom is dangerous?"

"Freedom is an idea that you shouldn't dwell on. It's largely an illusion at the best of times."

"Perhaps I like the illusion."

"That's hardly the point. Recovery can only come when you recognize your illusions for what they are."

"I always thought that freedom was reality, or maybe nothing else to lose."

"Don't paraphrase pop songs at me."

"They're my business."

"Your business is getting well."

"I got well when I stopped taking the medicine."

Kooning rubbed her chin.

"Perhaps we should talk about the way that you attempted to deceive those who were looking after you regarding your medication."

"I felt better than I do now. I'm so fucked up I can hardly count my legs."

"You can't be an objective judge of that."

"I can't? I thought how one felt was a pretty subjective thing."

"You decided to exercise your free will regarding your medication and all you succeeded in doing was to throw the whole regimen out of balance and precipitate this ridiculous display of defiance."

The conversation went on and on like this for more than forty-five minutes, and then, just as Gibson was thinking that it had to be over, there was a knocking on the door. Kooning looked up and frowned. Therapy sessions were never interrupted.

"What is it?"

"Urgent call for Doctor Kooning."

As she opened the door to the cubicle, two men pushed their way inside. They were dirty, unshaven men wearing stained duster coats and wide-brimmed hats. They smelled bad and had guns in their hands, grins on their faces, and Errol Flynn attitudes. Gibson's jaw dropped. The clinic had finally gone over the line with the medication and he was in total hallucination.

"How the fuck did you guys get here?"

Yancey Slide and Gideon Windemere were crowded into the small cubicle. The only thing that convinced Gibson he wasn't losing his mind was Kooning bleating with fury. "I'm going to call the police."

Slide laughed and pushed Kooning back down into her chair. "Can it, lady. We're having a reunion." He winked at Gibson. "We figured that we ought to get you out of here, particularly when we found that some associates of Rampton were picking up the tab."

"What took you so long?"

"We've both been kept a little busy."

Kooning looked as though she was about to explode. "You men are in very serious trouble."

Slide pointed his pistol at her and thumbed back the hammer. "You keep your mouth shut, Doc, or I'll do a job on your head, show you what trouble really is."

He turned to Gibson. "Are you ready to get up and go?"

Gibson nodded. "I've been trying to get up and go for months."

Gibson was so medicated that the race through the clinic and out through the front entrance took on an air of pure fantasy. On the final landing, a bunch of male nurses came at them but quickly backed away when they saw the guns. Undoubtedly they were straight on the phone to the cops, but this didn't seem to worry Slide in the slightest.

"We'll be long gone by the time the cops get organized."

The black Hudson was waiting at the curb. Gibson noticed with a smile that it was illegally parked. The three of them quickly ducked inside, Slide and Windemere in the front and Gibson in the back.

"Where's Nephredana? Is she okay?"

Slide glanced back and nodded. "Sure. She'll be where we're going by the time we get there."

Windemere turned and grinned at Gibson. "Christobelle will be there, too, so you may have a little sorting out to do."

Slide laughed. "Or they will."

"Where are we going?"

"Some secluded spot where we can get you dried out of all the crap that fucking place has been pumping into you."

"My dimension or yours?"

"Do you care?"

Gibson shook his head. "No."

They were now in the Midtown Tunnel running out to Queens. Gibson lay sprawled in the backseat. "So who are we all working for now? The God with No Name?"

Slide grinned. "You can't say His name anymore, either?"

Windemere looked curiously at Gibson. "How come you aren't demanding to know what's going on? You usually do."

Gibson closed his eyes. "I think I have a headache."

Windemere and Slide both guffawed. "And we're drunk."

"What weird shit are we being pitchforked into now?"

Slide shook his head. "No weird shit, kid. We can do exactly what we want to do for the moment. We're free men."

Gibson scowled. "We're men out of time."

"So make the most of it."

Gibson wished that he was drunk, too. "It won't last. Events have a habit of catching up with us."

Slide didn't seem to be in the mood for any negative input.

"Shit, kid, events are like cosmic waves. You just gotta ride them."

Gibson fell into line with a half smile. "Are you suggesting we all go cosmic surfing?"

Slide roared. "Exactly that, kid. Exactly that."

ABOUT THE AUTHOR

Mick Farren lives in Los Angeles and drives a white 1977 Cadillac Eldorado that is greatly admired by the guys at the carwash.

MICK FARREN
and
SCIENCE FICTION...

WERE MADE
FOR EACH OTHER...